BUT I'M NOT A SUPERVILLAIN!!!

Aoibh Wood

This is dedicated to all the women who make the world better.
Sometimes by hook or by crook.

And for all us supervillains.
May our evil schemes succeed amid adversity.

Books by Aoibh Wood

THE BOSTON PRETERNATURAL
INVESTIGATIONS SERIES

BLOOD RITUALS
BLACK MIRROR
GREEN RATH
DARK SISTERS (COMING 2024)

Other Novels

THE SENATOR'S WIDOW

Chapter One

Thirty seconds. It was only supposed to take thirty seconds. Sherry stared at the login screen, her finger tapping against her upper arm faster, with every passing moment. She stole a glance at her watch. Three minutes. Thirty seconds, her ass. Sweat beaded along her hairline. The guard would be back any minute now.

She double-checked the camera feeds. It was still clear, for the moment. People milled about in the impressionist wing, completely unaware. The Mayor and Police Commissioner were practically leaning on one of the Van Goghs, huddled with a half-dozen donors, their fake smiles plastered on their faces as they soaked up admiration.

Sherry allowed herself a brief smirk. Typical. Crashing their private party had been a breeze. After all, she knew the museum better than anyone. After working here for two years, she'd memorized all the entrances and exits, including the disused secondary loading dock, where the guards occasionally snuck out for a smoke.

She felt a shiver of excitement as a soft beep interrupted her thoughts. The login screen disappeared and was replaced by the main desktop. Windows opened and closed as if the system were possessed. Lines of code flew across the screen. The trojan was working. She watched in awe as the program looped the cameras, systematically erasing the past hour of footage. Her presence vanished. To the system, it would be as if she had never existed. A quick glance at the screens confirmed it: the cameras showed a feed from earlier in the evening, seamlessly stitched with a crossfade to keep the loop from being too obvious.

She snickered as the screen flashed, "Have a nice day!" A chibi image of a grinning hacker girl with a transgender flag appeared, her middle finger extended triumphantly—a calling card from Ghostwire. Sherry wasn't exactly friends with the hacker, but she had paid a pretty penny for her expertise.

Sighing in relief, Sherry yanked the USB drive out of the port and pocketed it. The security office was the nerve-wracking part. With all the glass and cameras, one wrong move, and she'd be caught. But everything had gone perfectly—so far. She slipped out of the office, her breath catching as the hallway outside seemed eerily silent.

The restroom door was just steps away, her sanctuary for the next few seconds. She hurried inside, leaning against the cold tile for a moment. Three deep breaths. Four. Then, she stepped out straight into the path of the guard.

"Sorry!" she exclaimed drunkenly, her voice carrying just the right amount of nervous laughter as she bumped into him, the hair falling to cover her face. Her fingers were quick and precise, reattaching his badge to his hip with the ease of years of practice.

The guard barely spared her a second glance. He was too preoccupied, lost in the monotony of his rounds. Perfect. Sherry gave him a sheepish grin before turning on her heel, her pulse hammering in her ears. A couple of minutes later, she was in the west wing, alone, as planned. The Rembrandt, *The Solitary Watchman*, was waiting for her.

Pulling on her gloves, it took her precisely five seconds to rig the pressure sensor and lower the painting from its hooks, swathing it in a silk bag she'd crushed into her clutch and slinging it over her shoulder. The two-foot-square frame was surprisingly light, a small blessing. With her heart in her throat, Sherry retraced her steps to the loading dock, her breath evening out as she slipped into the cool night air. No alarms, no guards. She disappeared into the shadows of the alleyway, unseen, unheard, undetected.

From start to finish, even with the delay caused by the trojan, the entire operation had been completed in seven minutes. It was a flawless execution, and no one would ever know.

There wasn't a single mention in the news. Not even in the police blotter. A crime that slick should've been on the home page of The Chronicle, but there was nothing. Sherry tossed her phone on the couch, where it landed with a sad little thud. She leaned back, irritated, but then she smiled. *Maybe they hadn't even noticed it was gone yet. Now, wouldn't that be funny?*

The most sophisticated museum security in the country, and she'd beaten it with a flat-head screwdriver, a hairpin, a wad of gum, and one very special USB drive. She pulled the USB from her clutch and turned it over in her fingers. "MacGuyver, eat your heart out," she chuckled, remembering the hundreds of reruns she'd watched with her mother.

After shimmying out of the ridiculous cocktail dress and into street clothes, Sherry wandered back into the living room, her gaze settling on the tiny Rembrandt. It rested against the wall in its absurdly large metal frame—ironically, designed to prevent theft. The little six-inch by six-inch oil-on-wood depicted a lone man standing guard at the edge of a forest, holding a lantern. She loved the piece from the moment she'd first seen it, and now it was hers, at least for a little while.

Sherry picked it up, letting the silk cover she'd used to bring it home fall to the floor. The sense of loneliness and stoic duty in the composition spoke to her. It was an early work but already showed the Dutch Master's signature chiaroscuro—the lantern light illuminated the trees while casting a deep shadow into the woods. Sherry felt the watchman's isolation, his silent resolve. She grinned and set the painting back down, basking in both the thrill of having stolen it and the emotions it stirred.

But the rush didn't last long. She sighed and let out a mirthless snort. A half-million dollars worth of a Master's in Fine Art, and where had it gotten her? A dead-end illustration job at a misogynist marketing firm, crushing student debt, and a deep appreciation for the art she'd stolen.

Not that she considered herself an art thief. On the other hand, she had stolen a priceless painting, so in that sense, it was art, and she was a thief, but it wasn't her usual line of work. This was her first time, and she'd done it for the money —a one-off. If Malka hadn't split and taken all their savings, Sherry never would've considered it. As if that made a difference. But she wasn't about to go crawling back to Sunbean Coffee for her old job. She had a master's degree, for God's sake. From Yale!

The irony was that her time in fine art had led her to this moment. She'd made plenty of contacts in the art world, some of them a little shady. Okay, a lot shady. One of those had been Mixxer, a fence specializing in antiquities. He'd hired her to coordinate the heist for his crew. She'd told him she didn't need them, but he'd laughed and said she wasn't experienced enough. He'd practically patted her on the head.

Sherry smirked at the Rembrandt. "That'll teach him," she purred smugly. "Asshole."

When she let Mixxer in on her success, Sherry figured her cut would be about three hundred grand. More than enough to keep her from losing her apartment, though nowhere near enough to pay off her debt. She'd left in a generous finder's fee so Mixxer didn't kill her for going behind his back. She hadn't planned much beyond that. Laundering the money would be the next hurdle, but how hard could that be?

She rubbed her forehead and swiped the George Dickel bottle off the counter, pouring herself a celebratory drink. "Here's to being a genius," she toasted to Barry.

Barry didn't answer. He was a dead houseplant—just another in a long series of distractions from her sorrow after Malka left. She'd promised herself she'd water him, but after a week, she'd forgotten about him. A week later, he was dead. A ridiculous feeling of guilt kept her from throwing him out, so now, the droopy, month-dead fronds sat accusingly in the corner.

Sherry glanced at the painting again as a naughty thought crept into her head. "No, no, no," she muttered in denial. "It was a one-time deal." But her mind nudged her along. *I got away with it, didn't I?* There were a few other things she could swipe, maybe lower profile, but just as fun. The thought brought a wicked curve to her lips. "I do have a fence."

It was tempting. With another score or two, she could pay off her debts and get on with her life. But if she was being honest, the money wasn't what enticed her. It was the high, the thrill of being in that private car with the painting swathed in silk by her side, making her escape. Nothing else compared.

Finally done musing, Sherry scrolled through her phone back to the homepage of The Chronicle. A publicity shot of Lena Swift caught her eye. She stood in her striking superhero costume of pink, white, and orange, her hands on her hips, out and proud, looking fierce. Gods, she had such a great ass. And that muscle definition... Sherry fanned herself with one hand dramatically. Lena was hot with a capital H-O-T. Sherry practically idolized her.

Being a superhero, though? Not for her. Chasing down chaotic nutjobs, maintaining a secret identity, a leotard creeping up her ass? No thanks. Not that Lena wore a leotard —her look was much more practical: a sports bra, leggings, hand wraps, and sneakers. Sherry couldn't deny that Lena made it all look very, very good.

The whole superhero/villain circus seemed like a hamster wheel to Sherry. Heroes caught villains, villains got locked up in The Penthouse, the revolving door of supercriminal justice, only to be paroled to maintain space and then caught again when they re-offended. The cycle did, however, have the benefit of keeping Lena Swift occupied. While Sherry had pulled off her heist, Lena had been busy with a guy called Snake-Charmer. The Gods only knew why.

"I deserve something better than this swill," Sherry griped, glaring at the whiskey bottle lurking on the counter like it had insulted her. She poured another drink and glanced at Breitweiser, her calico cat, who lazed contentedly on the couch. "Keep our booty safe, okay?" she cooed at him, petting his fluffy cheeks. He batted at her hands lazily.

"Mommy's going out," she said sweetly. She grabbed her jacket and helmet, locking the door behind her. She deserved a little celebration. Maybe she'd even meet someone. She snorted. "Yeah, right. Fat chance."

Kelly's bar sat on the corner of First and Vine, just two miles from Sherry's apartment. She didn't have the budget for a night out, but she didn't care. She was too wound up not to do something. Maybe Carl would be there playing pool. She could hustle a few bucks off him and the guys from the dock. Sherry wasn't a pool shark by any means, but she had a knack for it. Her dad used to joke she got her talent for busting balls from her mom—a sick joke to make about your child, but that was her dad, a consummate asshole.

She found an empty spot for her old Suzuki before heading inside. It wasn't the safest neighborhood, but no one would mess with her bike here unless they didn't know the area. She grew up here and still had friends around. If anyone touched her ride, odds were it'd be back by morning. If not, she could collect the insurance, which was worth more than the bike anyway. Another perk of an MFA—she'd learned how to twist insurance work for her, just like she'd learned how to twist an odometer back in the day on these very streets.

Sherry paused outside the bar, thinking about the last time she and Malka had come here. The memory wormed into her gut, stirring up that familiar mix of longing and betrayal. *Nope. Nope. Nope. Those days are over,* she reminded herself. *Malka's a big-time supervillain now, and she dumped you, remember?*

Inside, it was quieter than she expected for 9 p.m. on a Thursday. The usual crowd—ten, maybe fifteen people—was nowhere to be seen. Even Carl wasn't in his usual corner hogging the pool table. The bartender, Chuck, was chatting with a lone woman at the end of the bar. Some girlfriend, probably.

"Hey, Sherry," Chuck greeted with a wave. "Sorry, girl, I'm closing up early tonight."

Sherry pouted. "Come on, Chuck, help me out. Just one drink? Top shelf."

He raised an eyebrow. "Rough night?"

"Hardly. I'm celebrating," she said, adding some puppy-dog eyes to her pout. "Puhhleeease?"

Chuck sighed but held up a finger. "Fine. One drink. We're heading out soon."

"Yes!" Sherry grinned and trotted toward the bar.

"Who's your friend?" the woman asked. Sherry's steps faltered at the crisp British accent, and she glanced over.

Holy shit. The woman wasn't just hot—she was gorgeous: long chocolate-cherry hair, cobalt-blue eyes that could stop traffic, and a fit but curvy body. A red compass rose tattoo peeked out from her jacket cuff, too. Sherry's breath caught, and she quickly tore her gaze away, trying to play it cool.

"This is Sherry," Chuck said. "She's a regular. Usually less of a pest." He nodded to the other woman as he poured Sherry's drink. "Sherry, meet Jemma. She's an old friend."

Sherry gave a shy wave, jamming her hands into her pockets. *Relax, Sherry. It's just a compass rose. Doesn't always mean that.* "Sorry, I don't want to intrude. I can go."

Chuck snorted. "First off, I already poured it, so you're paying for it. You might as well drink it." Then he lowered his voice. "Second, she's more your type than mine, honey."

Sherry's eyebrows shot up, and her entire demeanor shifted. *She's gay?* And from the look of her—tight black jeans, leather jacket, sunglasses hanging from her T-shirt collar—she was exactly Sherry's type. Sherry grabbed her scotch and meandered down the bar, trying to be casual. "Hi, I'm Sherry."

"I know," Jemma said, pinning Sherry with her fabulous eyes and a crooked smirk of amusement. "I heard."

Sherry blinked, heat rushing to her cheeks—nice one. Chuck just told her that, you idiot. Jemma flashed a dazzling smile that sent all the heat in Sherry's face straight downward.

"So," Jemma began, her eyes dancing with amusement as she leaned closer. "What brings you out tonight? Did you say you were celebrating something?"

Sherry shrugged, trying to play it cool. "A personal best, of sorts. Thought I'd treat myself to a drink, maybe hustle a few bucks off the pool table." She grinned, swirling her scotch with the plastic stirrer. "You?"

Jemma traced the rim of her glass with a finger, her gaze never leaving Sherry's. "Chuck's an old friend. He invited me to a movie." Her lips curled into a slow smile. "Now I'm rethinking my plans."

Sherry's heart skipped a beat. She raised an eyebrow, fighting the goofy grin threatening to break free. "Oh? And what made you change your mind?"

Jemma took a sip of her drink, her eyes gleaming over the rim. "Well, it's not every day I meet someone who's so adorably awkward and still manages to be completely captivating."

Sherry nearly choked on her scotch, managing a laugh. "It's all part of the act."

Jemma leaned in, her voice dropping to a teasing whisper. "Oh, I don't know about that, but something tells me you're full of surprises."

Sherry's smirk grew, and she found herself leaning in, too, their faces only inches apart now. "Guess you'll have to stick around to find out."

Jemma's eyes flickered to Sherry's lips for a split second before she grinned. "I'm counting on it. You want to go somewhere?"

This time, Sherry snorted her scotch, coughing as she recovered. Of all the things Jemma could've said, that wasn't what Sherry had expected. "I…uh…yeah," she croaked. "As soon as I stop choking on my drink." Smooth. Real smooth. She couldn't believe how badly she was fumbling.

Jemma didn't seem to mind. She glanced at Sherry's motorcycle helmet. "You got a spare?"

Swallowing hard, Sherry nodded. She took another sip to

compose herself.

"Your place?" Jemma whispered, leaning in a little closer.

Sherry nodded again and downed the rest of her scotch. No point in wasting it.

"Put hers on my tab," Jemma told Chuck, taking Sherry's arm and completely ignoring her dumbstruck look.

"What about the movie?" Chuck called after them. "And your credit card?"

"Raincheck, honey," Jemma said over her shoulder. "And don't go buying a PS5 with my card."

"I can buy my own PS5," Chuck grumbled as the door closed behind them.

They climbed onto Sherry's bike, and Sherry's brain finally caught up with the moment. *This never happens to me.* But just five minutes down the road, Sherry felt a tap on her shoulder. Glancing in the side mirror, she saw Jemma staring at her phone, a deep red symbol reflecting off her faceplate. It looked like some kind of alert that techs used for downed systems. Shit.

Sherry pulled over, turning toward Jemma. "Emergency?"

Jemma got off the bike and removed her helmet, shaking out her silky hair. She gently lifted Sherry's face shield with one finger. Her lips twisted into a grim, apologetic smile. "Rain check?"

"Sure. What's up?" Sherry asked, trying to hide her disappointment. *Great. I'm never seeing this chick again.*

"Someone stole a bloody Rembrandt," Jemma muttered, sighing.

Sherry's breath caught. Uh-oh.

"Now I've got to deal with the insurance claim. It's what I do, recover art for insurance companies."

Sherry rued her rotten luck, but she kept her expression neutral. "Can I give you a lift somewhere?"

"No, I'll grab a ride share. I need to get changed and head to the scene before the police muck it all up."

Sherry pouted. "Alright."

Jemma undid Sherry's chin strap and pushed the helmet into her lap. "There, that's better." She leaned in, planting a kiss on Sherry's cheek. "I'm really sorry about this. It's not you, I promise."

Sherry's heart raced as Jemma's lips brushed her cheek. That kiss, brief but electrifying, sent a tingle through her skin and left her craving more. She swallowed hard, trying to focus on something other than the heat crawling up her neck.

"It's really not you," Jemma said, her voice soft as she leaned just a little closer. "I'd much rather be riding with you tonight."

Sherry forced a chuckle, her nerves buzzing. "Yeah, well, not everyone in fine art can be out of work these days. Someone must be making money."

Jemma's frown turned into a slow grin. "You work in art?"

"Off and on," Sherry replied, suppressing an arch grin.

Jemma laughed, a sound so warm it made Sherry's pulse quicken even more. "Well, it's not every day you meet someone like you, Sherry."

Sherry felt her cheeks burn under the compliment but managed a smile. "Someone like me?"

"Yeah," Jemma said, her cobalt eyes locking onto Sherry's with an intensity that made Sherry forget to breathe for a second. "Someone who struts like they can take on the world but still manages to be adorably flustered over a drink."

Sherry rolled her eyes, but she couldn't help the grin spreading across her face. "Flustered? Please. This is all part of the charm."

Jemma's lips curled into a playful smirk. "Oh, is that what it is? Well, it's working."

"You know, I'm available for flustering pretty much any day of the week," Sherry said, attempting to sound casual, but the words came out faster than she intended. She cringed a little on the inside, but Jemma only smiled wider.

Sherry glanced around. "You sure you don't want a lift? This isn't the best neighborhood."

"I'll be fine," Jemma said, flipping through her phone. "Here, do you have Artlline?" She held it out, the screen displaying a QR code.

Sherry fumbled for her cell and scanned the code, sending a

quick message to test it. Jemma's phone chirped like an old-school Star Trek communicator, and Sherry grinned. She loved Star Trek.

"There, all set. I'm busy the rest of the week, but how about Wednesday afternoon? Croissants and coffee?"

Sherry swallowed hard, trying to stay cool, but her brain was already fast-forwarding to their next date. Croissants and coffee? It sounded perfect—and impossibly romantic. "Uh, sure," Sherry answered, a goofy smile spreading across her face. "Still sure about that ride?"

"You're so cute," Jemma said, smiling as she walked away, pausing long enough to secure the helmet strap on Sherry's bike.

"Hey, wait!"

Jemma stopped, one eyebrow arched. "Yes, love?"

Gooseflesh ran down Sherry's arms at Jemma's accent. "Don't—uh—don't stand me up on Wednesday." Her heart hammered as she spoke. "I'm really looking forward to it."

Jemma's eyes softened, and for a moment, her teasing grin disappeared. "I wouldn't dream of it," she said sincerely. Then, with a wink, she turned, walking away, leaving Sherry to wonder how on earth she'd gotten so lucky.

Sitting on her bike, still watching the shake of Jemma's hips, Sherry couldn't stop herself from smiling like a total idiot.

"Why is it always the ass for me?" she murmured to herself with a chuckle as Jemma's silhouette faded into the shadows.

Chapter Two

Sherry leaned into the curve, seven-hundred-fifty cubic centimeters roaring between her legs, the warm night air rushing past her face. The city lights blurred in her peripheral vision, but all she could think about was Jemma. She couldn't stop smiling. Every engine's vibration echoed her excitement, the thrill of something new. The ride from where she dropped Jemma off was short, but it was just long enough to let the anticipation simmer. For once, the usual weight she carried— Malka's secrets, lies, and betrayal—felt lighter. Her mind drifted back to that last moment, the kiss on the cheek, the promise of coffee on Wednesday. A real date. Not a fling, not a stolen moment, but something that could grow.

The engine's hum matched the rhythm of her heart as she pulled up to her building, the cool metal of her keys clinking together as she dismounted. With a fluttering belly, she bounced a bit in the elevator. Her fingers fumbled with the lock in her excitement—a real date.

As the door swung open, a warm realization hit her like a wave: she missed this—this kind of normal, this anticipation of what could be.

"Finally," she murmured with a slight giggle, stepping inside. "The dry spell might be over."

Of course, nothing could ever be that simple. Jemma was an insurance investigator, and Sherry had stolen the painting she was after. But that was a problem for future Sherry. In a few weeks, the Rembrandt would be long gone, and three hundred thousand dollars would be sitting pretty in her account.

"Woo hoo, you hear that, Breit?" she called to her cat, tossing her helmet aside. But as she stepped forward, she froze, and her heart plummeted. "What the fuck?" she whispered, eyes wide, taking in the scene.

Burned into the carpet were a dozen footprints, like brands, leading from the wide-open balcony door to where the Rembrandt should've been. Gone. Oh, God. She was a dead woman.

Sherry narrowed her eyes at the scorch marks. "That bitch."

The footprints could only belong to one person—Malka, or as she now called herself, 'Lady Sin.' Sherry yanked her phone from her pocket, thumb stabbing Malka's Artline contact.

"That fucking—"

"Hello, darling," Malka's voice oozed from the speaker. "It's been so long, and I've missed you."

Sherry snorted. "Yeah, I bet. Is that why you took it?" She could picture Malka lounging in her office, probably in something super sexy. Sherry banished the prurient thoughts that tried to creep in. She missed her…no, no, no, she missed her body, that's all. She had to remember that Malka was an evil bitch now. Not that she really believed that. She was just pissed.

"I've called. I've emailed, but you never answer. How else would I get your attention, pet?"

"Don't call me that. I'm not your fucking pet, no matter how hard you tried to make me one."

"That's not fair. You know I had no control back then."

Sherry rolled her eyes, suppressing the familiar shiver Malka's Russian accent always triggered. "Just give it back, please? And fix my carpet. I don't want to lose my security deposit." Sherry's voice was pleading, and she fought to keep tears from her eyes. Malka clearly had no idea the danger she'd put Sherry in.

Malka chuckled softly. "I'll do both, I promise. But you'll have to come and get it. Tomorrow night? Eleven?"

"Fuck. Fine."

"Good girl," Malka practically purred. "Now, how's our cat?"

Sherry's eyes nearly rolled out of her head. She knew she'd have more success with honey than vinegar, but she couldn't help pointing out the obvious. "Breit's fine. You didn't want him, remember?"

"That's not my fault either, sweetcakes."

"Nothing is," Sherry interrupted. "You have no control anymore. Just sex and sin, right?"

The line went quiet. Sherry realized she'd gone too far. "I'm sorry," she whispered. "That was uncalled for."

"I know you're hurt," Malka said softly, her voice losing its slick charm. "I just wanted to see you. This is sometimes a lonely life, and you're the only person I know who hasn't been touched by it."

Sherry's hands clenched reflexively, her nails digging into her palms as Malka spoke. She hated how the sound of Malka's voice still had that effect on her—a warmth that spread from her chest to her fingertips, tingling with the familiarity and ache of a past that had once been her whole world.

Malka hadn't always been this way. Her mind was tugged back to those early days, and for a moment, she could almost feel the steady warmth of Malka's hand around her own, how they'd sat close and joked about grad school politics, imagining a future full of lazy Sundays and quiet nights together. Malka had even made Sherry's lackluster illustrating job bearable. But then everything changed.

The memory flashed through her mind. They had been at Maxxie's Italiano. Malka was enjoying tagliatelle, a bright smile on her face, adorable despite the bit of parsley in her teeth. A code green, she'd called it. Then, the world exploded. Sherry had thrown herself over Malka, taking the brunt of the debris. When she woke up a week later in the ICU, the restaurant was rubble, and a horned, red-skinned nightmare called Prince Lucifer was dead. Lena Swift had taken him down—maybe too hard.

But the blood that fell from his wounds had changed Malka, slowly turning her into the embodiment of carnal sin. She lost her job, opened a nightclub downtown, and tried to make Sherry her love slave. That was the final straw. They split, though the back-and-forth had dragged on for months. Sherry ended it for good, convinced Malka was sleeping with other people. Afterward, Sherry had learned she was right.

And yet, here Sherry was, still drawn in. Malka's words made her want to reach out, to tell her she didn't have to be alone, to take her hand and pull her away from this mess she'd become. But there was a pain beneath it, a betrayal she couldn't forget. Her hand twitched, wanting to reach for Malka as if she were right in front of her, but she curled it into a fist instead.

"Sher, darling?" Malka's voice cut through her thoughts. "You still there?"

"Yeah," Sherry croaked. "I'll see you tomorrow."

She hung up, leaning back against the door with a deep exhalation, blinking back hot tears that prickled like splinters. Tonight had started perfectly—a clean heist pulled off right under the Met's nose and a date with Jemma the Hot, as she'd taken to thinking of her. Jemma was everything Sherry had once admired in Malka: confidence, assertiveness, that steady command that pulled you in. But Jemma was also everything Malka wasn't anymore—untainted, genuine, warm without that ever-present undercurrent of menace.

She pushed off the door and headed to coax Breit from his hiding spot under the bed. Poor thing. Breit had once slept curled between them like a furry, purring buffer, but since Malka's transformation, he bolted at the first hint of her arrival. She'd blamed the smoke-like scent that clung to Malka now—something about it was alluring to Sherry, a seductive danger that called to some reckless part of her. But to a cat, she supposed it must be like a forest fire walking into the room. She knelt beside the bed, reaching out until her fingertips brushed his soft fur, feeling a pang of guilt.

"At least she doesn't smell like Prince Lucifer," Sherry muttered, half-remembering the sulfur stink as she shook a bag of treats to draw Breit out. "Did mean old Malka scare you? It's okay, sweetie, she's gone."

It hurt, that familiar gap where her life with Malka used to fit. But tonight, she coaxed Breit from his hiding spot with a few treats, and then, feeling his soft weight settle into her lap on the sofa, she did her best to relax. She'd have to see her one more time, and then she could get on with her life.

Sometime later, the delicate, thrilling flutter she'd felt at Kelly's returned. With a soft smile, Sherry reluctantly disturbed Breitweiser from his cozy perch, much to his disappointment. She drifted over to her easel, feeling that spark burst into creative energy as she began sketching the piece that had been taking shape in her mind in the last hour or so.

The prepped canvas had been sitting there untouched for two months. Part of the problem had been inspiration. The rest was motivation. It was hard to want to paint when life was just upside down enough to be rough but not so completely wrecked as to be truly stirring. Now, though, her imagination had been kindled.

"That's perfect," she thought as she drew the outline and added a few subsequent details to the figure, the street corner, and the lamp. For the colors, she took inspiration from Rembrandt himself—chiaroscuro to create powerful contrasts between her subject and the world around her. For the background, she selected ultramarine blue mixed with black for the sliver of sky seen in the distance. The walls of the buildings would be a mixture of warm amber, black, and deep, angry grays. For the street lamp, she went to a medium cadmium yellow. For the eyes, though, she selected cerulean blue, which she'd mix with a dab of titanium white, a stark contrast from the golden skin and the dark hair.

Once she'd laid down enough of the pre-work to ensure she wouldn't lose the image, she stepped back, drew a shroud over the canvas, and returned to the sofa, extremely pleased with herself. "That's going to be amazing," she said to her disdainful pet and flipped on the news.

"Holy shit!" she whispered in shock at the top story.

Chapter Three

Jemma watched as Sherry rode off, a mixture of longing and wariness twisting in her chest. She had a rule, a big one—no repeat partners, no emotional ties—but something about Sherry made her consider bending it. Maybe it was the bike. She had a thing for motorcycles. Or maybe it was Sherry's clumsy charm, that complete lack of game that somehow managed to be endearing. The way she'd been so concerned about her safety, it was sweet. But sweet was dangerous, and Jemma couldn't afford dangerous. Not again.

Jemma had been down this road before. Callie had started out as a fling, too, a cute distraction with bright eyes and big dreams. And when Callie had been caught in the crossfire of Jemma's life, well, the scars from that would never heal. So why the hell was she even considering coffee with Sherry? She mentally shook herself. She was just lonely, that's all.

She lifted off, air rushing past her face as the ground dropped away. The moment her feet left the pavement, a sense of weightlessness flooded her. It was always like this—the tension she carried melting away as she broke free of gravity's pull. She could go faster, much faster, but cramming air into your lungs at five hundred miles an hour was bad for you, and the memory of the expansion injury still clung to her like a bad dream. That first time, she'd passed out from the sudden compression of air rupturing her lungs. It had also torn off her clothes. She learned quickly. Breathe steady, don't overdo it. And don't go faster than you can see. There were other things in the sky: birds and bats. Hitting them didn't hurt much, but it was gross, and she felt bad for the animals.

Harborhaven blurred beneath her, the high, full moon casting silvery ripples across the water. The city was peaceful from this height, a stark contrast to the chaos she often found on the ground. She made her usual loop over Riverview Stadium, bathed in the lights of the evening's Leprechauns game. Jemma thought about swinging through to see the score, but she didn't have the time, so she flew on. The Anderson Insurance Tower, all lit up in rainbow colors, loomed ahead. That always irritated her. If they wanted to show their pride, they wouldn't be the preferred insurer of the RNC or Chirpy, the messaging platform owned by South African Nazi Pieter Merwe.

Finally, she crossed back to the Pillar District. There, sitting at the top of Barron's Hill, was The Greek Column. Some guy a hundred years ago had commissioned it in honor of a battle that never happened, well, at least not in Harborhaven. No one knew why it was still there, but now it was a landmark, so it stuck. She turned east from the column and landed lightly halfway down the hill on a wooden porch enclosed by slatted trellises on either side.

With a deep breath, she stepped into her little one-room efficiency. She passed the rolled-up futon and tiny dresser next to her desk. Above the desk hung a corkboard holding a few news clippings, magazine articles, and a bunch of mugshots: bad guys she'd either put away or for whom she was looking.

Her finger hovered over the corkboard, finally landing on the photo of Viktor Rostovich. Il Duce, he called himself—a stupid name that made her skin crawl. The man was muscle, power, and ego wrapped up in a package of brutality. The fact that he was Russian muscle and had a full head of hair only made him more absurd, but there was nothing funny about the damage he caused. Jemma didn't need a reminder of how dangerous he was, but every time she tapped that photo, she remembered the last time they'd crossed paths. The chaos. The blood. And the fact that next time, she might not be so lucky.

"Asshole," she muttered.

Finally, from inside the tiny closet, sandwiched between the short kitchenette and the miserable bathroom, she pulled out one of her outfits. She had six of them, all identical in a Lesbian Pride color scheme. She didn't call it a suit. That seemed pretentious.

The outfit had started as a joke—a costume for Pride, something to wear while dancing in the streets. Lesbo-girl she'd called herself. But that day had changed everything. When she'd flown up with that bomb to explode safely away from everyone else, she felt something she hadn't before: purpose. Saving those people had been terrifying and exhilarating all at once. And when it was over, she couldn't bring herself to stop. It wasn't just about the colors—it had become an instant symbol of what she could do, what she had to do. People, who probably never in their lives thought they would, thanked her, an out lesbian, for saving them. She'd never intended to become a hero, but sometimes the world made the choice for you.

These days, the hero bit was wearing thin. It was grueling, often painful, and interfered with every aspect of her personal life, but she'd become an icon, and she didn't want to let anyone down, especially not the fam.

Brushing aside the deleterious thoughts, she donned her trademark colors and wrapped her hands and forearms in nylon compression tape. She gave the wraps a quick slap to make sure they were tight and stepped outside onto the porch, silently lifting away into the sky.

Twenty-five minutes since she'd first gotten the call, she landed at The Met amid the three cruisers, including one with Fed plates. Tracy Dunbar, her usual contact, waited next to one, checking her watch and tapping her foot. Jemma cringed as she took in the young black detective, watching the curls of her impressive afro wave about in the light breeze. Well, there was nothing for it, so Jemma set down next to her.

"Took you long enough," Tracy bitched lightly. "Did you stop for coffee and a Danish?"

"Fuck you, too, D.," Jemma murmured softly with a grin. She kept her voice low, given the media presence just outside the cordon. It wouldn't do for her to disrupt her squeaky clean image. "It takes a minute to do my wraps." She held up her arms.

Tracy chuckled. "Why do you wear those things again?"

"You know why," she retorted with a wry look. "Now, what's the story? Why do you need me for an art theft? Do you want an appraisal or something?"

"Hardly," Tracy said with an amused snort. "Those guys want you." She pointed to a pair of suits next to a black suburban. One was tall, extremely broad-shouldered, and looked about forty. The other was a bit younger with brown hair and eyes.

"Uh-oh," she muttered dryly. They were from the FBI field office, probably Superhuman Affairs. This night was getting better and better. "Hey, kids," she said casually as they walked up. "So, what don't I know?"

"Agent's Parker and Bates," the first guy said.

She raised an eyebrow. "Which one of you is Parker, and which is Bates? You all look alike to me."

"Yeah, they told me you'd say something like that," the tall blonde retorted. "I'm Bates. This is Parker."

She shook both of their hands. "Yeah, I'm no one's favorite at the Bureau."

"You're mine," Parker said with a smirk and a wink.

Well, then, Jemma figured she'd need to be a little nicer, at least to Parker. Still though, gay or not, he was a Fed, and she had a thing about the Federal Government. They'd fucked up her life. "Thanks. So again, what don't I know."

"We got a tip this morning that the Rembrandt was being used to smuggle a sample of Lot 429, or at least a Russian attempt to duplicate it."

Jemma whistled. At least now she knew why they wanted her involved. Lot 429 was a nightmare. It had saved her from stage four breast cancer—at a cost. She was stronger, faster, near-invincible in so many ways, but the serum had killed every other person who had tried it, save one. She'd seen the effects firsthand, the slow, agonizing deaths of those who had believed they'd been chosen for something greater. She'd survived by sheer luck. Now, to hear that someone might be smuggling a knockoff into Harborhaven. It sent a noticeable shiver up her spine. The world wasn't ready for another Lot 429, and neither was she.

"Yeah, well, you know the odds on that. It'll kill whoever injects it." Her voice held a glib confidence that she didn't feel.

"It didn't kill you," Bates countered.

Jemma snorted a laugh. "No. But I only know of one other person that survived, and look how that turned out."

Parker spoke up. "That wasn't us. That was SPEAR, and it's been disbanded, but we had to do something with so many supers appearing seemingly out of nowhere."

SPEAR was the Strategic Personnel Enhancement and Advancement Research Agency. They had developed Lot 429, a toxic and radioactive serum laced with an antimatter isotope that wreaked havoc on mammalian physiology. SPEAR had tested it on terminally ill patients, hoping to create a government-controlled superhuman to counter a sudden rise in super-powered threats. Most subjects died, and the effects on survivors were unpredictable and often catastrophic.

For Jemma, the transformation had been agonizing and traumatic, but she was the only successful test subject. Despite this, SPEAR eventually deemed her uncontrollable and tried to eliminate her—a decision that hadn't gone as planned.

She turned the subject away from the painful memories. "So, which painting are we looking for?"

"The Solitary Watchman," Bates answered.

Jemma scoffed. "That's a six-inch by six-inch chunk of wood. How could they smuggle anything in that?"

"It had recently been reframed before it was shipped, so that's most likely," Parker cut in.

"And who brought it into the country?" Jemma asked, directing her attention to him.

"Russian Mob."

Bates scowled at Parker, irritated, and Jemma suppressed a smirk. Parker was in the know more than Bates, and he didn't like it. Too bad.

Parker continued, "Dimitry Rostovich, the oligarch in charge of Volganeft, is behind it, we think. He owns the painting and is connected with our Russian counterparts. That's all we really know. They can't be smuggling much. A dozen cc's, maybe, enough for two doses. The stuff costs billions to make, even in those small quantities."

Jemma nodded. "It's enough. But that's not much to go on. So, why did you call me?"

Bates shrugged. "We were instructed to read you in. The deputy director says you know the city and some of the less-than-savory characters here. She thought you could help, and you have a security clearance."

A warm, unbidden smile settled on Jemma's lips, which she quickly wiped away. Deputy Director Candice Fletcher was good people. She'd been the field agent protecting Jemma during her treatment, and she'd stopped two kidnapping attempts. She'd also sat by Jemma in a dismal cabin in Vermont while Jemma's body adjusted to its changes, which had not been pleasant, to say the least. "Yeah, I know someone, but it'll be tricky."

"Keep us in the loop, please," Parker said, his voice a little pleading. "We tried to work with Sentinel, but he never kept us apprised of anything."

"Wait," Jemma said, a puzzled look on her face. "I thought Sentinel was dead."

"He is—now," Bates said glumly. "Like Parker said, he didn't keep us in the loop. He went all lone ranger, and it got him killed. At least, we think it was him."

It took a moment, but then Jemma got it. Sentinel had been more private investigator than hero, but he could heal from almost anything and had incredible senses. Unlike hers, his mask had been multi-function. A lot of people couldn't imagine how miserable it was to be able to smell literally everything. Jemma had no idea either, but she could imagine. Compared to her strength, most people were like eggshells. She had to be extremely careful. Regardless, whoever had gotten to him must have been pretty thorough to finish him off. She shuddered to think about it.

"So," she said. "Any leads? Or am I on my own on that?"

Bates shrugged again. "Nothing solid. We don't even know who called it in. It was considered to be a low fidelity tip, that is until…" He gestured around at the police.

Jemma nodded. "Alright. Well, if there's nothing else, I'll be off."

"This is classified," Bates added a moment later. "Top Secret."

"I got that already. Don't worry. Mum's the word."

She shook each of their hands, took their business cards, which she stuffed into the side pocket of her leggings, and saw them back to their car. Once they'd left, she sauntered over to Tracy. "So," she said, drawing out the word. "How have you been?"

Tracy gave her a sideways glance, the faintest trace of hurt flashing across her face before she masked it. Jemma noticed it, though. She hated that she could never explain herself properly to Tracy. It wasn't that she didn't care, but caring was dangerous.

"You never call," Tracy said with a half-smile, but the edge in her voice was clear.

Jemma swallowed the guilt that crept up. "I've been… busy," she offered weakly, knowing it was a poor excuse.

Tracy sighed, shaking her head. "Yeah, I get it. You always are."

"Come on, Trace," Jemma responded miserably. Then she lowered her voice. "It's bad enough that we did it at all."

"Well, Lena," Tracy said, emphasizing the name. Tracy was one of four people who knew her real identity. "Who would have known? I wouldn't have said anything. Still, though, you could have at least called."

Jemma sighed. "Yeah, you're right. I'll try to keep in touch." She wouldn't, not because she didn't want to, per se, but because she was a coward. It just hurt too much. Trace deserved better. Sherry probably did, too. "So, did you find anything?" She asked, happy to get off the subject, if a bit inartfully.

"No. Whoever did it snuffed out the security cameras, disabled the alarm, and snatched the painting from right under their noses at closing time, no one the wiser. There was a wad of gum stuck to the pressure sensor, ingenious, really."

"GPS?" Jemma asked.

"No. The owner forbid it. That kind of leads me to believe it's an insurance scam."

Jemma glanced at the building, admiring the towering Corinthian columns. They supported a meticulously carved pediment depicting scenes from art history. The sleek wings of the building were encapsulated in smart glass that dimmed during the day, giving the whole thing a sort of Frank Lloyd Wright meets Ludwig Mies van der Rohe feel. The imposing bronze doors, etched with abstract patterns, led to a vast glass-domed atrium, hinting at the treasures within. She loved this building with all her heart, and in all the time she'd lived in Harborhaven, it had never been robbed—until now.

"Could be, but definitely an inside job," she probed.

Tracy turned and followed Jemma's gaze to the portico. "Looks that way. There was a dinner function here tonight, a lot of bigwigs on the list, along with art aficionados and some no names. We're checking into them."

"Don't suppose I can get that list?" Jemma asked. "There's some fuss about the painting that was stolen. Though, if I were going to steal a painting from this place there are far less conspicuous and more valuable ones to pick."

Tracy turned and looked at her thoughtfully. Jemma gazed back, her expression mixed of hope and contrition. Tracy sighed. "If a copy of the guest list finds its way into your hands, you wouldn't tell anyone where you got it, I'm sure."

Jemma frowned. "Of course not."

"Okay, I'll see what I can do. I'll hit you up the usual way."

"Thanks, Tracy. That helps."

"I get the collar if you find out who did this," Tracy demanded.

Jemma grimaced and shuffled her feet. "Can't promise that."

"Uh-huh," Tracy grunted. "This wouldn't happen to do

with your little chat with Bates and Parker would it?"

"Can't tell you that," Jemma replied, pressing her lips into a thin line.

"You know, you have no poker face," Tracy chuckled. "Yeah, fine. I get it. But you owe me."

"Thanks. And yeah, I owe you one. I promise."

"Limey," Tracy said lightheartedly.

"Yank," Jemma shot back in a whisper and lifted off, making a quick circuit of the city before heading home.

Despite the good-natured ribbing, Jemma's stomach churned. Seeing Tracy again, especially so soon after their brief fling, had stirred up more discomfort than she'd expected. But it wasn't just Tracy. The news about Lot 429 being reproduced tied her insides in knots. If it was on the black market, everything was about to get much, much worse. Jemma was the most formidable hero out there because of that serum, and Il Duce, or Il Douchebag, as she liked to call him, always went toe to toe with her. She couldn't imagine fighting someone like him who could fly. The collateral damage would be unimaginable.

Worse still, Jemma knew she shouldn't even be thinking of dating. Not with this hanging over her head. Not with the risks her life brought. It was reckless, and she was usually better than this. But still, she felt that thrill—something she hadn't let herself feel in a long time. Of course, that made the guilt even worse.

She clenched her fists, torn between what she wanted and what she knew was coming. There was no room for both, and that truth gnawed at her.

Chapter Four

Sherry sat on the couch, her heart hammering in her chest. Lena Swift was right there on the TV, casually talking to two men in suits—Federal Agents, by the look of them. Sherry's eyes flicked nervously to the empty spot where the painting had been.

"I should've locked the back door," she muttered. "Didn't expect my ex—who can fly!—to just pop in for a visit." Of course, that was Sherry's form of luck: bad. Malka had to choose today to drop in—the day she had an honest-to-God Rembrandt sitting in her living room.

She returned to the screen, watching Lena share more words with the Feds. Sherry took a shaky sip of shitty whiskey, her hand trembling so badly she nearly spilled it.

"I'm so screwed," she whispered to Breit, the cat purring obliviously under her nervous strokes. "You and Barry are gonna be homeless."

Unable to sit still, Sherry got up and paced, flipping through the cable news channels, searching for any sign this had gone national. It might explain why the feds were involved, but there was nothing. No mention of art theft or Lena Swift. "Maybe it's still just a local issue," she said to herself, but the unease gnawed at her, threatening to take her away. She took a deep breath. It would be fine. Lena was there for PR or something. "But then, why are the feds there?"

Her mind raced. "Probably some rich foreign asshole wanting his painting back," she tried to convince herself. "I'll get it back from Malka tomorrow and then hand it over to Mixxer when he returns."

Her gaze drifted back to the TV, landing on Lena's figure as she now spoke with a pretty detective in a cheap suit. Sherry stared, her stomach twisting. The thought hit her hard. If Malka hadn't stolen the painting… Jesus. Jemma could've walked in and seen it right there, sitting in plain sight. God! She felt so stupid.

Her heart pounded. "What the hell would I have told her? Huh, Barry?" She continued her angst-driven monologue a little shrilly, staring at Malka's scorched prints. "How would I have explained those? Do you have any idea? Because I don't."

The plant swayed in the air conditioning, offering no answers. Breit just licked himself, equally indifferent.

"I need to put my foot down," she muttered. "Malka's not allowed in my house, especially when I'm not here. This clingy bitch routine has to stop."

Her anxiety spiked. Lena would find out. She could see it now, Lena Swift appearing at her door, demanding answers. Sherry darted to the bathroom and threw up, clutching the toilet. "I'm going to prison," she groaned. "Lena always gets her man…or woman or whatever."

For all her whinging and worry, though, Sherry couldn't understand why Lena Swift would care. She did big world-ending events and supervillains that the cops couldn't handle, not art theft. Not that it mattered. She was involved, and Sherry was going to prison, and not a cushy prison like "The Penthouse," she would be going to Wentworth Federal Women's Prison where she'd be somebody's bitch, eating them out for smokes or something.

She didn't know if they still smoked in prison, but whatever. She'd still be somebody's bitch.

Sherry slumped back onto the couch, feeling tears prickle behind her eyes. "This sucks," she mumbled to Barry, who swayed silently in the air conditioning. At some point, she must have drifted off, because the next thing she knew, she jolted awake to the sharp buzz of her phone.

Fragments of a fitful dream clung to her mind: Malka's red skin and tail, Lena Swift's steely gaze as she shoved her into a deep pit. "And that's what we do to supervillains," Lena had declared, while Sherry begged for forgiveness. "I'm not a supervillain!"

Jemma had been there too, shaking her head in disappointment. "You're an artist. How could you steal it? It belongs to the world."

The phone buzzed again, insistent. Sherry groaned, grabbed it, and hit ACCEPT. Mixxer's face appeared on screen, his voice immediately grating on her nerves.

"Hey, Sherry Berry." He was as over-the-top as ever, with dark curly hair and a precisely groomed, bootstrap beard, lounging in purple pajamas and cradling a black cat like a wannabe Bond villain.

"What time is it?" Sherry grumbled.

"Just past midnight, your time," Mixxer replied, and Sherry glanced at her watch with bleary eyes. She'd only been asleep for an hour.

"To what do I owe the honor? And where are you anyway?" Sherry asked, trying to clear the sleep from her eyes.

"Monaco," He replied, then donned a conspiratorial tone. "As for why I'm calling, I caught a bit of news today, and—"

"Yeah, I've got it," she said, cutting him off. "I'll deliver it when you're back in the country. Just make sure the payment's ready."

Her pulse quickened when Mixxer's face hardened, his tone dropping. "I see. Well, normally, I'd be put out with you going behind my back like this, but I'm sure we can come to an arrangement. What did you have in mind?"

"Well, the cut of the entire team would be over half. So, I'm thinking three hundred."

Another uncomfortable pause. "That certainly benefits me, but the crew will be a tad upset. How do you suggest I handle them?"

Sherry suppressed a cringe and barreled onward, her voice full of bravado she didn't feel. "I feel like that's probably a you thing."

"Little girl," Mixxer said, his voice threatening. "I don't like to fuck about. You changed things. Now, you need to solve the problems that arise. That's what I'd expect from a professional, and you are a professional, aren't you?"

Sherry had wracked her brain over this, but she had no idea how to handle Mixxer's crew. "I am, but I just figured the hassle would be worth the extra two hundred grand. I guess not."

Mixxer laughed. "Touché. I'll send someone to pick it up."

Sherry's heart skipped a beat. "No," Sherry said. "I'll deliver it when you get back. I can wait, and I'll feel better than giving a priceless work of art to one of your flunkies."

"And I'd feel better knowing right where it is," Mixxer retorted, the menace returning to his voice.

"I have it stashed at Malka's," Sherry said. Fortunately, her phone slipped from her fingers then and hid her very noticeable grimace. She hadn't meant to tell him that. Scooping up the phone, she schooled her features and turned the camera back toward herself. "Sorry. Anyway, given the attention it's received, I'd like to keep it where it is until you return to the States."

"Darling, I think you need to be more worried about me than Lena Swift. That painting is very important to me. It had better be in my hands when I get back." The warning hung in the air, thick with menace.

"Of course, Mixxer," Sherry said. "I'm not stupid."

Mixxer flipped back to his usual pleasant self. "Good. So, let me ask you. I hired you because of your inside information, but there's something else I need. Assuming we can conclude this transaction satisfactorily, would you be available for another job? It's a little smaller, but I think it would be right up your alley."

"I might," Sherry said pleasantly. "What do you have in mind?"

"We'll discuss that when I get back. Kiss, kiss, Sherry Berry." Mixxer hung up.

"Shit," Sherry swore and tossed her phone on the cushions

at her feet, startling Breit, who took off. "If Malka decides to screw with me, I am so dead."

Chapter Five

Sherry made her way through the main floor of Sin City, Harborhaven's premier nightspot. The place was packed, as usual. Men and women danced on the central dancefloor, lounged at the two enormous bars and myriad tables, or showed off their outfits like they were walking billboards of personal style. Some were fire, like the girl in thigh-high boots owning the platform, but most were trying too hard. Usually, loud crowds and thumping bass would have put her in a catatonic stupor, her nerves stretched thin. But tonight, for whatever reason, she felt grounded, calm.

Sherry adjusted the collar of her black sleeveless jumpsuit, which clung just enough to show she meant business without revealing too much. The plunging neckline was her one risk, but with the belted gold chain and patent leather heels, she looked sharp.

She spotted Malka instantly, seated at her usual table and sipping on her signature dirty martini. Malka was the picture of old-school glamour—black dress, long gloves, heels, her black wings shifting subtly behind her with her mood. The short black horns on her head were as much a part of her outfit as her sultry expression. Even from across the room, Sherry could see that Malka was holding court like the queen of the night she was.

Pushing through the crowd, Sherry tried not to get jostled

by the near-moshing going on near the band. Along the way, she spotted a few of the city's lesser villains milling about, like Lull, sitting in the corner in black shades and a biker jacket, trying hard to give off a vibe that crossed Tom Sturridge with an emo frontman. Sherry smirked, amused at her private nickname for him, The Drowsinator. Lull's power was to make people sleep. And, like Malka's powers, it didn't work on her. He'd tried once. She had actually yawned, but then again, it might have been boredom. He liked to talk about himself. A lot.

Glancing around, she reminded herself how capable she was, her thoughts a little smug. She scoffed, "Posers." For all the supervillain talk around here, no one in the place, not even Malka, had pulled off something like that, but Sherry had, and all she'd had was her brains and a love of art. "Supervillains indeed."

Malka waved her over, her eyes glinting as she said something to the men at her table. They scattered.

"Alright, I'm here," Sherry said, dropping into a chair with a sharp edge to her voice. "Where's the painting?"

Malka pursed her lips, her eyes flicking to the band. "I can't hear you!" she yelled. "Come on!"

With a sigh, Sherry got up and followed Malka through the noise of the club and up the back stairs. She hated this part of Sin City—the second floor was where things got creepy. It was all themed rooms for pleasure; each one catered to a specific fantasy or desire. Some were relaxed and carefree, like the Tropic Room, complete with a small pool and screens that sported tropical vistas. You could even order a Piña Colada. Most of the rooms specialized in other kinds of fluid exchanges, some more risqué than others. She felt the oppressive silence as the door shut behind them, the soundproofing cutting them off from the chaotic energy downstairs.

Malka led her to the first door on the right—her office. At Malka's offer, Sherry placed her hand on the palm reader, and the door slid open.

"See?" Malka purred with a smile. "I've never removed

your access."

"I don't know why not," Sherry quipped, trying to sound more confident than she felt. "I did steal a Rembrandt from one of the most secure art galleries in the world."

Malka smirked. "Yes, well, we did work there together once. Remember the time we had sex in the impressionist wing?"

Sherry turned and glared at her. "Malka, stop. This isn't some cozy reunion, so don't bother. And if you're suggesting the only reason I pulled off the heist was because we worked there, let me tell you something—your club downstairs has thirty-six cameras, two thermals, which are new, and sixteen motion detectors. Each of the cash registers has gone all electronic, but you keep a fair amount of cash on hand for—"

Before she could finish, Malka moved fast, pinning her to the wall, her wings spread wide as one talon traced Sherry's cheek. The light scent of woodsmoke filled Sherry's mouth and nose. "I love it when you talk dirty," Malka whispered, low and husky, lips a hairsbreadth from Sherry's.

"Knock it off." Sherry shoved her back, her pulse racing. She struggled to keep her cool, but a part of her still missed this: the heat, the intensity, the insanity. Malka had always been bossy, but since her transformation, she had become entirely dominant. And, God help her, it turned Sherry on. But she couldn't let that show. Malka was her ex. Emphasis on ex. No matter how much she might still feel something, there was no going back. "I'm here for the painting. That's it."

Malka pouted, sticking out her lower lip like a child denied a treat. "You're no fun anymore."

That familiar pout tugged at something inside Sherry, but she pushed it down, taking Malka's hand with a small sigh. "I was never the fun one. That was you, remember? You were the wild one; I was the one making sure you didn't kill yourself."

Malka's expression shifted, her voice a little more caustic and a lot more sarcastic. "Oh, yes, the sober guardian. How could I forget? Don't be ridiculous." She tugged Sherry along.

Given her reputation for insatiable appetites and a succubus image, Malka kept her office decor surprisingly tame: dark gray walls, light gray carpet, and a massive obsidian desk perched on stainless steel legs. Even her chair was a plain, if cushy, black thing, though it was an Old Hickory Tannery worth probably about twenty grand. And right there, plain as day, in the middle of her desk, sat the Rembrandt. Sherry glanced at it but forced herself not to react. She didn't want to seem eager. This was a game, one she and Malka had played before. She had to keep an air of indifference.

"Why don't you sit with me?" Malka purred, motioning to the plush loveseat by the windows.

Sherry sauntered over, taking one of the single chairs. "Are you done messing around?"

The window was open, and a light breeze pushed Malka's stylized curls around. Malka smiled, more friendly than seductive this time. "You really make it hard for me to keep up my villain persona." She poured them both a scotch from the wet bar hidden in the wall. "So, tell me, what's turned you to a life of crime?"

Sherry snorted. "You did. You left me broke, remember? Then Mixxer reached out with an offer I couldn't refuse."

"Mixxer," Malka murmured, her smile tightening. "Tell me more."

"Not much to tell," Sherry said with a shrug. "He got my name from someone at the museum. For a while, I thought it was you, but then I realized even you wouldn't stoop so low as to steal a priceless work of art."

"Says the woman who actually stole it," Malka chuckled, and the sound sent a familiar shiver down Sherry's spine. "Well, I wouldn't have gone through Mixxer. If I wanted the Rembrandt, I would have asked you directly."

Sherry raised an eyebrow. "So, you know him?"

"I do," Malka said, her tone shifting slightly, becoming more languid. "If you've made a deal with him, you should stick to it. He keeps his promises. But don't disappoint him. If you want, I can call him for you and smooth things over—"

"No!" Sherry interrupted, maybe too quickly. She took a calming sip of her scotch. "I'll handle it. I don't need anyone else stepping in, but I do need the painting back."

Malka smiled knowingly, clearly enjoying the back and

forth. "You're so stubborn," she teased. "Okay, but first, let's catch up a little."

Sherry eyed the Rembrandt again but forced herself to stay cool. This was Malka's game: playful seduction, a bit of flirty conversation, and then pretending she was still the same. And, maybe she was, deep down. Malka wasn't just the demonic vixen she showed the world. There was still a part of her that Sherry had fallen in love with.

"So, how's life? I heard you lost your job," Malka said, easing onto the loveseat. "Was it that guy? What's his name? Fabio or Fernando?"

"Federico," Sherry corrected, sinking a little deeper into her chair. "Yeah. The company bought an AI art program. It can produce anything I could draw in a fraction of the time. Federico's still there, but I don't think he'll last long, either. If you've got a machine churning out art, why keep the department?"

Malka listened, nodding sympathetically. "Corporate world's brutal."

"You're telling me," Sherry said, sipping her scotch. "I get it now—this is how people at GM felt in the '80s."

Malka settled in beside her, that familiar gleam in her eye. She patted the seat next to her. "You know, I could use someone with your skills. Ever think about running Sin City with me?"

Sherry's eyes widened. "Wait, seriously?" She hadn't expected that. Usually, Malka's offers were teasing, more flirty banter than serious proposals. But this sounded… different.

"Think about it," Malka said, leaning back. "It's a real offer, and we have dental." She smiled at that last, revealing her pearl-white teeth, complete with elongated canines.

Before Sherry could respond, Timothy, Malka's inept bar supervisor, barged into the office, wheezing with effort as if he'd just escaped a burning building. Sherry and Malka both turned, Sherry with a glacial stare and Malka with an arched eyebrow, one corner of her mouth tugging downward in faint annoyance.

"They're here!" Timothy wheezed, gripping the doorframe

like a lifeline. "Charlie and Mary—they're here."

Malka's expression didn't shift from mild irritation. "So handle it."

Timothy's face crumpled. "But… they have guns."

Malka pressed two fingers to the sensitive skin at the base of her horns, her voice dry with barely restrained contempt. "Oh, for hell's sake."

Sherry watched Timothy as if he were something unfortunate under her shoe. Timothy squirmed, trying to avoid her gaze, one hand twitching instinctively—the same hand she'd broken with a beer stein when he'd tried one of his infamous unsolicited "friendly" touches. Sherry couldn't fathom why Malka kept him around other than for the amusement of watching him grovel. Maybe he had a particularly impressive "asset" tucked somewhere out of sight —though Sherry doubted it.

With a sharp glance at Sherry, Malka said, "Stay here." She swept past Timothy, tossing him one final look of disdain. "And do come along, Timothy."

Timothy nodded, visibly shrinking under Sherry's scornful gaze before quickly scuttling out after Malka, shutting the door behind him. Sherry leaned back, her lips curling with distaste as she savored the brief silence he left in his wake.

Sherry sat there for a few moments, staring at the door. What was that all about? After a minute, she wandered over to the desk, eyes drifting to the Rembrandt. Reaching out, she brushed her fingers along the edge of the frame, pausing when she felt a small groove along one edge.

Curious, she pressed on it. A hidden compartment popped open, revealing two small vials of blue liquid nestled inside.

"What the hell?" she whispered, picking one up carefully. The liquid inside shimmered, little crystal-like particles darting around in the light.

She was so engrossed in it that she didn't notice the commotion outside until it was too late. A loud pop-pop sounded from the club, startling her. She lost her balance, slamming both hands to the desk to catch herself. Glass shattered, and pain lanced through her palm as the blue liquid seeped into her skin.

"Oh, shit," she hissed, watching the strange goo disappear into her cut, leaving behind a thin blue line barely visible to the human eye.

Panic rising, she barely had time to register what had happened when the door burst open. Malka stormed back in, her wings flaring wide.

"Out the back. Now!" Malka snapped.

Sherry grabbed the Rembrand as Malka practically flung her toward the rear door. Stumbling, but with Malka helping her regain her feet, Sherry just managed to dodge the main door as it was blasted off its hinges.

Chapter Six

"Holy shit!" Sherry cried as she staggered, lost a heel, and crashed to the floor. Scrambling up, she bolted for the back door. But the second she threw it open, a flash of orange fur snapped at her feet. "Jesus!" she yelped, stumbling back onto her ass, kicking frantically at the snarling menace. It was a corgi—no, six corgis, all scrabbling through the door, surrounding her. She swung the metal frame at one, but it dodged as another sank its teeth into her ankle. "Help!"

Malka stormed into the pack barefoot, kicking the dogs with a heat that shimmered off her body. The fur on the corgis singed as she struck, but they didn't scatter. Instead, more poured in from the main hallway, and behind them followed the strangest sight Sherry had ever seen.

She blinked. Then blinked again. Marching in was the spitting image of King Charles from forty years prior, decked out in a pristine Gieves & Hawkes suit. In one hand, he gripped a gold scepter like a club. "I believe that will be quite enough," he said in a crisp, upper-crust British accent. Flanking him, men in full Beefeater uniforms followed, carrying assault rifles.

Sherry turned toward the rear door, only to see a woman dressed like Bloody Mary Tudor stride in, a pistol in hand. More henchmen filed in behind her, rifles raised. The well-trained corgis growled, baring their fangs as they circled her and Malka. "What in the fuck?" Sherry said, at a loss for anything else.

"I," the man said, voice dripping with genteel charm, "am King Charles, and this is my lovely partner, Queen Mary."

"The first," Queen Mary added confidently.

"And we are—pause for effect—The Royal Family. These are my faithful hounds, and these gentlemen here are some of my servants. We are here to relieve you of that painting, my dear."

Sherry burst out laughing. She couldn't help it. It was the most ludicrous thing she'd ever seen. "I'm sorry," she gasped between laughs. "I'm so sorry. I just…I can't…"

"Yes, meeting us can be quite a fright and set the senses afire, but I assure you, if you don't hand over that painting right now, I will be forced to put a bullet between your eyes." As he said this, he drew out a Walther PPK and pointed it directly at Sherry's forehead.

Malka's heat subsided as she eased over to Sherry's side, plucked away the Rembrandt, and whispered in Sherry's ear. "When I give the signal, run and jump out the window." Then she turned to King Charles. "Charlie, you know that Ivan will kill you for this."

"Oh really," Charles scoffed. "And where is he? No one has seen or heard from Ivan in eons. Almost everyone is convinced that you killed him yourself, and you're just using his name as a clever ruse."

Sherry snorted another laugh at the way he said ruse, drawn out and so stereotypically British as to be absurd. Mary scowled at her, and Sherry did her best to stifle her giggles as she pulled herself off the floor, hands raised. No matter what she did, though, she couldn't get the grin off her face. "This is ridiculous."

"Oh, do please keep taunting us," Charles said, the gun now pointed at Malka. "I'm sure—"

"Catch!" Malka cried and flung the painting at him. Charles dropped his gun in an attempt to catch the Rembrandt.

Malka grabbed Sherry, her wings snapping open as they leaped over the corgis toward the window. Sherry didn't need a signal. She sprinted through the pop of gunfire and dove headfirst. Before she even started to fall, Malka's arms were under her, gliding them both to the street below. They hit the ground rolling, narrowly dodging an oncoming bus.

A dozen black sedans squealed to a stop across the street in front of the club, vomiting a mass of well-armed men in suits. Malka pulled her off the ground. "I'll get the painting back, but those are Ivan's men, and you need to go. Now!"

"What about you?" Sherry asked, glancing up at the enormous picture window. King Charles glared at them.

"I'll be fine," Malka said, leaning in to kiss Sherry. The kiss was hurried and chaste, but it seared Sherry's lips like fire. "I'm sorry about all this. But it'll be okay. I'll make sure this doesn't come back on you. Now, go!"

Sherry hesitated a moment longer before taking off toward the subway entrance. There was nothing she could do here.

"Shit," she growled when she was safely headed toward her side of town. "Shit. Shit. Shit." Mixxer was going to kill her. She was a dead woman walking.

Chapter Seven

Jemma watched from high above as people streamed out of Sin City. She wasn't sure what was happening, but she'd missed the bulk of it. Several of Ivan's cars and vans were outside. She assumed the sporadic gunfire inside was from his security detail. Moments later, the gunfire turned silent, and two vehicles sped away from the club's back door: an old Jaguar XJ and a black Mercedes panel van. A few minutes later, Jemma watched Lady Sin herself walk across the street in a tattered dress. As she stalked inside, a dozen of Ivan's men came out, leaving in a hurry. Finally, the police showed up. Still, Jemma just waited. She wasn't here for a shoot-out between rival gangs, which she assumed this was. She was here to talk to Sin.

It was almost three hours before Sin's face appeared in the window, gazing down forlornly at the police cars. As soon as Sin disappeared back inside, Jemma decided that was her cue. Silently, she drifted down to the window and floated into Sin's office.

Sin sat behind her desk, tending to a couple of minor cuts with some gauze and alcohol.

"What happened here?" Jemma asked as she touched down softly on the carpet, one sneaker slipping slightly on what looked like dog drool. She didn't bother to hide her accent; there was no point. Sin knew Lena's cover, even if Jemma didn't know a thing about Lady Sin.

Sin looked up and sighed. "If you'd like one, the scotch is in the wet bar behind you, Jemma."

"I thought we agreed you wouldn't call me that," Jemma answered. "And I don't drink when I'm working."

Sin chuckled. "Well, then, be a dear and fix me one while I nurse my boo-boos, would you?"

Jemma shook her head but did as Sin asked. Sin held out her hand for the scotch, but Jemma just slid it across the desk.

"Still afraid to touch me?" Sin smirked, eyes twinkling. "Nice to know that Harborhaven's premier hero is afraid of something."

"Afraid? No. Cautious, yes. Especially after last time," Jemma said flatly and sat on the desk. Sin looked like she'd just been through hell, and Jemma was terribly curious as to what the fuck was up. "Please just tell me that no innocents were hurt."

"Well, Lull is definitely never coming back. He got a minor graze and had a fit," Sin said and winced as she wiped a cut on her forearm.

"You mean somnolence-man? That's no loss," Jemma laughed derisively. "I was referring to civilians, not wanna-be supervillains."

"No," Sin said, lifting the icy drink to her forehead. "No civilians. I do try to keep the peace."

"Good job," Jemma sneered.

Sin shot her a contemptuous glance. "I trust you're not here just to prattle on about the state of my affairs, so what brings you to my domain?"

"I'm looking for a Rembrandt. It was stolen yesterday from The Met. What can you tell me about it?"

"That's news to me," Sin replied, her voice relaxed and casual. "Which one?"

"It's called 'The Solitary Watchman,' I believe, and I'd very much like to find it."

Sin held her hands up in mock surrender, grinning. "Not a clue, darling. If I had it, don't you think I'd be bragging by now? Maybe hosting a private exhibition in some undisclosed location?"

Jemma rolled her eyes. "Very subtle, Sin. Just admit it—if you know something, just say so."

Sin shook her head with a chuckle. "Jemma, really. I'd love to help, but as shocking as it may seem, I have no hand in this one. I'd tell you if I did. You know how much I love an audience for my finest moments. On that note, art theft is a little below your pay grade, is it not, darling?"

Jemma smirked, leaning back with her arms crossed. "Professional curiosity. My day job, you know?" she said smoothly. It was a plausible story. "Maybe one day, you'll tell me about yours."

Sin chuckled, giving her a playful look. "Oh, it's best you don't know. Besides, I'm terribly boring when I'm not between the sheets, as you well know."

Jemma rolled her eyes. "Right. Boring. That's exactly how I'd describe you." Despite the glibness, her cheeks burned with the reminiscence. It had been a lapse—a regrettable, intoxicating lapse. An awful, sexy, hot, amazing, earth-shattering lapse. She hadn't planned on slipping into bed with Harborhaven's most infamous nightclub owner, especially not one with her… connections. But Sin's allure was like standing too close to an open flame, knowing she'd get burned and reaching in anyway. Even now, she couldn't say if it was the thrill or the guilt that lingered longer. That had been one hell of a walk of shame.

Sin, smirking, had insisted she'd never put the "whammy" on her, though Jemma wasn't so sure. Besides, it made a convenient excuse for her own lapse in judgment. Moreover, she'd been sloppy that night, leaving her kit out in the open for Sin to find. Just one mistake in a long list, but this one stung the most.

Because the truth was, Sin's charm had been like smoke—sultry and thick and thoroughly suffocating. Jemma had loved it. It called to a darkness in her that she kept tightly bottled. She had to. And, in retrospect, the knowledge of what Sin was tied up in, her association with Ivan and his web of shady dealings and penchant for violence, made Jemma's stomach twist. It wasn't Sin's reputation for sleeping around that made her skin crawl—Jemma wasn't one to throw stones there. It was that lingering shadow, the cold certainty that she and Sin were on a crash course. One day, they'd meet as enemies, not lovers.

"What?" Sin said, and Jemma realized she was staring.

"Sorry, I was just thinking," Jemma said, trying to recover. Sin grinned like the Cheshire cat. Just how dreamy-eyed had Jemma looked? She suppressed a shiver. "Anyway, I got a tip that Ivan had arranged for the painting to come to town. I wanted to find out why."

"Well, Ivan hasn't said word one about a painting." She put a bandage on one cut and then started tending to another, flinching again with the alcohol. This one was on her forehead and was bleeding a little more freely. Sin kept hitting just the edge of it, having no mirror to use and blood dripping into her eye.

Jemma shook her head, taking the alcohol and gauze from Sin's hands with a gentle firmness. "Here, let me." She guided Sin's hand aside and carefully wiped away the blood, focused on each movement as she tended to the wound.

Sin looked up at her with a familiar smirk, her dark eyes gleaming with warmth. "You going to kiss it better, too?"

Rolling her eyes but smiling, Jemma dabbed carefully at the cut and ignored the dig. "I don't think it'll need stitches," she murmured, pressing a fresh piece of gauze to the wound. She paused, her tone softening. "So, are you going to tell me what happened?"

Sin shrugged. "Territorial dispute with Charlie."

Jemma snorted a laugh. "Charlie? Are he and Mary still parading around with those ridiculous dogs?"

Sin chuckled, the sound warm and familiar between them. "Yes. You should have seen it—he's practically a clone of King Charles, or at least how he looked before… well…everything."

Jemma's smile softened, her tone growing thoughtful. "Yeah, I miss Lady Di, too." She gave Sin a meaningful look. "But why on earth would Charlie and Mary pick a fight now? And please tell me it's over?"

Sin's smirk faded, her brow creasing as she looked up, causing the blood to bead again. "Oh, it's over, alright," she said with a steely finality that surprised Jemma, her tone touched with a fierce indignation.

"I know that look, Sin. Please don't start a street war. I leave you be because you help keep things peaceful around here. I don't want to have to deal with you or Charlie. Especially Charlie."

Sin gave her a mock-hurt look, raising an eyebrow. "Why, especially Charlie? You sleeping with him, too? Two-timing me?"

Jemma snickered. "Not a chance; you know he's not my type. I was thinking about the dogs. The pound would put them down if things got out of hand."

"The corgis?!" Sin's voice rose, her eyes wide and incredulous. "You'd choose those pampered little mutts over me?"

Jemma laughed, picking up an adhesive bandage and spreading some antibacterial gel on it. She pressed it carefully to Sin's head, ensuring none of Sin's hair was caught underneath. "There," she murmured, smoothing the bandage. "All better. And don't worry—I'd almost definitely think of you before the dogs."

"Gee, thanks," Sin said sarcastically, but then she reached up with one hand to cover Jemma's, her expression softening. "Seriously, though, thanks." She sounded surprisingly sincere.

Jemma held her gaze for a moment, feeling the warmth of Sin's hand over hers before she cleared her throat. "So... Charlie just waltzed in and started shooting?"

Sin nodded, her mouth twisting in annoyance as she tended to a nasty set of punctures on her left hand. "Yeah, he swaggered into the bar like he was bloody royalty, then started shooting at my guys because Ivan was—how did he put it?— 'treading on his toes.' By then, though, it was already a brawl. No one was listening."

Jemma gently took hold of Sin's left wrist, turning it over to inspect the bite marks. "Looks like one of those little corgi brutes got a piece of you," she said, her tone soft as she poured alcohol over the wound and started to clean it, watching Sin wince just slightly at the sting. She grabbed a roll of gauze and wrapped it carefully, her fingers gentle but firm. "There," she said, admiring her work with a faint smile. "All bandaged up, ready to go a few rounds." She playfully waved her own wrapped hand at Sin, making light of the moment.

Sin gave a mock sigh, leaning back with a dazzling smile that sent a little shiver through Jemma. "Not with you, though. You'd kick my ass," Sin teased, her dark eyes gleaming with that familiar, mischievous heat. "But tell me—why are you so nice to me? I'm the 'villain,' or so I hear."

Jemma met her gaze, giving her a genuine smile. "Because you're the closest thing I have to a friend and because I'm wired this way. Hate just isn't in my vocabulary." She paused, chuckling. "Except for Il Douchebag. He's a well-deserved exception."

Sin snickered, her grin wide. "I'm sure he'd say the same about you, darling." She hesitated, then leaned a little closer, her voice dropping to a soft, enticing tone. "You know, you could stay. I've got a king-sized bed, and I'd bet anything you're still sleeping on that awful futon."

Jemma opened her mouth to protest, but Sin cut in with a look of mock innocence that did nothing to dim the spark of desire in her eyes. "I promise I won't do anything you don't want," she purred, her smile curling at the edges in that dangerously tempting way.

Jemma felt her cheeks warm again, but she rolled her eyes and shook her head with a laugh. "No. No way. I just came by to ask about the Rembrandt."

Sin tilted her head, eyebrows waggling mischievously. "What if I told you I knew something about that Rembrandt? Would you stay then?"

Jemma hesitated, feeling a twinge of excitement. Though whether it was the possibility of finding out about the painting or Sin's offer that went with it, she wasn't sure. Why did Sin always make her feel this way?

"I might," she replied, finally, her tone cautious. "So, do you?"

Sin watched her for a beat, a glint of amusement in her eyes before she shook her head. "No. Just wanted to see if you'd bite." She grinned, clearly pleased with herself. "But really, what's so special about this painting?"

Jemma moved away and lifted casually off the desk. "It's just a big payday," she lied smoothly, shrugging. "My honor is worth the commission."

"Uh-huh." Sin looked at her with a skeptical tilt of her head, clearly unconvinced but letting it slide. "Well, if anything comes across my desk, you'll be the first to know," she yawned. "But for now, I'm going to bed. Ivan left a couple of his goons downstairs, so Charlie and his circus won't be bothering me tonight."

Sin stood, stretching languidly, giving Jemma a full view of every inch of flesh exposed by her tattered gown. Then she sashayed toward the door, throwing a last, lingering glance over her shoulder at Jemma, one hand resting on the doorframe. "If you're not staying, you can see yourself out. Unless, of course..." She trailed off, eyes sparkling with invitation, before smirking and shooing her playfully toward the window.

"I mean it, Sin," Jemma said as she turned to go. "If you hear about the Rembrandt, I need to know."

"I heard you," she called back. "And I'll try not to start a war with Charlie, but I must do something. You know that."

Jemma just nodded, slipping out through the window, but she couldn't shake the unsettled feeling that lingered in her chest. She liked Sin, even respected her in a strange, unspoken fashion. Sin was sharp, witty, and charming in that infuriating way, and, unlike everyone else, she treated Jemma as an equal rather than someone to fear or worship. And as for the bed invitation? Jemma didn't really want that. Not with Sin, at least.

No, her mind kept drifting back to Sherry. The whole time she'd been tending to Sin's wounds, she'd been thinking about Sherry's laugh, her goofy grin, the way her awkward charm made her seem endearingly sweet. Sherry was the opposite of Sin's magnetic danger; she was warm and safe. There was an openness to her, something uncomplicated and without ulterior motives.

It wasn't that she wasn't interested in sleeping with Sherry. She most certainly was, but it was more that Sherry's sweetness—the genuine, guileless kind—was refreshing. It made her feel like, for once, she could relax, let down her guard. Despite her reservations, Jemma was already looking forward to their date, and a tiny smile played at her lips.

Airborn and away from Sin City, Jemma pulled her cell phone from her thigh pocket, her thumb lingering for a long time over Sherry's Artline contact. Should she call her? They already had a date scheduled, and she didn't want to seem like some insecure stalker.

Jesus. I've faced down mobsters, career criminals, and even lightning-wielding techno-nuts. Now I can't summon up the pluck to call a girl I just met? Of course, those guys could only give her a singe or piss her off. They couldn't smash her heart to pieces. And they wouldn't die if she screwed up.

But then again, she had learned a lot from her past mistakes, hadn't she? She was a little wiser, and she wouldn't get herself hip-deep before she knew what she was doing. Instead, she put her phone away and shot back home to change.

Chapter Eight

By the time Sherry got home, she felt like dogshit. Her head pounded, her stomach churned, and a cough rattled in her chest. She staggered into the bathroom, dropping her keys, bag, and phone on the couch. Somewhere along the way, she'd lost her other shoe—probably when she jumped out the window. Splashing water on her face, she shivered. She had to be feverish.

In the mirror, her reflection was pale, her eyes bloodshot. Every joint ached, head to toe. She glanced down at the thin blue line on her palm. "Oh, God," she whispered. "It's a biological weapon. I'm gonna die."

A sharp pain shot through her stomach, like she'd swallowed ground glass. She dropped to the linoleum and vomited up the scotch.

Should she go to the hospital? She hugged the cold toilet bowl. She knew she should. She should call an ambulance. But what would she say? "Hey, I stole a Rembrandt and got infected by a biological weapon someone smuggled inside." Yeah, that'd go over well. Isolation ward, then jail—if she even survived. "Fuck."

She crawled to the couch on her hands and knees when her legs refused to support her. Lifting her head to find her phone, the world spun, and she gave a few dry heaves. Tears slid down her cheeks. This was it.

Fucking Mixxer, the bastard had killed her. If he'd warned her, she wouldn't have messed with that compartment. Hell, she wouldn't have touched the painting in the first place. Worse, whatever she'd contracted was probably contagious. She might be the start of a pandemic. Mass murder by bio-weapon wasn't exactly on her to-do list this week.

For some reason, that thought made her laugh uncontrollably. It wasn't funny, but she couldn't stop. She rolled onto her back, hysterical, like it was the funniest thing she'd ever heard.

The laughter stopped abruptly, though, when everything went black. Panic rose in her chest. Her eyes were open, but she couldn't see. She was blind. "Oh God," she whispered, more hot tears flowing over her lashes. She weakly batted her hand around, trying to find her phone, but knocked it across the floor instead.

After a few minutes of fruitless attempts to move and find it, her stomach cramped up, and she doubled over, finally curling up fetal on the floor.

She lay there for hours, moaning softly, unable to move or think. Her phone rang a few times, but the pain was too much —her joints felt like they were on fire, muscles cramping constantly. Every so often, her heart fluttered painfully, like a bad palpitation, but a thousand times worse. How long had it been? It had to have been hours now.

Gorge rose in her throat again, and she rolled onto her side as hot, salty liquid spewed from her mouth. *Blood. It's a hemorrhagic fever of some sort. Some kind of super ebola.*

With what felt like a colossal effort, she swept her hand around the floor. Her trembling fingers touched something ice-cold—her phone. Sightless and barely able to control her violently spasming hand, she tapped her phone fruitlessly. She needed help. Somewhere, dimly through the agony, she knew she should've called an ambulance when she had the chance. Luck, though, was on her side that night.

Jemma had just gotten the makeup off the lower half of her face when her phone rang. She barked a laugh at the contact image. Answering, she pressed the phone between her ear and her shoulder. "Couldn't wait?"

People always assumed superheroes had some kind of sixth sense. In comic books, they did. But Jemma had never met anyone with Spidey-Sense—not one. And honestly, she was pretty sure spiders didn't have it either, just a bunch of creepy black eyes. What Jemma did have was the absolute certainty that if someone were going to attack a shopping mall or try to rob a government convoy, it would happen at the least convenient time. Like bedtime. Every. Single. Time.

"Sherry?" Jemma pressed when all she heard were scrabbling sounds. "You there?" Crap. A butt-dial. She was about to hang up when she heard it—a faint, agonized whimper that chilled Jemma's blood, followed by a bark of gritty, nasty-sounding coughing. Then, another whimper of pain.

"Sherry! Talk to me!" Jemma almost screamed.

Finally, a squeaking, tiny "Help me" emerged from the speaker, followed by a breathy, wheezing "Please."

"I need your address, honey," Jemma said as calmly as she could.

Sherry whispered the building name and croaked, "Eighth floor," then screamed. Ice filled Jemma's veins. She didn't wait. She snatched her underwear, sleep shorts, and shirt and balled them up in one fist. She didn't bother with shoes, but she did grab the one truly expensive thing she owned: her sapphire-lensed flight goggles and put them on. A split second later, clenching her phone in her free hand, she took a deep breath, held it, and launched into the night. Sonic booms trailed her the whole way.

In seconds, Jemma reached the building. Her flight goggles burned against her skin as she let them hang on her neck. After a quick scan of the eighth-floor exterior, she found Sherry's balcony, where she dressed, and peeked inside.

"Sherry!" she exclaimed, almost shattering the glass as she

opened the door.

Sherry lay facedown. A small pool of blood lay beneath her head, with some still trickling from her mouth. "Jesus, Sherry," she breathed and felt for a pulse. It was thready, and Sherry's breathing was shallow. Jemma pulled out her cell phone and called 9-1-1.

"9-1-1 What's your emergency?" A calm, professional voice said, sounding a bit bored.

Jemma rushed out a panicked response. "My girlfriend is passed out on the floor and bleeding from her mouth. There's a lot of blood. She's unconscious. I think she fell. Her pulse is weak and rapid, and her breathing is shallow. Please hurry." Without waiting for the operator to ask, Jemma gave her the address.

Eight minutes passed, a seeming lifetime, before the paramedics knocked. Both were female, one with broad shoulders and a butch haircut. The other was blonde and a bit smaller. While Butch-cut checked Sherry's vitals, the other took Jemma's statement.

"So, tell me what happened."

"This is how I found her." Jemma's demeanor crumbled, and her voice faltered. "I didn't want to move her in case she had a neck injury. That's all I know. Her pulse was one-ten, I think, and her respiration was quick. I…" It didn't make any sense. They barely knew each other. She'd seen people torn apart, shattered by impacts—always felt pity, maybe sadness— but gut-wrenching, breath-stealing panic? Never. But the thought of losing Sherry had Jemma spiraling, and she couldn't stop it.

"Ma'am," the woman said, placing a gloved hand on Jemma's shoulder. "We'll take the best care of her we can. Can you tell us anything else?"

Jemma shook her head and stood there, watching in abject terror as they placed a C-collar on her and put her on oxygen.

Moments later, three more medics arrived: a handsome older guy, barrel-chested with a graying beard, a young Asian woman who looked like she spent every off minute with weights and steroids, and a skinny blonde fellow with slightly bloodshot eyes who looked like he'd just woken up.

The older guy carried a backboard. "Gurney's outside the stairwell in the lobby. It won't quite fit in the elevator."

The butch paramedic sighed. "I was afraid of that. I guess it's the stairs."

Scowling as her temper spiked, Jemma flailed in anger. "Fuck. She's probably dying, and you're worried about a few steps? I should have just taken her myself."

The blonde and the butch girl stared at her for a split second, and Jemma took in a deep breath. "I'm sorry, that was uncalled for. I'm just scared."

Butch-cut gave her a sympathetic look, and then they lifted Sherry off the floor and carried her out. "Good God," the blonde blurted. "She's a lot heavier than she looks."

Jemma corralled her fear and anger. "Can I help?"

"No, ma'am," Butch-cut replied. "We've got this. It was just a surprise. She's pretty small. Why don't you ride with us." Jemma nodded and followed.

Once Sherry was in the ambulance, Jemma climbed in with the medics, gripping a bar near the door. Under the harsh fluorescent light, Sherry looked awful—ashen gray, tinged with green. Her eyes were bloodshot, pupils blown. Jemma's heart skipped a beat when she saw the pulse-ox: sixty-three percent. She didn't know much, but she knew that was bad, especially for someone in their twenties. "Jesus," she muttered.

The medic cranked up the oxygen, but Sherry's sats kept dropping.

Tears flowed freely from Jemma's eyes. Sherry was so nice, and Jemma couldn't understand how she could be so sick. It seemed so unfair and wrong, and a vice-like tightness clamped around Jemma's chest when the medic cut open Sherry's bra and placed leads. The heart monitor sprang to life, but it didn't beep.

"She's crashing," Butch-cut said flatly. "Epi." She banged on the cabin door of the ambulance, and the sirens wailed to life. The ambulance shot forward, pushing Jemma against the back wall. All Jemma could do was watch as Butch-cut started compressions. Jemma closed her eyes, struggling with her helplessness. For all her strength and power, she could do nothing. "God damn it! Sherry," she roared. "Don't you dare die on me!"

Abruptly, the heart monitor burst to life and beeped with a steady rhythm. Sherry sucked in a deep gulp of oxygen, and her eyes fluttered slightly. Then she let out an agonized moan. The blonde stood stock still, the epi injection still in her hand, unused.

"Holy shit," Jemma whispered as Sherry's eyes fluttered. Jemma looked at her sats. They had climbed to ninety-eight. A second later, Sherry screamed and jerked. With a nasty tearing sound and a bang, the nylon safety restraint across Sherry's chest ruptured. Sherry arched her back, then slammed back to the gurney.

"How much epi did you give her?" Butch-cut asked, her eyes and voice filled in equal measure with accusation.

Eyes wide, the blonde jammed the epi injection forward. "None. She started to recover before I could administer it."

The monitors wailed again, and Sherry's blood oxygen plummeted. Jemma glanced at the EKG it looked like static. The paramedics started working Sherry so fast she really couldn't follow, and every muscle in her body drew taught as she waited anxiously. Thirty seconds later, the ambulance pulled into the ER. They were the longest thirty seconds of Jemma's life.

Jemma stood there for a moment, her insides completely undone and twisted in knots as she watched Butch-cut ride the gurney into the ER, still doing compressions. A horrible sense of loss that she couldn't understand roiled inside her. She barely knew her, and it wasn't like Jemma to get caught up over a single victim like this.

No. Victims were the people she saw every day—killed or traumatized by the awful people who used their powers for destruction. But Sherry? Sherry was a person. And even though there were people out there who probably needed her, Jemma wouldn't leave Sherry alone. Jemma had learned long ago that her emotional needs had to come first. Callie had taught her that—before the accident. Callie lying face up, pale and cold with snow drifting across her face, came unbidden to her mind, driving the knife of grief further into Jemma's gut.

With a deep sigh, she found a secluded spot and rose into the night to go home and change.

Chapter Nine

Jemma stayed by Sherry's side for a day and a half. Assuming she was Sherry's girlfriend, no one asked her to leave. Jemma never confirmed it, but neither did she correct them. She wanted to be here. She didn't know why. She thought it might be how much Sherry reminded her of Callie, whom she couldn't save. Her therapist, Jennifer, would have a field day with that one. She was already suggesting that Jemma take a break from hero duty. Not because Jemma couldn't handle the emotional toll; she seemed to be doing okay, if not stellar, in that department.

Jennifer seemed far more worried about Jemma's regular visits to the women's section of 'the penthouse.' She felt Jemma was taking too much of an interest in the rehabilitation of the female villains she defeated, many of whom would almost certainly re-offend. Being a felon was a painful label to carry. But Jemma couldn't bring herself to stop.

Jemma breathed a sigh of relief when Sherry was finally stable and breathing on her own.

With Sherry out of immediate danger, Jemma turned to her own matters. She drove her gray Subaru Solterra—cliché, but electric, and she liked it—to the law offices of Dube, Chester, and Hauk. Or as she liked to call them, Dewey, Cheatham, and Howe. The joke was old and dumb, but it always made her chuckle, especially given the irony: Sanele Dube was brutally honest and almost pathologically ethical.

At the Brattleman Tower, the tallest building in Harborhaven, Jemma was led to a meeting room on the sixty-seventh floor. Out the eastern window, Harborhaven stretched all the way to the cape, a sprawling mix of glittering skyscrapers, quiet neighborhoods, and the endless shimmer of the bay. Her chest tightened with a familiar warmth, and goosebumps rose on her arms. This city wasn't just where she lived—it was a part of her. Liberal and welcoming, Harborhaven had been her sanctuary, a place that had embraced her identity without question, never making her feel like she had to hide who she was. It was where she'd found herself, fallen in love, and built a life that felt truly hers. And despite how that life had been tragically upended, the city still held her in thrall. Sure, the rising cost of living and the occasional crime from people like Il Duce or petty gangs brought their challenges, but nowhere else had ever made her feel this way—alive, accepted, at home. She couldn't imagine living anywhere else.

"Amazing, isn't it?" A male voice, a blend of velvet and smoke, rumbled behind her.

Jemma turned to see the smiling face of Sanele Dube, the tall, handsome black man and managing partner of the firm. A legal folder and pad sat clutched in his meaty hand. He smiled at her, his cut jawline softened slightly by a beard that would have given Common fits of envy. His high-skin fade was pretty tight, too, and highlighted the razor edge of his beard. Broad-shouldered and thickly built, even Jemma couldn't deny his natural charisma. The Armani suit and crisp British accent didn't hurt either. Beyond that, though, Sanele was a lovely man with an even temper and a strong sense of fairness. He was one of Jemma's favorite people, number four on the list of those who knew Jemma's alter-ego.

"Hi," she said with a confident smile. "How have you been?"

Sanele joined her at the window and hugged her shoulders. "I'm good. But how about you? Still living the bachelorette life?"

Jemma laughed weakly. "Trying not to, but my current interest is making it hard. I just met her, and now she's in the hospital. You?"

"Lana's great, as always." Sanele gave her a concerned look. "Do you need to do this later?"

"No," Jemma answered truthfully. She couldn't exactly lie around the man. Not only could he sniff out lies and half-truths like a bloodhound following a trail, but this close to him, she literally couldn't do it, a handy ability for an attorney.

"You know, we have this stunning view, and I seldom take any real time just to look. I'm always busy with one thing or another. Lana's trying to get me to retire, but then I steal just a moment in here by myself and think, 'But where would I get a view like this?'"

Jemma chuckled. "You'll never retire, Sanele. You love this too much. Besides, it's not your legal job that keeps you running around, and we both know it."

"You're probably right." He sat down in one of the chairs, gesturing toward the seat opposite. "Shall we?"

"Sure," Jemma dropped into the offered seat.

Sanele drew out her standard investigation contract. Jemma skimmed over it, but it was the usual, though she noted that the commission for recovery was twice the normal fee, which almost made her eyes bug out.

"They're willing to pay this?" She asked. "That's almost a hundred grand based on the valuation. I thought they would have gone with Frazier." John Frazier was a legend in the recovery space, and the reputation was richly deserved. He was also down to earth. He'd take on anything he thought deserved his attention regardless of how much it paid, and his ideas on that were somewhat eclectic. He'd once taken a case for a small bit of art worth maybe twenty grand just because he liked the artist and thought her work belonged on display, not in some criminal's living room. He was weird like that. More importantly, though, he had a track record of success that even Jemma, as a superhero, envied. She only knew of one case he'd ever chased where he hadn't fully recovered the target, some insane diamond necklace in New York. Even then, he'd recovered part of it and put the culprit behind bars.

"Frazier is in Paris at the moment working on a case of his own," Sanele answered. "You were their second choice."

"Remind me who the insurer is?"

"Rostovich is on sanction. He's paying out of pocket."

Jemma tilted her head. "Interesting. I'm assuming there's an escrow?" In a case like this, where Insurance companies were unable to do business with someone for legal reasons, it wasn't uncommon for wealthy owners to pay for recovery out of pocket, and Rostovich could afford it, but still, a hundred grand for recovery was a lot of money. Of course, that just told Jemma that Rostovich knew what was being smuggled with it. He was desperate to get it back, which for Jemma was good. It meant that the Lot 429 was still missing. The only problem was — "I can't take the case," she responded evenly. "Ethical reasons."

Sanele's eyebrows shot up, and he sat back, stunned. "It's a hundred grand, Jemma."

Kicking herself for her morals, Jemma shook her head. "I'm sorry, Sanele. I just can't. His brother heads the local Bratva organization, and Viktor is his enforcer. Besides, as you said, Rostovich is under sanction. He's also supporting a war of aggression in Eastern Europe, hence the sanctions. I just can't. If it were insured, I'd have done it to make sure the insurance company didn't get screwed, but direct? No. Absolutely not."

The big man sighed and slid the papers back into the folder. "I was afraid you'd say that. I was debating whether to keep it anonymous."

Jemma gave him an appreciative smile. "That's why I like dealing with you, Sanele. You're always above board, and I appreciate it. You'll have to give it to Smith."

Sanele snorted. "Smith couldn't find his arse with a compass and a map, you know that."

"Well, then give it to someone else. I have to take a hard pass. I'm sorry."

Sanele shrugged. "It's okay. I'm not thrilled with it, anyway. It's Travis's client."

Jemma chuckled. Travis Hauk, partner number three, was

the bane of Sanele's existence. Where Sanele was ethical almost to extreme, Hauk walked a fine line that skirted the edge of legal ethics. Jemma suspected that the reason she never saw Hauk and Sanele together was that Hauk couldn't help being totally honest around the big man, even if he didn't know why.

"Hey," Sanele asked. "Are you sure you're okay?"

Jemma swallowed hard, deciding whether to answer. "You know your abilities would make you a really good therapist," she said, delaying the inevitable.

"No, it wouldn't. Most people need some lies they tell themselves to stay sane. Besides, there are things I do not need to know. Trust me."

"I bet," Jemma said with a laugh before finally answering his original question. "I met someone I like, which wouldn't be an issue. Normally, it would be one night and done, but I can't seem to do that. Worse, I barely know her, but..." she trailed off with visible effort. He was way too easy to talk to.

A wide grin split Sanele's face. "Oh, girl, you are in trouble. You finally met someone who doesn't just make you think, 'I want to hit that and move on.'"

With a nervous laugh, Jemma shifted in her seat. "She's nice and all, but there is no way I can get involved with someone right now."

"Uh-huh," Sanele said, narrowing his eyes at her.

Jemma raised an eyebrow, her eyes narrowing ever so slightly, lips pressed into a thin line. She couldn't decide whether Senele was being deliberately difficult. "I can't lie this close to you."

"Unless you're lying to yourself," Senele retorted. "You can do that all day. So, are you going to see her again?"

Jemma thought about how to answer, fighting the impulse to simply spit out the truth. Ultimately, she couldn't think of a better option, even though she knew what Sanele would say. "As soon as I leave. Like I said, she's in the hospital."

Sanele lifted one of his bushy eyebrows. "Wait. You barely know her, and you're sitting with her in the hospital?"

Jemma blushed slightly, suddenly wholly unsure of her own feelings. She looked out the other window at the local tech college campus. "Barely is even a stretch. We met once for ten minutes, most of that with me riding on the back of her motorcycle. Now she's really sick, like dying sick. For whatever reason, she called me. I flew over and found her unconscious. I called 9-1-1, and she died several times on the way to the hospital. I…" Jemma stopped, realizing she was giving too much detail. Damnit. She'd let down her guard, and Sanele's ability had gotten the better of her.

Sanele placed a hand on hers. "It's okay. Obviously, you need to talk about it."

Jemma looked up at him. Her eyes probably looked a bit haunted, but she couldn't bring herself to care. "I broke the sound barrier last night getting to her place." She laughed mirthlessly.

"You flew naked?" Sanele's eyes turned to saucers.

Jemma flushed and giggled a bit. "Yeah. I didn't time it, but it was probably a personal best. My goggles were hot."

"What did you do for clothing?" Sanele gave one of his deep, booming laughs.

"Balled up in my hand. I didn't just walk in naked. Give me some credit."

"Well, she must be doing better since you're able to laugh about it," Sanele said.

Jemma had forgotten about his stellar insight. It wasn't superhuman, per se, but it was damned annoying. "Yeah, it was touch and go for a day and a half. But—"

Jemma was interrupted as the door opened, and Hauk walked in. "So, you are both pretty chummy. Are you going to take the case?"

"Can't," Jemma said, all humor leaving her voice. "Why are you even representing scum like Rostovich?"

Hauk opened his mouth, looked at Sanele, then closed it. Finally, he said, "Because there's money involved. Besides, even Russians under sanction are entitled to legal representation."

Jemma eyed him carefully. She'd hoped to catch him off-guard and maybe see if he knew anything, but he was too wary. She opened her mouth to ask another question, but

Hauk interrupted her.

"That's fine. We'll give it to Smith," Hauk said and stepped out.

"Well, that was uncalled for," Sanele said darkly.

Jemma shrugged. "Rostovich is a criminal, you know that, and I already think I've made it clear my opinion of the man."

"Yes, but Hauk handles a lot of our insurance business. You could find yourself in the cold."

Jemma waved her hand dismissively. "Anything big will go to Frazier, and Hauk knows better than to use Smith for anything Frazier won't or can't take. I'm not too worried."

She and Sanele exchanged a few more pleasantries, but the whole time, Jemma was distracted. Her mind flipped back and forth between the sick woman in the hospital waiting for her and the missing painting that she really should be focusing on. And why hadn't she taken the case? She'd already used the excuse as cover with Malka. She couldn't figure out what was wrong with her, and it bothered her.

Chapter Ten

Sherry opened her eyes, stretched her arms out, and immediately regretted it with a groan. Her chest felt like an elephant had been stomping on it. Glancing beneath her hospital gown, she noted EKG leads, wires, and a bruise the size of a watermelon on her chest.

"Did I die?" she asked under her breath. That sure looked like CPR bruising. She'd seen it before when her dad had had his first heart attack. He'd died on the floor, and they'd managed to bring him back.

She glanced around the hospital room. A glass wall covered with various compliance posters and guidance letters separated her from the hall outside. A few people in dark blue hospital scrubs passed by the door, heading in one direction or the other. To her left, a window looked out at a wall of bland brick. Beneath, a figure in street clothes slept on a tiny sofa, curled up and looking extremely uncomfortable. "Jemma?" Sherry said with a croak, her throat hoarse and sore.

The figure stirred and turned over. Long, pretty lashes blinked slowly over fabulous blue eyes until they finally opened. "Hey," Jemma said tiredly and pulled herself up. "How are you feeling?"

"My chest hurts like hell, but otherwise, I feel okay. How did I get here?"

"You don't remember calling me?" Jemma asked, worry

puckering her brow.

Sherry shook her head. "I just remember…" she broke off, trying to figure out what she last remembered. "It hurt," she whispered, then more loudly, "It hurt a lot. I threw up at some point, I think. Then I was on the floor."

Jemma reached into her back pocket and slid something across the table: Sherry's cell phone. "You've been out of it for three days."

Sherry blinked, and the finger of panic poked into her chest. "Three days? Crap." She held up a finger before snatching up her phone and unlocking it. Mixxer had called twice and had left a message. Sherry poked the voicemail button and pressed the phone to her ear.

"Sherry Berry, it's you know who. There's a bit more heat on than I expected, so do me a favor and stash the package somewhere safer. I'll be back in town on the thirtieth. We can take care of business then."

Two weeks. She had two weeks. Breathing a sigh of relief, Sherry set her phone back on the table, face down. "Sorry, something I thought was urgent was postponed. What were you saying?"

"No one could figure out what made you so sick. The doctors think you might have been poisoned."

Sherry nodded and felt every muscle in her body relax. It wasn't a bio-weapon. She'd been poisoned. Then she thought about the bruises on her chest. "I died," she said flatly. "Didn't I?"

Jemma nodded, and Sherry looked away.

"I'm sorry," Sherry said.

Jemma gave her a puzzled look. "For what?"

"For causing so much trouble."

"Did you poison yourself?" Jemma's voice was incredulous and accusing.

"What?! No! Just that you had to rescue me. I most certainly didn't poison myself." Sherry closed her right hand, hiding the blue mark. "I have no idea what happened." She hated the taste of the lie, but there was nothing for it. "I went to a bar last night. Maybe someone spiked my drink."

"Oh!" Jemma said, her relief evident, and Sherry frowned.

"Does that mean you wouldn't date me if I were suffering from depression?"

Jemma stared at her, emotions flashing across her face in quick succession. "No, I'm not like that. My ex suffered from depression for most of her adult life—childhood trauma, you know."

Sherry nodded. "Is that why you broke up?" Sherry put a hand over her mouth. "Shit, I'm sorry. That's none of my business. We barely know each other."

"No," Jemma said with a pained smile. "It's fine. She was killed in a car accident a few years ago."

"I'm sorry," Sherry said and sat up gingerly, reaching out her hand and wiggling her fingers for Jemma's.

Jemma stared at it strangely, as if it were a thing alive that might eat her. Then her hand twitched, and she had this guilty look, like she wanted to take it but didn't think she should.

Sherry pulled her hand away and looked down. She'd overstepped. "Shit, I'm sorry."

"Huh?" Jemma said, looking up. "It's not that at all. I was just surprised. Here you are, in the hospital after almost dying, and you're trying to comfort me. It should be the other way around, that's all." Jemma paused for a second, scooting the chair closer. "Anyway, it was a long time ago. Accidents happen, and you don't always get to do something about it. Sometimes, no matter what you do, you lose."

Sherry put her hand out again. This time, Jemma did take it, and Sherry gave her a sympathetic smile. "But you didn't lose this time. You saved my life, and I'm grateful. My mother raised me to appreciate people. I'm not very good at it sometimes, but I want you to know that I appreciate you."

"Ha," Jemma said. "You haven't gotten to know me yet. I'm a handful." Jemma smiled at her. It had been a joke, Sherry knew, but underneath, she detected that strange tinge of guilt. The confident woman she'd met at the bar wasn't here today, she realized, and this wasn't just a softer image Jemma was projecting; it was the real woman beneath the bravado. She was still self-possessed and poised, but there was a vulnerability about her. And Sherry found that damned attractive, not because she was vulnerable, but because she felt she could be vulnerable.

"So," Sherry said after they'd been sitting like that for a moment. "Are we still on for coffee?"

Jemma glanced up at her. "Sure," she said, and the confidence returned. "But I prefer tea."

Sherry chuckled. "Of course you do."

The door opened, and Jemma quickly pulled her hand away. A doctor, a nurse, and someone with a phlebotomist's kit walked in. Sherry chuckled for a moment at the image. It sounded like the start of a bad joke.

"I'm Doctor Carlsson, Ms. Broward. How are you feeling today?"

Sherry placed her left arm on the bed, palm up, as the nurse raised the head of her bed and checked her vitals. She took a moment to answer, taking stock of her body. "I feel fine. My chest hurts, but otherwise, I'm okay. Do you know what happened?"

The doctor was a man in his mid-forties. As he sat down on a stool and rolled over, he said, "You were pretty sick. Tell me, in the twenty-four hours before you came in, did you eat or drink anything strange, or had you been anywhere unusual?"

"Jemma said you think I was poisoned," Sherry said as he checked her pupils.

"We're not sure. Nothing came back on your toxicology panel, but we'll do another just to be sure." The nurse left, and Sherry flinched as the phlebotomist started taking blood.

"Would you like your girlfriend to stay? I need to check your chest and see how the trauma to your sternum is healing."

Jemma stood and turned a little pink and said, "I'll...uh... wait outside."

Sherry chuckled. "She's not my girlfriend." When Jemma had stepped outside and closed the door, she added, "But I wouldn't mind."

The phlebotomist, a middle-aged Latina, looked at her and grinned. "I don't blame you there, honey."

"I know, right? She's gorgeous."

The doctor continued as if they hadn't spoken. "Well, your labs are a little off. Your CK is 294. Your WBC is 17,000, which is much higher than I'd expect. And your AST, your liver enzymes, are 75. All of that implies that you're metabolizing something toxic. But all of the toxin assays I've run are clean. Do you use illicit substances?"

"Drugs?!" Sherry asked doubtfully. "Hardly. I drink more than I should, probably. But nothing crazy. I'm certainly not a binge drinker, and I don't get wasted."

"How many drinks would you say you have each day?"

Sherry laughed. "Each day? Most days, I don't have any. If I go to the club, I might have three or four, maybe, but I try to keep it to two Martinis, max. I did have three shots of whiskey on Monday, though. And I saw my ex last night, so I had a scotch on the rocks while we talked. That's it."

"With these liver enzyme levels, I'd like you to stay away from alcohol for a while."

Narrowing her eyes and feeling a bit of heat rising in her cheeks, Sherry snapped at him. "How many drinks do you have when you go out? You have a ruddy complexion that looks like telangiectasia. Your palms look like tomatoes, and you're lips are cracked. Those are all signs of advanced alcoholism."

The phlebotomist chuckled and then pressed her lips together.

Hightower blinked. "Your…uh…friend said you were an artist."

"I am," Sherry said, her temper flaring. "But I read a lot, and I don't want this dismissed as alcohol poisoning. I don't drink enough for that, ever. Not only that, I wasn't drunk. I came home feeling like I had the flu. I barfed, and then I started bleeding from the nose and mouth and went blind. I thought I had ebola or something."

The doctor took some notes on his pad. "Is there anything you could have been exposed to? Any chemicals? Or maybe inhaled?"

Sherry rubbed her right forefinger and thumb together

nervously. "No," she lied. "Nothing I can think of. How would I know?"

"Maybe a strange smell. Maybe you drank something with an odd taste? Or were you near any industrial chemicals?"

Sherry shook her head. "No, nothing like that. I was hoping you could tell me, but obviously not."

"Well, we'll see if we can find anything, but I'll get you out of here as soon as possible." Hightower made a few notes and left with an irritated look on his face. Jemma returned a moment later and resumed her seat next to Sherry.

"Damn, honey," the phlebotomist said as she was packing up. "That's one way to get yourself discharged."

"Well, he didn't even ask me how I got here when he walked in. He'd already decided I was a club rat who partied too much. He's a misogynist pig."

The phlebotomist barked a laugh, but she didn't defend the man.

"Well?" Sherry prodded with a grin. The phlebotomist looked at her, opened her mouth as if to say something, then clamped it shut. Finished drawing blood, the woman resumed packing her kit and left, still doing her best not to snicker.

"He's an asshole," Sherry muttered under her breath.

"I think I like you," Jemma said as she walked back in.

"I just want to go home," Sherry muttered, putting on a solid pout. "This place sucks."

"You heard them. You'll probably be discharged soon." Jemma placed a tentative hand on Sherry's. "Do you want a ride home?"

Sherry looked down at Jemma's hand and then back up at her face as she processed Jemma's words. "You don't have to do that."

Jemma gave her an earnest smile. "I want to."

Sherry grinned. "Then I accept." After a moment, more seriously, she added, "And thank you."

Chapter Eleven

Apart from a clothing run to Sherry's apartment, Jemma stayed by her bedside for the whole nine hours until she was discharged, talking & playing cards with a deck she had picked up on the way back to the hospital. They played gin for a while, then switched to Texas Hold 'Em, using a bag of Reese's Pieces as chips. Sherry lost every hand, but it kept her occupied, and Jemma had fun. They had a lot in common, and Jemma learned a great deal about her.

Sherry was twenty-nine and hated being forced to conform. She was a southpaw, which Jemma didn't find surprising since Sherry was an artist. Sherry loved music of all kinds and could play the piano, the guitar, and the hang drum, which Jemma found fascinating. Among her more interesting quirks were a tendency to be a bit flighty and a self-confessed need to rush into new things. She was also terrified of heights, or rather, 'splattering all over the concrete,' as Sherry had said bluntly.

Most of all, though, Sherry loved art. She loved not just making it but also looking at it and analyzing it. It captivated her. That alone made Jemma's heart leap. When they were done, they spent four hours talking about art of all kinds. Well, Sherry did most of the talking, and Jemma listened in rapt attention. All the while, a pleasant feeling welled inside her, like she'd finally met someone who really got her, and by the time the nurse walked in with discharge instructions, Jemma had a huge beaming smile that she just couldn't contain—and, if she was honest, a huge crush.

"Do you two live together?" the nurse asked as she organized the small sheaf of papers. "Or is there someone who can keep an eye on you for the next few days?"

"Um, we just met a few days ago," Sherry muttered, her face rapidly turning crimson, which Jemma thought was absolutely adorable.

The nurse looked pointedly at Jemma. "Well, the question still stands."

Sherry snorted a laugh. "We haven't had our first date, let alone our second, so we haven't had time to U-haul, yet. And my family isn't an option. So, no, not really."

Jemma covered her mouth to hide her grin, impressed at how Sherry hadn't missed a beat. "I'll look out for her. How long?"

Sherry looked back up at her. "Um…"

"Three days. If her improvement continues, she needs to be back here in three days."

"I'll take care of it," Jemma said, throwing Sherry a wink.

The nurse reviewed the discharge papers, and Jemma watched as Sherry half listened and periodically shot a glance her way. Jemma had no idea what she was doing, but her sense of right and wrong just wouldn't let her leave Sherry without any help. Sherry couldn't even dress herself, and not that Jemma was a stranger to helping someone, but getting this involved? It scared the bloody piss out of her. Worse yet was the warm flutter in her belly when she helped Sherry dress.

"Well, we're here," Jemma announced as they pulled into the garage beneath Sherry's building.

"Poor Breitweiser is going to be so pissed at me."

"Who?" Jemma asked, befuddled.

"My cat. He's been home for three days by himself. I hope he had enough food."

Jemma laughed. "Please tell me you didn't name your cat after Stéphane Breitwieser, the art thief?"

"My ex did. She's got a bit of a criminal mind. We used to work at The Met and found him beside the dumpster outside. He was just a kitten. I wanted to name him Patches, but my ex can be kind of pushy. In the end, though, I got him when she split, after she… uh…after she…" Sherry stuttered to a stop and paused for a long moment.

Jemma didn't pry. Whatever had pulled Sherry up short wasn't her business.

"Anyway," Sherry continued, "he's my buddy."

"Well," Jemma commented with a crooked smile of checked amusement. "He's fine. I did look in on him—twice. He has food and water, and his litterbox is clean."

Sherry's face bloomed with gratitude, and her eyes pooled. "Thank you so much. I really appreciate it. You're so sweet. You're my hero."

Jemma shrugged. "I just did what anyone would do."

"No. Just anyone would have ignored my call or told me to call 9-1-1. Just anyone wouldn't have stayed and made sure I was okay, especially for three days. Just anyone would not have taken care of my cat. You're a saint."

"I'm not," Jemma said, almost reflexively, and then hesitated. She quickly reached into her pocket, not wanting to linger on the thought. "I almost forgot," she continued, pulling out Sherry's keys. "Full disclosure: I didn't stay the whole time. I left a few times for work… and some personal stuff. Also, your carpet is wrecked, but that wasn't me."

"Yeah, the footprints. That's a long story. And I'm glad you stepped away to take care of yourself." Sherry's grin turned a bit mischievous. "For a minute, I thought you were some crazy stalker type."

"No," Jemma answered with a shy, nervous laugh. "Not a stalker."

"Seriously though," Sherry said. "You want to hear something funny?"

Jemma raised an eyebrow. "Okay," she said, drawing out the word.

"I had a really good time today. Isn't that nuts?"

"You know what's even crazier?" Jemma laughed. "I did, too. The best in a long time."

Sherry gave Jemma a peck on the cheek, then stepped out. She had to clutch the door as her legs refused to support her, eventually sliding to her hands and knees. "Whoa," she muttered, shaking her head.

"Sherry!?" Jemma jumped out and ran around. "You okay?"

"Sorry, I'm still a little weak, I think."

"Here, let me help," Jemma said and gently lifted Sherry into a bridal carry. "Is this okay?"

Sherry pressed her lips together momentarily, then grinned, "Yeah," she whispered. "Yeah, that'll do fine."

Beneath the antiseptic soap smell from the hospital, Jemma caught a whiff of what she could only describe as Sherry as she leaned into her shoulder. Jemma wanted to ignore it, but she couldn't. Sherry smelled really good, and the skin of Sherry's cheek lay soft against her collarbone. The paramedics had been right; Sherry was much heavier than she looked. It was a difference by degree for Jemma, as strong as she was, a bit like the difference between a one-pound and two-pound weight for a normal person, but it was noticeable.

"You must work out," Sherry murmured as Jemma elbowed the elevator call button.

"Sometimes," Jemma lied. Her metabolism was so high that she never had to work out again. She was lucky that way. Il Duce, as she recalled, had to work his ass off to keep his body bulging with muscles. If nothing else, he'd one day get old and slow, and Jemma, who barely aged, would put him down permanently.

Sherry reached down and unlocked the door with one hand, holding her bag of belongings in her lap, and Jemma carried her inside. The little calico lay on the sofa, staring balefully at them.

"I'm home, sweety," Sherry said when she saw him.

"So, what did happen to your floor?" Jemma asked as she set Sherry on the couch.

"It's—It's just stupid is what it is," Sherry said and pursed her lips. "I don't want to talk about it."

"Sorry, I just thought it was odd."

"It's not worth it," Sherry said, her expression closed.

Jemma schooled her face and changed the subject. "So, your cat has food, but you don't. And given that you practically fell out of my car, I'm going to run to the store. What do you like?"

Sherry stared at Jemma, blinking in surprise, and it was one of the cutest things Jemma thought she had ever seen.

"What?" Jemma asked when Sherry kept staring.

"You're just so sweet," Sherry said, turning suddenly a little bashful. "Not at all how I imagined when we first met."

"Well, if you want me to be an evil bitch, I can do that. I'm good at evil bitch."

Sherry giggled. "I doubt that."

"Seriously," Jemma said. "What do you like? Skies the limit."

"Really, please don't," Sherry replied, her cheeks flushing furiously. "I can order from a delivery service."

Jemma crossed her arms and raised an eyebrow, her voice turning semi-serious. "I'm loading your fridge. It's not a debate. Besides, you're stuck with me for three days, and I refuse to starve."

Sherry hesitated for just a moment and then folded like a cheap suit. "Okay, fine," she sighed. "Sandwich meats, bread, soy milk, and nothing too complicated to cook. I have a mild allergy to shellfish."

"Got it. I'll be back in a bit. Call or text me immediately if anything happens."

"I will," Sherry assured her, reclining on the sofa with a long yawn.

At the grocery store, Jemma grabbed a half-dozen pre-made dinners—high quality and easy for Sherry to just throw in the oven. She added staples like peanut butter, soy milk, and a few days' worth of ham and cheese. She also added in coffee. Sherry seemed like the dark roast type. Added to that was cream. Hopefully, Sherry wasn't Jewish. She figured Sherry would've mentioned if she kept kosher.

For herself, she grabbed a pack of hamburgers, buns, three

steaks, a dozen potatoes, eggs, instant grits, and a few other items. This was the price of her supercharged metabolism: a sky-high grocery bill. At least she wasn't a speedster. That life was miserable, as she understood it.

In the freezer aisle, Jemma paused at the ice cream, tapping her lips. "What kind of ice cream do you eat, Sherry Broward?" she murmured. Jemma's choice depended on her mood—chocolate on most days, something sweeter when things were good. Sherry, though? She seemed like a sweet tooth, maybe a dash of chocolate for the rough days, but…

"Ah ha," she whispered as she spotted the perfect flavor and snatched it from the freezer.

Half an hour later, Jemma walked back into Sherry's place, juggling four grocery bags, to find Sherry fast asleep on the couch. Smirking, she locked the door and carefully carried Sherry to the bedroom, tucking her in with the blankets pulled tight.

Jemma lingered, staring down at her. In the soft glow of the lamp, she could take in the details. Sherry still looked tired, shadows clinging to her cheeks, but she was beautiful. The curve of her jawline, the high cheekbones—regal, almost. Her nose was small, and though her mouth seemed comically wide when she yawned, it was softened by full, expressive lips.

"Good night," Jemma whispered, turning off the light and quietly closing the door.

After putting away the groceries, Jemma decided she'd had enough. She was exhausted. It wasn't so much that she'd done anything, but the ups and downs of the last three days had drained her emotional reserves. Unable to get comfortable on the loveseat in the tiny living room, Jemma finally stretched out her 5 foot 10 frame on the floor with a couch cushion. She lay for some time, just staring at the ceiling.

"What am I doing?" she muttered in the dark. "I should just go." It was an idle thought. She couldn't leave someone in Sherry's state until she knew they were safe. That wasn't her. It probably had a lot to do with her upbringing. Despite their old-fashioned values and the rift with Jemma, her family were kind people. They never turned anyone away in need, even her.

Jemma turned that thought over and over before sighing and rolling onto her side. She just needed rest. It took a while, her mind racing with a hundred little thoughts, but eventually, she drifted into a deep, dreamless sleep.

Chapter Twelve

Sherry felt Jemma's hands on her, though she couldn't see them. But another voice cooed in her ear, Malka's, with her thick Russian accent. "Just like me, now," Malka said. "You know you want it. I missed you, pet." Sherry shifted and moaned as hands drifted down and over her legs, sending a spark of pleasure through her.

"It's time to wake up," Jemma said, and her face loomed from the blackness. But it wasn't Jemma. Instead, Lena Swift's, clad in her trademark headscarf and mask. Her cobalt blue eyes bored into Sherry's, drawing a powerful need from deep within. "Come on, pretty lady," she said softly. "Time to wake up."

Lena's hand brushed against Sherry's cheek, feeling different, more real somehow. But Malka's insistent fingers, capped with her wicked nails raked gently down her belly toward her center, drawing out another moan.

Sherry turned her head, "No," she whimpered, her voice a mix of denial and ecstasy.

"Wake up!" Jemma's voice said again, more forcefully this time.

The visions fell away, leaving Sherry blinking in confusion, her chest full of longing and her body pulsing with need. "What. . ." Sherry slurred drunkenly.

Jemma perched on the edge of Sherry's bed, brushing a

stray strand of hair from her face with a cheeky smile. "Good dream?" she teased, eyes sparkling with a touch of mischief.

"Huh?" Sherry blinked, still groggy, as her face warmed. She tried to brush off Jemma's look but felt the blush intensify as Jemma raised an eyebrow, not saying a word, just watching her with a knowing smile.

"What?" Sherry finally muttered, turning her face away to hide her embarrassment.

Jemma chuckled softly but let it go. Her expression shifted, softening with a look of gentle concern. "Do you want a hand with a shower?"

"No," Sherry grunted quickly, trying to rise. "I can… get…" Lifting maybe an inch, her whole body shook with fatigue, and she fell back to the pillow, instantly exhausted. She burned with frustration. She hated being seen as weak. She'd always been independent, and, for a moment, she stubbornly considered just lying there. But three days unconscious in bed and all the things that went with it had turned her riper than an old, brown, fly-covered banana. She needed a shower. Breathing heavily, she finally looked tentatively up at Jemma and gave in, stuttering slightly. "You don't have to…I'm sure eventually. . ."

"Look," Jemma said gently. "It's okay. I'm just here to help. I promise. So, let me help you."

Sherry's brow furrowed in confusion, but she nodded her assent. She didn't understand why Jemma seemed so intent on helping her. She was grateful, but the woman barely knew her. And while the thought of being in a shower with Jemma was certainly enticing under other circumstances, the vulnerability, the dependence, it unsettled her. She was at Jemma's mercy. Yeah, Jemma was sweet, but Malka had been sweet, too, and, well…

Wrinkling her nose slightly, Jemma gently lifted away the comforter. Sherry still wore the jeans and T-shirt from the previous night.

Sherry took a shuddering breath. "I don't understand what's wrong. I didn't feel this weak yesterday. I'm getting worse."

Taking her arm, Jemma checked her pulse. "I don't think so. For all your effort, your pulse is a steady and strong fifty-eight, and your color is good. They wanted you to rest for three days, so let's take it one day at a time, okay? I bet it'll get better. Try to be patient."

Sherry gave a slight nod. "Okay."

She did her best to help scoot out of her clothes, trying to ignore the feel of Jemma's soft hands running down her legs as she removed her pants.

"Are you too cold?" Jemma asked, her voice kind. At Sherry's shaking head, Jemma gave a soft, coaxing smile and lifted her shirt, fingers brushing softly against Sherry's ribs.

Sherry found herself distracted and unsure of where to look. Her entire body ran with goosebumps, and heat flamed in her cheeks. "Huh?"

"Are you cold? You're trembling," Jemma repeated, the timbre of her voice drawing Sherry's gaze to her stunning blue eyes.

"I...uh," Sherry stammered in a whisper. "I—" she started again and then swallowed. "It's probably just the effort of sitting up," she finally breathed, an absolute lie, but her tremors had nothing to do with temperature either.

Usually, being sick made sex the last thing on her mind, but she didn't feel sick, per se. Nothing hurt. There was no nausea, no headache, not so much as a sneeze. She didn't feel tired, exactly, just weak, as if her limbs didn't want to respond. Consequently, there wasn't anything distracting her from Jemma's hands practically roaming all over her body. It was maddening

While Sherry lay there, helpless, Jemma slid her panties down. Sherry had to suppress a gasp as Jemma's warm fingers lifted away the waistband and tugged them off. *God, this is torture.*

At last, Jemma wiggled her panties over her feet and tossed them aside. "Okay, give me a minute to run a bath."

"There's a small handled hinoki bucket under the sink," Sherry said. "It might make things easier."

Jemma nodded, pulling the covers back over Sherry before

she left. A few minutes later, Sherry heard the bathwater running, and Jemma returned.

"You ready?" Jemma asked in an almost motherly tone.

"Sure," Sherry mumbled softly. She wasn't ready. Not one bit. She was nervous as hell, and she couldn't stop thinking about how great it would be for Jemma to drop on the bed and stuff her face between her legs. The fantasy played over and over in her head even as Jemma picked her up, easy as you please, and carried her to the bathroom as if she weighed nothing.

Stop it, brain! I'm sick, remember.

Jemma lowered her down, holding her just above the water. "See if it's too hot."

Sherry blinked, struck by Jemma's strength as she hovered there. Dipping a hand in, she found it perfect—hot but not too much.

Jemma slid Sherry in gently, placing a hand behind her head so she didn't bump it. Then she scooped up the scrubby off the counter. "Where's the soap?"

"The bar," Sherry said, pointing to a cheap, white block. At least her arms worked somewhat. "I feel like I got a rotten miracle from Miracle Max."

Jemma laughed. It was full-throated and deep and made Sherry's insides turn mushy. "He must have been rushed. You don't use liquid soap?"

"The bottles are bad for the environment," Sherry said. "Besides, bar soap is cheap. Starving artist, remember?"

Jemma snorted in amusement. "Been there, done that."

Sherry gasped as Jemma began running the scrubby across her back and neck.

"Oh, my," Jemma said, grinning dangerously. "Are we sensitive?"

Sherry shifted uncomfortably. "A little." In truth, she was sensitive all over, and prolonged or overly repetitive contact of any kind tended to overwhelm her. Jemma seemed to recognize this implicitly, though. She never lingered too long on any one spot and kept the pressure effective but light. Still, when she reached the bottoms of Sherry's feat, she tickled them a bit, drawing a bubbly laugh from Sherry's throat and a grin to her lips.

"Stop," Sherry said. "That is so not cool. I'm an invalid, remember?"

"Sorry. I'm not trying to take liberties, but your laugh is pretty. I like hearing it."

Sherry flushed from head to toe and looked away. The only other person who had ever done anything like this had, of course, been Malka. She'd had a way of knowing just the right things to do or say, making Sherry feel okay with being so close. The fact that Jemma seemed to share that with Malka might have bothered her, but oddly, it didn't even occur to her to feel anything but appreciative. It was nice, and she realized just how perfect Jemma seemed to be for her. It was early, and they barely knew each other, but so far, she was sweet and patient. Jemma didn't seem to mind her awkwardness either. Huge plus.

Her musings were cut short as Jemma finished washing her legs up to just above her knees and paused. "Well, this is a conundrum."

It took a second for Sherry to catch up and realize what had stymied the other woman. She looked up into Jemma's eyes. The playful gleam was gone, replaced by a slightly hungry expression.

Sherry's breath turned uneven and shallow, and her head buzzed a little with anticipation. She didn't know what to say. She'd never been this vulnerable with anyone, not really, and she certainly had never let a veritable stranger do as she pleased. And, though she might have fantasized about it once or twice, letting it happen in real life was something else entirely.

Still, something in Jemma's manner, her confidence and forthrightness, said it would be okay. So she let herself sag against the back of the tub and closed her eyes. She left her hand open and palm up to receive the scrubby if that's what Jemma decided. She waited, then, to see what Jemma would do. Would she continue? Or would she hand Sherry the scrubby to do it herself?

After a moment, a hand ran through her damp hair, pushing it out of her face. Then Jemma let out a ragged breath as she ran the rough pouf up and down Sherry's thighs.

"Is this okay?" Jemma asked.

"It's nice," Sherry nodded, her eyes still closed.

Almost involuntarily, Sherry's legs spread a little, at least as well as they could. A few drops of water splashed her chest as the scrubby landed in the water next to her, and a soft washcloth slid between her legs. She drew a harsh breath, which slipped out a moment later in a soft, high-pitched "hmm."

Jemma stopped, and Sherry swallowed as her chest heaved.

"Here," Jemma whispered as her hand slid behind Sherry's back, tilting her forward. Holding Sherry in place, Jemma ran the washcloth down Sherry's back and washed her posterior. Sherry let out a little squeak as the rag slid between her cheeks. Seconds later, it was all over, leaving Sherry flustered but embarrassed to say anything. She sat there in the cooling water, slumped forward.

"There," Jemma breathed, sounding a little hoarse. "All done."

"Hardly," Sherry muttered under her breath.

Jemma laughed quietly, and Sherry realized she'd heard her. *Oh, God, how embarrassing.* "I…wow…you must think…"

Jemma laughed a bit more, and Sherry detected a hint of nervousness. "Well…" Jemma said, her voice almost a whisper.

Sherry looked over. Jemma's mouth was pressed into a thin line as if opening it would reveal some dark secret. Her eyes lingered on Sherry's lips, and her chest heaved slightly. Sherry could see the hunger and want in those eyes, but Jemma's expression also revealed hesitation and worry. There was something there, something painful that furrowed Jemma's brow. Jemma wanted her, but whatever it was held her back.

"Hair?" Sherry whispered and cleared her throat, and hopefully, the awkwardness between them.

Jemma silently nodded, and the moment passed. Grabbing the little bucket, she dumped water across Sherry's hair and lathered it with the shampoo bar. Sherry blew out a breath to cool her thoughts and, coincidentally, clear the water from her mouth as Jemma's fingers gently kneaded her scalp and worked the shampoo through her brown locs.

Too soon, it seemed like only seconds, it was all done. Jemma opened the drain, refilled the bucket from the faucet, and rinsed her off.

"Do you think you can stand?" Jemma asked as she lifted Sherry from the tub and set her down on the dark blue bathmat.

"I don't know," Sherry replied dreamily. The warm bath and Jemma's careful touch had lulled her into a state of relaxation, and she didn't want it to end, but she couldn't flop around in the tub, and she was still thoroughly naked. Trying to rise, Sherry found her arms and legs still refused to support her, though they seemed to do better than on the bed. Maybe she just needed to get some movement going.

Jemma lifted her up and onto the commode lid, setting to work with a towel.

Sherry managed to keep herself upright as Jemma dried her off.

When Jemma started to hang the towel over the towel bar, Sherry caught her arm. "I'm okay," Sherry said. "So that you know, that was a wonderful experience, and I appreciate it. Honestly, I appreciate all that you've done so far. You're a saint."

"I'm not," Jemma denied with a dark frown and hung the towel. Then she looked down at Sherry, her lips curving upward into a wry smirk. "You have no idea what I've been thinking all morning."

They both laughed. Sherry knew very well what had been on Jemma's mind. It had been all over hers.

They spent the rest of the afternoon on the couch in pajamas, talking and watching television. At one point, Sherry put on an old public television special about Van Gogh. It was a one-man play, Vincent, starring Leonard Nimoy as his brother Theo. Through bits of some five hundred letters between the two men, it illuminated the tragedy and occasional dark humor surrounding the artist's life.

"That was fantastic," Jemma said. "I can't believe I've never seen it before. I didn't even know it existed."

Sherry gave her an arch grin. "It's one of my favorites. I'm not a huge fan of the impressionists, but Van Gogh always intrigued me, the way he saw color and the way he used both it and contours to express the world in a way that no one else did."

"So, what is your favorite period?"

"That's easy, baroque. I've always loved the contrast of dark and light. And the intense emotions each figure expresses. It helps me understand their feelings, at least in the artist's imagination."

Jemma turned on the couch, tucking one leg underneath. Her blue eyes caught the light, seeming to sparkle. "What about Vermeer? We talked yesterday about how his portraits always seemed so serene, without intense emotion."

One corner of Sherry's mouth turned up. "But that's just it. The Dutch Masters were so precise. If a figure didn't have an intense expression, that was on purpose. Sometimes, I find myself wondering just what they must have been thinking. But of all of them, I think I love De Bray the most. He was famous for portraying multiple figures, and his paintings captured the emotions of everyone in the room like a photograph. They're just amazing."

Jemma felt herself lighten. It had been so long since she'd been able to talk art with anyone in any depth. It was as if they'd been meant to find each other. "My favorite portrait has always been The Night Watch. There's something about the contrast between the little golden child and the darkness behind them. It's so. . . Dutch. The juxtaposition of civic duty and the threat of violence."

"Pop art!" Sherry squealed. "Honestly, Rembrandt is the only artist most people can remember from the Baroque

Period. If they even know what that is."

"Hey!" Jemma protested light-heartedly. "Rembrandt is not pop art. It's not like he painted soup cans or inkblots." Grabbing a throw pillow, she threw it at Sherry, who threw her hands up to block it and then tossed her head back and howled with laughter.

Jemma couldn't suppress her smile as she watched Sherry, who had been dying just days before, so filled with joy. "Feeling better?"

Sherry grinned wildly but then turned a little shy, her face pinkening. "Yeah. I am."

They went on like that, talking about every artist imaginable and watching more public television shows. Some were about art, but others were about literature or history, such as a show about the tombs of the Pharos, which enthralled Jemma and took them into another long conversation, this time about archaeology and, more importantly, old Indiana Jones flicks.

By nine o'clock, their tongues were tired, and Sherry was nodding off, a sweet little expression on her face.

"Can I ask you what you're painting?" Jemma asked as she picked up Sherry to take her to bed.

Sherry smiled as Jemma lay her down and began tucking her in. "It's not done, so don't go peeking," Sherry said. "I'm serious. I don't like people to see what I'm painting before it's finished."

Jemma nodded and held up a three-fingered salute. "Scout's honor," she said with a grin.

Sherry managed to struggle her way to the left side of the bed. Then she patted the right side. "You don't have to sleep on the floor."

Jemma hesitated, conflicted between her desire to stay near Sherry and knowing she should refuse. *I shouldn't be doing this.* It was just a whisper of a thought, though, and in the end, she dismissed it. It was okay to sleep in bed with Sherry. As long as they didn't have sex, she wouldn't get too involved. At least, that's what she convinced herself. It was a rationalization, she knew, but she couldn't—no, she didn't want to—say no. So, against her better judgment, she slid beneath the sheets and spooned up behind Sherry.

Sherry hummed in delight, wiggled a little to get comfortable, and closed her eyes. Jemma lay there, an arm draped across Sherry's midsection, her mind turning over and over, wondering if this was all a terrible mistake.

"Jemma?" Sherry prodded through a yawn.

"Mmhmm?"

"Thank you. I'm almost glad that I got poisoned. Isn't that funny?"

Jemma smirked. "Well, it certainly made for an interesting first date." And when Sherry's hand clasped her own, Jemma did her best to pretend it didn't matter. *It's okay. It'll all be okay.*

Of course, she paid absolutely no attention to the warm feeling that bloomed in her chest or the butterflies dancing in her stomach as she drifted off to her first peaceful sleep in years.

Chapter Thirteen

Sherry woke the next morning and, much to her surprise and delight, moved a bit more easily, more like herself, though every muscle hurt. She felt as if she'd just done a full CrossFit workout without benefit of a warm-up. *At least I can roll over.*

The bed was empty, and the smell of frying bacon wafted through the apartment. She pushed off the covers and wobbled her way toward the living room, keeping a hand on the wall. Her legs carried her, but her balance was way off, as if her body wasn't hers. She had to watch her feet with each step, carefully placing one foot in front of the other. Finally, she reached the living room and all but gasped. Jemma stood in the kitchen in nothing but a T-shirt and her panties. The sight of Jemma's fit and toned body, her powerful legs, and the bulge of her shoulder muscles left her momentarily speechless.

"See something you like?" Jemma said without turning around. "You should be resting."

"I'm fine," Sherry said, even as her face rapidly shifted from muted pink to full crimson. She stepped toward the couch, but it turned into a lurch as she lost her balance, almost falling to the floor. As it was, she impacted the back of the sofa with a thump.

In a flash, Jemma was there, lifting her up and placing her on the sofa. "I hate to say I told you so, love, but..." She trailed off as she set Sherry down.

Sherry, for her part, kept her lips pressed into a thin line to keep from grinning. Finally, she huffed out a breath. "You're sweet. Thank you."

Jemma gave her a crooked smile that made Sherry's heart jump and whispered, "I saved your life. Now I'm responsible for it. At least, that's what they say."

Sherry was acutely aware of Jemma's proximity and the heat radiating off her body. It made her want to squirm uncomfortably. She wasn't one to let others take care of her, but Jemma had a way about her, confident and light, like it was no big deal, that made Sherry want to lean into the experience rather than pull away. Besides, it wasn't like she was in any fit state to do much.

"Breakfast will be ready shortly," Jemma said. "Do you like black pudding? I bought some for myself, but I'm happy to share."

"I've never had it," Sherry answered, her voice coming out a little hoarse. "But I'd love to try it."

Jemma nodded, and then she gave Sherry a dazzling white smile. Leaning in close, she said softly, "You have to let go."

"Oh!" Sherry laughed, releasing Jemma's neck, where she was still hanging on. "Sorry."

Jemma gave a quiet little giggle and headed into the meager kitchen, giving Sherry a full view of her long, powerful legs. A gym rat, for sure, Sherry decided. Despite Jemma's demeanor, Sherry detected a quiet tension between them. It wasn't uncomfortable, per se, but it seemed delicate.

As she cooked, Jemma occasionally turned back for a brief glance, but she didn't linger. They were quick flirting things that made Sherry so bashful that she didn't know where to look.

Eventually, she just leaned back on the sofa to stare at the ceiling and listen. The faint sounds of Jemma moving around in the kitchen soothed her thoughts. Her mind was a swirling mix of emotions--attraction, confusion, and something darker, more familiar: Malka. She tried to banish thoughts of her, but with Jemma's warm presence so near, it was hard to keep her heart from lurching uncomfortably between the past and the present. It wasn't just the remnants of the poisoning that made her feel shaky. No, this was something else. Something more frightening.

The last thing she wanted was to have her heart broken again. The whole reason she'd stolen the painting had been to gain some independence and sense of self. To correct the injustice Malka had dealt her without going to Malka for money. She could have, she knew, but there was no way she would. That felt too much like—defeat. Of course, now the painting was in the hands of Charles and Mary, and Sherry had no way to get it back. But there was nothing she could do about it right then, so she ratcheted down on the spike of fear in her chest and tried to stay in the moment.

The aroma of breakfast filled the air, pulling Sherry out of her thoughts as Jemma unfolded a TV tray and set it up in front of the couch. Sherry blinked as Jemma carefully placed a plate of food on the tray: bacon, eggs, black pudding, and more. Her eyes flicked from the breakfast to Jemma, who sat down beside her, a plate of food in her lap, though she made sure to leave a careful gap between the two of them. The space felt both necessary and unsettling; this pull, this draw, toward someone she barely knew, someone who wasn't Malka, lingered in the quiet air between them.

Sherry looked at the black pudding. It didn't look at all appetizing, but she'd eaten weirder things in her life, so she took a tentative bite. Jemma watched her, fork poised above her plate, a bit of mushroom speared on the tines that kept a smidge of fried egg on the back.

"So, what do you think?" Jemma asked, her voice soft, as if she could sense Sherry's hesitation.

Sherry's throat felt dry. "About the food or...?"

Jemma gave her a small, knowing smile. "About the food. We'll start there."

Sherry let out a shaky breath, relieved by the lighter tone, chewing thoughtfully before responding. "It's good," she said after a moment, forcing a smile. "Thanks."

Jemma nodded, but she didn't take her eyes off Sherry, studying her quietly. Sherry shifted under the weight of that gaze, feeling exposed in a way she wasn't used to. It was unnerving how easily Jemma seemed to see through her walls, how she wasn't pushing but still…waiting.

"Really?" Jemma finally prodded.

Feeling a little guilty about not loving the stuff, she didn't look up. "Um…it's not my favorite, but it's edible."

Jemma chuckled. "More for me then. Do you mind?"

Sherry nodded and let Jemma take the remaining black pudding from her plate. "I guess you're not a germaphobe. That's good."

Jemma looked at her, face serious. "What's wrong with germaphobes?"

Sherry, taken aback, wasn't sure how to respond. "Um… Nothing. It's just…"

"Yes?" Jemma probed, an eyebrow arched.

"Okay, when I was in college, during undergrad, I dated this girl who was a total germaphobe. She insisted on not letting anything touch her food. Everything had to be near burnt before she'd eat it. I'm sure there are folks who can do that kind of relationship, but not me. Why?"

Jemma shook her head and then laughed. "I was just wondering. The way you said it, it sounded like there was a story there."

Sherry rolled her eyes to hide her discomfort. "Well, I can handle a lot, but not when you have to use anti-septic gel every time we touch. It drove me nuts."

Cutting off a bit of sausage and stuffing it in her mouth, Jemma spoke around it. "I was just wondering. You don't seem too uptight."

"What about you? Do you have any pet peeves?" Sherry asked, probably a little too forcefully.

Jemma frowned. "I'm sorry. I wasn't trying to upset you. I really was just curious." Then she sighed heavily. "I— I'm not very good at this. I've been living alone for a few years now, and I'm out of practice."

"I don't understand," Sherry said, screwing up her face in confusion. "You seemed fine at the bar the other night."

The other woman shrugged. "It's easy to be confident when

you're looking for a one-night stand. There's no commitment, nothing to be afraid of, and…" Jemma trailed off, pushing a bit of roasted tomato around on her plate.

"Oh," Sherry whispered. She understood. Jemma was afraid of commitment. Strangely, that made Sherry feel better, not worse. Yes, they shared that, but what it really told Sherry was that Jemma might want this to be something. Tentatively, she reached out a hand and placed it on Jemma's leg. "It's okay. I'm not upset. I'm a little out of practice myself."

Jemma gave a laugh so full of nervousness that Sherry could clearly hear her discomfort. "Well, then, aren't we a pair."

Sherry grinned then. "So it would seem."

Chapter Fourteen

Sherry opened her eyes. It was still early with the street light eight stories below filtering in through the curtains—not enough light to really see with, other than shapes. Her arm was draped over Jemma's midsection as she lay spooned in behind her. She buried her face into the mass of dark-brown hair. Leaning in until her nose touched Jemma's head, she breathed deeply, letting the scent fill her lungs. Jemma smelled so good, like warmth, neither bitter nor sweet, on a cold winter morning. Cozy, she decided, and even a little exciting.

A soft hand slid across Sherry's in the darkness, interlacing her fingers. "It's still a little early."

"I know." Her voice was just a breath as Sherry continued to take in the scent of her, feeling the press of Jemma's body. Every inch of taught muscle in her back and her butt was amazing. *Come on, Sherry. It's not like you've never felt a woman before.* Of course, she'd never been with a woman like this. Jemma was amazing, and she had an earnest kindness that her life to date had so lacked. Her mother was kind, but she'd always been so busy raising her brother and her. And her father, well, she preferred not to think about him.

Sherry scooted a bit on the bed as Jemma rolled over.

"How do you feel?" Jemma asked, and Sherry realized that she felt fantastic. A whole new her.

"Great. Nothing hurts, and I don't feel weak." She lifted her arm and waved it around.

"I'm glad," Jemma chuckled. "I won't lie, though. I could have used a few more days here. It's been—nice."

Sherry frowned despite her recovery, hoping that Jemma couldn't see her. She didn't want Jemma to leave. While she didn't want Jemma constantly taking care of her, and it had only been three days, she had already grown used to having her around. Watching TV, talking about art, movies, everything really. She enjoyed her company.

"Hey, don't frown," Jemma said and drew a hand up under Sherry's chin when she tried to look away. "Just because you're better doesn't mean we can't spend time together. I promised you a date, remember?"

"Just one?" Sherry asked almost shyly.

"I think we can do better than that," Jemma said, and without warning, she leaned in and pressed her lips to Sherry's. Unexpected as the contact was, Sherry didn't hesitate, wrapping one arm around Jemma and parting her lips. She felt the roughness of Jemma's lips that comes with the first moments of wakefulness and tasted the tang of her early morning breath as it flowed past her desperate tongue and into her lungs. Jemma's tongue swept into Sherry's mouth, eliciting a soft whimper of need and desperation.

Sherry shifted, pulling Jemma on top of her, parting her legs slightly, and letting Jemma's thigh slide between hers, pressing up against her wetness. It was the first genuinely intimate touch of something special, a promise of what could be. Her hands roamed Sherry's muscular back, feeling her fingers' soft, pleasant vibration as they slid across the skin. God, she wanted this. She wanted more as she pressed her hips upward, grinding against Jemma's leg.

Slowly, Jemma lifted herself up on her arms, leaving Sherry flushed with warmth and a rush of feelings that she didn't want to end.

"What's the matter?"

"Nothing," Jemma whispered. "I think we should wait to take the next step, is all. We still barely know each other, and since this isn't a one-night stand, I think we should spend some time doing stuff. See how we gel. What do you think?"

"I suppose," she grumbled. She wanted to tell her that sex was doing stuff, but she got the message. And Jemma wasn't wrong. Sherry did need to take stock of what she wanted from a relationship if that's where this was going. It was good advice, though she was loathe to take it.

Jemma lifted one arm, all of her weight impossibly balanced on one hand. She crooked a finger under Sherry's chin again. "That doesn't mean we can't keep making out, though. Does it?"

In answer, Sherry grabbed Jemma bodily and pulled back down, her lips greedily seeking Jemma's. Jemma traveled downward, nibbling at Sherry's neck. Sherry felt the gooseflesh rise on her arms as Jemma nibbled at the skin. In a flush of sensation and feeling, Sherry decided she wanted to be on top. She pulled Jemma over onto her back…and right off the bed. With the pop-pop of springing elastic, the fitted sheet pulled loose, and they landed on the floor with a thump in a tangle of arms and legs amid gales of laughter.

"Whoops!" Sherry chuckled as she found herself on top of Jemma, firmly bound against her by the top sheet and sandwiched awkwardly between the bed and the wall. "Are you okay? Did you hit your head?"

Jemma snorted. "No, I'm fine. Can you get up?"

"Umm. . ." Sherry wiggled a little left and a little right, but both arms were cinched against her chest, and her hands were resting…*Oh, God.* She shook her head vigorously. "No. No. I can't move." Her cheeks flamed as she fought to keep her hands perfectly still.

"Comfortable?" Jemma asked cheekily as her face broke into a wide grin, making it absolutely clear that she was well aware of Sherry's hands flat against her breasts. "Here."

Shockingly, Jemma lifted up, even with Sherry's weight on top of her. Sherry knew she was strong, but wow! Of course, Sherry slid right down to her knees and found herself buried once more in the sheets, her face pressed right against Jemma's hip. Jemma unwrapped her from the sheet, releasing Sherry from her captivity. She rocketed up, her head crashing into

Jemma's jaw.

"Ow! Shit!" Jemma exclaimed and stepped back, holding her chin.

"Jesus!" Sherry swore and dropped back onto the bed. "I'm so sorry. I'm such a clutz."

Jemma laughed again but then stopped as she looked at Sherry.

"Really," she whispered, the moment stripped of all its humor, and tears welling in her eyes. She sniffed. "I didn't mean to…"

Jemma sat beside her on the bed—probably trying to keep her tone soothing. "Hey, hey, it's okay. It was an accident. I'm not hurt. It just caught me off-guard. Really, it's fine."

Sherry didn't respond. Her thoughts drifted, light as smoke on the breeze. She wasn't sure where she went at times like this. She was just gone, lost in the haze. It took a minute before she registered the gentle shake of her shoulder.

"Huh? Oh, sorry. I…uh…" Slowly, she resurfaced. "Yeah, I'll be fine."

"Where did you go?" Jemma asked, her voice soft, feather-light, meant just for Sherry.

"Nowhere. Sometimes, when I'm overwhelmed, my brain just stops. It's hard to explain." Sherry's thoughts wouldn't stop with that, though. *No, it's not hard to explain. You're autistic. Just tell her.* That subtle fear she always felt niggled at her, though, keeping her silent. What if Jemma freaked?

Jemma nodded thoughtfully, her gaze understanding. "Well, no harm done. So, laze around in bed, or get food?"

"I need breakfast," Sherry said, energy bubbling back. "I've been cooped up for days, and I feel amazing!" She bounced off the bed with a burst of enthusiasm. "Dibs on the shower!"

Jemma's trailing laugh—warm and sweet—wrapped around Sherry like a hug, calming the noise in her head, bringing her back into focus. It was like the world settled with that sound, everything a little less sharp, a little more manageable.

Sherry headed into the bathroom, still feeling that afterglow of peace, and grabbed the shower handle—only to hear a loud snap. The brass handle broke clean off in her grip, leaving her staring at the pieces dangling from her fingers, confused.

"Well, fuck," she muttered, inspecting the bits of metal like they'd fallen apart on purpose. She blinked at them, her brain catching up slowly. With a heavy sigh, she tossed the pieces into the wastebasket. "Cheap crap."

Still naked and now shivering, she ran to the hall closet and dug in her tiny toolkit.

"Sherry? What is it?" Jemma called from the bedroom.

"Shower handle broke. I swear I need to have the appliances in this place checked by an inspector," she grumbled, rummaging loudly until she found what she was looking for. Returning to the shower, jawlock pliers in hand, she used them to turn on the water and stepped in, the cold fiberglass underfoot making her toes curl.

Chapter Fifteen

Sherry stepped out of the shower, toweling off quickly as steam swirled around her. Despite the broken-handle fiasco, the hot water had worked wonders on her aching muscles. She felt more energized than she had in days—maybe even a little too energized. A loud grumble from her stomach pulled her out of her thoughts. *Jesus, I'm starving.*

She wandered into the kitchen, where Jemma had set out some toast and coffee. Just the sight of it made Sherry's mouth water.

"Mind if I make something real quick?" Sherry asked, already rummaging through the fridge. "I'm starving."

Jemma glanced at the clock on the wall. "I mean, sure, but your appointment's at 8:30, and it's already 7:30. We should probably get moving soon."

Sherry waved it off, grabbing eggs, bacon, and sausages. "I'll try to be quick, but, honestly, I'm really hungry."

Jemma raised an eyebrow. "Sherry, you ate a whole pizza last night. How hungry could you be?"

"Just some scrambled eggs, sausage, and... yeah, some bacon," Sherry said without missing a beat. "Oh, and maybe some toast."

Jemma gave her a wry smile. "Some toast. You sure you don't want a fruit bowl with that?"

Fruit sounded good, and Sherry checked the fridge. "Oh, ha

ha. We don't have any fruit." She set to cooking while Jemma sat and watched, a puzzled and thoroughly amused look on her face.

By the time Sherry sat down, the plate in front of her looked like a small feast. She barely registered Jemma's incredulous stare as she devoured everything in front of her, even buttering six slices of toast before realizing she'd finished them all.

Sherry paused, blinking at the empty plate. "Did I just…?"

Jemma, suppressing a laugh, nodded. "You did."

Sherry rubbed her stomach, feeling a little sheepish. "Guess I was hungrier than I thought."

Jemma shook her head, laughing. "Come on, if we leave now, we won't be late. You sure you're not still hungry?"

"Let's just get going before I eat the table," Sherry said, standing up with a groan.

The subway ride to Harborhaven General helped clear her head, but Sherry couldn't shake how hungry she'd been. She never ate like that—like ever, not even as a kid. Now that she thought about it, she'd been eating solidly like that for two days straight. Yesterday's breakfast had been three eggs, two slices of toast, and two glasses of orange juice. Then she'd had a huge Reuben from Sapkiewicz's Deli down the street, famous for their monstrous sandwiches. Jemma had already mentioned the medium meat-lovers she'd knocked back the night before. She hadn't even noticed.

After the usual check-in process, Sherry found herself sitting on the exam table, tapping her finger nervously against her upper arm. Jemma sat in the corner, scrolling through her phone, but Sherry couldn't stop the nervous energy swirling in her stomach.

A nurse entered and took her vitals before asking her to step on the scale. She looked at the scale, then at Sherry, and then back at the scale. "165. That can't be right." Her voice carried a tinge of confusion.

Sherry blinked. "I'm only five-two," she muttered, eyeing the numbers like they might shift if she stared hard enough.

The nurse frowned and tapped the scale, as if that would change anything. "Let's try another scale."

Sherry sighed and shuffled into the next exam room, stepping onto a second scale. The nurse pressed a few buttons and waited. "165."

"Seriously?" Sherry stared at the nurse, incredulous. "Two scales are broken?"

The nurse offered a sympathetic smile. "Let's try one more."

Sherry threw her hands up, rolling her eyes as she trailed behind the nurse yet again, practically stomping to the next room. She stepped onto the third scale, hopeful for a different result. The nurse glanced down, then back up. "165. Well, you wear it damn well."

Sherry blinked. "What is going on?! Have I been sleep-eating? No way I've eaten forty-five pounds of food in three days."

Jemma, leaning casually against the doorway, stifled a laugh, shaking her head. "Sherry, you had a whole pizza, a Reuben the size of your head, and two huge breakfasts in the last two days. Add in this morning's latte. That's a lot of calories, and it's all still in you. And all you've done is rest."

"Rest? More like a coma!" Sherry shot back, bewildered. "I haven't left the house in days, and now I'm the Hulk?"

The nurse chuckled awkwardly and patted her on the shoulder. "Your vitals are perfect, and you're in excellent health. Nothing to worry about."

As the nurse left the exam room, Jemma smiled, her voice teasing. "So, 165, huh? Maybe you've got secret superpowers. Ever think about that?"

Sherry pursed her lips in irritation. "Don't be ridiculous. You're what, five-ten? You get on the scale. I'm telling you, it's borked."

Jemma held her hands up. "Oh, no. I don't do the scale thing. I work out. Scales are the devil."

Narrowing her eyes, Sherry crossed her arms. "Uh-huh."

The door swung open, and a young female resident with bright hazel eyes, close-cropped dirty blonde hair, and a clipboard tucked under her arm walked in. She offered a warm, professional smile as she glanced at Sherry.

"Morning, Sherry. I'm Dr. Taylor. Dr. Carlsson handed your

case over to me, so I'll be following up with you today."

Sherry nodded, fidgeting with the hem of her hoodie. "Good. Dr. Carlsson's an asshole. Thanks."

"Jesus, Sherry," Jemma exclaimed through barely controlled laughter as the doctor suppressed a grin.

"Well?"

Dr. Taylor pulled up a chair, flipping open the clipboard. "So, that aside, how are you feeling? Any lingering symptoms from—" The doctor frowned for a second. "Says here you thought you were poisoned?"

Sherry shrugged, trying to sound nonchalant. "I feel okay, but… I dunno. Some weird stuff's been happening."

Dr. Taylor raised an eyebrow, clearly intrigued. "Weird, how?"

"Well," Sherry began, "the shower handle broke this morning. I just turned it, and it snapped right off. That's… not normal, right?"

Jemma barked a laugh, quickly stifling it with her hand. Dr. Taylor smiled slightly but stayed focused.

"Hm, that's definitely interesting," the doctor said, scribbling something on her clipboard. "Anything else? Unusual weight changes?"

Sherry sighed. "Yeah. Apparently, I'm 165 pounds now. Which makes zero sense, because I haven't exactly been feasting, and it's not like I'm gaining muscle overnight."

"We just went over this, Sherry. You've been pigging out." Jemma said lightheartedly, then made a snorting sound and laughed.

Despite herself, Sherry laughed with her. "Fine. I know it sounds stupid, but still."

Dr. Taylor nodded thoughtfully. "I can understand your concern, but from what I can see here, all of your test results came back perfectly normal. In fact, you're in excellent health."

Sherry blinked. "Excellent health? I gained, like, forty pounds out of nowhere and snapped a shower handle in half. That's not excellent."

The doctor chuckled, shaking her head. "I know it feels strange, but from a medical standpoint, your body seems to be functioning perfectly. If you continue to experience any more unusual changes, we can run further tests, but for now, you're free to go."

Sherry exchanged a glance with Jemma, still processing what she'd heard. "So, I'm fine? That's it?"

Dr. Taylor nodded. "For now, yes. If anything else comes up, let us know. But based on the labs, you're in fantastic shape. Though, I'd really like to know what you were exposed to, just so you know what happened."

Sherry shrugged. "I really don't know." The lie tasted even more bitter than it had when she'd woken up three days before. And despite Jemma's gentle ribbing and the Doctor's dismissal, Sherry felt the specter of worry creeping up on her, even as she tried to convince herself that she had just eaten a lot and that the shower handle was defective or fatigued.

After Dr. Taylor left, Sherry slid off the table. "Great," she muttered, still confused as she dressed. She stopped, though, with one shoe on, and reached out, grabbing Jemma's hand and pulling her into a tight hug.

After she let go, Jemma looked at her. "What was that for?"

Sherry swallowed. It was loud in her ears. "I just wanted to say thank you, for everything. I know I'm a mess, but I really loved having you with me the last few days. And, well, I'd be dead without you, so there's that."

Jemma took Sherry's face in her hands. "Sherry, I like you, too. And I want to see where this goes. Besides, I think your quirks are cute." She gave Sherry a chaste kiss and released her. "Now, put on your other shoe. I have one more day set aside before I have to be back at work. What do you want to do?"

Sherry felt her cheeks flush, trying to stifle a grin. "I don't know," she muttered, hoping it sounded nonchalant, though inside, a thrill was bubbling up.

Jemma linked arms with her as they headed outside. "How about we hit Harborhaven Central Park? Fresh air might help clear your head, and besides, you'll be back to normal in no time."

Sherry sighed dramatically but nodded. "Fine. But if I gain

another 50 pounds, I'm blaming you."

The park was only a few blocks from the hospital and the sun was high in the sky, a gorgeous seventy degrees. T-shirt weather. They stopped briefly for coffee at a Sun Bean, where Sherry ordered a cafe mocha with extra whipped cream, and Jemma got a vanilla cappuccino. Sherry tried to treat them, but Jemma insisted on paying, reminding Sherry that she was out of work and not to waste her money on coffee and rolling her eyes at the humorous "yes, Mom" from Sherry.

The wide open green space offered a sense of relief as the warm summer air hit Sherry's face. The weight thing was still bugging her, but the park was doing its job at loosening the tension in her chest.

After a few minutes of quiet, Jemma spoke up, her voice casual. "We've got a few leads on the Rembrandt case."

Sherry stiffened slightly, keeping her expression neutral. "Oh yeah? What kind of leads?"

"We've also got some chatter that the Bratva might be involved," Jemma replied, sipping from her coffee. "The museum footage was erased, so we're looking for footage from other buildings around the museum."

Sherry's heart skipped a beat. The Bratva? And shit, she never considered there might be cameras around the loading dock. Were there? She couldn't remember. She forced herself to stay calm, but the questions were starting to pile up. She tried to shift the subject as smoothly as she could while still watching Jemma out of the corner of her eye. "So, are you… uh… working with Lena Swift?"

Jemma, mid-sip, choked on her coffee, sputtering slightly before recovering with a sheepish laugh. "Oh, uh—yeah. I've met with her. She's definitely… around. How did you know she was on the case?" Jemma wiped her mouth with the back of her hand.

"The news." Sherry raised an eyebrow, suspicion tickling the back of her mind, but she shrugged it off for now. "Must be pretty cool, working alongside a superhero."

Jemma's eyes turned a little tight. "It definitely keeps things interesting."

"Bullshit," Sherry stated flatly.

"Bullshit, what? What bullshit?" Jemma asked, giving Sherry a bemused look.

"Don't pull my leg. You're really working with Lena Swift? What's she like?"

"I'm not, but I wouldn't say I'm working with her. We're just working the same case," Jemma said. "She's nice, I guess. I mean, what do you even say to a superhero?"

Sherry barked a laugh. "You're serious? Maybe start with, 'Can I have your number?'"

Jemma sipped her coffee. "Not."

"What? Why not?" Sherry screwed up her face in confusion. How could Jemma work with the lady and not at least have tried. Though, if she had, and if Lena had said yes—Sherry let that thought go. She liked spending time with Jemma. She wasn't ready to make anything official, but like Jemma said, she wanted to see where this was going. It certainly couldn't go any worse than it had with Malka, and she'd survived that.

"Because," Jemma replied. "Unlike you, I'm not all a-gaga over her. I do have some chill. Besides, it's work. For all you know, we might have nothing in common except for being queer."

Sherry shook her head and grabbed Jemma's free arm, leaning into her. "Well, her loss is my gain."

"Indeed it is," Jemma said. "Besides, I think you're way prettier than Lena Swift. I'm kind of a brown-eyed-girl girl myself."

Sherry waggled her eyebrows and took Jemma's hand, swinging it lightly.

As they continued walking, though, Sherry's thoughts turned back to the earlier mention of the footage and the Bratva. She was sure her disguise had held up—mostly. But now, with Lena Swift sniffing around and Jemma casually dropping tidbits about the case, the walls felt like they were closing in. She needed to figure things out before everything unraveled.

Chapter Sixteen

Jemma returned Sherry home at almost ten o'clock, having walked all through the park and down Bayside Street, which ran, strangely enough, a block over from the river. They had spent the day perusing the eclectic bucket of shops along the street, everything from hiking to weird incense and crystal places. Despite Sherry's weird freakout about overeating and a defective shower handle, they'd had a good time. Jemma was beginning to get a picture of Sherry: Sweet, almost certainly autistic, and kind-hearted. She didn't seem to have a nefarious bone in her body. She was also tougher than she let on.

At some point soon, Jemma decided, maybe after a few more dates, she'd have to test the waters. See what Sherry thought it might be like to date a superhero, or perhaps, what she thought a girlfriend of Lena's might go through. With that thought, Jemma realized that it scared her. She really liked Sherry, and now she was thinking about maybe, one day, telling her who she really was. It felt like madness, especially after what happened to Callie. She didn't want to imagine anything like that happening to Sherry.

Sherry leaned in for a goodnight kiss as they reached her apartment. It wasn't as passionate or greedy as their impromptu makeout session that morning, but it was still toe-curling.

"Call me?" Sherry said as they parted.

"Definitely." Jemma stood at her car door, her eyes trailing Sherry until Sherry entered the building. She drove away, shaking her head. She hadn't been lying. She had enjoyed herself despite the circumstances. The last four of six days had been amazing, certainly the best time she'd ever had in a hospital, and as a cancer survivor, she'd seen enough of them. What impressed Jemma the most, though, was how fucking brilliant Sherry was. The woman had to have a genius IQ. It didn't seem so at first, but Sherry had that whole left-brain talking to the right-brain thing going on, and when they'd strayed to other topics, Sherry's knowledge was encyclopedic.

Ultimately, Jemma was glad she hadn't slept with Sherry that first night. It would have been one and done, and she liked her. Jemma couldn't deny that she was looking forward to their next date.

With a genuine and happy smile on her face, she drove home. Her grin vanished, though, as soon as she exited the car and her phone blared with a klaxon. "Shit," she groused, but she couldn't complain. She'd had six days without a single call other than Sherry's mysterious illness.

Some guy calling himself Voltstrike had just robbed a jewelry store. Sherry flipped over to the secure DOD app she'd been given by the Bureau and looked up his profile. His name was Jerry Walthers. He was an older supervillain who'd done time for mostly petty thefts and one grand larceny in The Penthouse. She wasn't at all surprised to find he was an electrokinetic, not with that moniker. With a sigh, Jemma ran upstairs and changed. A few minutes later, she was in the sky over Harborhaven.

The downside of dealing with electrokinetics was that getting hit with electricity hurt—a lot. It had to be powerful to put Jemma down, but it had happened before, and she hated fighting them. On the upside, though, they tended to be flashy —literally. So, when she spotted bolts of electricity sparking into the sky along Riverside Drive, she knew right where to go.

By the time she arrived, the excitement had left Riverside Drive and moved to Citizen Park along the riverfront. A crowd of people lay on the ground as Voltstrike and his crew huddled at Half-Dome, a concert venue in the park, fending off the police. Voltstrike and his goons were holed up behind a bunch of piled steel scaffolding haphazardly strewn on the lawn in front of the stage. Police cruisers had them boxed in on three sides, cutting off their escape.

Behind Voltstrike and his men sat the huge stone bandshell, about forty feet tall and at least fifty feet wide. He had to have superhuman muscle with him—someone strong enough to tear down that scaffolding and build them a fortress of steel in minutes.

"Great," Jemma grumbled as she surveyed the situation and looked for her opportunity to engage. She was most concerned about the twenty or so civilians that were lying in the grass. The police were trying to get them away, but lightning blasts kept flying out and sending the cops scurrying for cover. Maybe fifteen seconds after she arrived, Jemma saw her chance. A woman in the kilt and sports bra, the aforementioned muscle, maybe nine feet tall and built like a Mack Truck, grabbed a six-foot chunk of a truss and hurled it toward one of the cruisers to the left of the stage.

Jemma shot down and landed between the scaffolding and the cruiser. She managed to catch the massive piece of metal, but the momentum still carried her backward several feet, her shoes digging furrows in the earth. She went to throw it back, but a bolt of lightning struck the far end of the torn metal, jolting her muscles and sending her to her knees. She dropped the steel as soon as it subsided and decided a more direct approach was needed.

She flew low, maybe two feet off the ground, shooting straight in and praying none of the people in between lifted their heads or tried to stand. Another lightning bolt shot her way but missed, hitting one of the cruisers, creating a shower of sparks and scorching the side of the car. Doing easily a hundred, Jemma hit the big woman. With the crack of breaking bones, the woman flew backward into the curbstones under the stage. The woman didn't move after that. *Strong but not tough*, Jemma thought as she waded into the goons. A couple of them took shots at her. The bullets stung a bit, but they pancaked on Jemma's skin and fell to the ground.

It was a small crew, only five, not counting the downed heavy: four goons in balaclavas, cargo pants, body armor, and boots. Walthers, likewise, dressed for business. At least he wasn't wearing some stupid costume. She went through Walther's gunmen like tissue, dropping them quickly, but as Jemma grabbed the last goon, she got a face full of lightning that sent her to the ground. She could see Walthers advancing on her with both hands out. Electricity streamed from the stage junction box through him and right into her. It hurt, and it was scrambling her thoughts. She couldn't concentrate enough to fly away, and her body wouldn't respond. She was in real trouble.

Fortunately for her, Walthers wasn't the kind of genius that Sherry was. If he had been, he probably wouldn't have walked right from behind cover to try to finish her off. The dude obviously thought he was Emperor Palpatine, but as soon as he was exposed, he got a bullet in the head from one of the cops and dropped to the ground, dead. With a pained groan, Jemma rolled off her back.

"Shit, that hurt," she muttered to herself. Standing, she took a self-assessment. Her muscles had stopped twitching when the current stopped, and the discomfort had vanished. The electricity had burned her in places, but it had healed almost as soon as it happened. Otherwise, she was physically okay.

Her outfit was another matter entirely. The entire right side was cooked, melted in several places, exposing most of one leg. In her right pocket had been her phone, now a lump of fried plastic stuck to her leg. At least her bra had made it through intact. She'd had wardrobe malfunctions before, a few of them, and probably everyone in the world knew exactly what her left boob looked like. That had been embarrassing. She considered herself fortunate that she'd never been in a situation where her leggings were destroyed or torn off. That would be mortifying, and she really wished that one day someone would come up with some better stuff than nylon-lycra. Everything she wore got destroyed, so it didn't matter what it was.

Jemma glanced at Walthers, shaking her head in quiet dismay. "What a waste," she muttered before turning her attention to the big woman she'd knocked out earlier. She expected someone built like that, playing the role of muscle in a superhuman brawl, to be made of sturdier stuff. Kneeling down, she carefully turned the woman's wrist over, pausing as she caught sight of the bold, rainbow-colored tribal design on her bicep, but it was the medusa tattoo on her forearm that pulled her up short.

"Shit," Jemma muttered under her breath. She hated hurting people, especially people who already carried scars—physical or otherwise—from a life filled with violence. Killing them? That tore at her. She could count the lives she'd taken on one hand, and even that number haunted her.

The first had been Michael Jamal Willis, a street kid—just eighteen. He'd stolen a portable high-powered laser, rigged it up with help from some over-eager science nerds from Harborhaven University who thought lasers were the pinnacle of cool. Jamal had turned that laser into a weapon: a pair of goggles linked by a cable to a backpack, firing wherever he looked. Jemma hadn't known the details when she yanked the cord, thinking it would disarm him. She hadn't realized the backpack itself was the actual laser. When the optics failed, the backpack had exploded. Jamal never stood a chance.

Then there was Lucifer. That one she tried to give herself a pass on. The guy had overdosed on steroids, combined with Lot 429, which had twisted him into something monstrous. His heart had given out mid-fight. His death wasn't technically her fault, but it still lingered.

The third had been Erin Hae Park, known as Lady Chimera, a shapeshifter. Their fight had stretched across three city blocks, an epic brawl. In the heat of battle, Jemma had swung at her—just as Chimera shifted form. During the transition,

Chimera passed through her human form, vulnerable and weak. It had only been a split second, but Jemma's punch landed at the exact wrong moment. Lady Chimera died instantly. Jemma had retreated to her house afterward and didn't leave for a month. That was the day she'd considered quitting. Jamal's death had been an accident, Lucifer's an overdose. But Erin? That had been all her. It was Callie, her girlfriend, who had finally convinced Jemma to step back into the field.

Since then, Jemma had come to terms with one harsh reality: sooner or later, someone would die. She was powerful enough to move a city bus fifty feet with a punch, and with the stakes that high, it was inevitable. People who chose to fight her knew what they were getting into. Still, she tried not to hurt anyone.

She never let herself think about the fourth one. Not if she could help it.

Fortunately, the woman at Jemma's feet had a strong, steady pulse. She would live. A weak moan escaped her lips as her eyelids fluttered open, eyes struggling to focus. When her gaze finally locked onto Jemma, there was a weary resignation in them.

"We lost, didn't we," she said, her voice thick with a southern drawl.

Jemma knelt down, offering a small, sympathetic smile. "Yeah, you did."

The woman swallowed hard, her voice barely a whisper. "I didn't kill anyone, did I? Please say I didn't kill anyone."

Jemma shook her head. "No, you didn't kill anyone. But you could have."

The woman's gaze flickered with something—guilt, shame —before she looked away. Two paramedics were already moving toward them, but Jemma held up a hand, stopping them in their tracks. This conversation wasn't over.

"You want to tell me what happened?" Jemma asked, her tone gentle but firm.

The woman hesitated, her eyes still averted. "I'm not always in control," she said quietly. "I'm aware, but I can't stop myself. It's like something takes over."

Jemma raised a skeptical eyebrow. She'd heard this story before. Sometimes it was true, sometimes not. "What's your name?"

The woman looked back at her, conflicted. "Don't laugh," she replied glumly. "It's Amy Jekyll."

"That's a little on point, don't you think?" Jemma said with a slight grin. She had to admit, it was funny.

Amy shrugged, and a few tears ran down her face. "Just a freak coincidence. It's my real name."

"Can you stand?" Jemma asked.

The big woman tried to stand but gave a cry of pain and grabbed her back before falling back to the ground. "No. I think my back's broke."

"I'm sorry," Jemma said. She turned to the paramedics. "Will she fit on a backboard?"

"No," Amy grunted painfully. "I weigh almost eight hundred pounds."

Jemma frowned. "Give me a minute. We'll get you out of here." She waved in the paramedics.

They had to bring in special equipment, and Jemma had to help, but they finally loaded Amy into an ambulance, and Jemma climbed in for the ride with a sense of deja vu. She held Amy's hand the whole way.

"Thanks," Amy said, tears still rolling down her face as they waited in the ER. The paramedics were giving report.

Jemma pushed aside the mass of blonde hair. "It's okay."

Amy looked away, and a hiccuping sob escaped her lips. "No, it's not. It'll never be okay again."

With a sympathetic look, Jemma said, "Yes, it will. You'll recover from this."

"They'll put me in 'The Penthouse," Amy whispered. "They'll throw away the key."

"No." Jemma shook her head and gently squeezed Amy's hand. "They won't throw away the key. They'll treat you for your condition if they can or help you find a way to manage it. Trust me, they don't want you in there any more than you want to be there. It's not a for-profit prison, and it's designed for people like us. But it'll be lonely. I'll visit if you'll let me."

"Why would you do that?"

"Because I believe you," Jemma said earnestly, blinking to drive back her own tears. "And I think you deserve a second chance."

"You're a saint," Amy said.

"No, I'm really not," Jemma replied as a group of hospital staff wheeled Amy away.

Jemma watched her go, feeling a lump in her throat and the unshed tears floating in her eyes. The woman might have lied about losing control, but Jemma didn't want to believe that. She wanted to believe that this woman would be treated and go on to live a long, peaceful life.

When she got home, Jemma took a hot shower and dug a spare phone from her closet to replace the one scorched in the fight. It was her last. She'd have to get more. Once she got someone in support to activate it, she opened her little task application and flipped to the list called 'Visits.' On it, she added the name 'Amy Jekyll.'

Desolate and lonely, she turned out the light and cried herself to sleep.

Chapter Seventeen

Apart from daily visits to Amy's bedside— in costume, of course— Jemma spent the next few days hiding out at home. Fortunately, Amy wasn't paralyzed as Jemma had feared. The impact with the curbstones had caused something called spinal shock, but other than a minor fracture, there was no significant damage to her spine. Jemma had, however, broken Amy's scapula, three of her ribs, and her left femur.

Simply put, she had hit Amy way too hard, and while Amy didn't know it, Jemma was well aware of how close Amy had come to dying. Jemma was usually more careful, and she spent a fair amount of time figuring out if the issue had been an honest mistake or her distraction. In the end, she decided on the latter. There was only one distraction right now, and though it hadn't been at the forefront of her mind, she was sure the feelings being dredged up by this budding whatever it was with Sherry were the cause.

On the third day of wallowing, Sherry managed to break through Jemma's melancholy with some choice fine art memes and cat videos. The one that finally got her was *Portrait of the Officers of the White Flag of Delft* by Jacob Wilemsz Delff, with a big-letter caption that read, "Photobombing before it was cool."

Finally, having had enough of wallowing in self-pity and confident that Amy would be okay, Jemma pulled herself from bed and texted Sherry.

"Hey."

"Hey yourself," Sherry texted back, followed by a heart emoji and a waving hand.

"What are you up to?"

There was a pause as Sherry typed. "Just hanging here with Barry and Breitweiser."

"I was going to ask if we could go on that date today instead. But if you're busy. . ."

"I'm not busy. Barry's my zombie plant, and you know Breitweiser."

"I was wondering why you had a dead plant in the corner," Jemma replied.

"He's not dead," Sherry replied with a zombie emoji. "He's unnn-dead. There's a difference…well, shit." Swearing face emoji.

"What happened?" Jemma asked, raising an eyebrow.

"Now my sink faucet is broken. The handle just snapped. This place has issues."

Jemma put a hand to her mouth and laughed. "Ah. So you're a super, and you never told me."

"Hardly," Sherry texted. "The only power I have is super bad luck. Sigh."

Jemma sent a four-leaf clover emoji. "Wishing you better luck. So, is Breitweiser finally speaking to you?"

"Cat treats do wonders," Sherry texted back, followed by a big smile emoji. "Barry's still quiet, though." This was followed by both a plant emoji and a sad face.

Jemma chuckled and sent a coffee emoji, a question mark, and a pleading face emoji.

Sherry replied instantly. "LOL. Of course. Where?"

"Meet you at your place at one o'clock?"

"Bet."

The summer day was a perfect seventy degrees as Sherry and

But I'm Not a Supervillain!!!

Jemma strolled toward the Coffee Bean, sunlight casting a warm glow over the street. Sherry's steps were light, almost playful, while Jemma kept pace beside her, her gaze shifting between Sherry and the lively surroundings. The scent of blooming jasmine mixed with the faint aroma of Minerva, a local Indian restaurant that Sherry absolutely adored. The gentle hum of conversation floated from open storefronts, and as they passed by, a soft breeze stirred Sherry's hair, catching the sunlight in fleeting glints.

Jemma stopped suddenly, her eyes lighting up when she spotted a small, wrinkled pug waddling toward them on a leash. "Oh my God, can I pet him?" she asked the owner, practically bouncing in place.

The owner nodded, smiling, and Jemma knelt, scratching the little guy behind the ears as he snorted in delight. Sherry joined in, a bit entranced by how gentle Jemma was, her fingers carefully stroking the pug's tiny, wrinkled head.

When the owner and pug continued on, Sherry smirked. "You know, pugs have all kinds of health issues because of those squished faces. Breeding them is like the mad science version of cuteness."

Jemma shrugged, grinning. "I know, but they're so adorable. It makes up for them being walking, snorting science experiments."

Sherry rolled her eyes, but her smile softened. "Guess you're a sucker for troublemakers, then."

"Guilty as charged," Jemma said with a wink, linking her arm with Sherry's as they continued on their way.

"Keep up…ooooh!" Sherry exclaimed, tugging Jemma as they closed on Sheldon's Books and Paper a few blocks from the Cafe.

Inside sat a stack of the latest unofficial biography of Lena Swift: *Icon, The Lena Swift Mystery*. Splashed across the cover was Lena Swift, still in her mask and headscarf and with her trademark hand-wraps. However, she was clearly nude underneath and casually wrapped in a gigantic lesbian pride flag, her shoulders, hip, and one leg solicitously exposed.

Jemma stopped and moved back, looking inside, trying to

see what Sherry was looking at. "What is it?"

"The book cover," Sherry said with a grin. "She's just so cool."

"Huh, now who gave them permission to use that photo?" Jemma muttered as she looked inside.

"What?" Sherry asked distractedly.

"I said, what is it? What are you looking at?"

"Right there," Sherry practically squealed in her cutest fangirl voice, poking the glass window. "The Lena Swift book. Look at the cover! Duh."

"Who? Lena Swift? She's alright, I guess. If you're into that sort of thing."

Sherry turned to her and gave her an incredulous look. "You're kidding, right? I mean, she's not you, but she's certainly hot?"

Jemma grinned widely. "So you think I'm hot?"

Sherry laughed. "No, I said Lena Swift is hot." When Jemma's face fell, a bit of her chestnut hair dropping over one eye, Sherry chuckled and leaned in and pushed it aside. "You are much, much hotter."

Jemma waggled her eyebrows. "I figured that's what you were saying. But, come on, it's Lena Swift, even I'm not that hot."

"It's just the outfit," Sherry chuckled. "I wouldn't mind seeing you in some tight leggings. I bet you'd look just as good, maybe better. Maybe you could cosplay it."

"I do not cosplay," Jemma said flatly. "Especially not Lena Swift."

Sherry pouted in mock disappointment. "Oh, fine. There goes that fantasy."

Jemma laughed until she doubled over, wheezing.

"Oh, come on," Sherry said petulantly, pulling Jemma along toward the coffee shop. "It's not that funny. Jeez."

Jemma finally straightened. "Yes, it is. But seriously, is that how you see me, something to just dress up in a pair of tights and a sports bra? That's a little sexist, isn't it?"

Sherry scoffed. "Says the lady whose first words to me were, 'You want to go back to your place?'"

"That was different. You were hitting on me."

"Yeah, so."

"Now we're talking about a whole other person."

Sherry sighed. "First of all, I was kidding, at least mostly. Second of all, yeah, I like to look, and my sexy thoughts might be a bit close to the surface, but did I ever suggest once that we have sex?" Jemma didn't seem sure how to respond, which was just fine to Sherry, so she continued. "I just admire pretty women with muscles, and I'm not shy about it. If other people think that's shallow, then that's on them. Big babies. Grow some ovaries. Lena Swift is sexy. You're sexy. A lot of women are sexy. But that's in my opinion, and I don't assume that their only purpose is to be sexy or have sex. I'm not some guy."

"Yeah, but…"

"No buts," Sherry said, a bit of heat flaming her cheeks. "I'm a feminist. I believe that women should be treated with respect. I wouldn't catcall a woman or treat her like trash or act like she doesn't have a brain. Just because I think someone's hot doesn't mean I just want to screw them. I might want to sometimes, but I don't want some brainless blow-up doll. I want a woman with an opinion and isn't afraid to voice it."

Jemma put her hands up and took a step back. "Point taken."

"I'm not done," Sherry replied. She was on a roll now, and it was one of her pet peeves. "It's not okay to look at a woman's physical characteristics and think that's all she is, but it is okay to find a woman attractive and say so if it's not unwelcome. So, is it unwelcome? If it is, I'll stop."

Jemma swallowed hard. "Um, no," she said sheepishly.

Sherry pursed her lips and narrowed her eyes. "No, what?"

"It's not unwelcome."

"Good, because I think you're damned attractive, and funny, and sweet, and smart, and I love that you love art. But I don't know the first thing about Lena Swift other than she's a superhero, which I think is nutty, but I do think she's attractive, so that's what I remarked on. Frankly, she's hot with a capital H.O.T."

"Okay," Jemma said defensively with a weird look on her face, sort of a half-smile, half-shocked thing that suggested she hadn't been expecting a lecture. "I was always raised that stuff like that should be kept in your head."

Sherry looked at her. "If you were a guy, I'd say yeah, probably. But that's not because guys aren't allowed to think women are hot. It's because men have a history of objectifying women to such an extreme they try to make them slaves and make them feel bad about themselves, so I'd like to see them reeled in a bit. But I don't think you think that way, so I don't mind at all if you think someone's hot. Right now, at least, you're with me, and I'm okay with that. Don't be such a damn Millennial all worried about your feelings."

It was Jemma's turn to scoff. "I'm not being a Millennial, but my feelings matter."

Sherry's face was beet red. "Look, my mother raised me to drink from the waterhose and be in before dark. She never coddled my feelings or treated me any different from how her mother treated her. If I was bad, I got the switch. Was it the best way to raise a kid? I don't know, but she did her best, and she knew the world didn't give a shit about our feelings. That being said, I do think your feelings matter, and if it bothers you, I won't do it anymore, but I'm not a sexist. Women should be running this bitch."

Jemma blinked. "Wow." For a moment, she gawped like a fish, clearly at a loss for words.

"Sorry," Sherry said sheepishly, reining in her temper. "I just don't like being called a sexist. Everyone calls my ex a sexist, and I don't like being compared to her. Not that she actually is a sexist. She objectifies everyone."

Stepping forward, Jemma wrapped her arms around Sherry. "I'm sorry, I hadn't really thought about it that way. And you're not wrong. Lena Swift is kinda hot."

A slow grin parted Sherry's lips as she glanced up. "But not hot as me, right?"

"No, definitely not," Jemma replied with a giggle. "Besides, you've got a nicer butt."

Sherry snorted. "I wish. You've got a nicer ass than she

does, though."

Jemma laughed again. "If you say so," she answered as they continued down the street, holding hands.

"Do you think she has a good PR team?"

"I'm sure people think she does," Jemma said wryly.

"Well, I figure her PR team is shit. Someone needs to get her to do an endorsement," Sherry said absently. "I mean, I'm sure there's an athletics brand that would kill for it."

Jemma smirked. "I suspect she's much too principled for that kind of capitalist shtick."

"Maybe, but I can't imagine superhero work pays well, and there are people like Kronos in Manhattan who are practically covered in brands."

"Yeah, but they'd only endorse Lena for one month out of the year," Jemma chuckled. "Besides, I wouldn't want a big red target on my back, even for a month."

Sherry stared at her blankly, then caught on. "Oh, ha, ha. Well, they'd have to commit to year 'round because, too bad for them, she's gay all the time."

"Yeah, too bad," Jemma repeated with a chuckle. "Maybe you should be her publicist."

"Not my scene," Sherry replied. "But there is something I'm dying to know."

Jemma pulled open the door to the coffee shop. "What's that?"

"Why couldn't I have been that photographer? Lucky bastard."

Jemma smirked and raised a teasing eyebrow. "Oh, come on. You'd have been making awkward small talk the whole time. 'Is the flag comfortable? Do you need more lighting? Did I mention I'm a pool shark?'"

Sherry stuck out her tongue with a theatrical flair, and Jemma grinned, positively basking in her own cleverness and looking far too pleased with herself. With a roll of her eyes, Sherry pulled back the door of the café and scuttled in just ahead of Jemma, stopping short and sticking out her butt childishly just to make sure Jemma bumped into her.

"Rude," Jemma laughed.

Sherry turned abruptly and gave Jemma a sweet kiss. "I'm smoother when you get to know me. And I thought my awkwardness was part of my charm."

"It is," Jemma said, her humor replaced by sudden sincerity. "I think you're amazing."

Caught off guard by the statement, Sherry flushed and turned shy. She looked around, but with nowhere else to rest her eyes that felt natural, she glanced back into Jemma's. She expected to see them sparkling with humor, but they weren't. On the contrary, they were alight with an emotion that Sherry couldn't fathom. Something profound but not unpleasant, if the upward curve of Jemma's lips were any indication. Sherry's chest sank, and her stomach did somersaults. It took her a moment to gather her wits and connect the dots in her head, but eventually, she understood. This was that moment—another one for her little internal box. That moment when you looked at someone and saw just how beautiful and amazing they were. She could see it in Jemma's eyes, too. She knew instinctively that she and Jemma were sharing in that feeling. Usually, she had to work others' emotions out in her head, but not now, not with Jemma, and that made her heart rabbit away.

The moment was broken, though, when a man opened the door, and they were forced to move. Jemma took Sherry's hand with a soft smile and led her to the counter.

Sherry ordered a peppermint mocha with a few extra pumps, and Jemma got her usual vanilla latte coupled with an eclair, which she eyed for several minutes as she sipped at her latte.

Sherry stayed quiet at first, watching Jemma and her éclair. She seemed fascinated by Jemma's reticence to just scarf the thing down. In truth, Jemma was trying desperately to think of something to say, some way to recapture that brief feeling by the door.

A teasing smile crept across Sherry's lips. "So, what's the

story here? Are you planning on seducing that éclair or just admiring it from afar?"

Jemma raised an eyebrow, lips twitching in amusement. "What? Can't a girl enjoy her pastry in peace?"

Sherry leaned in, eyes gleaming with mischief. "Oh, I dunno. You're staring at it like it's about to propose."

Jemma chuckled, picking up the éclair slowly. "Maybe I'm waiting for the right moment. It's a commitment, you know."

Sherry folded her arms, smirking. "I bet. You'll be married to that thing before I even get a minute of conversation."

Jemma took a delicate bite, her grin spreading. "Don't be jealous. You've got your own charms."

Sherry rolled her eyes dramatically. "Yeah, sure. If only I tasted like that creamy filling, maybe I'd stand a chance."

Jemma nearly choked on a sip of coffee, laughing. "Okay, fine, I'll share. But only because I like you better than the éclair."

Things grew silent and awkward again until Jemma chimed up. "You have the cutest little mannerisms. When you're talking, your eyes trace the edge of your cup."

Sherry gave Jemma a bashful smile. "You noticed that?"

"Among other things," Jemma said. She watched how Sherry's eyes darted around her face, never quite locking with hers. "Autistic?"

"Yeah, I'm on the spectrum," Sherry replied just as her hair flopped in front of her face, concealing some of the fear in her expression, but Jemma saw it, almost as if Jemma might run away screaming at the pronouncement. It was preposterous, but Jemma had no idea how others might have reacted in the past, so she reached out her hand in a comforting gesture.

"May I?"

Sherry stared at the hand momentarily, a hint of surprise flashing across her face as if no one had ever asked her. "Sure," she said finally and placed her hand in Jemma's, a bit of a tremor flowing through it.

"You mask it well," Jemma said. "I didn't know. So, I'm sorry if I've made you uncomfortable."

"That's kind of the point of masking," Sherry said, meeting

Jemma's eyes briefly, "but you haven't made me feel anything but happy. I struggle with some things, but I'm pretty good at not putting myself in uncomfortable situations. Lots of practice. My ex was good about it, though." Sherry cringed inwardly. She hadn't meant to mention Malka.

Jemma gave her a soft smile. "Can I ask what split you two up?"

"She changed, and I didn't," Sherry said flatly, clearly wanting to avoid the topic.

"Well, if I trip over any of your triggers, I apologize, but you don't have to be afraid to tell me. I want you to be comfortable around me."

Sherry drew her hand back into her lap, then finally picked up her coffee. She lifted it to her lips but then stopped. "I am comfortable around you." She paused again before adding, "Very comfortable. I want you to know that. If you really didn't know I'm autistic, then you have some kind of sixth sense because you accommodated my condition surprisingly well, and I appreciate it."

"I'm glad," Jemma beamed and glanced out the window. Rain had begun to fall, but the sun still peeked through the clouds, giving the world outside that strange, happy grayness that blossomed from the promise of a rainbow and the smell of wet streets. Jemma treasured days like this. They reminded her of nothing so much as the works of J.M.W. Turner, with their muted colors and dark clouds set against stark sunlight or moonlight or white snows.

Sherry commented, as if she'd read her mind, "It's pretty, isn't it? The way the water drops splash in the puddles, distorting the sunlight, the deep clouds desperately trying to cover the land below in shadow."

Jemma's eyes snapped back to Sherry, who was also looking outside. "Were you made just for me?" The words came out in a whisper, almost unbidden, but the twitch in Sherry's mouth told Jemma she'd heard her.

"Maybe," Sherry said, a thin Mona Lisa smile curving the edge of her mouth. She sipped her coffee, eyes still glued to the world outside. "The Storm on the Sea of Galilee? No…"

Her expression turned thoughtful as she glanced at Jemma and then back outside. "Dutch Boats in a Gale? That's your favorite."

"Jesus," Jemma whispered. "How did you know that?"

Sherry shrugged. "I don't know. It was just a guess."

"Well, it's a fucking good guess because it's spot on."

Sherry turned back to Jemma, a dreamy look in her eyes. "Maybe I was made just for you." Without another word, she scooted her chair around the table closer to Jemma. "You have the prettiest blue eyes. They're so pure and deep and bright. They'd give Paul Newman fits. I want to fall into them and see the world all cast in blue as I gaze through their edges."

Jemma felt herself on her back foot for the first time since they'd met. She'd only touched the surface of Sherry. There was another woman there, far beneath, who had deep, turbulent emotions and an incredible depth of the soul. If Sherry wanted to fall into her eyes, Jemma wanted to fall into Sherry, to become lost in her hidden world, maybe never to return. Her breast swelled with that desire. It manifested as a pressure to touch her and a shiver of nerves and a hundred other sensations that scared her. She was in over her head. She hadn't meant to get so close, but now it was as if the current had taken her, and she couldn't fight it. She wouldn't call it love—this feeling—but it could be one day.

Swallowing loudly and choking a bit on her own emotions, Jemma spoke. "That's probably the most beautiful thing anyone has ever said to me." She couldn't help the tear sliding down her cheek, and she swatted at it. Not even Callie, whom she'd loved so much, had ever said anything half as wonderful.

Sherry, for her part, blushed furiously and pressed her lips together before looking back outside. "I'm sorry, that was really forward of me."

Jemma squeezed Sherry's hand. "No, it was—" She never got to finish her sentence as her phone blared with the Klaxon. Jemma closed her eyes in despair. Shit, it never ends, and it's always at the worst fucking time. She pulled out her phone and looked at it. Instead of a scroll of text with a villain designation and other information, there was just a message: Call Me.

Jemma pursed her lips in frustration. "Someone better be dying," she muttered.

"Someone steal another painting?" Sherry asked, a playful smirk tugging at her mouth.

"No, but it is work. Let me make a quick call," Jemma said with an irritated frown, stepping outside.

"Hey," Tracy said flatly when Jemma answered. "We have a problem."

"Okay? Is it an emergency?" Jemma asked, irritation plain in her voice. "I'm kind of doing something."

Tracy let out a sharp laugh. "Well, we've finally got some movement on the case."

"Okay, and this can't wait?"

"What's got you suddenly so busy?" Tracy's question held a trace of amusement, like she already knew exactly why. When Jemma didn't respond, Tracy continued, "Well, I need you here. I've got a stack of work, and there are things you need to see for yourself. So, how soon can you get here?"

"I'm on my way," Jemma sighed and hung up. "Bad news," she said as she returned to her seat. "Work."

Doing her best to smile through her disappointment, Sherry asked, "Find the Rembrandt?"

"Unfortunately, no, but it's related. Raincheck?"

"Sure, why don't you come by my place this weekend," Sherry blurted out before she could stop herself. "I'll cook!"

Jemma grinned. "And she cooks, too?"

"Sure," Sherry said sheepishly. "I cook. Saturday night? Movies and food? You're not allergic to anything, are you?"

"No. You're on," Jemma said, grabbing her coffee and leaving a peck on Sherry's cheek before she strode out the door.

Chapter Eighteen

Descending from the afternoon sky in her Lena Swift guise, Jemma landed outside Police Headquarters. The massive building loomed—no, crouched—at the corner of Trese and Bruge, a hulking granite and glass structure unapologetic in its brutalist design. Jemma's lips curled with distaste. Not because she hated the police—though authority never sat well with her—but because the whole place reeked of despair. It looked like a relic of Soviet-era efficiency, shipped block by block and dropped into her home, an artifact from Stalinist Russia that no one had asked for.

As she moved between the throngs of pedestrians and the cold shadow of the building, people raised their phones. She even lifted off the ground and posed for a few shots. She wasn't a fan of selfies; they often felt like they were chipping away at her life. But it was a public life, and one that she'd chosen. She could walk away if she wanted, but she wouldn't.

Her smile turned from plastered to genuine when confronted by a single mother pushing a pram. The baby inside, no thoughts in her adorable little head, wore a Lena Swift "Stay Proud!" onesie. Jemma grinned as the mother pushed the baby into her arms and snapped a photo. Jemma resolutely despised commercialized hero worship, but she ran a little merch site, and profits funneled into queer charities. Some attention couldn't hurt.

Inside the station, Tracy was already waiting by the desk, her eyes dancing with amusement. "That was adorable," she said, her tone full of a gentle tease. "That kid's gonna treasure that picture forever. And who knew you were so good with kids?"

Jemma huffed, eyes flicking to the ceiling as if appealing to the universe for patience. "I hate holding babies. They're like soap bubbles. One wrong move and pop."

Tracy leaned in, voice dropping to a conspiratorial whisper. "You didn't break me, and I'd say we were pretty wild."

Heat flushed Jemma's face as she hissed through clenched teeth, "Really? In the police station?"

Tracy's laugh was rich and full, the sound bouncing off the sterile walls as she led Jemma toward the elevator. "Come on, I've got something for you."

"It better be good," Jemma bitched. "I was on a date."

Tracy snickered. "Were you?" The way she said it suggested she knew something she wasn't telling Jemma, and it piqued her curiosity.

The fourth-floor cube farm, where Tracy worked, was positively claustrophobic. Detectives sat hunched over keyboards or lounging in their chairs, lit by the garish glow of overhead fluorescents. But in one of the smaller interview rooms, Jemma could finally breathe. As they sat, the door clicked shut, and Tracy slid a grainy, black-and-white photo across the table. "There she is."

Jemma's eyes narrowed as they settled on the image—a woman, her hair pale in the washed-out light, climbing into the back of a sleek SUV. The shot was distant and imperfect, but in the woman's hands was a black sack. The kind you carried something valuable in. Something square. Something about the size of a missing painting resting in its brand-new frame.

"Well, great, but this is a terrible shot," Jemma shrugged and slid the picture back across the table. "Can the photo guys clean it up any?"

"That's as good as it gets, I'm afraid, but here's the thing. That car was parked around the back of the museum next to loading dock number two."

Jemma cocked her head, her eyes narrowing. The impatience was plain on her face, the unspoken *get to the point* hanging between them.

Tracy, unfazed, leaned forward. "That dock hasn't been used since the early nineties. Most employees don't even know it exists. This has 'inside job' written all over it. One of the guards was headed out for a smoke—said he saw a blonde woman, black evening dress, getting into an SUV right around there. She wasn't on the list of attendees for the party either."

"Okay, so are there any other pictures of her? Interior surveillance?"

"No," Tracy said. "The cameras were looped electronically, the footage erased. But, the digital forensics tech was able to dig out the malware that was used—a piece of it, anyway. How much do you know about someone named Ghostwire?"

Jemma arched an inquisitive eyebrow. "The hacker? I think she works for Ivan Rostovich. Why?"

"Well, apparently, she always signs her work," Tracy said, leaning forward with a smirk. "And while the malware didn't get copied to the system outright, a chunk of it found its way into something called a pagefile. That chunk included this."

She slid a piece of paper over. Jemma's eyes widened briefly before a laugh slipped out. It was a cute, chibi-style drawing of a hacker, flipping off the viewer. The character was decked out in trans colors—pastel pink, blue, and white. It felt almost absurd against the seriousness of the heist.

"Cute," Jemma muttered, sliding it back across the table. "Real professional touch. So how do we know no one at the party was in on it?"

"We've accounted for everyone's whereabouts for pretty much the entirety of the party. More importantly, the painting was stolen in a seven-minute window. The guard supervisor, who also runs the surveillance room at night, went on rounds because the museum security team is currently short-staffed. He claims he ran into a blonde woman whom he was sure was drunk."

"Okay?" Jemma said, not following. "So?"

"His badge was used to enter the surveillance room while he was on rounds. Then, the door was opened three minutes later. He ran into the same blonde woman shortly before returning to the surveillance room."

"Maybe he was involved?" Jemma said, stating what she thought was pretty obvious.

"That's what we thought, but we can't find any other evidence to support that. Also, the guy's been with the Museum for ten years. It's still a possibility, but after interviewing him, I don't think so. I think our mystery lady has some seriously light fingers."

"I see." Jemma sat back and pursed her lips. "No other suspects, then."

Tracy shook her head. "No. And the guard never got a look at the mystery lady's face, either. We've got him under surveillance and are monitoring his bank accounts and credit. If he's involved, we'll find out eventually. There was one thing —" Tracy snapped her lips shut.

Jemma couldn't decide if she hadn't meant to say something or if Tracy was just baiting her. "What thing?"

Tracy frowned. "It's probably not important."

"Tracy," Jemma prodded. Tracy was definitely baiting her.

"The guard called a local nightclub shortly after the theft. I don't think it's important, but I've had difficulty chasing it down. No one there seems to know who he talked to."

Jemma narrowed her eyes. "Let me guess. Sin City." Tracy nodded. Maybe Jemma did have spidey sense after all. Of course, if something seedy were happening in the city, Malka would know what it was if she wasn't already right in the middle. It wasn't a terribly educated guess. "I see. It's probably nothing, but I'll check. I'll also contact my sources and see if I can find anything on Ghostwire, but that's her moniker for a reason. She's a ghost. Very few, if any, people know who she is. Anything else?"

"Nothing I can discuss." Tracy closed the folder and leaned back in her chair, her eyes glinting like an inquisitor getting ready for a torture victim. "So. . . How have you been?"

An innocent enough question, but Jemma braced herself

anyway. She could tell Tracy was chumming the water. "I'm Fine. Why do you ask?"

Tracy didn't answer right away, letting the silence hang for just a second too long before taking a slow sip of her coffee, her grin peeking out from over the rim. "A little bird told me you were in the emergency room… with a new girlfriend."

Jemma's mood immediately shifted, irritation flaring. "Sounds like your little bird is committing a HIPAA violation," she said, her voice clipped. The thought of someone blabbing her personal business made her blood heat. Worse, the idea that Tracy might be keeping tabs on her was like sandpaper against her skin.

"It's not like that," Tracy said, feigning innocence, but Jemma could just hear the self-satisfaction at getting a reaction. "It was a cop who happened to be in the ER when Miss Broward was brought in. He said he saw, and I quote, 'that girl I used to hang out with,' coming out of an ambulance in her pajamas." Tracy looked entirely too pleased with herself.

"This fucking town is too small," Jemma cursed. "She's not my girlfriend. I was helping her out, that's all."

"In your pajamas?" Tracy asked incredulously.

Jemma's face turned the color of a blooming rose. "It's what I was wearing when she called me."

Tracy smirked. "For three days?"

"Tracy," Jemma responded sharply. "It's none of your business. Honestly. This is getting a little creepy."

Taking a deep breath, Tracy leaned back. "Look, I'm not stalking you. You said that having someone in your life is unsafe—for them. We were friends long before we slept together. I'm just making sure you're okay."

"Well, I'm fine," Jemma snapped angrily. She wasn't really mad at Tracy. She just hated being embarrassed, even though she couldn't figure out for the life of her why she should be. "Sherry's really nice and she was really sick. Besides, that's what I do, you know?"

"Help people," Tracy replied dryly.

"Yes, help people."

"Did you help yourself into her bed?" Tracy asked with a

chuckle.

"Tracy!" Jemma responded, trying to sound scandalized, but she could feel her cheeks flame ever darker.

Tracy cackled. "I knew it. Look, I was never sore about us not being a couple. And I won't even bitch about the fact that clearly this girl is right for you, and I'm not. I get that, too. I was pissed off because you ghosted me; we've been friends for years."

Jemma frowned and looked away with a deep sigh. At least Tracy had stopped digging at her. "I know, you're right. But Tracy, be honest, would you go to an art exhibit with me—like ever?"

"Hell no," Tracy laughed. "Museums bore me—just a bunch of paint and statues."

"My point exactly. But I promise I won't avoid you anymore. I'm sorry for that. I just felt guilty."

Tracy nodded to her. "I know. And I appreciate the apology. Just don't do it again." Standing up, Tracy opened her arms, and Jemma hugged her. "Now," Tracy continued. "When we go out there, no blubbering. I don't want the guys to think I've gone soft. Lunch?"

Jemma laughed. "Dressed like this? No thanks."

Tracy gave her a sly smile. "Sounds like you have plans elsewhere."

"I don't. But I do have a lead to run down. Some other time." *Like in a few years when I don't feel guilty for sleeping with a friend.*

"Sure," Tracy said with an arch grin and pointed toward the elevators. "Drop your visitor's badge at the front desk on your way out."

Outside, Jemma gave a few more waves to the scattered fans lingering by the entrance, her practiced smile still in place. Then, with a quick glance around, she lifted off, the cool air rushing past as she shot upward, leaving the police station—and Tracy's questions—behind.

As she soared higher, the city stretched out below her in a patchwork of light and shadows. She angled toward the harbor, its waters covered in whitecaps from the heavy breezes below, reflecting the sunlight like sparkling crystal. The steady rhythm of her flight was calming, soothing her irritation. For a few minutes, it was just her and the sky.

Then, feeling a bit mischievous, she spotted a passenger jet gliding toward the airport on today's landing pattern. With a smirk, Jemma zipped close to the plane, skimming past its windows just for fun. She knew better than to get too close, but it was one of those days where she needed the distraction.

A teenage girl in one of the windows noticed her, wide-eyed and disbelieving, her face pressed against the glass. Jemma slowed down, grinning as the girl waved enthusiastically and blew her a kiss. With a playful glint in her eye, Jemma waved back before pressing a conspiratorial finger to her lips. Then she shot off, disappearing before the girl could do more than stare.

That little moment—it was precisely what Jemma needed. A reminder that despite everything else weighing on her, there were still people out there who looked up to her. People who loved what she did. And for now, that was enough.

Chapter Nineteen

"Deep house," Sherry said as she sipped her martini and enjoyed the mellow music at Sin City a few days later. "Nice."

"It can't always be boom-sha, boom-sha, you know?" Malka commented, doing a fair imitation of a dance music drum beat. "People get bored. Hell, I get bored."

Sherry smirked. Sometimes Malka was downright cute, like right then, saying something completely down-to-earth and goofy. And it was in those moments that Sherry missed her. Despite her changes— the red skin, the horns, the wings—it was still Malka's face, her mannerisms, her silly sense of humor, and her beautiful body, mostly, anyway. But Sherry also missed the blonde hair and sparkling green eyes. Sherry could remember thinking that no one should have eyes that green. And with an intrusively dark feeling, she realized that no one did.

"Can I confide in you?" Sherry asked, shaking off the creeping melancholy.

Malka raised a delicate black eyebrow and leaned into the conversation, resting her chin on the backs of her interlaced fingers. "Please do."

Her sudden smile was a little disconcerting, and Sherry thought better of asking for advice about Jemma. "Maybe it's not a good idea," she said, fiddling with the toothpick and plucking one of the olives off the end.

But I'm Not a Supervillain!!!

Adopting a more pleasant grin, Malka took the toothpick from her hand. Her obscenely long tongue snaked out and wrapped slowly around the olive, its intrinsic muscles rippling suggestively. With the gentlest squeeze, the olive slipped off and into her mouth. "Blue cheese," she murmured around the olive, "is my favorite. Seriously though, I promise I won't laugh."

"I'm being serious here, Mal, I need advice."

The succubus's eyebrows slid up. "With a woman." It wasn't a question.

Sherry nodded. "We've gone on a couple of dates, right?"

"Expected," Malka replied with a wry expression. "Do go on."

"Well, I want to make a good impression. We went on a date for coffee, and I was so awkward. And she had to run off in the middle of it. I thought I'd bombed it, but then she apologized for leaving, and we decided to have dinner." Sherry's expression turned sheepish as she looked away, mumbling. "I offered to cook."

"Wait, what? That's funny; from over here, it sounded like you offered to cook. That can't be right."

Sherry looked up at Malka, the flesh around her lips white from pressing her lips together so hard.

Malka laughed. "You? Cook? Are you trying to poison her?"

"Please, you've got to help me. I really like this woman. She's amazing. I don't want her getting food poisoning or something. I really want to wow her."

With an incredulous snort, Malka leaned back in her chair. "Does the walking dead have a name?" She asked, taking Sherry's remaining olive into her mouth the usual way this time.

"Jemma Caldwell," Sherry said.

Malka coughed violently and made a choking noise, one hand to her neck.

"Jesus, Malka, are you okay?" Sherry almost jumped up, but Malka held her hand up and recovered her poise. With a last cough and a bit of croak, she said, "I'm sorry, I didn't catch that. What was the name again?"

"Jemma Caldwell," Sherry repeated. "Have you met her before?"

"Sherry," Malka chided playfully. "There are six-hundred-thousand people in this city, what are the chances that I know her?"

"Good point. That was a dumb question, wasn't it? See, that's what I'm talking about. I'm not sure what to do. She's nice and fun and has a great sense of humor, but I feel like I'm blowing it. Mostly, though, she's so smooth, and I'm, well, me. This really needs to be good."

Malka's face broke into a wide smile. "I seriously doubt that you're blowing it. Do you remember when we met?"

Crimson crept up Sherry's cheeks, and she rolled her eyes with embarrassment. "How can I forget? We were in the commissary, and I spilled red jello all over your sweater."

"No," Malka said. Her tone turned deadly serious, but she couldn't hold it and started to giggle. "You were trying to pick me up in the commissary, and we were talking about Vermeer, and you jerked your hand to your ear because somehow you thought I didn't know where an earring went, sending your spoon and half your gelatin into my face, then it landed on my sweater. It was one of the most adorable things I've ever had the pleasure to witness. What was cuter, though, was how apologetic you were, so goofy and profuse."

The embarrassed blush in Sherry's cheeks bloomed into something just north of scarlet, and she looked down. Truth be told, it was a fond memory, but not one that she and Sherry ever talked about, not since—

"Hey," Malka said, waving her hand to get Sherry's attention. "None of that, now. No regrets. We had a great relationship, but things happened. It wasn't your fault, and I miss parts of it, too, but now, we're talking about your would-be true love. So, I'll give you the best advice I have ever given anyone."

Sherry raised an eyebrow. "And what's that?"

"If she doesn't like you just the way you are, then fuck her. " Her voice was stern, protective, supportive in that Malka way. "It's that simple. You're a great woman, Sherry. Yeah, you can really get into things, and sometimes you're clumsy, but that really is part of your charm."

"Gee, thanks, Mom," Sherry said dryly. "Just be yourself wasn't what I was hoping for."

"Christ, Sherry, you're in your late twenties. You're not a teenager. I'll tell you something that helped me move forward after," she gestured to herself, "after all this. Remember how disgusted I was with myself? I felt like I couldn't control my libido, and I started lying all the time."

Sherry's face fell, and a rock slowly sank into her stomach. "It was two years ago, Malka, not a lifetime. Of course, I remember." Sherry watched as Malka swallowed hard, a touch of liquid glistening in her eye.

"I didn't have any control back then," Malka said. "I left because I was through with hurting you. You didn't deserve it. I wasn't in a good place. Anyway, that's not what I'm talking about. So here I was at thirty. I'd lost everything I ever wanted in life. The Met fired me. You and I were on the outs, and I had nothing."

"Except our savings," Sherry said bitterly. "There was that."

"No, this was right before that. And I have tried to pay you back several times, but you won't take it."

"I don't want the money," Sherry said caustically. It was harsh, but it wasn't stupidity. Taking money from Malka felt like a payoff for her feelings so that Malka could erase her guilt, and Sherry was still too hurt to let that happen. It was petty, she knew, and probably pointless, but it made her feel a little vindicated, and she refused to let go of that. She had to be the bigger woman. In truth, though, it felt like it had just turned to stubbornness. She pushed that aside. "Anyway, you were saying."

Malka leaned forward, and the hand she placed on Sherry's was almost hot to the touch. Over the few months that they'd still tried to work it out after the change, Sherry had learned a lot about Malka's new body. The heat in her body reflected her feelings. When she was angry, embarrassed, or surprised, her body temperature spiked. Or if she was horny or having an enjoyable time. The problem was knowing which was which sometimes.

"I watched this little clip on the internet of Michael Caine. He was rehearsing a stage play with this husband and wife pair on stage during an improvised fight scene. They got carried away and started throwing things. A chair they'd thrown had gotten lodged in the door through which he was supposed to enter. He told the director he couldn't get in because the chair was there. The director told him to use the difficulty."

"I've seen it," Sherry said with a little laugh. "If it's a comedy, you trip over the chair. If it's a drama, you push it out of the way in a way that supports the character. Stuff like that."

Malka swept her hand around the room. "I was desperate. I couldn't hurt you anymore, I knew that, but I didn't want to be homeless or on the street, so I took the money and opened the club."

"And left my ass broke," Sherry bitched. "Glad you got your difficulty out of the way."

"Oh, quit being such a child and grow up, Sher. I told you then that I'd repay you, but you were too angry and hurt to accept it. Now you're just being a pain in the ass about it." Malka waved to the waiter walking by and ordered two more martinis for them. "And you do that so you can hold it over my head. You think I don't know that?"

The rebuke stung, mainly because Sherry knew it to be true. She looked away, not wanting to meet Malka's eyes.

"Was it pride?" Malka asked.

"Was what pride?" Sherry said, now thoroughly irritated at the direction of the conversation.

"The Rembrandt, was it pride?"

Sherry glanced around furtively. "Keep your voice down," she hissed. "No, it wasn't pride."

"This is a supervillain bar, Sherry. No one cares." Malka said, waving her drink around imperiously. "And you should be proud of yourself. You stole an iconic painting from The Met with no trace, no evidence, and no one the wiser for hours. That takes talent."

Sherry blushed again, this time at the compliment, and she couldn't help the shit-eating grin that spread across her face.

"See," Malka said. "You think I don't know you, that I've turned into some monster, but I do know you, and you're as much the criminal as I have ever been. And how did you like it?"

Dropping her head, Sherry let the long wave of her hair fall across her vision as she whispered. "It was fucking amazing."

Malka barked a laugh. "Ha! I knew it. It's thrilling, isn't it? Last time you were here, you said I was the risk taker, but didn't you go on all those adventures with me? Tell me that you regret the rock climbing, or the rappelling, or the skydiving."

Sherry realized that she couldn't. It was a stunning pronouncement that left her reeling. "Shit."

"Now, take a deep breath. You have difficulty talking to pretty girls, and if you're coming to me for help, this girl must be gorgeous. But she's asked you for a second date, so you can't be bombing it. Just be yourself, and if you find yourself feeling like an idiot, use it. No one suspects the bumbler, either. Try to remember that. It's perfect camouflage."

"I guess," Sherry said. She was practically sabotaging the compliments, and she knew it.

"Oh, stop," Malka said with a dismissive wave. "How did you know how many cameras I'd installed since you were last here?"

"I counted," Sherry said flatly. "It's not hard."

"You haven't been here in over a year and a half," Malka scoffed.

"You know I have a head for it. I always have."

"And you always wanted to rob something," she finished for her.

"Yes, I mean, no, that's not it," Sherry sputtered. "I had no choice."

Malka raised that skeptical, questioning eyebrow again and then donned a wicked grin as the air around her rippled slightly. "Liar."

Fortunately, their drinks arrived, saving Sherry from any

further prevarication. Malka was right. She could have just asked Malka for the money. Hell, she could have asked Malka for a job, a real job. She had known that, but she didn't because Mixxer had approached her and asked if she could help him with a plan for his goons. Instead, she'd stolen the Rembrandt out from under everyone's nose.

Sherry twirled the olives in the martini, deciding whether to have a second one. She looked up to find Malka staring at her, the corners of her mouth twitching.

"Villain," Malka said, and the depraved smile blossoming on her face left no doubt in Sherry's mind why the heat was blooming around her. "Come on, let's go."

Chapter Twenty

"Jesus," Sherry whispered in awe as she stepped across the hardwood floors, eyeballing the top-end appliances. "Your kitchen is bigger than my whole apartment."

Malka scoffed. "Don't be ridiculous. It's two hundred square feet; our apartment was three times that."

"Fine, add in this pantry, and it's half the size," Sherry quipped, her eyes roaming the shelves of the walk-in storeroom. She'd never stepped foot in Malka's condo before. Hell, she hadn't even known where she lived until today.

Malka had the entire penthouse of One River Place, a brand-new building that overlooked Riverside Drive and the Devon River. As with her office, the sparse decorations contradicted Malka's saucy reputation for the most part, though several walls were adorned with acrylic and watercolor paintings of nude or partially nude women in various poses: some smoked in chairs, others lounged on setees, a few were standing. Each one was different, and they all expressed disdain as if being painted had been a supreme inconvenience that they barely tolerated.

Appointed in a minimalist style, each room was decorated for maximum space with a minimum of pointless or small decorations. Sherry thought perhaps that they were set up so that a careless sweep of Malka's wings was less likely to topple something. One room, off the main living space, was a library filled with books, not just on shelves but stacked on the floor and lying on tables. The art histories that filled the shelves weren't much of a surprise; the relatively large collection of lesbian romances, however, was. Curiosity burned in Sherry to see the bedroom, but she knew better than to go anywhere near that. "So, what are we doing here, anyway?"

"I'm going to teach you how to make a simple meal that will knock your girl's socks off. What was her name again?"

"Um. . . Jemma. What can I make that would possibly impress her?" Sherry asked, now finding a spot at the center island as Malka poured them each a generous helping of white wine. Sherry was glad they'd left before they'd started their second round of Martini's. She was already feeling a little buzzed as it was.

"Shrimp scampi," Malka said. "You always loved it."

Another pang of negative feelings washed over Sherry, and she did her best to brush them aside. "You think pasta and shrimp will impress her?"

"Yes, I do. On one condition. You bring her by the bar next week, but do yourself a favor and don't tell her who I am."

"Why?" Sherry asked, her eyes narrowing.

"Because I want to make sure she's worthy of you."

Sherry rolled her eyes. "Fine. But the scampi recipe better be fire."

"Oh, it will be," Malka said, scooping up her wine glass and marching deeper into the apartment. "I'm going to get changed. You probably should, too."

Sherry all but panicked. Looking down at herself, she realized that her skimpy black club dress probably wasn't appropriate for cooking, but the idea of following Malka into the apartment further left her breathless for every reason imaginable.

Malka poked her head back around the kitchen doorway. "Are you going to cook in that?"

Pressing her lips into a firm line and squeezing her hands into fists, Sherry tried to move, but her legs wouldn't answer her. She was stuck fast, her heart running like a jackrabbit. "Um. . . Maybe this wasn't—"

Malka didn't wait for her to finish the sentence. Instead, she returned and grabbed Sherry's hand, pulling her behind her into the living room and then down the hall toward the master bedroom.

"Malka, you know I don't like it when—"

Stopping abruptly in the hallway, Malka spun on her heel. "I won't hurt you," she whispered gently. "You used to trust me. I know I did things I shouldn't have, but I never put you in any danger." With a squeeze of her hand, Malka slowed her pace but continued dragging Sherry along.

Sherry tried desperately to get her breathing under control, as they reached Malka's bedroom. She counted the bits of furniture, trying to focus on each one, taking it in. A huge, canopied bed sat against one wall, and a vast picture window looked across the river. The buildings of Harborhaven University glowed on the far side. Wall sconces shed dim light across the room, illuminating a wall hanging of Sherry. In the portrait, Sherry lounged on the sand beside rolling waves, barely covered by a white button-down shirt. Malka had painted it years ago, and it was the one thing she'd taken when she'd left. Seeing it didn't help at all, and Sherry panicked.

Head buzzing from alcohol and the edge of hyperventilation, she wanted to tell Malka to stop, that this was a bad idea, but her voice refused to work right. Everything sounded like a squeak. "Please, Malka. . . I. . . Please. . ." Her entire body trembled with a mix of fear, anxiety, and anticipation. She was losing control of her emotions. In seconds, now rocking on her heels, she tore her hand loose and flapped her fingers in the air. It was an expression of anxiety, one she'd fought hard to suppress. Some dim part of her knew that, but she couldn't stop herself. Her conscious brain had all but shut down.

Malka stepped forward, her face a mask of concern, and spread her wings, enveloping them both and blocking out the light. "May I take your hands?" Malka whispered.

Despite their soft tone, the plosives in Malka's words sounded like gunshots in her ears. Still, Sherry managed a nod, unsure if Malka could see.

Malka grasped Sherry's hands and gave three quick strokes of her knuckles before letting go. "It's been so long since… I didn't realize. I'm sorry."

Still stuck, Sherry nodded and swallowed hard. Finally, her voice returned, if only in a whisper. "I'm scared" was all she could get out. It wasn't quite how she really felt, but she had no words for that. She wasn't sure it was fear, exactly. And it wasn't anxiety. She couldn't name it.

"Take your time. Do you want to sit down?"

Sherry slowly knelt on the floor, and Malka settled with her. The comforting enclosure of Malka's wings settled Sherry's nerves over the next few minutes. Her breath was still heavy, but she no longer felt on the edge of panic. Malka said nothing; she knew how to deal with this from their time together. Just snuff out the light and stay close without smothering her.

Slowly, after a few more minutes of rocking, Sherry began to come around. "I shouldn't have come here. This was a bad idea."

"No, it's not your fault," Malka said. "I should have just brought you some clothes. I should have known better. It's just. . ." Malka's voice trailed off. Then, after a moment, she said. "Do you want me to take you home?"

Sherry shook her head. "No. I just need a few minutes. Why don't you get changed?"

"You sure?" Malka's voice was low and soft, so familiar, even with the strange reverberation it carried now.

"I'm sure," Sherry said, her eyes following the pretty patterns on the Persian rug. "I'll be okay."

Malka furled her wings behind her, letting the light in once more as she slowly stood, turned around, and dropped down again. Her wings slid to the floor on either side of Sherry. "Do you mind?"

Sherry blinked slowly, comprehension coming to her in fits and starts. With a trembling hand, she reached out and undid the fasteners over each wing and slid the zipper down. Malka probably could have done it on her own, but Sherry understood somewhere in the back of her mind that Malka needed to know that Sherry was okay, that she hadn't just traumatized her. This was her way of grounding her feelings and absolving herself of needless guilt. It wasn't Malka's fault. She'd just forgotten.

Malka rose, her dress pooling elegantly around her feet. As Sherry's senses sharpened, her gaze traced the line of Malka's column-like legs, following the curve upward to the strong expanse of her back, where the supracoracoideus muscles tightened with each flex of her massive wings. A shiver ran through Sherry. Her ex was breathtaking and, if she were honest, even more stunning now than she had ever been. Sherry watched, mesmerized, as the ripple of strength traveled across her back in a smooth, powerful stretch.

Those delicately powerful movements became a rhythm she could cling to. It wasn't sexual—though Sherry could admit, on some level, the grace with which Malka moved was a little arousing. But more than that, the fluid motion of her muscles, the way they flexed and released beneath her skin, captivated her in a way nothing else could. Sherry's mind, which threatened to spiral into isolation and stimming, instead focused on the ripple of sinew as Malka shifted her weight, the subtle dance of tendons, giving her something solid to latch onto. The tension pulling her under loosened, replaced by the silent, steady beat of Malka's body.

Malka pulled a nightshirt over her head, adjusting it so the slits in the back lined up with her wings. Bending down again, Malka knelt as Sherry buttoned the hem of the nightshirt around the muscular joining of wing to back. Malka stood and pulled on a loose pair of drawstring pants. Finally, she turned to face Sherry and held out her hand patiently.

Sherry took it and let Malka pull her up off the floor. Their faces were inches apart, and the smokey aroma of Malka filled Sherry's nose. It was like the late embers of a campfire, a bit ashen but not unpleasant. Sherry blinked and took a deep, shuddering breath, letting it out. Then she drew in another, letting the scent fill her up inside. Her duplicitous thoughts tugged at her. *God, I miss her.*

"I'll get you some clothes," Malka whispered, her lips so

close that Sherr could have pursed her own and met them. But then, Malka drew away and found a shirt and another pair of drawstring pants for Sherry. They were too large, but Sherry made do.

Sherry was about to turn and leave the bedroom, but Malka lifted a hand to her cheek. Instinctively, Sherry leaned into the touch and closed her eyes. It felt so soft and silky against her face. Malka's soft lips met hers, and Sherry melted. She expected Malka to deepen the kiss, but she didn't. Instead, she backed away and took Sherry's hand. "Let's go get you ready for your date."

With her body a roiling tempest of confused emotions, Sherry let Malka lead her from the room and back to the kitchen. Malka walked Sherry through the steps of making the meal. Carefully, she explained everything, showing her how to prepare her ingredients, mise en place. Her hands drifted over Sherry's as she performed each step, making gentle corrections.

Sherry was intensely aware of how close Malka hovered: breasts occasionally brushing her shoulder blades, fingers guiding hers, a hand at the small of her back. The experience was slow and sweet and achingly needful. The entire time, Malka never mentioned the kiss she'd stolen or anything else that had happened that evening. They just made food.

When they were done, they ate, and Malka made encouraging suggestions on which white wine went best with the meal and the best presentation of the dish. Malka even placed a pick-up order for Sherry for everything so she wouldn't have to do any shopping. Sherry loved shellfish. The problem was that her body didn't, or so she had thought. She hadn't eaten it in years, but she still expected to break out in hives. She didn't.

"I'm sorry, I don't have any antihistamines," Malka said as they ate. "I just hope you don't break out too badly."

Sherry shrugged. "I'm fine for the moment. I'll take something when I get home. I wouldn't miss this for the world." She slid her hand across the table and touched Malka's forearm. "Thank you for this. I really don't want to screw this up."

"Are you sure this is the relationship for you?" Malka asked. It was a simple question, carrying none of Malka's usual snide tone.

"I think so," Sherry said as she twirled angel hair onto her fork and then stabbed a shrimp. "I know what you're going to say, and it's the one thing I'm worried about."

"You're a thief, Sherry," Malka nodded. "You have the bug. Like you said, it's not the money; it's the thrill. You love pitting yourself against people when the stakes are high, especially given your innate gift for all things electrical. It's why you didn't just boost bikes. You stole the really expensive ones."

Sherry gave a slight nod of her head, but she didn't respond. She'd been thinking that same thing since the night of the heist. She liked bucking the system. No. She liked beating the system, whether it was a high-end security system like the Met or popping the KIM-U keyless ignition on a Ducati. The more complex the system, the more tempting it was. Now that she'd let herself back into that mindset, she wondered if she could give it up, even for Jemma. Malka knew her too well, and she found it unsettling.

After dinner, Sherry changed back into her dress. The evening had done nothing to settle her nerves or clarify her feelings—quite the opposite.

"Why are you doing this?" Sherry asked as she prepared to leave.

Malka gave her a gentle smile and placed a hand on her cheek. The gesture was tender and loving, and Sherry tilted her head into Malka's soft fingers, closing her eyes and feeling the dagger-like nails just brushing her neck and ear.

"Because," Malka said as she ran her thumb across Sherry's cheekbone. "You deserve happiness, and I'm not at all sure I could give it to you. I think I could, but we've been down that road. So the least I can do is help." As Sherry opened her eyes and looked into Malka's face, the succubus gave a devilish smirk. "Of course, if it doesn't work out, you know where to find me."

Sherry felt unable to breathe. A deep part of her just wanted to let go and wrap herself up in Malka, but the memory of pain and betrayal kept her still. She knew how it would turn out, and she couldn't go through that again.

"One last thing," Malka said. "Your new carpet arrives tomorrow. And I know that you didn't ask, but I covered the mortgage for this month until you get paid."

"You shouldn't have done that," Sherry said before she could stop herself. Then she snapped her jaws shut, pushing down her pride. "I'm sorry. Thank you for that, but I'll manage. Okay?"

Malka nodded, kissed Sherry's cheek, and walked her to the door. Sherry bid Malka goodbye and took a cab home. The entire way, she sat in a daze as her heart tried to tear itself in half right there in the back seat.

Chapter Twenty-One

Jemma scanned the room, biting her lip to fight the rising gorge in her throat. It was a blood bath. There were six bodies. Mixxer was dead, shot through the head behind the desk of his posh home office. The rest of the room was destroyed. Even Mixxer's infamous full bar, where he'd earned his nom de guerre, lay in splinters, torn apart. Three of the bodies had their heads crushed manually. That took far more strength than any normal man could manage.

"Rostovich," Jemma said, her voice tight. "This is Ivan and Viktor's work. A nice topper to my morning of dress shopping."

Tracy gave a curt nod and a guilty grimace. "Sorry, I thought you ought to see this. From left to right, that's Quentin Dillard. He's an electronics specialist." Dillard's head wasn't crushed, but the depression in his chest was too deep to be a survivable injury. Something had hit him like the end of a telephone pole, crushing his torso into the ground.

"That's Andrew Carlton, wheel-man," Tracy continued. "I think that's Karen Schilter and her brother Emil. They're well known for stealing antiquities. Finally, that's Wilmar Jackson. He's a former Marine infantryman turned hired muscle."

Jemma didn't know how she recognized Karen, Emil, and Wilmar, given how mangled their faces were. "You said this was related to the case?"

"Take a look at the desk."

Jemma hovered her way over to the desk to avoid disturbing any evidence. She was wearing booties, but it was best just to avoid contact altogether. Mixxer's head was upturned, eyes sightless. On the desk in front of him sat the floorplan of the Met, mostly covered by books and other odds and ends. Jemma lifted the pages with a gloved hand, getting a glimpse of four more underneath. It was the entire facility, including below-ground storage, equipment rooms, and exterior access points. "They were planning the Met heist? I don't understand."

"If I were to guess," Tracy responded, stepping across the bodies to the desk. "Mixxer planned the heist, and someone else beat him to it. I suspect that's why the plans are buried underneath all of this other garbage. With this whole crew here, he must have been meeting someone. For another job, maybe?"

"Ivan's guys?" Jemma wondered aloud. "But if that's the case, why kill them? It doesn't make sense. As I understand it, Mixxer's supposedly done a dozen jobs for Ivan. I wouldn't call them friends, but I didn't think they were on the outs."

Tracy shrugged. "You think maybe Dmitri wanted the painting stolen? But if that's the case, why not have his brother ship it directly to him?"

Jemma turned in the air and faced Tracy. "They were smuggling something into the frame. I can't discuss it in more detail, but if you ship a piece of artwork to a private individual, it might be inspected. Museums have agreements to prevent that to avoid damaging the paintings, at least in many instances. Because priceless paintings aren't typically convenient ways to smuggle anything large, like a drug shipment or explosives, they're considered low risk. One less thing for customs to care about. If I wanted to smuggle something small—a million in cut flawless diamonds, we'll say —I could stash them in a frame, have it shipped, and then have someone steal it on the back end. It's not a great route for regular smuggling, though. There are only so many priceless paintings, and it's difficult to arrange."

"Unless you own the painting," Tracy stated flatly.

"Unless you own the painting," Jemma repeated in agreement. "Let's talk about this outside."

Tracy snorted in mild amusement.

"Won't you get in trouble for letting me into the crime scene?" Jemma asked once they were standing in the driveway.

"I needed your expertise," Tracy answered. "It looks like a superhuman crime, and who better to ask? That's my story, and I'm sticking to it. "

Jemma chuckled. "I guess that makes sense. Not that you guys don't deal with superhuman crime plenty."

"Yeah, still, though, I thought maybe you might be able to help me out. We're coming up with not much on the actual thief. Looking at that mess, I'd say that Ivan hired Mixxer to steal the painting, and someone pulled the rug out from under the lot of them, so he sent Il Duce to clean up."

"Yeah," Jemma said. "Whoever masterminded the heist probably screwed 'em. Our mysterious blonde, I'm betting. There's obviously a detail we're missing, though. Ivan wouldn't have killed Mixxer under normal circumstances. It wouldn't be like him to kill an entire crew for something like that. Unless he thought they'd gone behind his back. But if that's the case, where's the painting now? And still, why did Ivan have them killed? I'm assuming it's Ivan. It sure looks like Il Douchebag's handiwork."

"I'll say this much," Tracy murmured. "I wouldn't give a rat's ass for our mysterious blonde's life right now. We need to find her before Ivan does."

"You had lunch yet?" Tracy asked.

Jemma snickered. "No, you interrupted my morning with this horror show. Thanks for that, by the way."

"There's a spare set of sweats in my trunk. You can change on the way. How do you feel about a Chicken Parm from Vito's Deli?"

"What about the scene?" Jemma asked, watching the evidence techs filing in and out of the mansion.

"Jennings will finish it from here," Tracy said casually,

referring to her partner, Christine Jennings. Jennings was a relatively new detective. Jemma hadn't met her yet, but she was sure she would.

A half-hour later, Jemma, now in an HHPD sweatsuit, sat by the window of Mama Vito's Italian Deli, across the street from police headquarters. They really did have the best chicken parmesan sandwiches in town, and Jemma ate hers with gusto. "Oh, this is so good," she said around a mouthful of food. "I had forgotten how good."

"The best," Tracy murmured, wiping a bit of marinara off her lips with a napkin. "So, let's noodle this. Mixxer is planning to steal the Rembrandt. Let's say he's doing it for Ivan. One of Mixxer's crew manages to snag it out from under him, apparently solo. No small feat. So what, then? Ivan is pissed that they were taken in by one of Mixxer's guys?"

Jemma shook her head. "No. That's just not Ivan's style. He wouldn't go after Mixxer for that unless—" A germ of an idea began to take root in Jemma's head. "Maybe Mixxer was in on the solo heist and wanted to keep the money for himself and sell it to the highest bidder." That was a thought. Mixxer was a fence. He had more than enough contacts to sell the painting, especially if he didn't know what was in it. That was a terrifying thought. If Mixxer sold it to just any old schmoe, who knew what would happen if Lot 429 was really in the frame? If she were lucky, it would just sit on someone's wall until she tracked it down, but she was never that lucky.

"It's possible, but if that happens, how will we know who has it?"

"Watch the hospitals. See if anyone comes in with strange symptoms, unexplained illness with a sudden and just as unexplained recovery."

But I'm Not a Supervillain!!!

Chapter Twenty-Two

The following day, at the crack of dawn, Sherry had been yanked from a fabulous dream. In it, she'd been flying side by side with Lena Swift over a city she didn't recognize. The interruption, though, had been welcome: carpet installers.

Sherry curled her toes into the thick wool carpet, reluctantly impressed. When Malka made a promise, she delivered. This was the most luxurious thing she'd ever felt underfoot—better even than when she'd dropped Malka's glass of Cristal at Sin City. The padding beneath had a satisfying bounce, and the false flooring underneath had fixed that annoying squeak by the door—perfect timing for her movie night with Jemma.

Malka had even thrown in a plush sofa from Ward & Flannery. The polyester upholstery was so soft it felt like velvet, a clear peace offering after the corgi fiasco. And it was bigger—much better than the old loveseat. Honestly, Sherry was glad to see that thing go. Curling up with Jemma on what had once been hers and Malka's had felt too weird and moderately uncomfortable.

"What do you think? Huh, buddy?" she asked Breitweiser as she unfolded and stretched out on the big sofa, her feet sliding nimbly behind Breitweiser's curled-up little body. The cat lifted his head and turned his patchy little face toward her before dropping back to his usual mid-day nap. "I'll take that as approval. How about you, Barry?"

Barry sat in the corner under the window, looking pleased with the entire arrangement. Sherry suspected he was just grateful she hadn't allowed the delivery guys to take him away with the old loveseat. In the midst of reveling in her new furnishings, Sherry felt her cell vibrate under her butt.

She frowned. "Maybe if I ignore it, they'll go away," she muttered drowsily, and it stopped. A few minutes later, though, the phone buzzed again, and she finally scooched a bit and lifted her ass, much to Breit's dismay. He threw her a baleful look as she slid the phone from her pocket, hit the connect button, and put it to her ear.

"Hello?" she answered through a yawn.

"Hey, Sherry Berry! How are you? Do you have my painting?" Mixxer, of course.

Sherry froze; she felt like her heart had stopped. It had undoubtedly skipped a beat, probably several. "Hi there," she said as smoothly as she could. "About that. The thing is—"

"I don't like bad news. So think carefully before you speak." Mixxer's voice sounded tight, and despite his bouncy demeanor, she could detect a building edge.

"You see, so. . ." She drew out the word, trying to keep her voice level. "I got the painting from Malka, as you said, but then I was attacked by The Royal Family and a gang of little dogs. I know it sounds preposterous, but they took it."

There was silence on the phone for several agonizing seconds, and Sherry felt tears welling in her eyes. She was fucked.

"Well, that is disappointing," Mixxer said finally. "I don't have to tell you that my buyer is most impatient, and I know I don't have to repeat just how frustrating I find procurers who don't deliver."

Sherry swallowed hard. "No, Mixxer, you don't. I'll get the painting back, I promise."

"You better," Mixxer demanded. "If it's not in my possession in seven days, you might want to consider getting your affairs in order, Sherry."

"Seven days?" *That wasn't enough time. No way was that enough time.* "I thought you were out of town for two more weeks."

"Seven. Days." His voice had gone ice cold. "I'll have someone come and pick it up. I do know where you live, in that nice mid-rise by the docks."

"Fuck," Sherry swore loudly. "This sucks."

Sherry leaned back on the sofa and stared at the ceiling, her mind racing with possible outcomes. With an almost palpable effort, she thrust aside her panic and decided on a course of action. She didn't want to do it, but now, she had no choice. Malka seemed to have her meathooks into the entire city, so if anyone would know what to do, it would be her.

"I need to find King Charles," Sherry told Malka as she sat in her office that evening. Her gaze lingered on the sky outside as she wrung her hands and her legs shook. "I'm in real trouble. Mixxer is going to kill me if I don't find the Rembrandt and get it to him."

Malka moved around from behind her desk and took Sherry by the hand, leading her to the couch. "Come over here and tell me what happened."

"Yesterday morning, after you had that carpet delivered—thank you, by the way. The couch was way too much, but I appreciate it. Anyway, After they put the carpet down, Mixxer called. He's demanding I get the painting back from King Charles. I know that if I don't, I won't have to worry about not getting paid. He's gonna kill me." Sherry put her head in her hands and cried. She had no clue what to do. "I didn't know where else to go."

"That's it," Malka stated, heat coming off her in waves and her eyes glowing just a little brighter. "We need to put an end to this. I'll talk to Mixxer later and deal with him."

"What are you going to do?" Sherry asked, her voice trembling.

"I'm going to explain that you're my friend. I'm going to make sure his buyer gets their damn painting and that you get paid. That's all."

"Malka," Sherry said. "I don't think they're just going to give it up, and I don't want them hurt."

Malka frowned, and her wings shivered slightly in agitation. "Sherry, darling, I don't think you realize the world you're a part of now. We can't accept no for an answer. It's that simple. Let me worry about how I'm going to deal with it." She paused for a minute and turned Sherry's hand over, examining the back side. "Have you been working out?"

Sherry said nothing.

Narrowing her eyes, Malka lifted the hem of Sherry's shirt, feeling Sherry's abs as she did so. Sherry jerked back, pushing her shirt down. "What are you doing?"

Malka's face was a mask, utterly devoid of emotion. "Sherry, you're built. I can see it in your shoulders and the veins on your hands. You look like you've been lifting. I know every inch of that body. Something's changed. What's going on?"

Sherry looked out the window at the puffy pink clouds hovering off to the west against the darkening sky. A slight breeze blew into the office and ruffled her hair. She closed her eyes and sighed, deciding how much to tell her. In the end, she needed someone to talk to about what was going on. She sure couldn't talk to Jemma. She'd ask way too many questions. She wrestled internally for a few seconds before finally saying, "Yeah, I've been working out."

Sherry was sick of lying to everyone but didn't know what else to do. Jemma couldn't know about the Rembrandt, and Sherry didn't want Malka to know about the blue stuff inside. Who knew who Malka would tell? She was on the edge of getting it back, and she didn't want to blow up what she felt like might be her last chance to get things squared away and get out of this mess.

The only problem was that Malka clearly wasn't buying it. And why should she? Sherry had examined herself just that morning. She wasn't just fit; she was ripped. She had boulder shoulders and washboard abs. Her thighs were so muscular that she had taken to wearing loose-fit jeans. It hadn't been as noticeable at Malka's home, but now.

"Uh huh," Malka said finally. Maybe she wouldn't pursue it. "Well, I'll get to work on getting in touch with Charlie and Mary and get the painting back. Let me worry about that."

"What do I do in the meantime?" Sherry said. "What if Mixxer calls again?"

"He probably will, but not until I talk to him. If he calls, do as he says," Malka answered, her tone calm, matter of fact. "It'll be fine. I promise."

Sherry ran a sweaty hand through her hair. Her leg was again bouncing. "I never knew you had so much pull."

Malka gave Sherry a half-shrug. "I have a few favors I can call in. Don't worry."

Sherry leaned into Malka, resting her cheek on Malka's chest like she used to do when things got too emotional. She hated her life sometimes. Most of the time, she was fine. She could fend off heavy personal interactions and keep herself level. But nothing had prepared her for all of… Her thoughts stuttered for a second as a wave of something washed through her. Malka's body was so warm. She just wanted to—she jerked away. "Stop it," Sherry demanded, moving away from Malka on the couch. "I know what you're trying to do."

Malka raised her hands defensively. "You were melting down. I just wanted to ease your stress. I promise."

Sherry's shoulders slumped. "I'm sorry. I'm just—" She couldn't finish the sentence, and she started to pace. "It's—It's —"

"What?" Malka replied, her voice calm, easy.

"Something's happening to me. I don't know what it is or if it's going to stop. I can't really talk about the details, but I wanted to ask you something."

Malka raised an eyebrow, her hands folded in her lap as she waited for Sherry to continue.

"After—" Sherry broke off again, unsure if she should start down this road. "After your—"

Leaning forward slightly, Malka waited.

"After Prince Lucifer, how did you deal with things? I mean, how did you make it right?" Sherry started to get more agitated. She needed to slow down. Finally, she sat down next to Malka and leaned in. That calm feeling returned as Malka's arm wrapped around her shoulders. Sherry's fingers found purchase on Malka's dress and dug in, holding her close. She swallowed hard. It sounded awful in her ears, like something slithering down her throat.

Closing her eyes, she started again. "After Prince Lucifer and after you left, how did you come to accept these changes?"

Malka stroked Sherry's hair and spoke almost lovingly. "Ah, that. Eventually, I realized two things. One, my life was never going back to what it was. I would never be the same, and there was simply nothing I could do about it. That allowed me to look at the benefits. I can fly, Sherry. I don't often, and it's hard work, but I can jump out that window, flap my wings, and be off into the night. It's very liberating."

"And the other changes?"

"I don't pay much attention to them. I'm stronger than most people but not what one might consider superhuman. As for the big boobs and hips?" She shrugged. "They're a mixed blessing. Again, I dress for whatever part I'm playing at the time. Secondly, and more importantly, I learned quickly that I am in charge of my own life. I can make my own decisions. Not out of desperation, like when I left and took our savings. I feel my own power, not because of what I can do, but because of who I am. You could give these gifts to a dozen other people who might not do as well with them. Being feared isn't fabulous, but it does have its advantages, and I use that. Now, why do you ask?"

Sherry stayed silent, mulling Malka's words. Could these changes be a blessing? Maybe. But right now, all it instilled was fear. Like everyone, she'd read stories on social media. Rumors of a secret government facility where they used people like lab rats. People who had died horribly. There were even some pictures. And everyone knew about SPEAR. Lena Swift had brought them down years ago. She wondered if this blue stuff running through her veins was part of that, and it terrified her.

Finally, though, she decided not to tell Malka anything. "No reason," she said, finally. "I was just wondering. I've been going through some things." After a moment of more silence, she whispered. "I never got over it."

"I know," Malka murmured, nodding slightly. "But you will. It'll get better. You never told me how your date went. How did she like the shrimp?"

Sherry smiled, enjoying the way Malka slid her hand around, never lingering on one spot. *She remembers.* Sherry took a long, deep breath and sat up. "That's not until the day after tomorrow, but I'll let you know."

"Okay," Malka said and stood. "Why don't you go home and get some rest? I'll deal with Mixxer and Charlie. Once I've arranged things, Mixxer will give you a call."

Sherry nodded, standing and gathering up her helmet. "You're a good friend, Malka. I'm sorry I was gone so long."

Malka smiled, but Sherry could see a tightness in her eyes, something unsaid. "What is it?" she asked.

"Nothing. You should get going."

Sherry wanted to stay. She felt safe here, but she knew it was a bad idea. Her libido was doing little happy dances, and she didn't want to risk indulging that. So, she gave Malka a quick hug, a light kiss on the cheek, and with another soft "Thank you," she left and headed home.

Malka had been sweet and helpful, but she couldn't just do nothing. She needed to find that painting, and soon. Maybe Malka would find it, but Sherry decided it was time she took matters into her own hands. She'd gotten herself into this. She was going to get herself out.

Chapter Twenty-Three

One might have thought that somewhere in the vast online archives of the Harborhaven Chronicle, Sherry would find a mention of "Charlie and Mary." She did—plenty of them, in fact. The pair were suspects in several crimes but had somehow evaded arrest each time. Of their real identities, however, there wasn't even a whisper. They were like ghosts. But Sherry had grown up with a librarian and knew that the information she wanted was out there. When the online world came up empty, she knew exactly where to look next.

The Harborhaven Library's Caldwell Building was a masterpiece of Beaux-Arts elegance. Its oxidized copper cornice, adorned with dolphins and seashells, paid homage to Harborhaven's maritime past. Three carved seals framed the entrance, representing the library, the city, and the state. Inside, grand arches soared above, and the reading halls felt almost cathedral-like, with ceramic tile vaults and marble floors that added a soft echo to every footstep.

Sherry had stationed herself in the library's lower archives for two days now, cashing in a favor from one of her mother's old friends who still worked there. The hum of the microfiche machine and the warm glow of ancient clippings transported her back to childhood, to nights spent here nestled in marble grandeur. When she wasn't out hustling, painting, or even stealing motorcycles, she would often find herself here, wrapped in the familiar scent of old wood and worn paper. Sometimes, she even thought she caught a faint whiff of her mother's floral perfume, mingling with the library's air.

By now, Sherry knew just about everything there was to uncover about The Royal Family. They had first surfaced in Harborhaven ten years ago, with a strange and violent debut linked to the murder of a dog kennel owner in Brattleford, Maine, a small, isolated town. Back then, they had been seen wearing balaclavas emblazoned with the Union Jack. Since then, they had become increasingly active in Harborhaven's underworld, mainly as weapons brokers to third-world buyers. Though they kept their operations discreet, Sherry had connected them to three high-stakes robberies involving military contractors and advanced weaponry.

She had pieced it all together from the scant details available and a few FOIA requests she'd stumbled upon in the library archives. The details were heavily redacted, but a few rather obvious clues—like a note signed "Courtesy of The Royal Family" and sightings of trained corgis at each scene—had pointed back to them.

And now, she had found the final piece. Sherry stared at a small news article from the police blotter, dated twenty years earlier. Looking back at her were Charles and Mary McGowan, two proud dog breeders posing with a fat ribbon from the Westminster Kennel Club dog show. Charles had clearly had some work done since then, but Mary still looked every bit like a portrait of Mary Tudor. The article was brief: someone had burned down their kennel, killing all but one of their beloved corgis.

"Gotcha," Sherry whispered as she read. By all accounts, Charles and Mary McGowan were a perfectly ordinary couple who bred corgis, and Sherry wondered what had pushed them to embrace a life of crime.

She zoomed in on the photo. It had been taken at the puppy farm, pre-fire. Behind Charlie and Mary and their award-winning and quite adorable corgi sat a mailbox. Twisting the knob, she brought it into focus and pressed the print button, sending it to the big printer in the corner. She pulled it off the printer and stashed it in her bag.

With the address and notes tucked safely in her backpack, Sherry strode toward the exit. Outside, she swung a leg over the seat of her motorcycle, pulling on her helmet in one smooth motion, and fired up the engine. The familiar rumble felt grounding, chasing away some of her anxiety. She revved the throttle and muttered to herself, "Alright, McGowans. Time to see what's left of that old farm."

As she sped down the road, the wind whipped past her, cool against her neck and tinged with the scent of fallen leaves. Her mind spun through her leads—she'd already narrowed down their old property, found some transfer records, and spotted that tantalizing mailbox in the background of their kennel photo. That old farm might be abandoned, but she wasn't counting on it. Not after they'd somehow slithered around Harborhaven's underworld for years without a single arrest.

"Could it be that obvious?" she muttered to herself as she rode. She didn't have high hopes, but it was her next best stop.

A grin crept onto her face as she leaned into a turn, she was actually having fun. It wasn't quite as thrilling as the heist, but it was close. Chasing down a bunch of assholes who'd taken what she'd rightly stolen had a poetic quality. Of course, it could be that she watched too many movies.

She made some mental notes as the road straightened out, marking her stops: first, the property itself, then maybe a few conversations with anyone left in the area. And if that turned out to be a dead end, she'd still have the kennel clubs to work through. "They can't stay ghosts forever," she muttered under her breath.

The old farm was a good hour's ride out of Harborhaven, and with each mile, Sherry's excitement grew. If there was anything left out there—a stash, a lead, even just a scrap of paperwork with their handwriting—she'd find it.

The old McGowan puppy farm came into view just as the sun was dipping below the horizon, casting long shadows across the barren fields. Sherry cut the engine, coasting the last few yards before hopping off her bike and tugging off her helmet. The place was worse than she'd expected: the barn roof sagged, vines strangled the fence posts, and the whole property looked like it had been swallowed by years of neglect. The house and kennel were both gone, their burnt remains reclaimed by the weeds.

"Damn it," she whispered, hands on her hips as she took in the scene. She'd been so sure this would be the place. So sure there'd be some trace of their past here. But if anything was left behind, it was likely buried under layers of dust and debris. With a resigned sigh, she pulled a flashlight from her bag and started scanning the property.

In the corner of the barn, tucked away behind a stack of moldy crates, she spotted a narrow metal filing cabinet, rusted and on the verge of collapse. She jimmied open the drawers only to find empty file folders and a dead mouse.

"Gross," she groaned and shivered as she took it gingerly by its desiccated tail and tossed it aside.

She was about to close the bottom drawer when something caught her attention. Kneeling, she tugged it open as far as it would go—and there it was: a lone, crinkled envelope. Sherry's fingers brushed over the faded yellow forwarding sticker. The name was unreadable, but the address beneath it made her stop cold.

She put her flashlight in her teeth and scrambled for the microfiche inspection loupe in her bag. With narrowed eyes, she held the lens over the label. The dot-matrix print was barely legible, but she could still make out enough: 2303 Commerce St. She recognized it instantly—an old, abandoned water processing plant on the east side, practically on top of the sewer lines. And not just any sewer lines. These ran right under her old neighborhood, only six blocks from her apartment.

"Of course," she muttered, her mouth curling in a mix of frustration and grudging admiration. "Villains can't leave the underground alone, can they?" Charlie and Mary must have repurposed it, turning the plant into some kind of hideout. Growing up, she'd passed it a thousand times and never thought twice about it.

Back on her bike, she felt a pulse of anticipation. She'd have to get changed—this wasn't just a recon mission. If she was going to track down that Rembrandt and reclaim it, she'd need to be ready to get in and out without detection.

Once she returned to her apartment, she shed her casual clothes and dug through her old boxes for her "business" attire: a black turtleneck, reinforced cargo pants, and a pair of old, worn combat boots. She hadn't worn them in forever, but they still fit. Her picks and other "tools" were still in the crossbody bag she used to carry, and she inventoried them with quick, practiced movements. Then came her gloves, and finally, she tugged her hair back, pulling on a dark beanie.

She glanced in the mirror one last time, taking in the steely look in her eyes. Tonight, she wasn't Sherry Broward, a mild-mannered artist. She was Sherry Broward, the thief who'd once swiped high-end bikes in under thirty seconds. And she was taking back what was hers.

Chapter Twenty-Four

Sherry left her bike in the back alley behind Kelly's, just three blocks from the plant. She kept to the shadows, and it was as if her body had a memory of its own. God, she hadn't done this in so long, but it felt natural. There was a sense of familiarity in creeping through the darkness that made Sherry feel strangely relaxed. As a kid, this had always been the worst part. Once she was on a bike, she knew she could make good, but on the ground, she'd always felt exposed. Tonight, however, it was different. She was older, more experienced, and, though some might argue otherwise, more mature. This was old hat, and it felt good.

She came to the fence and crept along the darkened perimeter of the water plant, her movements silent until she found a gap where the galvanized links had failed. Someone else had come this way in the distant past. A small section had been torn and twisted back, just wide enough for her to squeeze through. She crouched, sliding through the opening, careful not to snag her clothes on the jagged metal. Once inside, she moved quickly, sticking to the shadows until she reached the base of a rusted-out, rickety staircase bolted to the outside of the main, warehouse-like building. Each step groaned under her weight, and she winced, pausing every few seconds to listen for movement inside. The only sounds were the soft creaks of the stairs and her own steady breaths.

At the top, she peered through a grimy window, taking in the unexpected sight: the inside of the plant was a mix of the old, abandoned structure and newly renovated space. One area, sectioned off with fresh drywall and industrial lighting, was clearly a residential setup. It had no roof, and she could see into every space, including the bathroom. It was thankfully unoccupied, but *eww*. This was definitely quarters for The Royal Family's Beefeater henchmen. There was even a larger bedroom, likewise unoccupied, that Sherry assumed was for Charlie and Mary. Clearly, they had no qualms with the crew hearing them in the throws of…well, whatever throws they did. Again, *eww*.

However, sitting against the wall in that room was her prize. If she inched across the trusses supporting the roof, she could rappel down the other side, snag the painting, and use her ascenders to climb back up, no one the wiser. The support structure was plenty dark. No one would see her, she hoped.

An occasional, pitiful whine echoed from the other side of the building, giving Sherry a sigh of relief. "Thank God. The dogs are kenneled." She tried the window, finding it unlocked. Apparently, they didn't expect prowlers. *Oops, their bad.*

"Home sweet home," she whispered wryly, slipping through the open window. She carefully made her way onto a narrow beam just below the A-frame ceiling, balancing with practiced skill. The truss creaked faintly, but she could handle a tightrope situation. And from up here, she had an even clearer vantage over the whole floor. Men milled about below, moving crates of whatever. Charlie and Mary were lounging in an enclosed office chatting. Sherry edged forward.

Just then, harsh voices sounded at the far door, loud and menacing. She froze, looking down to see three large men striding into the open space, all wearing dark jackets and sporting tattoos: Bratva. Great. Ivan's goons, or were they minions? She could never tell. She knew it had something to do with whether they believed in 'the cause.' In any event, Sherry began to wonder if she shouldn't have just taken Malka at her word. Well, too late now.

Ivan's men fanned out, and she watched as they started inspecting the place, talking in low voices that bounced off the walls. She strained to hear, picking up snippets about "the painting" and "payment in full." She figured they had as little love for Charlie and Mary as she did. Eventually, they were confronted by some of the Beefeaters, and the conversation turned heated. *Good, they won't be looking for me.*

She was just about to start inching forward again when she felt something—a twitch, really, just below her foot. She looked down. And there, to her horror, was a massive rat—no, a family of rats, nestled against a support attached right at the center of the beam. She shivered involuntarily. *Fuck.*

One of the rats scampered toward, sniffed her, and then made its way forward before crawling onto her boot, its tiny claws scratching against the canvas fabric of the ankle. She suppressed a gasp and fought to keep her balance as the rat sniffed her pant leg with unnerving curiosity. "Don't you dare," she whispered to it through gritted teeth.

Unimpressed with her threats and, in her mind, deliberately mocking her, it scuttled further up Sherry's boot, then sniffed at her calf. She couldn't shake it off without risking a fall, and any sudden movement would give her away to everyone below. To her horror, the rat looked up, almost meeting her eyes before scratching its way onto her pant leg, moving higher with each second.

Desperately trying not to panic, Sherry took a slow, deep breath. The three men below her were in a heated argument with the Beefeaters now. Charlie and Mary had abandoned the office and joined in, their voices filling the air.

Sherry decided to make her move—but as she shifted her weight, the rat latched onto her pant leg, climbing upward in determination.

"Motherfucker," she muttered, shaking her leg as carefully as she could. The rat slipped but caught itself, now clinging more stubbornly. She tried a few more strategic shakes, trying desperately to dislodge the creature without making a noise. It only gripped harder, inching closer with every shake, like it was on a mission to torment her. Her back foot kept sliding with each shake perilously close to the edge of the beam, causing her to windmill slightly.

"Fuck," she whispered and shifted position again. The sound of her boots scraping on the beam sounded like sandpaper to her, but no one below seemed to notice. She looked down.

Ivan's men seemed to be escalating their argument, with one of them jabbing a finger into the chest of the tallest Beefeater. They were certainly distracted—but not enough to miss her if a fat-ass rat dropped on one of their heads. Worse yet, the truss was unstable, swaying. One wrong step, and she'd be right in their crosshairs, dangling above them with an aggressive rat as her sidekick.

Finally, in a desperate bid, she twisted her foot sharply, shaking just enough to send the rat skittering off to the beam, where it slid off into the open air. It landed on the floor below with a loud thump, immediately catching the attention of the men. They spun toward the sound, weapons drawn, and one of them swore in Russian before they all laughed and pointed at the rodent, picking itself up and scrambling away.

Taking advantage of the chaos, Sherry scrambled forward, slipping along the truss until she was near the opposite wall. She peered down, catching sight of an open vent into the air system that led toward the other side of the building. Without a second thought, she swung down, squeezing herself silently into the vent just as the assembled group returned to their argument, oblivious to her escape.

As she crawled through the narrow duct, she let out a shaky breath. If that was the worst that Charlie and Mary's lair had in store, she'd be golden—but she somehow doubted her luck was that good.

It wasn't. A pop-pop sound echoed through the building. It was on. Someone had started a firefight in the warehouse. More gunfire and a bullet zipped through the vent, passing precariously close to Sherry's head.

"That's it. Fuck this," she muttered and scrambled to a vertical shaft that led straight down into the residential area. Kicking out the grate, she dropped through and flattened a

Beefeater who'd been standing right below it. Fortunately, she landed with him face down. He started to stand, but she grabbed his shoulders and pulled. His whole body slammed to the ground with a sickening crack, his legs folding over his chest before swinging back. He was out. Sherry stared at him for a moment, stunned. The guy was huge. He must have weighed at least two-forty, and she'd levered him down into the carpet-covered concrete like a five-pound bag of potatoes. Yay for leverage. If only Malka could see her now.

To her left was a steel door in the exterior wall, guarded by a fat crossbar. It opened inward, but with the clap-clap of gunfire, some of it now automatic, she decided she'd overstayed her welcome. The Rembrandt would have to wait.

So, without further ado, she kicked the door. The shot was as solid as she'd ever felt, and the door gave way under her foot. The hinges tore from the interior wall, and the door flew out, sliding across the gravel outside.

"Just like the movies," she said, dipping under the crossbar and not stopping for a second to wonder about that little miracle as she made her way back into the night, empty-handed but alive.

That was too close.

Her relief didn't last as she pulled the beanie and slid onto her bike at Kelly's. She could only hope that Ivan's guys won and retrieved the painting. She didn't dare tell Malka about this. She'd just wait for her call or Mixxer's. Malka said she'd straighten it out. Still, though, Sherry wondered where her ex had gotten so much pull as to have Ivan doing little pickup jobs for her.

In any event, Jemma would be coming by tomorrow, and they could sit on her brand-new couch and watch Star Trek II. That was first on the list for their dinner and a movie night.

Chapter Twenty-Five

"Kaaaaahn!!!!" they both screamed, as Jemma and Sherry watched Captain Kirk scream into his communicator at a buff-chested Ricardo Montalban.

Sherry snatched up the remote and paused the movie, assailed by uncontrollable laughter. "Oh, my God! I love the over-acting! It's amazing."

Jemma nodded her head vigorously. "William Shatner. Total Ham-asaurus. He's chewed so much set, I bet his stomach is woodchips."

"Yeah, he's fun to watch, but he's an ass," Sherry commented, her lips pursed.

Jemma looked as if she'd been struck. "What?"

"You don't know? He's a narcissistic pig. Half the cast of the old series hated him. And he was nasty to Wil Wheaton when he was sixteen. Gene Roddenberry had to make Shatner apologize. And he did it in a note written by his assistant. He didn't even bother to do it in person."

Looking completely crestfallen, Jemma crossed her arms. "Well, that sucks. Fuck that dude."

Sherry laughed. "Yeah, he's a lot like my dad, unfortunately." Sherry snapped her jaws shut as she got off the couch and headed into the kitchen to make dinner. She'd just blurted it out. It was a habit, a bad one. But did she really want to talk about her dad? The guy was a prick. All he ever thought about was himself. It wasn't a pleasant subject, and they were having such a nice time. She tried to change the subject quickly. "Anyway, he was on Boston Legal with James Spader, who is super nice. Did you ever watch 'The Blacklist?'"

Jemma followed her into the kitchen, slipping slightly on the linoleum in her sock-clad feet. "Yeah, I've seen it. I don't see how people can think that Red isn't her mother. They drop a million hints."

"I know, right?" Sherry responded, feeling her shoulders drop and appreciating Jemma's perceptiveness. "It's just ridiculous. Of course, having Reddington selling Jesus on the Sea of Galilee in the first season was genius."

"I laughed so hard." Jemma's smile and voice reflected her unabashed delight.

"Where have you been all my life?" Sherry said, doing her best to hide her blush and shy smile. She often worked to keep her personal emotions quiet. Being too outspoken had never served her well. Her sense of humor was often considered strange, and she could never read a person, let alone a room. But with Jemma, Sherry realized, she couldn't help herself. The woman just drew it out of her, like Wonder Woman's magic lasso.

Jemma grinned, leaning against the counter as Sherry peeled the shrimp. "I was doing other things," she teased. "But I'd gladly make up for lost time if you'd like."

Sherry shot her a playful look before turning back to the stovetop, where butter and garlic sizzled in the pan, filling the kitchen with a rich aroma. 'Low heat, don't scorch the garlic. Then white wine, lemon, shrimp,' Malka's instructions echoed in her mind. It was oddly soothing, this step-by-step rhythm, almost like Malka herself was there in the kitchen, guiding her.

As Sherry poured in the wine, the pan hissed, releasing a fragrant steam. Jemma watched her quietly, her gaze attentive, almost soft. "You're really good at this," she said.

Sherry shrugged, stirring the shrimp as they turned pink. "My ex taught me. Believe it or not, my mom and I didn't have much home-cooked food growing up." She hesitated, not used to going here. "My dad… well, he was a narcissist. Everything had to be about him, all the time."

Jemma's face softened as she listened, and Sherry felt a small warmth in her chest—like Jemma really got it. "He left when I was five," she continued, voice low. "But before that, he never bothered to understand me. I was a little kid with autism, and all he saw was a problem. He screamed and tried to… beat it out of me." Sherry's mouth twisted in a bitter smile. "He thought he could discipline me into being 'normal.'"

Jemma's hand found her arm, gentle and grounding. "I'm sorry. That must have been… so hard for both of you."

"Yeah," Sherry said, her voice barely above a whisper. "My mom did her best, but he left her in pieces. Guess I picked some of those up." She took a deep breath, giving Jemma a wry smile. "And here I am, making shrimp scampi for the first time and not burning it." She plated the food, her heart racing as she handed Jemma a dish. "So I guess… some things worked out."

Jemma accepted the plate, her smile warm and understanding. "Yeah, Sherry, I'd say they did."

"So," Sherry said as they sat down to eat. "What about you? Are you close with your family?"

"No," Jemma said with an exaggerated roll of her eyes. "I was raised LDS." Sherry's brow furrowed, and she opened her mouth, but Jemma cut her off. "Yes, there are Mormons in England. Not many, and they're not very well respected."

"I'm guessing they weren't thrilled that you're gay," Sherry commented, taking a tentative bite of shrimp, silently hoping the lack of hives the other night was a trend. In her flustered state, she'd completely forgotten to take an allergy pill when she got home, but the expected breakout never happened.

"No, they were not. But it wasn't that I was gay, exactly. It was that I refused to stay in the closet and act like a good little girl. I'd wanted to go to Oxford, but my parents basically forced me to go to BYU. After that, I'd hoped they might be a bit more supportive. The church's stance had softened somewhat, but they weren't. When I finally summoned the nerve to come out, they were, at best, lukewarm to the idea. Three of my sisters simply tried to ignore it, and when that didn't work, they ignored me instead. My mother wrung her hands and griped as if it was about her. My dad made a bunch of noise and bluster and called it a phase. Only my youngest sister, Hannah, accepted me."

Sherry twirled a bit of angel hair on her fork and stabbed a bit of shrimp, separating the tail with her knife. "But they didn't kick you out or anything?"

Jemma shook her head. "They did, kind of. I wrote a missive to the President of the Hyde Park, London Stake, condemning the church's approach to same-sex couples and marriage. I was young and full of myself, thinking I could take on the church. I thought at most I'd get some kind of written reprimand."

"But that didn't happen?" Sherry asked, her fork hovering over her plate, clearly enraptured with the story.

Jemma gave a mirthless snort. "Of course not. I was hauled up in front of the disciplinary council. Church guidance gave them quite a bit of leeway, but it was downtown London. I really didn't expect it to be all that serious." With a sigh, Jemma took a sip of her wine before continuing. "Never in a million years did I expect to be excommunicated from my faith."

"Jesus," Sherry whispered, horrified. "That's awful."

"It gets worse. Because of that, I was barred from seeing any of my sisters get married. Hannah was beside herself over it, but my father steadfastly refused to have the wedding at all if I was invited."

"Oh, Jemma," Sherrry said. "I'm so sorry that happened to you."

Jemma just shrugged. "It's ancient history now. Hannah's twenty-seven and lives in Salt Lake City. She teaches at a local elementary school and has been happily married for five years. I don't see her much, though."

Sherry tilted her head. "Why not?"

"Her husband is a bigoted ass. He doesn't want me around my two nieces. He thinks I'll get the gay on them or something. The arguments between Hannah and her husband, Jack, almost ended their marriage. I don't want to be the cause of that, so I stay away."

"Dear God," Sherry muttered, shaking her head. "But, if their marriage comes apart because he can't handle his gay sister-in-law, he's the cause of that. I know it's not my place to judge your family, but you're amazing, and anyone who doesn't see that can fuck right the fuck off. "

Jemma laughed out loud and leaned over, giving Sherry a soft kiss on the cheek. "I really wish you'd been around when I was going through it. I could have used that kind of support."

Sherry grinned at the compliment. "Probably not. I only have two responses to confrontation: running into a corner and hiding or drawing blood. I know what I would have done in that instance, and I'm not prison material."

"I can't see you in prison, Sherry. You just don't have it in you."

With a snort, Sherry turned her face away and sipped her wine. Jemma had no idea.

Chapter Twenty-Six

Once they'd finished dinner, they made their way out onto the balcony. Sherry stood, arms resting on the railing. One thing about living in such an industrialized neighborhood was that it was quiet, deathly so. Her building was the first in what would invariably be a long line of upscale apartments meant to gentrify the East Side. Quietly, she gazed up at the stars. When Jemma's soft hand landed on hers, Sherry finally spoke. "I don't like being alone."

"I know," Jemma acknowledged. "Neither do I. My life is hard, and sometimes there's risk. People who steal things don't like what I do. They can be. . . violent." There was something in Jemma's tone, a loneliness and a deep sense of loss, but before Sherry could ask about it, Jemma continued. "So, I've taken to living a solitary life. I have a tiny apartment, a few art books, and not much else."

"That sounds sad, and I would know," Sherry waved her hand around, indicating her apartment. "That's the life I live." Her eyes traced Jemma's profile from her soft forehead and angular nose to her strong chin. She paused for a moment, lingering on Jemma's beautiful lips. "Please don't hurt me," she whispered, a pleading tone in her throat. "If you don't want to be with me, that's okay, but…" She broke off, afraid she might chase Jemma away.

Jemma's mouth curled into a smile, and she turned her

head, gazing into Sherry's eyes. "I'll try not to, but I am horribly out of practice. I haven't even considered dating anyone in over six years."

The very idea stabbed at Sherry's heart. Jemma was sweet and seemed to care about everyone she met. The thought that she'd closed herself off to even the idea of a loving relationship seemed horribly wrong. Of course, that's what Sherry had done. But then again, Sherry didn't feel she had anything to offer. She was a failed art thief who was hung up on her ex. She didn't think she deserved Jemma, or perhaps that Jemma deserved better, and yet, she couldn't let go—she didn't want to let go. Jemma was everything Sherry had ever wanted. She was beautiful, honest, and kind. She said what she meant and didn't seem to keep secrets. That last made Sherry feel like an absolute heel, and her heart twisted with hopelessness. She'd begun to feel that her decision to take the Rembrandt would drown her entire life, and soon.

"What are you thinking about?" Jemma asked, and Sherry realized she'd been lost in Jemma's pretty face during her musings.

"Just that I think you're pretty wonderful." Sherry lied as she slid up to Jemma, bumping shoulders with her as they both leaned against the railing. Their eyes met. Sherry burned inside with a desire for Jemma that nearly stole her breath. She'd heard stories of people who found the one person meant for them, but she never believed them—until now.

Slowly, as if drawn by mutual gravity, they both leaned in. Sherry's eyes darted across Jemma's face, looking for any indication, any hint, that she felt the same.

In answer, Jemma closed that tiny space between them and kissed her. As they hungrily explored each other's mouths, Sherry gently pushed Jemma back onto the outdoor chaise and straddled her hips. Pulling back to look at this goddess she'd somehow ensnared, Sherry noticed that, for the first time, Jemma was the one trembling. Despite her challenges, Sherry could see that Jemma was scared. She pushed the hair away from Jemma's face and dipped back down to kiss her once more.

Jemma's tongue swept Sherry's mouth, and Sherry's need bloomed into a raging desire. She whimpered slightly with its intensity. It had been so long since she'd felt like this as fireflies danced inside her, and her chest felt lighter than air, as if they could fly away to the stars. Amid the embrace, Jemma rolled them off the chaise, and, to Sherry, it felt as if they both just floated down to the decking. Jemma dug her fingers into Sherry's hair and pressed her hips between Sherry's parted legs.

"Please," Sherry whispered as Jemma began placing soft, wet kisses on her cheek, her chin, her throat, until she reached the spot just below her ear. Gooseflesh popped all across Sherry's body, and she uttered a soft, breathy "Oh."

Jemma's hand slid down her side and then back up, pushing up her shirt, fingers lighting on her ribs. She hummed with pleasure.

Jemma slowed her ministrations and looked down into her eyes. "This wasn't something I planned." Her voice held so much depth that Sherry couldn't quite piece it out: fear, worry, need. It was all wrapped within. "I tried not to," Jemma said, continuing her confession. "But I can't seem to stop. It's all I want."

"Then don't," Sherry whispered hoarsely.

In answer, Jemma lifted Sherry's shirt, trailing kisses down her belly and back up. "Would it be too much if I asked if we could go to bed?"

"No," Sherry whispered. "Please."

Jemma lifted Sherry off the deck, and once more, Sherry was taken aback at how she lifted her so effortlessly, even with the recently added weight. It only served to heighten her arousal, and a tension built in her chest: anticipation. Burning anticipation.

They slipped quietly through the apartment and into Sherry's bedroom, where Jemma set Sherry on her feet and stood before her. Sherry swallowed a little nervously as she lifted Jemma's T-shirt over those fabulous shoulders and let it fall to the floor. Her fingers played across the rippling muscles in Jemma's arms. But then, those beautiful blue eyes caught her. They were dark and full in the dim light of the table lamp. Within, Sherry spied the raw need and desire, but something else lingered as well: vulnerability.

She stepped around and unfastened Jemma's bra, a finger tracing the overlapping muscles—so well defined. She knew that Jemma was strong, but the definition peeking through the skin still surprised her. She reached around and heard a gasp as her hands cupped Jemma's breasts. For all her sculpted strength, Jemma's chest had a fullness Sherry hadn't expected, adding a certain allure to her already captivating presence. Sliding her fingers in the crease, she let her hands drift back around and felt a shudder pass through Jemma as she ran a finger along the edge of Jemma's deltoid.

Carefully, she undid Jemma's pants and slid them down over her bare feet, noting her pronounced flexor tendons. She longed to run her fingers along them and feel the power they obviously held.

Sherry's eyes traveled upward, following the length of Jemma's body. There wasn't a mark on her, not a single scar or blemish. Her entire body was impossibly perfect. If scars were what defined us, then Jemma's skin was a blank canvas, primed and waiting for the first brush stroke. If ever a goddess of beauty walked the earth, Jemma Caldwell would be her chosen vessel.

Jemma turned then and tugged at Sherry's shirt. "You've been working out," Jemma commented quietly as she slid her incredibly soft fingers across Sherry's abdomen. The muscles spasmed slightly, so unused to being touched like this.

"What?" Sherry whispered, lost in the slow voyage that Jemma's fingers were making. Looking down, she saw what held Jemma's attention. She had washboard abs, even more defined than they'd been just the day before. And not just those. Sherry's anterior serratus and pyramidallis also bulged beneath the skin. Further down, her quads were a little larger, too. The definition shocked her. She looked—athletic. "Oh. I think that's just diet and basic exercise," she dismissed before slipping out of the wireless bra. "I promise, I haven't seen the inside of a gym in over a year."

"Oh," Jemma said with a cheeky grin. "So you're that girl."

"What girl?" Sherry asked with narrowed eyes. "Think carefully before you answer. My hand is dangerously close to your nipple."

"The one who always looks good no matter what she puts in her body."

"Oh," Sherry shrugged. She didn't think so, but she wasn't going to argue. "Well, it's not like you aren't built like a cross-fit goddess, so it's not much comparison."

"My job keeps me fit," Jemma said.

Sherry raised an eyebrow. "Insurance investigations keep you fit?"

Jemma spluttered. "No, I mean, it keeps me going to the gym. Sorry, that came out badly."

"Oh. Must be rough," Sherry grinned, her voice dripping with sarcasm. She placed a finger on Jemma's lips. "Now, no more talking."

With a sly grin of her own, Jemma lifted Sherry up and dropped her on the bed with a husky, "That's my line."

Sherry let out a squeal of delight. "Oooh, you're so bossy. I like it!"

"You have no idea, missy," Jemma chuckled softly. "Now, shush."

With a raised eyebrow and a grin she couldn't hide, Sherry slid up the bed, meeting the headboard with a soft thud. Jemma followed, moving to straddle Sherry, her expression no longer playful but filled with greedy desire. Sherry swallowed nervously, feeling a sudden luscious trepidation.

It didn't last long, though, as Jemma smothered her in a heart-pounding kiss, pressing hard and nipping at Sherry's bottom lip.

"Oh, God," Sherry moaned against Jemma's mouth in submission. She wanted only for Jemma to take her. No control. She wanted none.

"You can trust me," Jemma whispered in her ear and sucked gently on the lobe, sending a shiver down her spine and gooseflesh sprouting all over.

Sherry slid down, letting her head sink into the pillow, her body buzzing with anticipation. She wrapped her arms around Jemma, seeking comfort in the warmth of her skin. But before she could settle, Jemma's hands slipped back and clasped her wrists with a grip like iron wrapped in silk. She pressed Sherry's arms back to the bed, her touch a command rather than a gesture.

"Keep them here," Jemma ordered, her voice low and thick with intention.

"Yes," Sherry breathed, the word leaving her like a prayer. She closed her eyes, feeling her entire body float in the stillness. A shuddering breath escaped as she soaked in the intensity of the moment, every nerve alive. The sharp edge of fear mingled with excitement, a potent mix that made every inch of her skin hum. She craved this—this surrender. For the first time, her senses begged to be overwhelmed, each touch sending a ripple of electricity through her body.

Jemma shifted, her movements deliberate and sure, and without warning, she flipped Sherry roughly onto her stomach. Sherry gasped, a whimper rising from her throat as she felt the press of Jemma's weight against her. She could no longer distinguish her feelings. Did she feel fear? Pleasure? Want? The lines blurred until her emotions were tangled, swirling together like a storm inside her, making her head fuzz over in delightful oblivion.

Fingertips traced a slow, deliberate line down Sherry's spine, the touch feather-light yet commanding. Sherry arched instinctively, her back curving both into the touch and away, the sensation almost too much and yet not enough. A loud, desperate moan escaped her lips as her body trembled beneath Jemma's control. She felt utterly exposed, every nerve screaming for more.

The overwhelming sensations that often pushed Sherry to retreat now drew her deeper, pulling her into a space where touch became all encompassing. Every caress, every breath, every small shift in the air around her became magnified, an intricate web of sensations that wrapped around her mind and body, leaving her helpless and yet yearning insatiably for more.

Jemma ran her tongue across her buttocks and down each leg, lingering and licking at the backs of her knees. Sherry lost track of where Jemma stopped, and she began. Then, suddenly, it ended.

"Roll over," Jemma demanded. Sherry obliged, no longer truly conscious, blissfully trapped in all that was Jemma, even as her body responded.

Jemma dropped down, her shins pinning Sherry's arms, her wetness pressed to Sherry's mouth. "Now, take it," Jemma ordered.

Sherry hungrily pulled Jemma's clit into her mouth, sucking and licking it, pushing the flat of her tongue across it. The buzzing in her head finally ceased, and the moment snapped into a sharp clarity. She wanted to pleasure Jemma, to give her all that she could and leave her wanting more. From airy disconnectedness, she'd rocketed into fiery lust. Nothing less than having Jemma ride her hard would suffice.

Jemma moaned. Sherry's arms, pinned as they were, left her helpless. She loved it. Jemma slid back and forth, her hand pressing into Sherry's head, pulling her lips painfully to Jemma's body. And it continued like that. Sherry couldn't get enough, even when Jemma's violent moans and the shifting of Jemma's hips all but suffocated her. Jemma came, her head thrown back and howling her rapture from deep in her throat.

Sherry was on the edge of coming herself, but Jemma lifted off of her and slid down.

"Not yet," she whispered, pressing a finger to Sherry's lips as she made her way to Sherry's breasts. "Don't you dare."

Jemma nibbled and bit at her skin. Teeth pressed into a nipple, and Sherry gasped in pain and pleasure as the buzzing resumed and her thoughts fled. She couldn't remember who she was, where she was. There was only sensation as it seemed a thousand fingers slid across her body, caressing her ribs, raking painfully across her stomach, and running a bruising grip down her legs. It was all she had ever wanted from a woman. A memory flitted dimly in her head somewhere, gossamer and hard to catch. This was better than she'd ever had, even with—no! She pushed it aside.

Her breathing hitched momentarily with remembered loss, but then Jemma found her center and pushed two fingers fiercely into her, and the memory skittered away, bringing her back into this moment, this woman, this second.

Sherry gave a harsh, guttural groan of pleasure as she felt Jemma inside her, slick with her wetness. Then Jemma's mouth was on her, too, finding that perfectly sensitive spot on the underside of her clit and flicking it with her tongue over and over.

Sherry lifted her legs, resting them on Jemma's biceps. As the orgasm grew and overtook her, Sherry slapped her hands to the backs of her knees and growled, her head thrown back in absolute ecstasy. It was a gravelly sound, loud and full of her fury, her pent-up passion. She came harder than she ever thought she could, back arched, hands digging into her own flesh. And yet, Jemma continued, and only seconds later, she was begging.

"Please," she gasped. "Please. No more. I can't…I can't… take…" Another orgasm washed over her in waves, eliciting another rough sound from her throat, a series of rising and falling grunts.

Jemma released her and slid up her sweat-soaked body. Sherry's arms and legs wrapped around her.

"Dear God," Sherry whispered, just a breath in the air, seeming like a bit of smoke puffing away in a moment of synesthesia.

Jemma lifted herself, carrying them both to a sitting position, Jemma on her heels, Sherry in her lap. She crushed her mouth to Sherry's and forced her tongue inside. Slowly, the press of her lips grew more gentle, eventually becoming light and tender. Finally, the kisses ceased, and Sherry's forehead dropped against Jemma's chest as she panted, totally spent.

They sat there for a long time, Jemma just caressing Sherry's back in slow, languid strokes with irregular pauses. Boneless, Sherry finally let go, flopping back to the bed. She couldn't look at Jemma as embarrassment took hold, so she curled on her side and pulled her knees up.

"Are you okay?" Jemma's voice had a worried tone.

Sherry nodded. "That was amazing. I was just...I was so loud. And you..."

Jemma laughed. "I assumed that meant it was good."

"The best," Sherry whispered. "The best."

Jemma slid down next to her and pulled the covers over them to ward off the encroaching chill of the apartment. Strong arms enfolded Sherry and held her close.

"Is this okay?" Jemma asked.

"It's perfect." Sherry's feelings, which had seemed so torn and confused, solidified into something beautiful. Inside, a sudden clarity burst into being. Jemma wasn't just perfect; she was perfect for Sherry. She was loving and caring and kind and strong and confident. Jemma understood implicitly how to handle her, whatever her state. And most of all, she was patient.

And Sherry let herself believe, for just a glimmering moment, that she might be perfect for Jemma. Jemma needed love, and it was all Sherry wanted just to give it to her. She refused to give in to the dark clouds that swirled in the back of her mind. This was a beautiful moment, a pearl that deserved to be treasured in a way that she felt no one would understand. But that was okay.

She knew.

"How would you like to go on this year's Art and Wine Cruise?" Jemma asked later, in the quiet darkness, when Sherry was spooned up behind her and couldn't see the shit-eating grin on her face. The response was priceless and made her secret smile even wider.

Sherry sat bolt upright. "What? Are you fucking with me, Jem? You better not be fucking with me because that's not funny. No one gets tickets to that except rich assholes. I've always wanted to go on that cruise. And this year, it's Bethany Silver. She does female form in every medium. Wait. Are you serious? You better not be kidding—"

Jemma rolled over and placed a finger on Sherry's lips, unable to contain herself. She reached back, flipped on the bedside lamp, and slid the tickets from her book, holding them up. "Two tickets. One for you," she said, tapping them against Sherry's nose. "And one for me."

"Ohmygodohmygodohmygod." Sherry squealed out loud. "Ahhhh." Then she threw her arms around Jemma and started landing kisses all over her face, making Jemma laugh.

Once Sherry had finished, she sat up against the headboard, feeling rather smug, but it wasn't long before she slid back beneath the sheets and fell into slumber.

She never felt Sherry stir next to her. So soundly did she sleep that she never noticed that one side of the bed was empty. And not a single brush stroke did she hear as Sherry finished her painting, working into the wee hours until it was perfect.

Chapter Twenty-Seven

Jemma was swamped with work for the next two days. She'd just spent four hours in court as Lena Swift, dealing with the arraignment of that idiot, Snake Charmer. Fortunately, he wasn't Special Class like Il Duce or herself, so a regular cell would suffice just fine, consequently, no bail. After that, she'd received a case involving a diamond and emerald necklace stolen from Carrie Villa, a top-tier jewelry designer. The necklace was worth about two hundred grand. If she could find it, it would net her around twenty thousand.

It had taken all day Saturday just to get the contract signed and get started. Travis Hauk had been an asshole the entire time, bitching about why she wouldn't take the Rembrandt contract. In the end, she realized that her refusal was pointless. She would find it eventually anyway; she always did. So, she relented and signed the paperwork.

Outside Brattleman Tower, Jemma pulled out Special Agent Parker's card. It was Sunday, and Parker would likely be pissed, but this couldn't wait. She dialed his number. The phone rang a few times before he answered with a familiar, gruff tone.

"Special Agent Parker."

Jemma always wondered why cops never gave a full greeting. It was always just their name. Tracy was the same.

"Morning, Parker. It's Lena," she said, her voice steady. "I need to know what you learned about that 'discount' Lot 429."

"It's my day off, Swift," Parker grumbled, clearly irritated. "And this isn't a secure line."

"Think of it as a favor for international relations, and do you really want to meet me in the office for a few quick answers?" Jemma quipped with a smirk he couldn't see. "So, what's the story?"

He let out a reluctant sigh. "Alright, here's what I've got. Turns out, it's not some 'discount' version. The Agency got wind that the Russians have been building a hyper-collider out in the middle of Siberia."

She froze, piecing together what he was saying. "Wait, you're telling me they built a hyper-collider? This isn't some watered-down knockoff—this is the real deal?"

"Looks like it," Parker replied.

She stared up at the cloudless sky. Fuck. That was not what she wanted to hear. "Okay, what else?"

"They got the specs through a data breach at SPEAR. We think it was unintentional spillage by one of the original scientists. Another idiot taking work home, I suspect. I'm still tracking that down, but... well, this isn't some low-budget imitation."

Jemma felt the weight of the news sink in. "If they have the original formula, then they've had time to test it. But why send it here?"

"Your guess is as good as ours at this point...but I have a sneaking suspicion."

"Viktor," Lena said, and a spike of fear sank into her chest. "If he takes it, and survives..."

"You ever see 'The Boys?'" Parker asked.

"Unfortunately," Jemma said. "Homelander." Homelander was a comic character who was a psychopathic, narcissistic Superman. Unstoppable, totally violent, and completely unhinged. The kind of villain that would be Jemma's worst nightmare. "But it's still lethal. Even for existing supers."

"The department is officially calling you guys meta's now. They think it's snazzier and yet still politically correct. But yes," he continued with a sigh, "generally, it's still fatal, but..."

Parker paused ominously.

"But, what?" Jemma had a really bad feeling about this.

"It's unconfirmed, but the rumor is that they've learned to improve the odds through tailoring the formula. Not the powers, thank God. Those are still fairly random, something to do with quantum probabilities."

Jemma closed her eyes. "Shit. So someone had a person in mind for this."

"Like I said, it's unconfirmed."

"So, what are we doing about the hyper-collider?" Jemma asked.

"Nothing we can do."

Jemma's eyes narrowed at no one in particular. "Nothing *you* can do," Lena confirmed, putting the emphasis on 'you.' She could do plenty.

"Now, Lena, don't do anything reckless. We can't afford an international incident right now. Something like that could spark World War III."

She scoffed. "Reckless? Me?" She forced a lightness into her tone, hiding the anxiety clawing at her. "Thanks, Parker. I mean it. This helps… in the worst way possible."

"Happy to ruin your Sunday, too," he muttered before ending the call.

Jemma lowered the phone, the pieces starting to fall into place. The hyper-collider in Siberia was unsettling enough, but the location sparked another realization. Her search for intel on the Rembrandt had led her on a convoluted trail of hints and dead ends, but one piece of information from a friend in the UK had been gnawing at her until just now. The painting had been transferred to a gallery in Novosibirsk before it was sent to Paris and then on to Harborhaven.

She'd brushed it off as odd at the time. Even remote places deserve to see great art. But now, it clicked. The Rembrandt, the hyper-collider, Lot 429—it had all been neatly planned. And it was so simple. Ivan, wherever he hid, was just one compatible test subject away from turning this nightmare into reality.

Despite the lurking danger of the serum, she was still no

closer to finding it. Saturday night, she'd called Sin City. Malka had been more than happy to let her talk to everyone in turn, but no one knew who the guard had spoken to. It was maddening. She felt like she was closer than it appeared, but every avenue turned up bubkis. For the moment, there was just no more she could do.

Finally, sick of worrying about it, she decided that a Sunday lunch with Sherry was in order. Truthfully, it was as good an excuse as any to spend time with her.

"Any chance you could swing by Brattleman Tower and pick me up?" Jemma asked when Sherry answered the phone. "I'm dying for a good lobster roll."

Sherry didn't hesitate. "Absolutely, be there at eleven-thirty."

"Perfect."

Sherry arrived promptly on her motorcycle, the engine's purr announcing her presence. Sherry was in a dark red patterned skirt, hiked and cinched to keep it away from the gears, a black tank, and knee-high motorcycle boots. It was a fabulous look.

"Ready for an adventure?" Sherry asked, handing her the extra helmet.

"Always," Jemma grinned, her eyes reflecting the tower's shimmer as she hopped on in her business suit, hiking up her skirt and slinging her messenger bag across her body.

Once she was mounted up and had her arms firmly around Sherry's waist, they sped off toward the East End.

Twenty minutes later, they pulled up to the Wild Lobster, a cozy spot with a spectacular view of the skyline from the waterfront. For Sherry, hands down, it was easily the city's best seafood. It was also in the neighborhood, not far from her apartment. The salty sea breeze mingled with the rich aroma of fries, lobster, and steamed crab as they found a table up against the exterior of the building. Harborhaven had allowed restaurants to take the sidewalks for serving areas during the pandemic and let them stay afterward. People liked having a place for outdoor dining, even if it was right on the street.

As the server set their plates down, Sherry took one look at her lobster roll and sighed, feeling a mix of horror and betrayal. "They put celery on it. Who does that?" She glared at the offending flecks of green like they'd personally wronged her. Irritated, she pulled out a pair of tweezers from her purse and wiped them on her napkin. Then, beneath Jemma's amused gaze, which she ignored, she began the meticulous work of picking the celery bits off, one tiny piece at a time.

Jemma leaned her chin on her hand, watching with rapt attention. "You're really committed to the purity of that lobster roll."

"It's not commitment," Sherry said, eyebrows knit in frustration as she carefully removed yet another celery bit. "It's the principle of the matter. If they're going to do lobster, they should do lobster. I didn't ask for celery."

"Just send it back," Jemma offered.

"No," Sherry's voice was intense, and she shook her head, not even looking up. "This country wastes enough food to feed half the planet. I won't contribute to that if I can help it. Besides, contrary to present evidence, I asked for a hot-buttered lobster roll, not a lobster roll with celery. That's why I order them that way and not cold."

Jemma chuckled, shaking her head. "You sound like you're preparing a legal case."

"Call it what you want," Sherry replied with exaggerated dignity, finally taking a triumphant bite of her roll--now celery-free. "But a true lobster roll should be about the lobster, the split-top hot-dog bun, and hot butter. Anything else is just… garnish abuse."

"Is it now?" Jemma laughed out loud at that before taking a bite of her own lobster roll, which, as it happened, she'd ordered cold. Just the way she liked it. "That's interesting, though," she said around a mouthful. "I can't wait to see what you'd do if I ever bring over pasta with a bit of parsley."

"Don't even joke about that," Sherry shot back, mock-serious. "Good taste is serious business."

"Clearly," Jemma teased, grinning. "Well, then. I can't wait to see what you cook up for our next meal. Just make sure you give the celery a restraining order."

Sherry scoffed. "Fine, laugh it up. Just don't come crying to me when you realize I was right all along. I see what you're eating there."

Jemma chuckled, but her laughter faded abruptly, her gaze drifting past Sherry and her expression sharpening with a flicker of concern. "I'll be right back. Bathroom," she said, sliding out of her seat and disappearing into the restaurant.

Sherry blinked, slightly puzzled, but shrugged and took another bite. Then she heard it—the unmistakable screech of tires, followed by a wail of sirens. She looked up, her heart skipping a beat as she spotted a Porsche tearing down the street, with police cruisers in hot pursuit.

The car lost a tire, sparks flying as it spun out of control, veering directly toward the café, and their table. Sherry tried to get up and move, but her cross-body bag was caught on the arm of the chair, causing her to flop back into her seat.

In a flash of pink, white, and orange, Lena Swift dropped down like a hammer, the sheer strength of the impact rippling through the air. With both hands out, she grasped the front bumper. Her feet dug deep furrows into the asphalt as the car came to a jarring halt no more than a meter away, the front end crumpled almost completely around Lena. The people inside, two boys no more than seventeen, looked unhurt as the airbags deflated into wrinkled Nylon blobs.

Sherry's jaw dropped, her mind struggling to process what she'd just witnessed. Lena Swift. Harborhaven's very own superhero had just saved her life. Applause and cheers erupted around her, but Sherry remained frozen, wide-eyed.

Lena Swift turned and extricated herself from the car, her gaze softening as she looked at Sherry. She cocked her head and gave a small, reassuring smile. "You okay, love?" she asked, her voice warm.

Sherry's mouth opened, but all that came out was a faint stammer. "Uh… I… y-yeah… I think so…"

As the police began to pull two embarrassed-looking teenagers from the car, Lena Swift gave Sherry a nod and a wink, the faintest flicker of a smile in her eyes before she took off, disappearing into the sky. Sherry just stood there, staring after her, her brain still caught in just how blue her eyes were. And God, her backside was even more legendary in person. She fanned herself with one hand.

Moments later, Jemma came jogging out of the restaurant, looking flustered and out of breath, one shoe on her foot and the other clutched in her hand. Her skirt sat a little crooked, too. She rushed to Sherry's side, her hands gently brushing over Sherry's arms and shoulders, her face full of worry. "Are you okay? I came running as fast as I could."

Sherry blinked, her mind racing as she tried to piece together the whirlwind of events. "Y-yeah, I… I'm fine. Lena Swift just… she saved me," she said, barely believing her own words.

Jemma gave a relieved laugh, brushing a stray lock of hair from Sherry's face. "Well, lucky she was nearby, huh? Good thing she has a habit of showing up at just the right time."

But something nagged at Sherry as she looked at Jemma. The timing of Jemma's sudden disappearance, the odd familiarity of Lena's stance, her figure… and that word, 'love,' typically a British term of endearment, one she'd occasionally heard from Jemma herself. Sherry glanced Jemma up and down, recalling the striking similarities, even down to her fabulous blue eyes and… her ass. Could she?

The suspicion itched at her as they sat back down, and a flustered Jemma put herself back together. A moment later, though, Sherry's train of thought was derailed and lost. A sudden blur of fur zipped through the tables, pulling Sherry's attention as it weaved between the legs of diners. Sherry's hand shot out instinctively, catching the collar of a corgi with a plump, proud chest and an eager, panting face. She petted it and stroked its cheeks, just like she would Breitweiser.

"Where's your owner, girl?" she asked as the dog started licking her face. Grabbing the collar and looking at the tag, she froze—a finely detailed royal crest, the emblem of King

Charles. Her mind raced, recalling the gunfight at Charles and Mary's hideout, the Bratva storming in, guns blazing. The memory sent a chill down her spine.

Had Charles and Mary survived the ambush, or had the Bratva taken them down? She looked around. There was no sign of either Charles or Mary.

The odds had been in the Royals' favor—over a dozen of their henchmen against just three Bratva—but the uncertainty gnawed at her. And what about 'The Solitary Watchman?' She'd planned to return for it in two days, but now, with this little reminder of the Royals running loose, she wasn't so sure.

Still brushing her hair back into place, Jemma leaned over with a warm smile and joined Sherry in her pampering of the little pooch. "Well, hey there! Who let you loose?" It's little butt wagged as it enjoyed all the attention.

Sherry forced a casual laugh, eyes still on the corgi's collar. "Maybe she just wanted to check out the lobster rolls."

Jemma chuckled, watching the dog pant happily. "If this little furball had a taste for seafood, I'd say we have a new best friend on our hands." She gave the corgi one last affectionate pat before sitting back.

As the corgi settled comfortably under their table and snacked on some old french fries that had fallen from someone's plate, Jemma tilted her head, eyeing the dog thoughtfully. "Well, as cute as she is, we can't exactly take her home. She's got to belong to someone around here."

Sherry bit her lip, glancing around for any sign of an owner. The last thing she needed was for Jemma to dig into the dog's origins. "Maybe she's just on a little adventure."

"Right," Jemma replied, rolling her eyes. "But I don't think her adventure includes lobster rolls. She's got a collar; someone's got to be looking for her."

Sherry watched, amused but cautious, as Jemma pulled out her phone. "I'll call animal control. They can scan her tag and find her owner. It'll be better than letting her wander into traffic."

"Yeah, probably," Sherry said, scratching the corgi behind the ears one last time as it licked her hand, oblivious to all the fuss it was causing. As Jemma spoke to the pound, Sherry whispered to the dog, "You've got a lot of nerve showing up here."

The corgi just looked at her with wide, innocent eyes, blissfully unaware of Sherry's tangled thoughts as Jemma wrapped up the call. "They'll send someone to pick her up in a few minutes," Jemma said, leaning back with a satisfied smile.

Sherry nodded, keeping her expression neutral. "Good. Wouldn't want her to get into any more… adventures."

As she put her phone away, Jemma's bag fell over, and papers spilled across the table. Sherry started helping Jemma scoop them back until one caught her eye. Her eyebrows rose in mild surprise, the title read, 'Hyper-collider Anomalies and Antimatter Research.'

"Someone has a secret geek hobby," Sherry teased, arching a brow and holding out the paper to Jemma. "Is it particle physics or quantum mechanics? Or, maybe…it's anti-matter research."

Jemma took the paper from her with a smirk. "What do you know about hyper-colliders?"

"Oh, you'd be surprised," Sherry said, snatching back the paper before Jemma could put it away. She waved it around dramatically as she spoke. "You know, hyper-colliders aren't just smashing particles for fun. That's what super colliders are for. Hypercolliders are designed to produce complex antimatter—and, more importantly, to contain it for later study."

Jemma tilted her head, raising an eyebrow. "Oh, really? And how exactly does that work, Ms. Frizzle?"

"Well," Sherry began, leaning in with an intense expression. She loved this stuff. "It all starts with energy—serious energy. When particles like protons are accelerated to near-light speeds and then smashed together, they release an enormous amount of energy in that split second of impact. According to Einstein's $E=mc^2$, that energy can then convert into matter. But here's the kicker—it doesn't just produce regular matter. For every particle created, there's also an antiparticle, like an electron's antimatter twin, the positron. That's what an ordinary super-collider does."

Jemma's eyebrow lifted a little further. "Ordinary, mmmkay. Go on."

Sherry waggled her eyebrows, warming to the subject as she returned the paper to Jemma. "One particle of matter, one particle of antimatter. They're opposites. Hyper-colliders accelerate particles much faster, where time nearly stops for them. The magnetic fields are incredibly precise, ensuring a much more reproducible experiment, though not perfectly so. But, instead of measuring weird stuff like Higgs-bosons and whatnot, it is specifically designed to produce more complex types of antimatter, like antiprotons and antineutrons—the building blocks of anti-atoms. But because antimatter annihilates the instant it touches regular matter, they have to use magnetic fields to trap and contain it, keeping the particles suspended in a vacuum."

"I get all that, but how do they keep it from exploding?"

"In theory, it never should," Sherry said, thrilled that she had someone to discuss it with who wasn't glazing over at the bare mention. "When complex anti-matter comes into contact with normal matter, it doesn't just annihilate like an electron. Anti-protons and anti-neutrons are made of anti-matter quantum particles. It only takes one of these to annihilate and destabilize the whole anti-proton, which then decays in bits through other processes. Which begs the question," Sherry waggled her eyebrows conspiratorily. "What caused the Socorro hypercollider to explode?"

"And what's the answer?" Jemma's voice wasn't teasing. She was paying attention—rapt attention to Sherry.

"No one knows. Anti-matter is collected in magnetic bottles —basically a—"

Jemma smirked and interrupted. "I know what a magnetic bottle is."

"Oh, good," Sherry said. "Anyway, that's where they store these anti-particles and, with a little effort, coax them into more complex anti-atoms. At least, that's the theory. Though, now that I think about it, with a strong enough array of magnetic lenses, you could..." Sherry trailed off, lost in thought.

Jemma let out a low whistle. "How do you know all this?"

Sherry blinked, snapping back to reality. Then she shrugged, suddenly feeling self-conscious. This was where it always got weird with people. "I read up on it...right after the hypercollider explosion in New Mexico."

Jemma's mouth twitched. "So you just randomly read up on theoretical physics?"

"It's applied physics," Sherry corrected, voice flat. "And yes...I know it's a geek thing, but I can't help it. Stuff like this fascinates me." She looked down. "Sorry, I know it's weird."

Jemma's hand landed on hers. "No. You don't have to apologize. I think it's amazing. Can I ask you a personal question?"

Sherry shrugged noncommittally. "Sure."

"What's your IQ?"

Sherry looked away. "Does it matter?"

"Absolutely not. I was just curious. I think you're amazing either way." Jemma's voice shifted, turning gentle. "I'm not afraid of intelligence, Sherry. I won't bolt. I'm not insecure about dating smart people, no matter how smart, as long as they're as interested in me as I am in them."

Sherry drew in a deep breath and blew it out in relief. The sense of acceptance that she felt with that simple remark was liberating, and a feeling welled inside her that she couldn't articulate. It felt like affection or maybe love, but not exactly. It was one of those things that happened from time to time that flummoxed her vocabulary skills and her emotional understanding, which wasn't all that hard. Emotional connection was always a struggle for her. And yet, even without being able to describe it, she felt connected on a deep level with Jemma. Something had just clicked, and she liked it.

"One sixty-four," she mumbled, still feeling weird saying it. She never told anyone that. It was a sore point for her. When people found out just how smart she really was, they usually ridiculed her, tried to tear her down, or accused her of outright lying.

Jemma didn't do that, though. All she said was, "I figured.

So, tell me more about hyper-colliders."

Sherry looked up, mouth agape in shock for a moment before she continued on. "Hyper-colliders push the boundaries of what we can do with particle physics. If they can produce enough complex antimatter, who knows? Antimatter could power reactors, spacecraft, all sorts of things. But there's a dark side. There's a fringe theory that even a small anti-matter annihilation could conceivably have reality-altering effects at the quantum level."

Jemma looked at Sherry, a teasing half-smile on her face. "You are the most adorable nerd."

Sherry chuckled, her eyes still glinting. "Hey, it's your paper. Besides, what's the harm in knowing a little more about what goes on in places like these? We still don't know what happened at the Socorro collider. The government says it's fine, but…"

Jemma rolled her eyes, but she was smiling. "I think you might be just a little too interested in this, Sherry. We know what happened: three people died of gamma radiation poisoning. Seven people were horribly burned, and the rest were safe. The collider's functioning again."

"Yes, but think about it. Anti-quarks are quantum particles. We don't know much about how they interact with normal quantum particles. We don't even know if they could be long-lived. They might last much longer than the anti-neutrons that they make up. They could have strange effects on normal matter, even cellular biology." She stopped, and her eyes took on a teasing twinkle. "I have a better question, though."

"Yes?" Jemma replied, dragging out the word.

"Why are you dabbling in subatomic physics."

"Hey, everyone needs a hobby," Jemma replied, tucking the paper back into her bag with a little smirk. "Some people read novels; I read up on particle physics."

"I'm sure it's a real page-turner," Sherry quipped. She grabbed a stray piece of lobster from her plate and flicked it at Jemma, who dodged, laughing.

"Maybe I want to be just like you," Jemma said, picking the flicked lobster off her tray and popping it solicitously into her mouth.

"No," Sherry said, turning abruptly serious. "No, you don't."

Jemma's face fell. "Did I say something wrong?"

Sherry shook her head. "No, nothing. It's fine."

Jemma didn't pursue the discussion, thankfully, letting Sherry off the hook. She didn't like herself sometimes, and she wouldn't wish the worst parts of her life on anyone.

"So, what else do you read?"

Sherry gave a shy grin. "The occasional steamy romance."

Jemma leaned forward. "Any favorites?"

"Vampires, werewolves, spies, whatever suits my fancy. You can dig into my e-reader the next time you're over if you like."

"I'd like that."

Sherry took another bite of her lobster roll, and Jemma gasped, causing her to pause mid-chew, mouth full. "What?"

Jemma eyed Sherry's plate. "Wait a minute—I forgot. Aren't you allergic to shellfish?"

"Oh, it's nothing. Shellfish doesn't make me sick," Sherry replied with a dismissive wave. "Sometimes I get a few hives, but it's no big deal. I'll take a Benadryl when I get home."

Jemma threw a hand to her forehead in an exaggerated swoon, her voice syrupy sweet. "You'd risk breaking out in hives to feed me lobster roll? What a chivalrous, selfless woman you are."

Sherry laughed. "I do like them too, you know?"

"Now, don't ruin it for me. I was just thinking that you might fancy me."

"I do," Sherry whispered softly, the corners of her mouth crooking upward.

Jemma didn't respond at first. She just placed her hand on Sherry's and watched her. After a bit, she said, "I fancy you, too. More even than Lena Swift. I still can't believe I missed her. That sucks."

Sherry shrugged, chuckling to herself that she'd ever thought that Jemma could be Lena. "Yeah, well, I'll see if I can't fall off a building or something so you can get an autograph."

"No thanks," Jemma said with a smile. "I'd much rather you kept your feet on the ground beside me. Lena Swift can bite me."

With a nervous laugh, Sherry raised her beer bottle. "Deal." They clinked bottles, grinning over the remains of their lunch. As Animal Control arrived and took away the little corgi, Sherry gave him a last pat and waved goodbye. Good riddance. Then she made a mental note to pick up that Benadryl. Then she remembered one other thing. "Um, I have a question."

"Another one? I think you've hit your limit for today." Jemma teased and knocked back the remains of her beer as they stood to leave.

"Will you come with me to Sin City tomorrow night?"

Jemma raised an eyebrow, looking non-plussed. "Sin City? Why?"

"My ex works there, and I had to promise to bring you by as payment for her help with dinner the other night. She wants to meet you."

Pursing her lips, Jemma narrowed her eyes. "Okay, but I don't want to stay there long. It's a supervillain bar. It makes me…uncomfortable."

Sherry nodded. "Just a quick stop for a drink, and then we can go."

"Okay. One drink, and we leave."

Sherry nodded. "I promise."

Jemma looked at her watch. "I need to get back to work. Oh, don't forget a dress for the harbor cruise."

"I've got one," Sherry lied. She didn't have one, but Malka did. And she was sure she could borrow it. She kept that wisely to herself, though.

Chapter Twenty-Eight

Jemma stared at the crowd, making their way into Sin City. To say she was uncomfortable was an understatement. It was one thing to come here and chat with Malka as Lena. There was a sense of comfort to her anonymity as Lena Swift. Even if Malka knew her identity, no one else did. If something went down when she was Lena Swift, she could just take care of it. As Jemma Caldwell, well, she had to be careful.

"Hey!" Sherry said, taking her arm from behind.

The touch startled Jemma, who was still utterly confused as to why they'd had to meet Sherry's ex here and not elsewhere. As much as she despised the idea, they were here now.

Sherry began tugging her to the VIP line, past all of the wanna-be villains, groupies, hangers-on, and thrill-seeking twenty-somethings.

Jemma found herself nose to back with a behemoth of a man, seven feet tall and almost as broad. As he turned to wave at someone, he bumped Jemma.

"Hey, watch it!" she barked, and the man turned. *Shit.* It was Il Duce himself, Viktor Rostovich.

"Oh!" Viktor said, giving her a relatively pleasant smile, at least as pleasant as his shoddy gulag dental work allowed. "My apologies, ma'am."

"No problem," Jemma said through gritted teeth. Of all the people she would encounter, this was the last person she wanted to see or had expected when Sherry had said she wanted her to meet her ex. She should take him down out here and arrest him, or at least try. But she couldn't. It was incredibly frustrating. She hated this man, and here he was, being an absolute gentleman. It was an act. Of that, she was certain. Rostovich had a reputation for getting aggressive with women. He might seem polite in person, but he had absolutely no qualms about hitting a woman.

The doorman pulled aside the purple velvet rope and let them in. Rostovich peeled off toward the righthand bar, and Jemma whistled. "Wow, I haven't been here in two years. This place has been totally renovated."

Sherry cast her a glance sidelong. "I didn't know you'd been here before."

"It was a long time ago," Jemma said, trying her best to sound casual. "I had a fling with someone who worked here."

"Oh, really? Who?" Sherry asked, taking Jemma's hand and dragging her through the club.

"No one you'd know," Jemma said.

Tonight's motif was big band. The bandstand was stacked with a full house orchestra, including trumpets, drums, timpanis, even a full xylophone.

"You'll like my ex; she's pretty cool, though try not to piss her off too much. She can be," Sherry paused briefly, looking for the right phrase before settling on, "a lot."

Before she knew it, Jemma found herself at the back left corner table, closest to the back stairs. "Shit," she muttered under her breath as everything became clear.

"Jemma, this is my ex, Malka," Sherry said. "Malka, this is Jemma."

Malka raised an eyebrow and donned a wide smile full of wicked, wicked promise.

Jemma hesitated, unsure what to do. How was Malka going to play this? Would she expose Jemma right here?

"It's a pleasure to meet you, Jemma," Malka said, offering her hand. "Welcome to Sin City. I really hope you enjoy your evening. Sherry has told me all about you. And I'm sure she's mentioned me."

Not in so many words. "It's…uh…nice to meet you, too." Tentatively, Jemma took Malka's hand.

Malka drew it to her lips, leaving a tender kiss on Jemma's knuckles. As she did so, Jemma felt Malka's soft tongue brush between her index and middle finger, and a shiver flew down Jemma's spine, forcing her to repress a shudder.

"Do sit," Malka said, waving to the seats at her table and scooting around to sit on Jemma's right, her leg right up against her. "Tonight is on me for the two lovebirds."

"Malka," Sherry warned, narrowing her eyes.

Jemma shifted uncomfortably. *You have got to be fucking kidding me.* Malka, the supervillain succubus of Harborhaven, the woman who had her hands in every nefarious scheme in the city, was Sherry's ex-girlfriend. How the fuck had that happened?

"A martini for Sherry," Malka said with a grin and then turned to Jemma. "And, don't tell me, let me guess—a scotch on the rocks for you, I bet."

Jemma narrowed her eyes at Malka. "Don't," she mouthed.

"What?" Malka mouthed back, giving Jemma a sly wink, just as Sherry glanced at their approaching waitress. When Sherry looked back, Malka was the picture of innocence, except, of course, for her 'cat that ate the canary' grin. Jemma was in for a very, very long night.

"Scotch is fine, thanks," What really baked Jemma's noodle, though, was that Sherry, sweet, innocent Sherry, had been in a relationship with Lady Sin. She tried to picture it and just couldn't see it.

Their drinks arrived in record time. Jemma eyed hers warily, wondering if Malka would try to poison her. It probably wouldn't work. It had been tried, but the experience was unpleasant. She didn't like vomiting, but then again, who did?

Malka leaned in, a sly smile curving on her lips, her eyes glinting with mock interest. "So, Jenny," she drawled, her voice as smooth as silk. "What is it that you do for a living?"

Jemma's smile stayed fixed, but her fingers tightened ever so slightly around her drink. "It's Jemma," she corrected, her voice steady, "and I'm an insurance investigator."

"Oh, insurance," Malka purred, drawing out the word with exaggerated relish. "Bet that's thrilling. You must be good at digging up people's dirty little secrets." Her gaze lingered on Jemma, a little too long, a little too knowingly.

"Not exactly," Jemma replied, irritation simmering beneath her calm tone. "I'm an independent contractor. Mostly, I help people find missing items… like paintings." She held Malka's gaze, her eyes icy. "And sometimes, when people misplace a little cash, I help with that, too."

"Jemma!" Sherry hissed under her breath, nudging her arm. "I'm sorry, Malka—she's just… it's been a long week."

Malka waved her off, her voice saccharine-sweet. "Oh, Sher, darling, think nothing of it. It's kind of cute, really. I think it's sweet how much she cares." She cast a playful, mocking smile at Jemma, as if daring her to push further.

Jemma's face flushed red, realizing too late she'd played right into Malka's hands. Plastering on a polite smile, she shot Malka a narrowed glance. Malka's game was clear: goad her, push her buttons, make her slip up. If Jemma wanted this to work with Sherry, she'd have to do better at keeping her cool. But why did this have to be so infuriating?

Malka, still smiling, gave Jemma an appraising once-over. "You know, Jemma, you look absolutely fabulous… especially for someone in insurance. I'd almost expect something a bit more… conservative," she added, letting her words settle like a slow-burn insult. "You know, all pinched and proper." She tilted her head with a feigned look of genuine admiration, as though the jab were a true compliment. Then she turned to Sherry, her face lighting up with amusement, sharing the joke only she truly understood.

"Malka," Sherry groaned, giving her a look of warning. "Not you, too."

"Of course not, darling. I am the epitome of a gracious host," Malka replied, her gaze sliding back to Jemma.

"Perhaps you could give me some pointers. I hear 'streetwalker chic' is back in style," Jemma shot back with a cool smile, unable to resist the jab.

Sherry's eyes widened, darting between them, clearly

caught off guard.

Malka laughed, completely unfazed, giving an exaggerated toss of her hair. "Oh, honey, you can do better than that. I prefer the term 'woman-of-the-night couture,' thank you very much." She winked at Sherry, clearly reveling in the exchange. "It's all about style with a touch of danger."

Sherry's wide-eyed stare bounced between Malka and Jemma. "Alright, you two. Can we please just have a polite drink?"

"Absolutely," Malka replied, voice dripping with innocent amusement. "I am being polite, don't you think, Gina?"

"It's still Jemma," she replied, forcing a tight smile. "And yes, I appreciate the…hospitality."

Just as she said this, Jemma felt something warm and snake-like begin to slide up her leg under the table. Her eyes darted to Malka in a mix of surprise and outrage. But if she reacted, Malka would play innocent to make her seem paranoid, and Jemma knew it. She tried to ignore the sensation, though her pulse quickened.

Malka's grin widened, her eyes glinting dangerously as she bared her fangs just a fraction in a sly, knowing smile.

"So," Malka said, her tail still snaking its way past Jemma's knee, sending a chill up her spine, "how did you two meet?" The amusement in her tone was unmistakable as Jemma slapped her hand against her leg under the table, halting Malka's tail from creeping any further.

Sherry, oblivious to the whole exchange, smiled dreamily, ready to recount the story. Meanwhile, Jemma's blood simmered, and she pinched Malka's tail through her pant leg —hard. Malka squeaked and jerked, rattling the entire table.

Jemma's hand snapped out, keeping Malka's wine from spilling as she gave Malka a pointed look. Fortunately, Sherry's drink was in her hand.

"Are you quite alright?" Jemma asked, the corner of her mouth ticking slightly in checked amusement.

"Perfectly," Malka said, voice tight. Jemma could see her rubbing the tip of her tail under the table.

"You know what?" Sherry said, eyes narrowed at the two of

them in annoyance. "I'm going to the bathroom. When I get back, you both had better be acting more like the ladies you are." Sherry stood and stalked away.

Jemma whirled on Malka. "Knock it off."

"Oh, Jemma. It's just a spot of fun, honestly."

"Well, it's not bloody amusing. Besides, I thought we were friends."

Malka's expression shifted abruptly, going from smiling and friendly to serious. "We are, but I don't want her getting hurt. Your line of work gets people killed."

It was a low blow, but it landed squarely. Jemma's eyes went wide for a moment as guilt twisted her gut. She did her best to deflect. "And you thought that the best way to express it was through petty torments?"

"No. I'm just screwing with you because it's fun, darling. Besides, you love it."

Jemma pursed her lips in aggravation as an unbidden memory of just what Malka could do with that tail popped into her head. "No," Jemma said flatly. "I don't. And if you do that again, I'll break the fucking thing."

"Spoilsport," Malka said. "Truce then?"

Jemma's gaze flicked over Malka, her lips pressed together, barely holding back the exasperation simmering just below the surface. Her brow furrowed as she studied Malka for a beat.

Finally, she allowed a thin smirk to tug at one corner of her mouth, almost as if it was happening against her will. "Fine," she said, eyes narrowed, and her voice carrying the barest hint of amusement beneath her irritation.

Timothy shuffled over, interrupting them as he leaned down to whisper something urgently in Malka's ear, his breath a little too close for her liking. Malka's expression soured, and she held up a hand, silencing him with a snap of her fingers. "I'm busy, so deal with it." As he turned to go, she added, "Oh, Timothy, get Jemma another scotch—a MacAllan thirty, I think." Her voice was cold and dismissive.

A flicker of irritation passed over his face, clearly insulted at being reduced to a barback. Malka caught the look and arched an eyebrow, daring him to say something. With a sullen sigh, he turned on his heel, slinking off in his usual defeated hunch.

As he left, Jemma raised a brow, giving Malka an amused look. "Why do you keep him around, anyway? You're always complaining about him."

Malka leaned back with a wry smile, eyes following Timothy's retreat. "Oh, he's harmless enough as long as I keep him from skimming the till. And I do enjoy watching him squirm every time I catch him slacking."

"Fair enough." Jemma downed her scotch, grinning to herself.

As she leaned back, Sherry sauntered back and slid into the seat next to her, giving Jemma a sidelong, appraising look. "Are we getting along better?" she asked, a glint of dry humor in her eyes.

"Much," Malka answered smoothly, wrapping a lie in the truth. "I was just telling Jemma how much I love Grimshaw's 'The Lady of Shalott.'"

"Good," Sherry replied, taking a sip of her martini before continuing. "So. In answer to your question. I met Jemma at Kelly's." She gave Jemma's hand a gentle squeeze and giggled slightly. "You know, at first, I thought she was Chuck's girlfriend."

"Sherry, sometimes you're so clueless," Malka laughed.

"Yes, well…" Sherry paused momentarily, a frown crossing her face that Jemma couldn't decipher. "Anyway, I tried to be smooth and fell completely on my face."

Jemma stepped in. "It was absolutely adorable. Tell me, Malka, is Sherry good at billiards?"

"She's an ace," Malka said, and Jemma thought she detected a hint of wistfulness. "I've never beaten her, but she is the undefeated champion of the annual tournament at Kelly's, as I recall."

"Really?" Jemma raised an eyebrow and turned an appraising glance at Sherry.

"Oh, yes," Malka continued. "Don't ever let her convince you otherwise. She hustled pool in her teenage years, back when she was stealing motorcycles."

Jemma did a spit take into her drink and stared at Sherry

gape-mouthed. "Stealing what?"

Sherry leaned back in her chair, shifting uncomfortably, but a hint of pride flickered in her voice as she spoke. "I was a straight-A student, a total bookworm at home. My mom loved it—she thought I would be some kind of genius."

"You are a genius, darling," Malka oozed, adding color.

Jemma was suddenly intrigued and terribly confused. It hadn't occurred to her one bit that Sherry might have the bottle for felony theft. Clearly, she'd misjudged her. "So, what happened?"

Sherry's smile turned a bit rueful. "That was just the cover story. On the streets, it was a whole different game. I used to hustle and scam. I committed a little larceny, boosting motorcycles, mostly. The expensive ones." Her eyes grew distant as she recalled those days. "Once, I got my hands on a Ducati. It was probably worth more than my mom's house."

Jemma raised an eyebrow, half-amused, half-horrified. "And?"

Sherry shrugged, a slight grin tugging at her lips as she twisted her Martini glass, her eyes following the toothpick-bound olives as they rocked. "I fooled everyone for a while. My mom thought I was hanging out at the library, and sometimes I was, but most of the time, I was out finding bikes for a local chop shop. It wasn't about the money, though; it was about seeing if I could pull it off. I loved the thrill."

Malka smirked, taking a sip of her drink. "Sounds familiar." She shot Jemma a sideways glance, clearly enjoying the shared hint of rebellion in Sherry's story. Of course, that had been what had attracted Jemma to Malka in the first place when they'd had their fling. She'd had a thing for bad girls after Callie, but those days were long behind her, and she had to remind herself that Sherry was talking about high school, not present day.

Sherry grinned and chuckled a bit. "This one time, I was trying to hotwire a BMW, and a cop rolled up."

"I love this," Malka interjected, swirling her olives in her martini.

"What did you do?" Jemma asked, genuinely intrigued

despite herself.

Sherry shook her head, grinning. "I started walking the bike and told the cop that my 'boyfriend' had let me ride it, but I chickened out. And this guy—oh, he really leaned into his 'hero cop' moment. He gets out and starts giving me all these very serious pointers on bike riding, like I'm about to star in Fast and Furious. Meanwhile, I'm sweating bullets, just waiting for him to realize the key wasn't in it. He even pats the bike like, 'You'll get there, kid.' Finally, after two blocks, he gets another call and takes off. As soon as he's gone, I finish hotwiring it and fly out of there."

They all burst out laughing.

"That's brilliant," Jemma said, eyes wide with genuine admiration.

Sherry shrugged, a faint smile on her lips. "I do okay under pressure, as long as I don't have time to, y'know… actually think about it." Her voice grew quieter, and she looked away, her fingers brushing the edge of her glass.

Jemma reached across, her hand resting gently over Sherry's. "Hey, it's okay," she said softly. "I know. And I'm here—no matter what."

Sherry's eyes met hers, a bit of the tension easing from her shoulders.

Malka watched them for long moments; then, she slid her chair away from Jemma. Jemma glanced at her and caught a hint of something there. It wasn't jealousy exactly, more like longing. Sighing inwardly, she turned back to Sherry, suddenly hurting for Malka. Malka clearly still loved Sherry, and not just as a friend. Jemma realized that neither of them should be with Sherry, not if they cared about her. She'd known that, of course, but now, it was apparent, and the feelings it stirred were miserable and painful.

Jemma forced a smile. "Did you ever get caught?"

Sherry sighed, her grin turning sheepish. "I got too cocky. I tried to boost a Harley in broad daylight. Cops nailed me red-handed. I thought I'd be going to prison for sure. My mom was ready to disown me."

"But you didn't?" Jemma asked, her tone softer now.

Sherry shook her head. "Nope. Somehow got off light—community service and probation. Guess they saw a kid who could be 'saved' or something." Her smile faded, becoming more reflective. "I think my mom went after my dad for more child support unless he pulled some strings. He had a friend in the district attorney's office back then."

Jemma's expression softened. "She must care a lot."

Sherry exhaled slowly. "Yeah, she does. She did her best, even after my dad walked out."

Jemma leaned forward, her gaze warm. "You've been through a lot."

Sherry smirked, though her eyes looked tired. "Yeah, but I'm still here. That counts for something, I guess."

"It counts for everything," Malka said. "Why don't we order some food."

The rest of the evening passed pleasantly enough, with Sherry, Jemma, and Malka sharing stories and laughs. They even had a nice dinner of duck and lentils, but after they left, Jemma realized she had to do something. Malka had been right. If she weren't careful, Sherry would end up caught up in Jemma's life and get hurt.

So, as the warm summer air wrapped around them and they walked toward the subway, Jemma agonized. She glanced up, desperate for any hint of how best to handle this, until she realized that it would hurt both of them no matter what, and she screwed up her resolve.

Sherry glanced at her, still smiling and oblivious. Her world wasn't supposed to be mixed up with the Bratva or dangerous figures like Ivan Rostovich. She clearly didn't know the extent of Malka's connections, the threats they could bring to her door at any time. Jemma couldn't explain her own situation without revealing everything, so she took a different approach, her voice soft but firm.

"Sherry," she began, her tone almost hesitant, "I know you don't see Malka much, but I need you to understand… she's dangerous. Really dangerous. She's not just an ex. She's tied up with the Bratva. With Ivan Rostovich. That's serious."

Sherry looked at her, and her face immediately hardened. "I

know exactly who and what Malka is, Jemma. Those are my risks to take."

Jemma realized she'd forgotten who she was talking to. Sherry was sharp and perceptive despite her sometimes bumbling nature. And obviously, she'd underestimated her, given Sherry's penchant for motorcycle theft. Wrong as it was, it took real guts and calm to pull off. She shook her head, the worry and frustration rising beneath her calm facade. "It doesn't matter how often you see her. Being around someone with ties to people like Ivan—like the Bratva—puts you at risk and, by extension, me."

Sherry's smile faded, her face a mix of confusion and hurt. "What are you saying?"

Jemma swallowed hard. She was being a coward, and she knew it. Sherry was right about one thing, it was her risk to take. On the other hand, though, Jemma didn't want to be the one to bring that risk to her doorstep.

She wanted to tell her it was over, but she couldn't get the words out. Instead, she said probably the worst words anyone in a budding relationship could say. "I don't know if I can do this. I...I need time to think it over."

"What? But Jemma..."

"No, Sherry," Jemma interrupted, her voice rising more than she wanted it to. "That," she pointed back toward the bar, "is Lady Sin in there, not some ex who knits and likes trail mix. I counted at least four criminals in there who are wanted, including Il Duce, who we all know is a murderer despite the fact that he's never been convicted. I can't be around that. You know what? I just need to figure out what to do. I'll call you."

"Jemma, wait..." Sherry called to her back, but she kept walking. Even in her own ears, it had sounded contrived—total bullshit. No matter what she did, Sherry wasn't going to stay away from Malka. She would still be in danger. And if the tears now streaming from her eyes were any indication, she was making the worst mistake of her life. She spun around just before she turned the corner, but Sherry was gone, lost in the press of people heading into the subway.

"Shit," she muttered and disappeared into the city shadows.

Chapter Twenty-Nine

Sherry still sat on the couch with her head in her hands. She hadn't slept a wink all night. Everything was spinning out of control. Her night with Jemma and Malka had been a disaster. Mixxer would return soon, looking for his painting, which she didn't have. If she were lucky, he wouldn't just send someone over at the drop of a hat to kill her. That thought pulled her up short. What if Malka couldn't convince him to wait? What if she didn't find Charlie and Mary? Mixxer could be on his way or sending one of his goons right now.

As if in answer to her thoughts, a knock sounded at the door. She glanced around, panicked and eyes wild, but there was no place to run or hide, just the eighty-foot plummet from the balcony. Resigned, she took a deep breath and stood. The banging sounded again, followed by a crisp British accent, "Sherry, you asleep? I saw your bike down there. I just want to talk."

Filled with relief, Sherry did her best to dry her puffy eyes and hide her worry before she unlocked the deadbolt and opened the door a crack. "Hey," she said with a miserable sniff, wiping her nose with a tissue.

Jemma stayed silent for a second, her eyes scanning the sliver of Sherry's face. "I'm sorry," she said finally. "I wasn't trying to make you cry. I…" She broke off, not sure what to say, but the sight of Sherry's sad expression broke her heart.

Sherry slid off the chain and opened the door all the way. "Come in."

Jemma stepped inside. However, before Sherry could close the door, Jemma ran a smooth hand across her cheek and looked into her eyes. "I'm sorry. I just worry for you. I don't want to see you hurt."

"Come sit down," Sherry said, sliding onto the couch. At Jemma's approach, Breit moved over and made room. Sherry gave him a wary eye. "You don't move for me like that. What gives?"

Jemma sat and stroked the little calico's fur. "They're such neat animals," she said. "The way their coloring extends into their eyes." She chuckled slightly. "It makes them look like they were cooked up in a lab, like some superhero."

Sherry smiled wanly at the comment and turned, pulling one leg onto the couch. Breit dropped into the crook of her knee and curled up. "Look, I know who she is, Jemma, but I know her better than you do. Malka wasn't always that way. We met in the last year of our Master's Program. We had the same thesis advisor. Back then, she was sweet and loving. Her emphasis was art restoration, and we worked on a few projects together at the Met. That's where she worked. She was detail-oriented, though probably still a bit wilder than me."

Jemma shifted and mirrored Sherry, looking at her straight on. "What happened?"

"One bad day," Sherry said with a shrug, hands in her lap. She spoke slowly, the painful memories tugging at her and making her feel things she didn't want to: hurt, betrayal, grief. "Luke Luck. You know? Prince Lucifer?"

"Oh, no," Jemma whispered in horror. "You were there." It wasn't a question.

Sherry gave a confirmatory nod, and when she looked at Jemma, the depth of feeling she saw reminded her that Jemma did seem to care about her. "I tried to cover Malka, you know? A bit of concrete or a brick or something hit me in the head. I've still got a tiny plate back here where they had to fix it because part of my skull was pulverized." She swallowed. "I was only in ICU for a week before they sent me home to recover. I thought we'd just get on with our lives, and it seemed like it was better than ever. Malka always seemed so happy to see me, so into it in bed and stuff." She paused for a long moment, looking at Jemma, who seemed about to cry. "You okay?"

Jemma sniffed. "Yeah, sorry. I was there, too. It was a bad day for everyone, I guess."

Eyes wide, Sherry mentally berated herself. *Great, nice job.* "I'm sorry. I didn't realize, and I don't want to make you remember something—"

"No!" Jemma interrupted, scooting closer and clasping Sherry's hands. She sounded almost desperate. "No! I was fine. I didn't get hurt or anything. Keep going."

Sherry looked down at their hands. She felt Jemma letting go, but she stopped her, squeezing those hands a little harder, like they might disappear if she didn't have contact. "I went back to work for a few hours to check in. When I returned home, I found Malka sitting on the couch with her head in her hands. Her right eye had turned that bright yellow that they are today. They didn't glow as much, though. Black lines spidered out from her eye, down her neck, and all down her right arm. I thought she had a fever or a blood pressure problem because some of her skin had turned red."

Jemma did cry then, just a few tears and she pulled her hands loose to wipe them. "Sorry, I'm sure that was hard to see."

Sherry shrugged. "I was just scared. We went to the hospital. We saw specialists. No one could help her. The best we could guess, some of Prince Lucifer's blood got in her eye. At least, we think that's what happened. We don't actually know. But, I mean, look at her: horns, tail, most of the same stuff. At least it didn't make her head look like a goat, I guess."

"Is that when she changed?" Jemma's voice sounded choked with emotion, and she wrung her hands. Sherry thought to stop, but Jemma just waved her on. But the look of guilt in her eye left Sherry puzzled.

"That's when the big changes started," Sherry continued. "She wanted sex all the time, and she started taking reckless risks. She stopped going to work, and she was angry a lot. She was never violent, and I was never afraid of her, but I was afraid *for* her. The horns grew painlessly for the most part, except at the beginning. But when her wings sprouted, it was torture. She screamed and screamed for two days. I stayed up with her, rubbing her back, her face, her head, anything that might soothe her. It was all I could do. No amount of painkillers helped. Then it was over. She woke up one morning just as you saw her, but she was stronger, and she had her powers. I tried just to accept it." Sherry gave a wan smile. "And it didn't hurt that the—" She stopped abruptly, about to say something to Jemma that she wouldn't want to hear.

"The what?"

Sherry shook her head. "Nothing." She picked up her water bottle from the end table, taking a swig before continuing. "After that, Malka started sleeping around. She kept it hidden, but there were too many people, and eventually, I found out. We argued, and she tried to take over my mind. It didn't work. Well, it did for a few minutes, but then it just stopped. I don't know why."

"What did you do?" Jemma asked in a whisper. "Is that when you left?"

Sherry snorted and shook her head. "No, Malka was so horrified by what she'd done that she's the one who left. Of course, she emptied our savings from our joint account a few days later. I tried to get her to come back home, but she wouldn't. She told me that she couldn't control herself anymore, that our relationship was stifling. She didn't go into detail, and I was in no fit state to ask, so I just kept hoping.

"Every so often, she would call and ask me to come over to the club. We'd have sex and chat for a while, but then she sent me on my way. I tried to get her back, but she just kept telling me that it wasn't something she could do. So, a few months later, I blocked her number and stopped answering her emails. In the meantime, my life completely fell apart—" She lowered her voice. "I...I fell apart."

"That's awful," Jemma murmured, taking Sherry's hands again. "I'm sorry. I'd say I should have asked, but you were right. It was none of my business."

"No," Sherry said flatly. "You needed to know. And you're right, she's dangerous. I don't love her anymore, not really. I mean, I care what happens to her, but the Malka I knew is gone. I don't know why I've tried so hard to be friends with her."

"Because you still love her," Jemma said. "Sherry, we don't stop loving people when something bad happens to them, even like that. It's okay that you love her and care about her. And I know you're not in love with her. I just—" Jemma looked down. "What am I trying to say?" She took a deep breath. "I'm saying it's not a deal breaker, but I like you, and it makes me worry, you going over there. Sin City is a supervillain hangout. Bad things happen there all the time. Nothing anyone can prove, but I've heard of people going there and not coming back, you know?"

Sherry gave Jemma an odd look then. "What?"

Jemma nodded. "Four women, in the last six months. They were last seen going into the bar and never came out. No one's seen them since."

"I didn't hear about that," Sherry said. "Was that in the news somewhere, and I just missed it?"

Jemma flushed and stammered. "I—I—I don't know where I read it. But I read it somewhere. I'm pretty sure it was in the news."

Sherry made a mental note to check into it. "Are you really that afraid of Malka?"

Jemma shook her head. "No, it's not that. I told you that I haven't dated anyone in six years."

Sherry nodded.

"Six years ago, I was involved with a woman, Callie Summers. We met at, of all things, a beach volleyball tournament. We hit it off right away. Before long, we were living together. It was amazing. She was smart and beautiful and funny."

"She sounds nice," Sherry said when Jemma paused for a breath.

"She was. Our life wasn't without its problems. I told you

that my ex suffered from depression. It was pretty severe, and I wasn't in the best headspace at the time. My life was going through a bunch of changes." Jemma paused for a second and looked up, tears floating in her eyes. "I…uh…" She stopped again. "Things were so screwed up for a minute, and I thought that maybe if we made a big change, we could get past our problems. I decided I was going to propose. I bought a ring and everything."

Sherry scooted closer and put her hand on Jemma's forearm. "What happened?"

Jemma sniffed and pawed at her eyes. "I had decided I'd do it on Christmas Eve, but I'd left the ring in my office, so I went back to get it, telling Callie I needed a file. Callie insisted on going with me. I told her it'd be fine, but I think maybe she thought I was cheating on her. I wasn't. I was just working long hours. Anyway, I got the ring, and we headed home.

Sherry watched as Jemma spoke. She'd taken a bunch of courses in reading people to help compensate for her inability to clue in on people's emotions, but with Jemma, now, she needed none of it. Jemma was in horrible pain, and Sherry wished she could just whisk it all away. She had a hunch about where the story was going. She seemed to remember seeing something in the news about a car accident and a death. It had something to do with Lena Swift, she thought.

"As we were driving home across the University Bridge with the blizzard in full force, we hit something." Jemma was crying now, tears spilling over her lashes. She stopped for a moment and hiccupped a sob. "The car went off the bridge and into the river. Callie died on impact. I almost drowned."

"I found out later, that it was a bear, modified by some supervillain who called himself Dr. Carnifex." She shook her head. "I have no idea where these guys come up with these ridiculous names."

The lightbulb finally went on in Sherry's head. "The papers said it was after Lena Swift, but that no one knew why it was on the bridge."

Jemma shrugged. "That's certainly the mystery of my lifetime."

"Wait. Didn't Dr. Carnifex die shortly after?"

"He was found dead the next day. He'd been beaten to death. His body was…" Jemma stopped, and when she looked up, she had the most haunted look in her eyes.

Sherry all but launched across the couch and took Jemma in her arms, whispering, "Oh, Jemma, I'm so sorry." It all suddenly made sense. Jemma wasn't afraid for herself, Jemma was afraid for her. She could understand why she didn't want her around Malka. Finding out that Lady Sin was her ex and that they were still in touch was probably triggering as hell.

She crooked a finger under Jemma's face and gently drew those fabulous blue eyes, shimmering with tears, to look into her own. "Listen to me. I will stay away from Malka. We have something special here, and I won't ruin it. If I have to make a choice between Malka and you, that's easy."

Jemma shook her head. "No, that's not fair to you. I just need to get over it."

Scowling, Sherry shifted her tone, turning sharp. "No, that's not how it works. Grief is a long process. You don't just get over it. But if it'll make you feel better, I promise I'll be careful, and we can revisit it later. Okay?"

Jemma looked conflicted, but eventually, she nodded. "I'm sorry," she whispered finally. "I shouldn't have put you in that position. It's just…I…I'm a little scared, is all."

Sherry pulled Jemma close and hugged her tightly. "Me too. But we'll be okay."

Once Jemma had dried her eyes and it seemed her emotions had settled, she stood up and held her hand out. "So, can I take you out for an ice cream or something? Maybe make up for being a shithead?" Jemma asked, looking extremely contrite.

Sherry chuckled and donned a sly smirk. "You know, the Marshmallow Tease Latte is back at SunBean. I'd love one of those."

Jemma laughed. "You want a Latte?"

Sherry nodded. "Uh-huh."

"Topped with marshmallow fluff and with marshmallow syrup."

Sherry nodded again, a little more excitedly and with a broad grin. "Uh-huh! Uh-huh!"

Jemma cupped her cheeks. "You're so adorable," she whispered and kissed her.

Sherry leaned in and hummed contentedly. Jemma tasted like spearmint and heat, filling Sherry with warm thoughts. It was long moments before they pulled apart.

Jemma had a shy look on her face. "Sorry, it just struck me. I hope it was okay after..."

Sherry raised an eyebrow, then a slow grin spread across her face, and she laughed. "Yeah," she said finally. "It was wonderful."

A few minutes later, on their way out, Sherry grabbed the door handle and turned it. The entire handle snapped off in her hand, and the knob fell out of the other side. "Well, shit. I swear this place is definitely not up to code."

"What do we do now?" Jemma asked, examining the destroyed lock.

Sherry dug into her closet and found her old slim-jim, which she used to jimmy out the latch bolt so they could at least open the door. As they stepped out, Sherry pulled the door closed by the empty knob hole and locked the deadbolt from the outside. Fortunately, it was keyed on both sides, not that anyone but a toddler could get their arm through the hole to open it.

"There. That'll keep the burglars out until the lock is fixed." She scooped her phone from her purse and dialed maintenance. "Shall we go?" she said to Jemma with a grin.

Jemma just shrugged and took Sherry's hand. "Let's do."

Chapter Thirty

Standing on the pier, the air heavy with the scent of saltwater, Jemma couldn't help but smile as she watched Sherry, her gaze fixed on The Cape Clipper. The massive vessel glowed softly in the fading light, stretching over 150 feet, its sleek white hull reflecting the last traces of daylight. Sherry stood motionless, utterly captivated. She bounced up and down on her toes in front of the gangway.

Jemma's eyes traveled her gorgeous leg, visible via the scandalously high slit of her long red evening gown. The dress and the black patent leather heels looked suspiciously like something from Malka's closet. Jemma doused the worry that went with them. She'd promised Jemma that she'd be careful, and Jemma had to trust her. Instead, Jemma kept her attention focused on how amazing Sherry looked. Malka had nothing on her. She'd gone all out to look good for the occasion. Again, it suggested she'd had succubus help, but Sherry's allure was undeniable.

Dusk softened Sherry's features, highlighting her wonder as she stared at the yacht. When Sherry looked over at her, positively vibrating with excitement, Jemma returned the giddy smile with a warm one of her own.

"I don't know if I told you," Sherry said, her voice low. "But you look amazing."

"Thank you," Jemma said, shifting uncomfortably at the

praise. She had wanted to look her best for this adventure. Her hair was elegantly styled, side-swept and curled into long waves that cascaded over her left shoulder. She certainly stood out among all of the long gowns and dresses in her black crepe sleeveless bodysuit and sheer skirt. The neckline dipped daringly low, offering a tantalizing glimpse of soft curves. The fabric barely clung to her form, teasing the eye with the shadowed valley between her breasts, revealing just enough to suggest but not quite enough to satisfy. It ensured that Jemma garnered quite a bit of attention, none of which she relished and all of which was strictly for Sherry's sake. She wanted people to wonder who they were and how these two women looked so stunning.

The last hints of orange and purple spread across the sky, casting shadows that danced on the water. Sherry, still entranced, murmured, "It's like something out of a dream," and Jemma chuckled quietly to herself. She had seen that look before—on Callie. Jemma had taken her to Big Bend National Park for a week-long birthday trip. She'd stared at the brilliant sky just like that. And for the first time, the memory didn't conjure up anything more than a mild bittersweet reminiscence. There was no jolt of gut-wrenching grief. Somewhere in the last few weeks, the empty hole in Jemma's heart had begun to fill. She wondered if it was Sherry's presence in her life that had dulled the pain. Maybe she could find love again.

Jemma's attention was drawn away from Sherry briefly as she spied four men and two women in wait staff uniforms march on board, pushing several catering carts. One of the women looked a little familiar, but Jemma couldn't remember where she'd seen her. It could also be that she just looked like someone she knew, she wasn't sure, but it niggled at her. She longed to move closer and get a better look, but they were first in line, and the gangway would be open any minute. Besides, it was probably nothing.

Finally, after a few more minutes, a man in a spiffy 'ice cream' white uniform opened the gangway and took their tickets. "Welcome aboard, ladies," he said with a bright smile.

"Enjoy the cruise."

As Sherry and Jemma stepped onto the yacht, they were immediately enveloped by its air of refined sensuality. The dining deck gleamed under soft lighting that reflected off polished floors, creating an intimate, inviting glow.

The buffet table was a masterpiece—a long, elegant spread that dominated the center of the room. At its heart stood a towering seafood display, the pinnacle of luxury dining, with layers of oysters, lobster tails, caviar, and other delicacies. A massive plate of perfectly arranged shrimp glistened under the soft lighting. Around it, an array of hors d'oeuvres beckoned—delicate canapés, fresh cheeses, artfully arranged fruits, and a gorgeous plate of foie gras.

Perfectly arranged across the floor were nine round tables for the forty-five guests. They sat empty for the moment, but it wouldn't be long before they'd moved further into the harbor, and dinner would be served.

It was the artwork, though, that hushed even the most boisterous of the crowd. Striking paintings of nude female forms in seductive, intertwined poses adorned the walls, each piece more enticing than the last. In the center of the floor stood a massive statue in bronze of Oshun, an African goddess of love. Like all of the works, this one depicted her nude in all of her glory, long braided hair hung down her back, twisted and worked into delicate waves. Beneath her, four women, likewise nude, prayed at her feet, their expressions needful and, to Jemma's eyes, full of hunger. Oshun's face had a subtle expression that seemed to change depending on the angle of the light. It gave the illusion of being watched.

The paintings, with their tender yet risqué depictions, stirred something primal, blending art and desire seamlessly into the elegant setting. The room felt alive with subtle tension, balancing luxury with an undeniable erotic allure. Jemma had expected a display of so many nudes and, well, so much sex to be overwhelming, but it wasn't. The entire arrangement came off as elegant and beautiful rather than overdone.

Sherry was clearly awestruck. The dreamy look in her eyes told Jemma everything she needed to know. She'd done it right. She'd given Sherry a special gift tonight, and that was all that mattered to her. She and Callie had promised each other they would do this one day, but they'd never had the pull or the money, and while Callie was gone, Jemma felt like she would probably appreciate her sharing it with someone.

"I did it, Callie. I finally found someone," she whispered quietly to herself. Then, with more volume, she asked Sherry, "Well, what do you think?"

Sherry turned to face her, batting at tears. "They're lovely. It's all so…It's just perfect." She took Jemma's hand and all but danced them around until they found their table.

Once everyone had piled into the dining room, there was a flurry of movement outside as the ship cast off from the pier and began lumbering its way into the harbor.

"How do they keep them from sliding around?" Sherry asked, in awe of the amazing spectacle.

"Something about bolts and magnets," a man standing next to them replied hushedly. "They can basically disengage the flooring, and the tables simply slide around. If you return on most nights, there's seating for almost a hundred passengers."

He was a white man with a greying beard, about six feet tall. His face had seen a fair number of sunrises and sunsets by the weathered look of his skin and the harsh wrinkles around his storm-filled gray eyes. He stuck out his hand. "I'm Clint Mercer."

Jemma shook his hand. Mercer's firm handshake and easy smile conveyed warmth, but there was an unmistakable weight behind his presence. She could just hear Sherry now. This was Clint Mercer, the well-known investor and one of Harborhaven's most generous patrons of the arts. During the lean years following the housing bust, he'd even funded the city's public school art programs, keeping creativity alive for kids who'd otherwise go without.

"I'm Jemma Caldwell, Mr. Mercer," Jemma said, a sly grin crawling across her face. Sherry was obviously stunned by his very presence, so what Jemma said next would likely floor her. It felt good to surprise someone with something perfectly normal for a change. It didn't happen often. "We've met before. You might remember. I helped recover your '57 Vette three years ago."

"Oh yes," Mercer said. "I remember. And I appreciate it. I know the insurance company didn't pay much for your work, but she's special to me."

Sherry's jaw dropped, and Jemma reached over, delicately pushing it closed. Mercer had to notice, but he was too much of a gentleman to say anything.

"This beautiful woman is my date for the evening," Jemma added quickly. "Miss Sherry Broward."

"Broward, Broward," Mercer said, his eyes searching Sherry's face. "James Broward wouldn't happen to be your father, would he?"

Instantly snapped out of her starstruck stupor, Sherry finally spoke, sounding completely non-plussed. "Yes. He is." Then she added, "Unfortunately. How do you know him?"

Mercer sipped the scotch in his hand, then swirled it, letting the fat ball of ice slide around. "I spent a round playing golf with him at last year's Harborhaven Classic. He's got a bit of a temper."

Sherry pursed her lips as if she'd just sucked on a rotten lemon. "Yes, yes, he does. Tell me, how many clubs did he break?"

Mercer chuckled. "None, but not for lack of trying. I'll never understand how a body can get quite that angry over a charity sporting event where most of us were dropping snowmen."

"Snowmen?" Jemma asked, already lost at just the mention of golf.

"Over eight strokes," Sherry said acidly. "James always has to win. It's a flaw. One of many."

Mercer gave Sherry a crooked grin. "Since I'm sitting with you, I think we should table the discussion of Mr. Broward. It's obvious that his daughter is better mannered, and he's probably not worth the conversation."

It was Jemma's turn to have her jaw drop, but Sherry stuck her leg through the slit in her dress and nudged Mercer's chair out. "Grab a seat," she said with a smile. "I think I like you. So, are you always this plain-spoken?" Then she grabbed the nearest waiter and ordered a glass of MacAllen Twenty-Five.

"Thatta girl," Mercer said as he sat down.

"Woman," Sherry corrected, obviously over her initial bedazzlement.

"Young lady," Mercer replied. "I'm seventy-three years old. Pretty much every woman I meet except my wife is a girl in my eyes, so no need for offense. And to answer your question, I am who I am. I'm sorry if I've offended you."

Sherry chuckled. "No, not really. I like people who speak their minds. You always know where you stand."

"Good," Mercer replied, slapping the table. "I hate having to be coy with people. I do that all day in business. It's not in my nature, though."

Someone else at the table that Jemma didn't recognize got Mercer's attention, and Sherry turned to her date. "Oh, my god," she hissed. "You didn't tell me you knew Clint Mercer. He's a legend."

Jemma shuffled her feet, suddenly feeling a little off-kilter. "Yeah. I didn't realize he was so…uh…blunt. Sorry for that."

Sherry gave her a puzzled look. "What are you talking about? He's not one of my idols because of his manners. He funds an autism education foundation. The Mercer Artistic Scholarship Award helped pay for some of my tuition at Yale. He's my fucking hero."

Jemma blinked. "Oh. Wait, you went to Yale for your MFA?"

Sherry laughed. "Yeah. Don't be so shocked. I may be awkward and a clutz, but I'm not stupid."

"I think we've covered that," Jemma said seriously. "I think you're fabulous."

Sherry's expression softened, and a warm smile spread across her face. "I know." She placed her hand on Jemma's but pulled it back as her scotch arrived. "Oh, thank God," she murmured and took a sip. "Just what I needed. My nerves are already on edge."

Jemma frowned at that. "I thought you wanted to be here."

"I do, more than anything, especially with you. It's just there's a lot of people and a lot of money, and well…it's intimidating."

But I'm Not a Supervillain!!!

"Try to remember that they pull their pants on one leg at a time," Jemma said. "Tell you what, why don't we try the hors d'oeuvres?"

They stood and made their way to the massive hors d'oeuvre table just as six people entered the dining room from the back. Two had shotguns out. The others were all carrying sidearms.

"Wallets, watches, necklaces, bracelets, and earrings. On the table now. Phones in this bag," a tall blonde with a shotgun said, the supposed waitress that Jemma had spotted earlier.

"Every damn time," Jemma muttered under her breath.

Up close, Jemma realized why the blonde was familiar. She'd put her in jail a year ago. Her name was Catherine Capote. She was a low-rent supervillain who had enhanced strength and not much else. She was generally smart, though. This was an absolute disaster. With all the people around, Jemma could do nothing. She wouldn't let anyone die, but revealing herself would be a last resort.

One of the men began moving around with a bag, collecting phones. Jemma and Sherry had theirs out, waiting their turn. But when the guy strode toward Sherry and reached out to snatch her phone, Sherry balked. The guy yanked at it. Sherry yanked back, setting up a ridiculous tug of war.

"Let go," the thug hissed.

"Just give it to him," Jemma whispered, trying to keep things calm. "It's not worth the trouble."

But Sherry, ever stubborn, clutched her phone tighter. "Like hell," she muttered.

The robber tugged harder, but before he could get another word out, Sherry swung her left arm, backhanding him across the face. The man spun, staggered on jelly legs, and hit the floor with a dull thud. Jemma blinked in disbelief.

"Sherry!" she hissed, more amused than shocked, but Sherry simply shrugged, staring down at the unconscious man.

"They can't have my phone. I can't afford to replace it," she said flatly. With a determined expression, Sherry turned, grabbing the nearest plate—the massive shrimp platter from the buffet—and hurled it at the other thieves. The word pirates came to mind, but Jemma decided it was too grand for this bunch. Shrimp flew everywhere, smacking Capote square in the face.

"I'm allergic!" Capote gasped, stumbling back, spitting shellfish out of her mouth. Her face was already starting to swell, and she fell to the floor, dropping the shotgun and desperately trying to fling the shrimp away as her wheezing worsened.

"Seriously?!" Jemma exclaimed, stunned.

While Capote struggled, another rushed forward, only to step right into the big plate of foie gras, which Sherry had apparently knocked to the floor when she'd flung the seafood. The man's foot slid, and before he could regain his balance, he crashed into a steel support beam with a loud thunk, knocking himself out cold.

Jemma couldn't help herself. She barked a laugh.

The remaining guests, emboldened by either Sherry's ridiculous luck or the hapless nature of the thieves, rose from their seats to wrestle with the other thugs. Amidst the chaos, Jemma quietly moved through the crowd, slipping behind the bandits unnoticed. With quick, precise strikes—an elbow here, a punch there—she knocked the other three out, one by one, her super strength making quick work of it. No one even realized it was her.

When the dust settled, the last of the robbers lay unconscious on the floor, surrounded by shrimp and half-destroyed hors d'oeuvres. Sherry stood over the scene, catching her breath, while Jemma looked as cool and composed as ever.

"Well," Sherry said with a smirk, "that was… something."

Jemma simply smiled, her eyes gleaming. Finally, she laughed and shook her head, taking Sherry in her arms. "You really do ride with the angels, you know that?"

But I'm Not a Supervillain!!!

"What? It's my phone. My life is in there," Sherry said, and the genuine innocence in her expression made Jemma laugh all the harder.

Chapter Thirty-One

Jemma arrived at Police Headquarters, her heart still fluttering from thoughts of Sherry. The past few days had felt like an unbroken streak of pure, giddy joy—a kind she hadn't felt in years, maybe ever. She'd catch herself smiling at the smallest things: a memory of Sherry's laugh, the warmth of her hand, even the way Sherry scrunched her nose when she got serious. It was like every color around her had brightened, every sound softened, and every task seemed lighter. She was pretty sure that nothing could bring her down.

"I think I found our mysterious blonde," Tracy said as Jemma leaned against the wall heater behind her desk.

"Really?" Jemma crossed her arms and put her back to the window, letting the sun shine on her shoulders. It really was a beautiful day outside.

"So, you might want to sit down," Tracy said, her tone a little icy, her expression deadly serious. "I don't think you're going to like it."

Jemma pulled over a chair. "Okay, I'm sitting. So, who is it?"

"I did what you asked and looked into any hospital visits with strange illnesses that just magically vanished. I found exactly one." Tracy picked up a folder from her desk and handed it to Jemma.

Jemma opened the folder. All the color drained from her face. There, staring back at her, was a picture of Sherry

Broward. It was a shot of her at her graduation from Yale. Malka, pre-transformation, stood next to her, also in cap and gown, one arm around Sherry's shoulders. "That…that doesn't mean she stole the painting. It could have just been a poisoning, like the doctor said." Now that she said it, it sounded like a rationalization, even to her.

"There's more. I filed a warrant for your girlfriend's cell phone." Tracy held up a hand at Jemma's betrayed look. "I didn't have a choice, Jemma, you know that."

She handed over a sheaf of papers. Highlighted on the first page, in brilliant, damning yellow, was a single call the night of the heist: Malka. The second page had more highlights. Handwritten in the margin next to each one was the same name over and over: Mixxer.

Sherry leaned forward. She felt sick. She almost fell out of the chair, suddenly racked with fatigue and a gut-twisting feeling of betrayal. Sherry had all but told her. She'd been freaking out about her sudden bursts of strength. The shower handle. The doorknob. The man she'd knocked cold with a casual backhand on the harbor cruise.

"Jesus," Jemma whispered. "Shit."

"I'm sorry," Tracy said. "It doesn't look good, and there might be an explanation for all of this…"

"No," Jemma interjected. "It's her. She's the right height, and she is…or was, rather, the right build. I should have seen it. It was staring me in the face the whole time." All the muscle that Sherry had put on, seemingly out of nowhere. Jemma had been blind. No, she'd blinded herself to the possibility. And Malka had been in on it. Everything instantly fell into place. Setting aside that the paramedics had brought her back, Sherry had died. Her recovery was beyond miraculous. Who's up and walking without a mark on them three days after being poisoned to the point of dying? And what happened to the CPR bruising? She hadn't even noticed. "God, I'm stupid."

Tracy placed a hand on her knee and stooped over so she could look Jemma in the eye. "No. We see what we want to see. And from what you tell me, she seems sweet. Be careful before you judge her too harshly. From what I can tell, two years ago, her life was torn apart when Luke Luck plowed through Maxxie's. She had a juvenile record, but it's sealed."

"Boosting motorcycles," Jemma commented, her heart feeling as if it were in a vice. "She got arrested once for stealing a Harley."

"Well, she's been clean as a whistle ever since, so I don't know if…"

"She lied to me!" Jemma barked, her voice shrill. "All this time, she knew I was looking for that fucking painting, and she played stupid."

Tracy gave her a puzzled look. "You make it sound like that's irrational. She committed grand larceny. What did you expect her to say? 'Oh yeah, I've got the painting right here.'"

"Why are you defending her?" Jemma shot back hotly. "She's a lying, manipulative bitch."

Eyes wide, Tracy shifted her chair back slightly. "No, ma'am." She stated firmly. "You know better than that. And I'm not defending her. I had a juvenile record as a kid, too. It's never that simple. Anyway, what I'm trying to tell you is that, had I been in your shoes, I might have missed it, too, and I'd probably be just as angry. You'd be sitting right here trying to make me see that I wasn't stupid and she wasn't evil. Unfortunately, she is a criminal."

Jemma stood. "I have to talk to her."

"I don't think that's a good idea, Lena. You're angry."

"I'm not going to kill her," Jemma argued. "I just want to know the truth. Did I mean anything, or was she just stringing me along to stay ahead of the investigation? God, I'm so stupid."

Jemma stood and stalked to the stairs, taking them two at a time to the roof, where she lifted off into the night.

For a long time, she floated high above the city, well away from any flight patterns. Below her, the city stretched out in every direction. Tears rolled down her cheeks. Her chest hurt, and her stomach felt like a block of stone. She took a deep breath to steady herself. She needed to sit and think. So, she went to the top of Brattleman Tower and sat on the roof.

From the top of the building, the entire city came into

perspective. It helped calm her roiling emotions and gave her time to consider. Sherry had stolen the Rembrandt the night they'd met. The footprints had to be Malka's, so for some reason, Malka had been there. Jemma wouldn't think about why. It didn't matter.

Somehow, Sherry had been exposed to the Lot 429 knockoff in the painting. Unlike Jemma, though, her powers weren't manifesting all at once. They seemed to be coming in fits and spurts, and they were weak. At least so far. That's assuming, of course, that she hadn't been the guinea pig. Ivan's guys had killed Mixxer and his crew, which meant that Sherry would be next.

Jemma didn't bother to ponder more. Whatever she'd done, she cared for Sherry, might even love her, she didn't know. But she wasn't going to let a bunch of Bratva goons kill her. She shot off into the night, headed for Sherry's.

Chapter Thirty-Two

Sherry's phone rattled on the end table. She glanced at it and felt her chest sink in panic. She blinked slowly and took a deep, calming breath before answering, praying that this wouldn't go the way she expected. With trembling fingers, she lifted the phone and answered on speaker.

"Mixxer," she said, unable to keep the quaver from her voice. A firm knot twisted its way around her insides.

"Sherry Berry," he said, his voice jovial and polite, and yet still holding that grating edge she hated. "How's my favorite thief today?"

She clasped her hands to keep them from shaking. "Hi. . .um. . . What can I do for you?"

His voice dropped. It wasn't quite menacing, but neither was he happy. "So, you should have called me sooner. As it is, you've created some significant difficulties for me. Why on God's green earth did you leave it at Malka's?"

"I honestly thought it would be safe there," she said, a little of her courage returning. "I think a better question is how did Charlie and Mary know about it?"

Mixxer ignored the question. "She called me, you know."

Sherry swallowed around the lump as it returned to her throat. Her mouth abruptly parched, and she licked her lips, trying to wet them. "Oh? What did she have to say?"

"Well, she casually mentioned that she thought you were a

brilliant thief and could have a long career ahead of you. And, yes, she did tell me that those idiotic royalty try-hards stole the painting, but they couldn't have possibly known it was there. She said it was a territorial dispute."

Sherry had no idea. She supposed it was possible that it was a theft of opportunity. It wasn't as if they could wait around to ask questions. Charlie and Mary were going to kill them. "So, what now?"

"'What now,' is you are going to retrieve the painting for me," Mixxer said, giving the word 'you' an ominous emphasis. "I have made a deal to have it returned. Here's the address." He quickly rattled off an address for a building under construction in the seaport, and Sherry wrote it down.

"Got it," she confirmed and read it back to him.

"You have one chance to fix this, Sherry. Then I'll decide if we're square."

Sherry bristled at that. She didn't like being under anyone's thumb, and despite her better judgment, she said, "Wait, what do you mean 'decide'? I thought we were good. I thought we had a deal."

"I meant what I just said. However, if you can retrieve the Rembrandt for me and you can do so without any further complications, you will need to make good for a while. I have a few problems that need solving."

Sherry nodded quickly and sniffed back tears. She would be in debt to Mixxer forever. She knew that. Her life of crime wasn't over; it had just begun, and there was nothing she could do. "I understand. Am I still getting paid?"

There was a long pause. "I always pay my debts, of that I assure you. You'll get your money. I may take a small fee for my inconvenience, say twenty-five percent."

"Mixxer, I was trying to protect both our interests. Twenty-five percent seems steep."

His tone softened back to his usual business demeanor: super fucking annoying. "Perhaps, and, in principle, I agree that it should have been acceptable, and yet, it was not. Sad really. But this is the reason I wanted to have my crew steal it." That niggled at Sherry. She hated that Mixxer had been right.

She hadn't had enough experience to do this. "But," he continued brightly. "You did successfully steal the Rembrandt, so that's something. And I'm sure you learned quite a bit. Still, though, it's twenty-five."

Sherry didn't argue with him. "Why aren't we on video call?" Sherry asked, just looking for something to poke at.

"Data service here is atrocious, Sherry Berry," Mixxer said. "Does it matter?"

"No," Sherry answered, dejected.

"Good. Now, do as I ask, and we'll see what we can work out, pet."

"Fine." Sherry disconnected and scowled at the phone. She hated when people called her pet, especially like that. Mixxer had never been quite that condescending before.

Sherry went into her closet and found a pair of black leggings, a black T-shirt, her motorcycle jacket, and knee-high motorcycle boots. She did up her makeup a little on the goth side and checked out her appearance. She looked badass, though a little more cute than she would have liked, but what could she do with that round face? Not much. All the contouring in the world wouldn't make her face any more narrow. Still, though, it was a good look.

As she admired her appearance, her mood improved dramatically. This would all be over soon, she thought. Yeah, she might have to help Mixxer with a couple more jobs, but at least she'd be flush with cash. He did say he'd pay her, and Malka said that he always stuck to his deals. All in all, he'd been far more forgiving than she'd expected.

She stopped and stroked Breit. The cat stared at her from the bed with his bright, mismatched eyes. "You're a good one," she whispered as she kneaded his cheeks. "And with any luck, all this will be over, and I won't have to worry about Jemma finding out. Now take care of Barry for me. I'll be back soon, and we'll see about a place where the appliances don't fall apart."

Another thing occurred to her down in the parking deck as she fired up her bike. She had a job. It was an illegal job, but it would pay a shitload better than the cafe. Yeah, it wasn't part of her plan, but plans changed, and she would just have to settle for being in Mixxer's debt for a bit, whatever that turned out to be.

Jemma hovered just off the balcony, her arms crossed and her thoughts on fire after hearing the exchange between Sherry and whoever was pretending to be Mixxer.

"Oh, Sherry," she whispered to herself. "What did you get yourself into?" Lips in a thin line, she watched Sherry go about her business, getting dressed, cuddling with the cat, and grabbing her helmet and keys. The whole time, all Jemma could think about was how she would get back the painting and get the 429 to the Feds.

Now that she'd had time to think, her anger had softened. It didn't matter that she was Lena Swift, and the hard stone of betrayal in her gut wasn't reasonable. Sherry had never outright lied to her. Sherry had been nothing but nice and kind. Yeah, she was dumb, or so it seemed, getting involved with Mixxer, but she couldn't believe that Sherry had the kind of twisted mind to play her like that. She wouldn't believe it, and listening to Sherry on the phone, it was clear she was way over her head.

Jemma should warn her that Mixxer was dead. She should go in and lay it all on the table, but she didn't. She had to get the Lot 429 back; that was the priority. As much as Jemma hated it, she'd have to let Sherry walk into something that, Jemma hoped, wasn't a death trap.

She waited until Sherry was on her bike and followed her from above, staying in her blind spot directly overhead. Sherry eventually stopped at a construction site in the Seaport District, not far from Maxxie's, and Jemma pulled back to assess the situation.

While Jemma watched, Sherry made her way onto the site, quickly navigating the closed but unlocked construction gate. Beyond, Sherry parked her bike next to the green Jaguar and the black panel van. She walked inside the construction office, a one-story double-wide portable on cinder blocks. With a frown and a deep sigh, Jemma floated down and silently followed a few minutes later.

"Hello?" Sherry called from somewhere ahead. It sounded like she was in one of the offices off the main hallway.

Jemma crept along, listening to see if she could hear any conversation. There was none. The entire place was like a tomb, silent and foreboding. A shiver crept up Jemma's spine. This was bad. Something was very wrong here. If Jemma was supposed to meet Charlie and Mary here, then where were they? Their cars were outside, but none of their guards were anywhere to be seen. Her gut sank like a stone as she realized something else was missing. There wasn't a single bark. The dogs were silent. It didn't make any sense unless, of course, it was a trap. And the air, it smelled like—

"Holy fuck!" Sherry cried, and Jemma darted through the hall to the back office.

Sherry stood just inside the doorway, staring at the floor where King Charles, Bloody Mary, and their henchmen lay slaughtered. Even the dogs were dead. Sherry had the back of her hand to her mouth, and tears flowed over her lashes.

"This is what happens when you get involved with career criminals," Jemma said softly.

Startled, Sherry leaped back and placed a hand to her chest, nearly tripping over the outstretched foot of one of the corpses. "Holy shit! Don't creep up on me like that."

Jemma stared at her, arms crossed. "What are you doing here, Ms. Broward? What have you gotten into?"

"I—I—" Sherry stammered and looked down, back at the pile of bodies. "Jesus, what happened? And those poor dogs."

"I asked you a question," Jemma insisted, stepping forward and putting a hand on Sherry's shoulder, tugging the other woman around to face her. "Why are you here?"

Sherry closed her eyes and lowered her head, flushed with shame. "I fucked up," she whispered, voice cracking with either guilt or fear. Jemma wasn't sure, probably both.

"You were the thief. You stole the Rembrandt."

But I'm Not a Supervillain!!!

"How do you know my name?" Sherry asked, her eyes finally registering something other than shock.

Jemma narrowed her eyes and raised her voice, her incredulity evident in her tone. "That's what you're worried about?! Look at this! These people are dead! And more are going to die if I don't get that painting back… or, more importantly, the frame!"

Sherry opened her mouth to respond, but nothing came out. She looked at her right palm and then closed it. "Well, these guys stole it," she muttered, finally seeming to understand the gravity of her situation. "Someone stole it from them."

"Yeah, so it would seem. So, why are you here?" Jemma just wanted to see if Sherry would lie.

"I got a call. I was told I would find it here. Oh my God!" Sherry turned around and bolted for the door.

"What is it?" Jemma asked, moving in front of her and blocking her way out.

"My friend. If they knew it would be here, then she's in danger."

Jemma raised an eyebrow. "Or your friend killed them." Jemma all but spat the word friend, giving it an ugly, demeaning sound.

"No! She wouldn't do that!" Sherry said.

"Who are you trying to convince?" Jemma asked, her eyebrow still firmly planted on her forehead and a hand out toward Sherry's chest. "You know what? I'm tired of this." Jemma reached up to pull off her scarf and mask. Consequences be damned. Her fingers had just reached the silk when all holy hell broke loose.

The front of the building exploded in a hail of gunfire, artillery fire, you name it. Holes appeared everywhere. If Lena hadn't been in front of her, Sherry would have been riddled. As it was, a few of the bullets passed close enough to send drywall and wooden splinters spraying onto Sherry's face and hair.

"Get down," Lena said, shoving her roughly to the carpet and taking off. She wasn't gone long as she came sailing backward through the wall and landed next to Sherry in a heap.

"You okay?" Sherry whimpered as the hail of bullets continued.

"Yeah," Lena said with an irritated expression. "That idiot, Il Douchebag, is out there. He hit me with a car door."

Sherry couldn't help herself, she barked a laugh. "You mean Il Duce? The eight-hundred-pound boxer?"

"Yes, be right back." Lena drew herself up and flew out through the hole she just made. The gunfire stopped abruptly, and there was a lot of grunting and pounding outside that shook the building and sent tiles down from the drop-ceiling.

"I don't need to be here," Sherry said to herself as she drew herself up to run. Hopefully, no one would shoot anymore before she could get out of the crappy little trailer. A loud bang from outside startled her as she entered the hallway, and she turned to look. Another loud boom made her flinch, and something hit her hard in the gut. She stumbled backward with the shock of it and fell, the wind knocked out of her. She'd been shot.

She expected the world to turn black or for the pain in her gut to flare, like in the books she'd read, but there was neither. Remarkably, whatever had hit her obviously hadn't been hard enough to hurt her, and the pain died quickly. She looked down at her stomach and almost puked.

The hole in her leather jacket was enormous, easily the size of a grapefruit or maybe a large orange. The skin beneath was bright red but otherwise unmarred. The monstrous shell, she certainly couldn't call it a bullet, she didn't think, lay in her lap. Bits of brass surrounded it, but the bullet itself looked split like a banana peel.

"Get up!" Lena said, appearing from nowhere and dragging her roughly out of the hallway and into a side room. "Are you okay? Are you hit?"

Sherry blinked in shock. "What?"

"Are you hurt?" Lena shouted over the resuming gunfire.

She shook her head. "No. No, I'm okay. But—"

Lena was gone in a blast of wind that rattled the walls.

Sherry stayed put and pulled her legs up to her chest. She looked at the blue mark on her left hand again and then back at the hole in her jacket. "Oh, shit," she breathed.

Something hit her in the head and bounced off. "Ow!" she grumped, rubbing the top of her head. It felt like a golf ball. Glancing around the floor, she spotted another bullet, also deformed like the first, but much smaller this time. Her heart stopped, and her stomach fell. It didn't take a genius to understand why everyone wanted that fucking painting.

"Okay, I gotta get you out of here. Viktor's down, but not for long," Lena said as she slid back into the room. She reached down and hoisted Sherry off the floor.

That was as far as they got. Sherry's ears rang with the explosion. The world twisted away from her. Then, she was lying on her back under a massive girder, staring at the sky, the wind knocked out of her. The construction shed and the top four floors of the building next to it were gone. The remaining concrete and steel teetered precariously above her. She was pinned, barely able to breathe, and she couldn't wiggle out from under the girder. Lifting it was out of the question. Her clothes were a blasted wreck of fabric bits that clung to her body.

"Oh, God," a voice said near her. She couldn't see her, but she knew that Lena had survived. Slowly, Lena stood and coughed. Dust and debris covered her and caked her face. Lena's outfit was remarkably still in one piece, at least mostly. It had several holes and a few long rents. Her handwraps were shredded, though.

"Fuck," Lena muttered, and Sherry thought she heard her hiccup a sob. "Fuck, fuck, fuck. No." She sounded distraught, tossing bits of debris away, searching around.

"Hey," Sherry coughed, finally getting air from her traumatized diaphragm. "A little help."

Lena's head turned and stared at her, eyes wide. "Sherry? You—you're alive!"

Gone was Lena's midwestern nothing accent, replaced by

crisp British. Sherry blinked and spotted something on Lena's left arm. There, on the wrist, was a tattoo, a stylized and pretty red compass rose. Sherry closed her eyes and laid back. "Are you fucking kidding me?" She breathed. She shook her head at the irony of it all. No wonder she'd been so taken with Jemma's ass. Her voice sharpened into a wry tone. "Can I get a bit of help here—Lena!"

Chapter Thirty-Three

Jemma looked down at her and then back at the pile of men. With a quick glance over the piled rubble to ensure that Il Duce was indeed still unconscious, she lifted the girder off of Sherry, tossing it aside before picking her up and leaping into the air, shooting into the sky above Harborhaven.

"Oh, God," Sherry wheezed. "I'm going to be sick." Sherry squeezed Jemma, holding on for dear life.

"Please don't," Jemma whispered as they darted across the harbor toward the Pillar District.   Moments later, Jemma touched down softly on the rear balcony of her tiny apartment off of Corinthian Street. "We're here; you can open your eyes now."

Sherry cracked an eyelid and glanced around. They were on a charming little balcony, surrounded by wooden railing. Bare trellises rose up on either end of the deck in a criss-cross fashion, and little metal fairies hung from the gutters. It was adorable.

Through the gray dust and grit on her face, Jemma smiled at her. "You okay?"

Sherry nodded and smiled back.

"Cool," Jemma said and then dropped Sherry on her ass. "How long have you been an art thief? And how long have you been a super? I feel like such an idiot. Jesus, Sherry."

Rubbing her butt, Sherry stood. "Um. . . So, the Rembrandt

was my first heist. I needed the money." Of course, that was only part of it. "And as for the other thing. . . I didn't know. Not until today."

Jemma stood there and glared daggers at Sherry, arms crossed.

Sherry cringed. "I'm sorry. I wanted to tell you—" Sherry stopped abruptly and looked down. She needed to tell Jemma the truth if she'd salvage anything of their—whatever this was. She didn't know, but she didn't want it to end. "No, that's a lie. I wanted to get rid of the painting so you'd never know. It's not my career or anything. I'm not an art thief."

Her girlfriend just gave her a wry look. "So, where is it?"

Sherry cringed again. "Um. . . Would you believe I don't know?"

Jemma continued to glare, then stomped inside the sliding glass door. Sherry followed her through the tiny apartment, appointed with all kinds of retro stuff like a globe, some bookshelves that looked from an ancient library, and a desk that Charles Dickens might have used if she didn't know better. A tiny twin-sized futon mattress lay curled up in one corner.

"You live here?" Sherry asked, but Jemma didn't answer.

Finally, they reached a bathroom where Jemma began scrubbing ash and crap off her face in the sink. There was also a bit of blood.

"Oh my God," Sherry breathed in shocked surprise. "You're bleeding—and—and you have a black eye."

"Il Douchebag hits hard," Jemma replied in a low voice, still washing her face. "It'll be fine by morning. So you were saying?"

"Oh, yeah. So, here's what happened." Sherry quickly related the story about the painting, Malka, the corgis, finding the little vial of blue goo in the back of it, and Mixxer's ultimatum.

When she was done, Jemma shook her head and gave a dry, sad bark of laughter. "You suck as a thief," she said. "Why don't you find a job in the art world? Good grief, Sherry."

"You gonna turn me in?" Sherry asked sheepishly. "I wasn't

trying to get into all this. I was just broke. Malka took everything I had, and I lost my job a few months ago. This economy sucks, you know."

Jemma stared at her, disbelief all over her face. "Of course, I'm going to turn you in. You've stolen a priceless Rembrandt, nearly caused an international incident, and put the city in more danger than you can imagine. Not to mention the fact that you're an unregistered super. We have a name for people like you. Super. Villain." She emphasized both words before her tone shifted to something more world-weary. "But it can wait until tomorrow. I'm tired. I just got into a grudge-match with a quarter-ton Russian boxer with a fist the size of my head, a shitty attitude toward women, and a stupid Italian moniker. I need sleep." She started to strip out of her clothes and turned on the shower. Without turning around, she said. "I'll understand if you're not here when I come out. I don't feel like another fight, especially not with you."

Sherry stared at the floor. "I'm sorry," she muttered. "I'm not that person. I'm not a villain."

Jemma whirled on her, face burning, as if to say something else, but then she just shook her head, turned around, and climbed into the shower.

Sherry left her there, thinking it wise to say no more. She thought about calling a ride-share and just going home, but she wanted to talk to someone who might understand. Poor Breit was probably worried sick, but still, she found an old landline on the desk and dialed the number she least wanted to call.

"Hello?" Malka's Russian cadence was quiet and reserved.

Sherry spoke in subdued tones—small. "Um. . . Can I ask you to come get me? I'm in trouble."

There was a long silence on the other end before Malka came back, her voice kind and gentle. "Of course. Tell me where you are."

"Meet me at the Pillar," Sherry said as tears started to flow, and she swallowed hard. "I'll be there in about fifteen minutes." With a last glance through the bathroom doorway toward the shower curtain and Jemma's silhouette, Sherry left through the front door and followed the exterior stairs down to the ground.

"Good God, Sher," Malka said as the window of her limo rolled down. "What happened to you?"

Sherry swatted at her tears. "Only the worst night of my life. Lena Swift busted me, and Jemma dumped me."

"That can't be all. You're barely clothed? Is this the new emo look, or were you in an explosion?"

Sherry cracked a wry, empty smirk. "It's hard to explain." The last thing she wanted anyone to know was that she was a super. Besides, it might go away. She hoped it would go away. It was the last thing she wanted. "I went to get the Rembrandt, and those Russian idiots were waiting for me. Lena Swift was following them. But the Rembrandt wasn't there, and now I'm stuck. No Rembrandt. Mixxer's going to kill me," *if he can*, she added in her head. "And Lena Swift knows I'm an art thief. And did I mention that Jemma does now, too? That's why she dumped me."

"Wait, how did Jemma find out?" Malka asked.

Sherry wanted to tell Malka everything, but she couldn't. She wouldn't. Maybe Jemma would turn Sherry in, but she'd never tell a soul who she was. It was just—wrong. "She was investigating the case."

Malka twitched slightly in surprise. "Of all the dumb luck, sweetcakes. That sucks."

"Yeah," Sherry said and leaned against Malka, who wrapped an arm around her.

"Do you want me to take you somewhere safe?" Malka asked softly as they pulled away from the ridiculous monument.

"No," she said. "Just take me home. I need to get some sleep, and Breit needs me."

Malka looked disappointed, but she nodded and called up to her driver, "East Meridian and Grove, Transport District."

"Yes, ma'am," the driver replied, and then he raised the privacy shield.

"You know why paintings make a good means of smuggling for small things?" Malka asked.

Sherry's gaze shot to Malka's eyes, and something there terrified her. Those glowing yellow eyes seemed sharper, more penetrating, almost predatory. It made Sherry's voice tremble as she spoke in an almost hoarse whisper. "Because as long as it's small and the painting is being delivered gallery to gallery, it can bypass inspection."

"Correct. And the Met, being, well, The Met, has transfer agreements with every major gallery in the world. One could put almost anything inside." Malka's voice took on a sly, oily tone. "Like expensive and experimental chemicals. The kind that the US government would prefer not to acknowledge existed."

"What chemical?" Sherry asked, trying and failing to keep her breathing steady. This conversation wasn't going at all where she thought it would, and little lightbulbs were starting to turn on in her head.

"Say, a formula to make another Lena Swift. But, as I said, such a thing would be extremely experimental." Malka stroked the side of Sherry's face, and despite the sweet smile, Sherry could hear the superior tone in her voice, as if Sherry were all hers to do with as she saw fit. "It likely has side effects, you know?"

Sherry's heart sped up. "What—" her voice cracked, and she cleared her throat. "What side effects?"

"Depends on the person, I would think," Malka replied, her tail snaking around Sherry's leg. "But apparently, they're never good. Hypothetically speaking, of course."

Sherry gave Malka an annoyed look and lifted off her shoulder. "Stop, Mal. I'm not doing this."

Malka grinned mischievously and pinched Sherry's cheeks. "Sorry, Sweetcakes, it has a mind of its own, I'm afraid. And it just loves unregistered supers."

Malka's tail slid up over her knee. Sherry glanced down, meaning to push the thing off, but Malka's free hand slapped a cloth across her mouth and nose. Sherry got a solid whiff of chloroform before the world winked out.

Chapter Thirty-Four

Jemma stared at the ceiling. She needed sleep, but she knew that was a lost cause. She'd heard Sherry make the phone call —knew who it was she'd called. Jemma couldn't blame her. Sherry needed a shoulder to cry on.

"Fuck," she grumbled, letting her forearm rest above her head. Well, at least she didn't have to worry about Sherry getting hurt. That was a plus. A big plus, really. The fact that she was classed as a supervillain was a considerable minus.

She thought about Sherry and how inept she seemed at times. Despite the seriousness of it all, the adorable way that Sherry had asked if Jemma would turn her in had been like a kid caught stealing a cookie by her big sister. It made Jemma chuckle, inside at least. Sherry had this adorable smile that tickled Jemma in all the right places. She was sweet. What an idiot, Jemma thought, and she didn't mean Sherry. She couldn't send Sherry to prison. Then she really would be classed as a supervillain, an ETE or Enhanced Threat Entity, as the FBI called them. They'd give her a number, 897, if Jemma's memory was correct—that was the next one. Of course, who knew how they were describing them these days?

None of that actually bothered her. Sherry Broward, a local street kid, had stolen a priceless Rembrandt in a two-foot by two-foot metal frame straight from the Met, and no one had noticed it was missing for two hours.

"Damn," Jemma murmured. Despite her goofy demeanor and the dumb stuff she did occasionally, Sherry was brilliant. Jemma needed to talk to her before Malka convinced her to work for her and, by extension, the Russian Mob. Maybe she could find a way to get Sherry out of this mess.

Jemma pulled herself out of bed, put on a spare outfit, flight goggles, and flew out into the night.

An hour later, she plowed through the window at Sin City. She'd stopped at Sherry's expecting to find her in tears, or at least upset. Sherry had looked like a kicked puppy when she'd left. But her apartment was empty, and Jemma had a bad feeling.

Malka's office was likewise vacant, and Jemma frowned. She wasn't jealous—not exactly, though the idea that Sherry might have sought a different kind of comfort in Malka did make her feel a niggle of betrayal. No, Sherry had gotten a call from someone pretending to be Mixxer telling her to meet Charlie and Mary at the construction building. Then Ivan's men had shown up with Il Duce. And what had Malka said when she'd mentioned Il Duce? Something about her dislike of the man being mutual?

She made the rounds of the upstairs rooms, still working her brain into a lather over what she knew. Sherry had stolen the Rembrandt. Sherry said her powers were new. Sherry had bitched about breaking the shit in the apartment. She'd had no clue that she was developing powers—powers just like Jemma's.

"Fuck," Jemma swore. "What am I missing?" She needed to find Ivan and get him to talk. He would have the answers she sought, but no one had seen him in months.

Jemma marched back into Malka's office and rifled across her desk. "Doesn't this woman have a fucking file cabinet? Or a damn computer?" But there was nothing, just a few shipping invoices for booze and a manifest from a cargo ship, "The Severnyy Star," out of Minsk. Sherry put her knuckles to her mouth.

She looked back at the shipping manifest. She pulled out her phone and hit the icon for the aptly named Suzie: Your AI

Assistant.

"Hello, Ms. Swift, how may I assist you today?" the soft AI voice said. It was cheerful and yet slithery in a seductive kind of way. It reminded her of that movie she could never remember the title of, the one with Scarlett Johansson—friendly and sweet but with a sneaky sort of sex appeal. She snapped a shot of the manifest.

"Translate this, please," Jemma said into the phone. She cringed. She needed to stop using this thing so much, she'd just said please to a big fat database. Of course, it sounded so human she sometimes forgot. The app made some tapping noises, and then, a few seconds later, it began reading out the manifest.

"This is a cargo manifest for The Severnyy Star out of St. Petersburg by way of Rotterdam. The date appears to be incorrect. It details a cargo shipment delivered to Rotterdam seven days from today. It shows seventy tons of aluminum, three-hundred-fifty cases of rum—"

Jemma hit the interrupt button. A Russian ship wouldn't be carrying aluminum or rum, not from Rotterdam. They were shipping something else, and a lot of it. This was a bogus manifest to be swapped out when the ship arrived in Rotterdam. "Who owns the Severynyy Star? Check the Internet, please." Jemma added that last because Suzie would just make something up if she didn't.

"The Severnyy Star is owned by Hanover Imports, a subsidiary of SC Limited, Harborhaven. SC Limited is co-owned by Malgorzata Morozov and Aurora Capital Ventures."

She didn't know who Malgorzata Morozov was, but she had a hunch. She did, however, know who Aurora Capital Ventures was: Ivan, Viktor, and Dmitry Rostovich. It all made a terrible sort of sense. Malka had known all along about the Rembrandt. Mixxer had gotten wind of it and hired Sherry to steal it. Malka had wanted the serum, but somehow, Sherry was exposed. The Royal Family had found out about the painting and its contents, which is why they were dead. Malka was going to kill Sherry, and if the 429 knockoff worked like Jemma's formula, there was only one sure way to kill her.

"Suzie, you still there?" Jemma asked. Then she grimaced. Of course, it was still there.

"What waterfront properties does Aurora Venture Capital own in Harborhaven?"

Suzie rattled off a list of residential condo buildings. "No," Jemma muttered. "They wouldn't take her to a residential building. They'd take her someplace where they could hold her, but it would definitely be right on the water."

"Malgorzata Morozov is the owner of a warehouse on West National Drive," Suzie chirped.

Jemma hit the stop button. She hadn't intended that to be a question, but the Suzie app had the best model in the business, which was why Jemma used it. She stuffed her phone in her hip pocket, sucked in a deep breath, and flew out the window, rattling the windows all around Caster Square as she broke the sound barrier and hoping her uniform didn't shred along the way.

Chapter Thirty-Five

Sherry struggled with the chains, but it was pointless. They were huge, monstrous, clearly designed to hold someone much stronger. Maybe she was suddenly hard to kill, but she wasn't super strong or super fast or super anything else. She was just Sherry Broward, Art Certification Specialist turned would-be thief and a bad one at that. So, she just lay there, trussed up like a pig in a blanket. She struggled to adjust herself as the chains were pressing on her chest and making it difficult to breathe. With any luck, they'd suffocate her and put her out of her misery. Of course, they had to be ice cold, like the floor she lay on.

Sherry looked around as best she could. At least they hadn't chained her head. She was in a warehouse. A few scattered crates lay around, along with two large cargo containers stacked in one corner. Above hung a disused bridge crane that looked like it hadn't been operational since the forties. Several of the windows were broken. And through one, she could see the light of the harbor comms tower. She chuckled. She knew right where she was, two blocks from Kelly's, not that it did her any good. Heels clacked on the pavement behind her. Someone was approaching.

"I'm sorry, Sweetcakes," Malka said. "I wish I didn't have to do this. I really do. It wasn't supposed to go this way. But, you're a shitty burglar; you know that? Still, though, you show a lot of promise. You just need to up your endgame."

"You know," Sherry wheezed, though her breathing felt just a little easier. "That's not the first time I've heard that, this evening even. Maybe the Rembrandt was a bad choice, but it was the only thing in my size."

"Clever," Malka giggled. She crouched down, one hand lightly rolling Sherry onto her back. "Better?"

Sherry nodded, though her lips were still pursed in agitation. "You know you could just take them off."

"These were supposed to be for someone much worse than you, you know," she murmured, her eyes briefly meeting Sherry's with a hint of guilt.

"But why do this?" Sherry asked, struggling to breathe. "After everything…"

"Because it's too late to go back," Malka said softly. "But… part of me wishes I could." She sighed. "As for you… you were never my enemy, Sherry. But she—she leaves me no choice."

Sherry's eyes went wide, and she tried to wiggle free, but she could barely move. "I won't be your bait."

A silky laugh slid over Sherry's skin as Malka bent over, examining her. "Too late. She's coming. I happily left clues for her to follow, even."

"As for you, after I deal with Jemma…"

"Leave her alone. I'll stay with you. Do whatever you want!" Sherry blurted, her voice pleading. She had no idea what Malka had in mind, but if she wasn't running, she thought she had an edge.

Malka's face softened, her usual veneer of confidence wavering. "It's too late for that, Pet," she murmured, a trace of sadness in her voice. "I can see how much she means to you—and that hurts more than you know." Her gaze dropped, a flicker of vulnerability breaking through. "I always knew someone would come along, someone who could offer you a better life than I could. I just… never expected it to be her." She spat the word out, bitterness lacing her tone. "Why *her*?"

Sherry's mind reeled, her anger giving way to confusion. "What does it matter who…." Her voice trailed off as memories of the night at Sin City came flooding back. The way Jemma and Malka poked at each other over drinks—she'd thought it was just new-girlfriend, ex-girlfriend rivalry. But now, the subtext hit her like a slap, and she cursed herself for not seeing it sooner. Everything had been right in front of her: all those pointed glances and mocking words. And now, when it was far too late, she finally understood. "Oh, my God. You and Jemma."

Malka's lips tightened, and she gave a small, bitter nod. "Yes. Shortly after we broke up. She was alone and hurting. I was…well, where I was." Her eyes flashed with a mixture of anger and regret. "It was a one-night stand, and besides, I wouldn't let myself try to settle down again after what I'd done to you.

"You know, it's funny. I had thought I was over it, but then when I heard about your job, I felt something. I missed you. I tried to bring you into my world, but that just pushed you further into hers. It's infuriating. And now, I have to fix this before this complete cock-up buries me, too."

Sherry's eyes widened, realizing what Malka meant, the horror settling in. "You can't—Malka, please, don't do this. We can still find a way!"

Malka shook her head slowly, a look of helplessness crossing her face. "There's no other way, Sweetcakes. You're too close now; you know too much. If I let you go…" She paused for a moment, and Sherry thought she saw the glimmer of tears floating in Malka's eyes. "If I let you go, it's me they'll take."

Sherry sighed, but then her brain caught up to what Malka had said. "Wait. Bring me into your world? You hired Mixxer!" Sherry cursed herself mentally.

"That's my girl," Malka said, her voice bittersweet. "You always tease out the answer in the end. Yes, I had Mixxer arrange the heist. It was my job, sure, but I picked you for a reason. I wanted you close, Sherry. You're the smartest person I know. You had the brains we needed. And I thought… if you got a taste of this life, you'd understand me, maybe even want to be part of it." She paused, letting out an exasperated sigh.

"It doesn't matter, now. It's all pear-shaped, damn it."

Sherry lay there, still stunned. "That's how you knew I had it. That's why you just came and took it."

"I had an insider at the Met who told me the moment it was missing. And as soon as he did, I knew it was you. Mixxer needed five men. But you? You did it alone with your eyes closed."

Raising an eyebrow, Sherry craned her neck to follow Malka's movements as she walked around her. "But then, Charlie? And Mary? And why did you kill the dogs? The dogs didn't hurt anyone."

"I'm more of a cat person, you know that," Malka said wryly as if that explained it. "And Mixxer knew what was in the frame. He sold us both out to Charlie and Mary. So, he had to die. He was a two-bit fence who crossed the wrong woman. The same was true for Charlie and Mary. I would like to say I feel bad about them, but as they say about omelets and eggs."

Sherry frowned. "Wait, Mixxer's dead?"

"Oh, do catch up, darling." Malka dropped down and sat on Sherry's hips. From that angle, she looked like a giant, especially with her wings fanned. "Hey, Sherry Berry," She said in a perfect imitation of Mixxer's voice. "What do you think? Could I take it on the road?"

"You almost got me killed."

"That wasn't intended. We were there so I could confront you with the truth, show you how far you'd gone. Make you understand. But then she showed up, and Viktor...he went crazy."

"Ivan doesn't know about any of this, does he?" Sherry asked, still stalling for time, trying to keep her talking and hoping Malka would give her something she could use. Some bit of leverage that would get Malka to let her go...and leave Jemma alone. Malka didn't take reckless chances. If she thought she could kill Jemma, she probably could.

"Ivan died three months ago from a heart attack," Malka said. At Sherry's scandalized expression, she added. "I had nothing to do with it. He was old and fat. Though, honestly, it was convenient. I took over his interests and have made far more of his operation than he ever could."

A set of aircraft-sized doors opened at one end of the warehouse, stopping their conversation and ending Sherry's stalling. She looked up and saw an SUV pull in.

"That'll be Victor," Malka said.

"What are you going to do to me?" Sherry asked, the edge of panic in her voice.

"We'll try to make it as painless as possible. I can't use what I have planned for Jemma, so there's only one other way."

Sherry's eyes turned to dinner plates as she got it. "No! No, Malka, you can't." She didn't want to die like that: alone, in the dark…and the bitter cold.

One sagging corner of the SUV lifted as the monstrous Russian, Il Duce, squeezed out of the rear passenger seat. He still had quite the shiner under one eye, about the size of Jemma's fist. Malka lifted off her and strode toward Il Duce.

"Shit," Sherry breathed and tried to struggle. The chains weren't as heavy as she thought. It was probably the after-effects of the chloroform that had made them seem that way, but for all her straining, all they did was rattle. "Shit. Shit. Shit," she squealed, still trying to get loose.

With a deafening roar, a section of the ceiling buckled and then exploded inward. Jemma slammed to the ground with enough force to send a shockwave through the floor. The entire building shuddered and creaked from the impact. Chunks of buckled metal and torn aluminum rained down in her wake. "You okay, love?" she called, glancing back at Sherry through the settling dust, her eyes blazing.

Shocked, Sherry just blinked. "Jemma, thank God. It's a trap."

Jemma smirked. "You think?"

"Well, get me out of these," Sherry griped, wiggling enough to jangle the chains. "Let's get out of here."

"Come get some, bitch!" Il Duce shouted, his voice echoing in the wide-open warehouse.

Jemma's expression shifted from cocky confidence to outright fury. She turned and shot across the warehouse with a loud crack, hammering Il Duce with a right hook before he could get his arms up. He slammed back into a steel support, causing the entire building to groan violently. He didn't go down, but that hit rocked his world.

Malka took that moment to rummage through one of the containers behind her, where she pulled out a nasty-looking rifle with a long cord. Sherry struggled in the chains again, trying to get loose. She couldn't do anything about Il Duce, but she could do something about Malka. Clearly, Malka thought that weapon was her ace in the hole. Sherry tried to shout a warning, but caught in combat, Jemma couldn't hear her.

Jemma loosed a brutal barrage on Il Duce, battering him relentlessly. The man was tough and strong, but he wasn't fast, he wasn't particularly agile, and he couldn't fly. Jemma, on the other hand, was all those things, and she was pounding him to dust.

Sherry remembered the videos of Jemma fighting with various villains. She always seemed to be holding back, trying not to hurt them. She was going to kill; Sherry could see it in her face. Jemma was like an angry honey badger. Every hit Il Duce landed just seemed to piss her off more. By contrast, Il Duce was already bleeding from a dozen cuts; his face had swelled more, and he looked a bit punch-drunk. In moments, Il Duce was down and struggling just to lift his body.

A thunderclap echoed through the warehouse, wringing dust from the damaged ceiling and rattling pebbles from the floor. To Sherry's shock, Jemma dropped like a stone, landing in a heap on the ground, a gaping hole in her left shoulder. Blood poured from it. Sherry glanced back at Malka, who had the rifle connected to some kind of fat backpack on the ground next to her. A green light climbed up the barrel toward the tip.

Malka did take a moment to gloat then. "This is an M303 US Military issue rail gun made by Stahler Energy," Malka said, a vicious gleam in her eye. "It fires chunks of depleted uranium wrapped in magneto-ferrous metal. They were deemed impractical for the battlefield by the military years ago, but the rise of supers has, it seems, changed their point of view."

Il Duce was still struggling to rise. Jemma was pulling herself off the ground. The hole in her shoulder—and it was a significant hole—was starting to close, but it wouldn't be enough.

For Sherry, the world turned a nasty shade of red, and the only thing she wanted for all the world was to kill Malka Morozov and her beefcake sidekick.

But I'm Not a Supervillain!!!

significant hole—was starting to close, but it wouldn't be enough.

For Sherry, the world turned a nasty shade of red, and the only thing she wanted for all the world was to kill Malka Morozov and her beefcake sidekick.

Chapter Thirty-Six

One minute, Jemma was beating Il Duce to a pulp; the next, she was lying on the ground, her left arm hanging uselessly at her side. The pain was unimaginable, like nothing she'd felt since her transformation. She groaned in agony and coughed. Blood spattered onto the ground. Whatever had hit her had been moving like a meteor and left a massive hole. The only thing that saved her was that it had missed her heart, probably by a few inches, but she couldn't move very well, and the building started to swim even as the pain ebbed. She was going into shock, she knew, but she had no way to stop it. She just tried to muscle herself awake.

The ominous click of Malka's heels on the concrete sounded muffled and strange, like it was in slow motion.

"This is an M303 US Military issue rail gun made by Stahler Energy," Malka said. Jemma could hear the malicious glee in her voice. "It fires chunks of depleted uranium wrapped in magneto-ferrous steel. They were deemed impractical for the battlefield by the military years ago, but the rise of supers has, it seems, changed their point of view."

Jemma struggled and raised her head. Through the haze, she could see Il Duce pulling himself up. *Shit. We're fucked.* She'd left Sherry chained up because it would keep her out of the way, and, secondarily, she needed her to stick around so they could figure out how to get her out of this mess. That had been foolish. Now, they were both going to die.

"That won't kill me," Jemma lied with a grunt, stalling for time. "I'm already healing. I'll be up in a second."

"Maybe not, but I know what will," she said.

Il Duce grabbed Jemma by the leg and wrapped a thick steel cable around her. She had no idea where he'd gotten it, but this was an industrial warehouse, so it could have been lying around for all she knew. She still couldn't muster the strength to get loose.

It was the wound. Healing from physical trauma always took a bit out of her, and she'd never been hurt like this before. She hazarded a glance at Sherry, who had an almost demonic look of rage and was rattling the hell out of those chains, but she wasn't going to be getting out of them anytime soon.

This was it, Jemma realized. And strangely, it didn't bother her as much as she'd thought it would. The only thing that bothered her was that she'd failed to save Sherry.

Jemma knew that one day, she'd face someone who was more than a match for her. If not today, then tomorrow, or the next day, but someday it would happen. That day just happened to be today. She was a bit irritated that it was Malka, though. She'd completely misjudged the woman. She'd always thought that she was a low-ranking flunky running a nightclub. It had never even occurred to her that she was Viktor Rostivich's fucking partner. She felt even more like an idiot.

She couldn't even blame it on the distraction of Sherry. She'd known Malka for two years. And in that time, Malka, or Malgorzata Morozov rather, had risen from flunky to Mob Boss in one of the most misogynistic and brutal organized crime entities in the world. Jemma thoroughly underestimated the woman, and now she would die for it.

Il Duce hoisted her into the air and limped toward the door that led to the docks. He was going to throw her in the water. She'd drown, and despite all of her powers, she still needed to breathe. The big Russian kicked down the door and stepped outside with his struggling trophy.

Jemma struggled as hard as she could, but she simply

couldn't break free. Then, rather suddenly, she was tumbling through the air toward the edge of the dock, which was odd. She thought Viktor would just toss her in. Was he going for style points?

As she flipped over and spun, she spotted something that blew her mind. Il Duce was flying through the air, too, tumbling toward the water. A comical look of shock was painted all over his face. And there, on the docks, stood Sherry, beautiful Sherry, with dirty hair, half-naked in her wrecked outfit, and rage on her grimy, soot-covered face. One boob hung out where the explosion had destroyed her top.

Jemma would have laughed at the irony, but she landed hard on the edge of the concrete and fell into the water with a splash. With the steel cable wrapped around her, she sank like a stone, and her arm screamed as the salt water infiltrated her wound. She struggled, trying to get loose, but she knew it was hopeless. Moments later, she lost her breath, and the sea swam down her throat into her lungs. She convulsed once, then twice, and then blackness closed in.

Chapter Thirty-Seven

The chains shattered with a series of loud bangs as Sherry broke free, sprang up, and sprinted across the warehouse. She snatched the railgun from Malka's stunned grip and snapped the barrel as if it were a twig. With a swift shove, Sherry sent Malka flying across the warehouse into a stack of crates. Malka hit her head and slumped to the floor. Dead or not, Sherry didn't care. Her focus was on Jemma.

Charging through the busted doorway, she found Il Duce holding Jemma overhead like a trophy. Sherry closed the distance in an instant and delivered a bone-crushing uppercut. Il Duce's feet left the ground as he rocketed off the pier. Jemma tumbled out of his grasp, and for a heartbeat, Sherry thought she'd land safely on the dock. But dread twisted her stomach as Jemma missed the edge with a loud oof and plunged into the harbor. Il Duce splashed down a moment later, disappearing into the black water, dragged down by his own weight.

"Shit," Sherry cursed, diving in after Jemma. The water bit at her skin like daggers, freezing and sharp, but she pushed deeper, realizing with surprise how far down the pier's edge dropped—easily twenty feet.

When she hit bottom, Sherry paused, listening. To her left, a loud gurgle echoed through the dark, but then, from her right, she heard a metallic scrape. Blind in the murky depths, she kept feeling along the floor until her hand landed on something—a sneaker. Relief flooded her as she felt upward, her fingers tracing the shape of an ankle. She followed it up to a cable wrapped tight around Jemma's leg, then further to her waist.

Her head throbbed in time with her heartbeat as she strained against the cable, but Jemma's weight made it impossible to swim upward. She tried to break the binding, pulling and praying for strength. Still, it wouldn't budge, slipping through her fingers as her lungs screamed for air. Weakness crept in, but she refused to let go. Finally, she was rewarded with a faint tink, then another, until the cable tore apart. She grabbed Jemma's shoulder, but she was still tangled.

Out of breath, Sherry shot to the surface, gulped as much air as her lungs could hold, and dove again. Precious seconds ticked by as she found Jemma and tore at another section of the cable. It gave way more easily this time, but still, Jemma wouldn't come free. Another section stubbornly resisted, forcing her to surface for breath again. Panic threatened to seep in, but Sherry squashed it down. She wouldn't give up—she couldn't.

Diving a third time, she grabbed another section of cable, snapping it with raw determination. Jemma's arm floated free, and Sherry pulled her loose at last, cradling her tightly as she kicked for the surface, her lungs on fire. Breaking through with a gasp, she dragged Jemma over to a nearby ladder, hoisting her out of the water as if she weighed nothing.

Bending down, Sherry checked for breath. Jemma was still, her lips pale. Sherry turned her onto her side, pressing at her diaphragm until seawater spilled from her mouth. Flipping her onto her back, Sherry began CPR, grateful for the day she'd once dated a paramedic who'd drilled into her that "they aren't dead until they're warm and dead."

The water was freezing. But that meant there was still hope.

She chattered the words of 'Staying Alive' by the Bee Gees through her teeth as she did compressions to keep her rhythm, stopping every thirty to give a breath.

She didn't know if Malka was still lurking in the warehouse

or on her way back to kill them both. Not that she was worried about Il Duce. The man weighed a quarter ton—he wasn't coming back up. She supposed she should feel some remorse about killing him, but she couldn't bring herself to care. The only thing that mattered was Jemma, who still wasn't breathing.

Stopping to deliver another breath—her eighth in two minutes—Sherry muttered, "Fuck. You better get up! God damn it." She huffed, her arms burning from the relentless rhythm of compressions. A normal person couldn't keep this up. But then, she reminded herself, she wasn't a normal person anymore. She pushed that thought aside, leaning in for breath number nine. Finally, Jemma coughed, spewing seawater from her mouth.

Sherry rolled Jemma onto her side and let out a sigh of relief as Jemma began to retch. She checked Jemma's neck—her pulse was strong and steady. Even the wound on her shoulder looked markedly better. Leaning down, Sherry whispered in her ear, "Are you okay? Can you hear me?"

Jemma gave a quick nod, still coughing up what probably felt like half the ocean.

"You scared the absolute shit out of me," Sherry gasped, sinking back onto the pier as tears sprang to her eyes. "I thought you were dead."

Jemma managed to push herself onto her hands and knees, shooting Sherry a wry look. "Pretty sure I was. I saw a bright light and my entire ancestral line going back a thousand years."

Sniffling, Sherry gazed into Jemma's cobalt eyes. "Really?"

"No, not really. The last thing I remember, everything went black. Then I woke up to some crazy bitch trying to crack my sternum."

"Fuck you," Sherry muttered, her voice hollow with relief. With a grin, she leaned over and began to pepper Jemma with kisses. "You." Kiss. "Fucking." Kiss. "Asshole." Kiss.

"Where's Malka?" Jemma croaked, rolling onto her side and taking a long, shuddering breath.

"Inside. She might be dead. I don't know. I hit her pretty

hard." Sherry got up and peeked through the door. Malka was still where she'd left her, lying motionless. She watched, shivering from the cold, until she saw Malka's hand twitch, her chest rising and falling slowly.

"Come help me up," Jemma called.

Sherry walked over, picking Jemma up in a bridal carry.

"I said help me up, not pick me up," Jemma bitched.

"Yeah, well, you still have a shoulder wound, and you shouldn't be walking around after a near swimming."

"A near swimming?" Jemma snorted a pained laugh. "Ooh, that hurt. Don't make me laugh."

"Yeah, I dated a paramedic during my freshman year at Yale. That's what she called a drowning."

"What happened to Il Duce?" Jemma asked, glancing around. "And put me down, will you? I can walk, at least."

"Fine," Sherry said and dropped Jemma right on her ass.

Jemma looked up, shocked. "What the fuck?"

"Serves you right," Sherry said sternly. "That's for dropping me on my ass on your porch after playing all nice. Feels pretty shitty, doesn't it."

Jemma, taken aback, gave her a defiant look. "Oh, is that how it is? Bring it on, then."

"Nope," Sherry said, feigning innocence. "I don't think I will." She leaned down, grabbed Jemma by the arm, and helped her up. She started to walk away but turned back, hands on her hips. "Actually, I do have something to say. Did you think being shot, blown up, and having a building fall on me wasn't enough? You had to rub it in that I messed up?"

"Hey," Jemma interrupted. "I'm not the one who stole a priceless painting for some two-bit hustler and got cozy with a mob boss."

"Oh, right," Sherry shot back. "And you're just the one lying to me the whole time. And—oh!—the bookstore, where you let me go on about how hot Lena Swift is. I bet you just loved that. You made me look like a fool."

"You did that all by yourself," Jemma retorted. "And calling me a liar. That's rich coming from you. You're a fucking thief and not just any thief. You stole one of the most dangerous substances on Earth. You were trying to get one over on me so you could just go about your thieving ways without getting caught."

Sherry gave a mocking laugh. "My 'thieving ways'? Really?"

Their argument was interrupted by the sound of an approaching helicopter and sirens. They exchanged a tense look, Jemma clearly expecting Sherry to bolt. Instead, Sherry turned and stomped over to Malka, checking her breathing. She needn't have bothered, though. As soon as she leaned down, Malka's eyes fluttered open.

"Lover's quarrel?" Malka smirked, groaning as she touched the back of her head. "Did you really have to throw me into those crates? That fucking hurt."

"Oh, shut up," Sherry muttered, tearing off a strip of her shirt to press against Malka's head. "You were trying to kill me and my would-be girlfriend."

"Is this where you cuff me, Sweetcakes?"

"Don't call me that," Sherry said, rolling her eyes. "I'm not your sweetcakes. Besides, we're going to jail together, so I'll be in cuffs right along with you. On the bright side, we'll have plenty of time to chat about my," she raised her voice, "'would-be girlfriend.'"

Malka snorted. "We won't see each other. They'll throw us both in The Penthouse. And your abilities make you Special Class, like Jemma. You'll be in solitary."

Sherry shrugged, checking to see if Malka's bleeding had stopped. She'd do her time. She'd earned it—and so had Malka.

Chapter Thirty-Eight

The FBI hadn't been there long before they pulled Jemma aside for her statement, piecing together bits of the story before leading Malka away in cuffs, her wings bound with a thick zip tie. They loaded her into the back of a large transport van. Jemma hadn't mentioned Sherry's involvement to Parker; she knew she should, but she couldn't bring herself to do it.

"Thank you for saving Lena," the young agent said, introducing himself to Sherry. "I'm Agent Parker."

Sherry stepped forward, wrists extended. "I'd like to turn myself in. I caused all of this. I stole the Rembrandt. I'm also an unregistered super."

Parker stared, visibly taken aback, while Jemma's jaw dropped. Sherry gave Jemma a superior, if a bit wan, smile.

"Don't bother cuffing her, Parker. They won't hold her," Jemma said, fighting a mix of anger, grief, and irritation. She hadn't wanted Sherry to end up in a place like the Penthouse, but apparently, Sherry believed she deserved it. And maybe she did. Jemma's feelings were about as clear as butter.

"It doesn't matter," Sherry replied. "I'll come quietly."

Parker sighed, glancing at Jemma. "429?"

Jemma nodded, looking away to avoid Sherry's gaze.

A voice called out from somewhere inside the warehouse, "We found it! It was in the office."

Jemma turned and watched as an agent carried out the

painting—the object that had caused all this chaos. They passed it to a man in a lab coat, who carefully removed the second vial hidden within the frame. Jemma exhaled, relieved. "At least that part is over," Jemma muttered.

"You did well, Lena," Parker said with a smile and whistled at two men, waving them over and gesturing toward Sherry. "Take her into custody—unregistered meta, special protocol."

Jemma watched, heart heavy, as they escorted Sherry to a car and loaded her into the back. Finally, she turned to Parker. "No, I didn't do well," she admitted quietly. "I got completely blindsided. Il Duce threw me into the water, and if Sherry hadn't come after me, I'd be dead. That has to count for something."

Parker shrugged. "Not my call. The U.S. District Attorney will sort it out. But if you believe she deserves a chance, put in a word. It can't hurt."

Jemma nodded slowly. "Yeah," she said softly. "She's worth it."

It took a few hours for the Feds to finish clearing the warehouse and taking statements before Jemma was allowed to leave. As she flew off, a heavy feeling lodged in her stomach. All she could think of was the hurt and despondency in Sherry's eyes. It gnawed at her conscience. She was glad she hadn't turned Sherry in herself, but it didn't feel like a victory. It felt like a stain, a mark that blurred the line she'd tried so hard for so long to keep clear.

Her thoughts wandered back to Il Duce. She didn't regret his death—only that she'd been on the brink of killing him herself. She'd cut loose because they'd threatened Sherry just like she had when Carnifex had killed Callie. And maybe that was just who she was, and she'd have to accept it—one day.

"What a mess," Jemma muttered when she landed on the balcony of Sherry's apartment. Once inside, she started gathering up Sherry's belongings, tossing things she might need into a bag. Then her eyes caught on the covered canvas. She walked over and lifted the shroud to see what Sherry had made. Her breath caught, and tears pooled in her eyes. It was a portrait of Jemma from the first time they met, capturing her mid-step, glancing back as she walked away.

It was breathtaking, depicted in the dramatic chiaroscuro that Jemma had always adored, with darkness pooling around her figure like the deepest shadows of 'The Night Watch.' The amber light fell over her shoulder, catching the subtle contours of her face, drawing out every detail with that rich, haunting contrast she loved so much. Sherry had captured her in a way that felt almost ethereal, as though she were emerging from the shadows and yet drawn back into them—a fleeting moment caught in time.

Every brushstroke pulsed with warmth and intensity as if Sherry had poured her soul into the paint. In the background, a sliver of sky loomed in deep blues and blacks—a cold, distant void that echoed the depths of sorrow. The buildings rose in somber tones of warm amber, rich browns, and stormy grays, their colors blending in a way that suggested both solidity and decay, a world worn down and yet still strong.

The street lamp glowed a muted yellow, casting a soft light that barely touched Jemma's outline. It was as if the world was conspiring to keep her half-hidden, caught between the shadows and the light.

But it was the details that held Jemma in thrall—the cobalt blue of her eyes, painted with a touch of white that seemed to make them glimmer with life—the soft pink of her lips, muted in the dim light. Against the backdrop of her golden-toned skin and dark hair, her gaze seemed piercing, capturing a complex mix of strength, defiance, and vulnerability. Sherry had rendered her with such care, as though every drop of acrylic were a tribute to that first encounter. It was the work of a genius.

Jemma felt herself unravel, tears slipping down her face. She sank onto the couch, unable to tear her eyes from the painting, one hand reaching out absently to stroke the cat who padded over, meowing softly. She stayed there for a long time, sobbing quietly as she held the memory close, as vivid in her mind as it was on the canvas. "What a mess," she whispered again, this time to herself, struggling to pull herself back together.

Finally, with her tears dried, she scooped up the last of Sherry's things, placed Breitweiser in a cat carrier, and locked up the apartment. The cat meowed mercilessly all the way to her own place, his plaintive cries tugging at her heart, each one sounding like he was calling for Sherry.

"Sherry will be gone for a while, so it's you and me, fella," Jemma said softly as she set him free in her apartment. "I'll get you a litter box in the morning, don't worry."

After a shower and tossing away yet another outfit, Jemma rolled out her futon and curled up with Breitweiser. She put out the light and listened to the crickets as she stroked the cat's head. But despite her fatigue, sleep just wouldn't come. She grabbed her phone. The screen was cracked, and it wouldn't charge, but it still worked. She'd replace it in the morning. She opened her visit list and put the name Sherry Broward at the top. Tears slowly rolled over her lashes, blurring her view of the screen, so she shut it off, turned on her side, and cried.

Echoes of self-recrimination danced in her head as she thought about the last few weeks. She'd just had to go on one date—and then another, and another. And she'd just had to let herself fall in love. It wasn't a question. She knew how she felt.

She'd corralled a dozen supers, or metas, rather, who'd made the same excuses Sherry had. I was broke. I needed money for my kids. This wasn't what I'd planned. Most of them she hadn't believed, but Sherry? She'd seen how sweet and naive she was. She had no idea the world she had entered when she'd stolen the painting, and now she would pay the consequences. And she hadn't run. She'd checked on Malka, making sure she was alive. It was something Jemma would have done. Sherry was going to take her lumps, that much Jemma knew. The thought of Sherry in a Special Class cell at The Penthouse tore at her heart.

The first birds of morning chirped outside her window before she ever got to sleep.

Chapter Thirty-Nine

Sherry rocked back and forth on her bunk, knees to her chest, trying to soothe herself. In her head, she was in and out of that place she kept secret, full of an imaginary alternate life where someone cared for her. It had been a place she'd had since childhood, and it had helped her weather some very tough times. Today, though, it brought little comfort.

The cell was colder than she expected, but she shouldn't have been surprised. In every movie that she'd ever seen, jail was a place where people huddled up under too-small wool blankets and prayed for help. Sherry didn't bother. She'd been here three days. It was a guess based on the number of meals she'd been served. They'd been good-sized, but because of her now racing metabolism, they hadn't been enough.

Her sleep had been, at best, fitful, but not because of the temperature. Every night had been filled with nightmares, grueling ones. Malka had said the serum had side effects. She hoped that this wasn't one of them. They were driving her batty.

No one would tell her anything, and she hadn't been able to make a phone call, so she was shocked when a man appeared at her cell door. He was tall, black, and objectively handsome. At least, Sherry thought so. His beard was well-kempt and an obvious source of pride for him. He wore an expensive suit, clearly too smart for the public defender's pool, but he was an attorney, an expensive private attorney.

"Are you going to let me in to talk to my client?" the man asked, brows raised, to someone in the hall. His gorgeous British cadence reminded her instantly of Jemma and caused her eyes to pool. She tried to blink them back, but a few tears slid down her cheeks. She wiped them on her sleeve with a sniff.

The door opened, and the man stepped in. A guard came in carrying a small folding table and a chair. It was Carrie Ford. She typically worked the night shift and stood or sat outside her cell from ten at night until six in the morning. Of the guards, she was the only one who didn't look at her like she was the devil herself. She didn't talk much, but she seemed nice.

As she set up the table and chair next to her bunk, she threw Sherry a sympathetic smile and spoke to her for the first time, just a whisper. "It'll be okay. You'll survive this."

Sherry continued to rock, watching Carrie retreat and the attorney sit on the stained and rickety folding chair. It groaned slightly under his weight. Ford left, and the door slammed shut behind her with a clang that rattled Sherry's teeth and banged in her ears. Above, the camera that watched her rotated upward, and its demonic little red light went out.

"Ms. Broward," he said smoothly. "Can you hear me?"

With a nod, Sherry slowly unfolded a bit. "Are you a public defender?"

He shook his head and slid a business card across the table. "My name is Sanele Dube. I am an attorney and senior managing partner of Dube, Chester, and Hauk. A mutual friend has asked me to come and see if I can help you," he said, tapping the side of his nose.

"Am I in solitary, Mr. Dube? Is that why I've had no contact?" she asked, her voice was flat, emotionless. She hurt desperately inside, but her ability to manage that had grown overwhelmed hours after she'd arrived and the severity of her predicament had set in.

"It's Senele, please. And may I call you Sherry?" the man said, his kind eyes and steady demeanor washed over her.

His presence was so comforting that Sherry's anxiety simply vanished, as though someone had waved it away with a magic wand. Yet when she spoke, her voice still carried shadows of the pain twisting her gut. "Sure."

"This case is classified. Fortunately, I do a fair amount of work for the government and hold a clearance. If you'll accept me as your attorney, I promise I will do my best to get you out of this."

Sherry shook her head. "I don't want out. This is all my fault. Lena Swift almost died because of me."

Sanele sat back. "But you did save her life, so let's do the best we can to make sure you're treated fairly, no?"

That seemed reasonable. "What do you think you can do?"

"If you plead guilty, I believe I can get your sentence down below a year. We have a good case for justifiable homicide with respect to Mr. Rostovich. The man was a criminal. In addition, you did not use excessive force on Ms. Morozov, despite the fact that she attempted to murder Ms. Swift."

Sherry interrupted him. "What will happen to her? Malka, I mean?"

Sanele tilted his head and gave a warm smile. "You really do care," he said, his voice tinged with curiosity and a touch of surprise.

"Yes, I do. I feel bad for her. It's not all her fault, you know."

"She's facing felony attempted murder, assault with a deadly weapon, and dozens of other charges based on what they found in the warehouse. Honestly, she is in serious trouble."

"Can you help her, too?" Sherry asked.

"She's retained an attorney. The DA will expect you to testify against her," Sanele said flatly, and Sherry knew that it would be the price of any deal she might get.

"I know," she said. "I expected as much, regardless."

"So," Sanele said. "Tell me everything."

And Sherry did. Over the next three hours, Sherry told him way more than she wanted. Once she started, she just couldn't stop. Everything came out: how she'd stolen the painting, been exposed to the serum, Charlie and Mary, and her feelings for both Malka and Jemma. She even blurted out some of the more prurient things about her relationship with Jemma, though Sanele helped her move past that, thankfully. It was as if she could hold nothing back. Finally, near the end, she broke down, confessing her love for Jemma and her desperation in trying to salvage their budding relationship.

Sanele paused, then set down his pen. "Ms. Broward, you need to stay focused on your situation right now. Your relationship with Ms. Caldwell will work itself out as it should, one way or the other."

Sherry swallowed the lump in her throat and sat back against the wall, feeling the cold of the concrete press into her back. "I know. It just hurts."

"I will speak to the DA and see what I can arrange. Just stay strong. Keep yourself in check. Being a model prisoner can only help your case."

Sherry nodded and bid Sanele goodbye, watching him leave. As the door closed behind him, the camera whirred back into position, and the red light came on. They were watching her again. On a whim, Sherry gave it a half-hearted wave. This was her life now.

Ford returned a bit later and removed the table and chair. "Do you want a visitor?" she asked.

Sherry looked over at her. "Who?"

"Your mother is here. She'd like to speak with you."

"Oh, God," Sherry groaned. "What am I going to say to her?" She was lying on her bed and threw an arm over her forehead. Finally, with Ford hovering at the door, she held up a thumb. "Sure, why not." The door opened, and Ford stepped out.

Moments later, Sherry sat up as Erin Broward, Sherry's mother, stepped inside. The door closed automatically, and her mother flinched. Sherry always thought her mother was beautiful, though her long blonde hair had gone gray, and she'd shorn it down. Sherry chuckled to herself, thinking that she might not look out of place at any of the lesbian bars she'd frequented in her youth. She hadn't seen her mother in quite a while.

"Hi, mom," Sherry said with a meek smile. "Nice haircut."

"You like it?" Erin asked with a soft smile. "I felt like I needed a change."

Sherry grinned. "It's…um…different." She didn't move, though. The space between them felt like a gulf, wide and painful.

Erin charged across the intervening space and scooped her daughter into a fierce hug. "Are you okay?" she murmured softly. "It'll be okay, I promise."

Sherry broke down, sobbing into her mother's shoulder. "I'm sorry mom, I…" She choked on the next words, unable to say anything.

Erin let go and sat down, patting the bunk. "Why didn't you call me? Why did I have to hear it from your girlfriend? You know I would have come."

"They didn't let me have a phone call. At least, not yet. The case is…I was told it's classified."

"Maybe so," her mother said, a spark of anger in her eyes. "But that doesn't mean they just get to ship my daughter to jail without her rights. I threatened to make a stink and go to the news if they didn't let me in to see you."

Chuckling, Sherry sat and leaned back against the wall. Leave it to her mother to get all mama bear on the US government. "I love you, mom," Sherry said. "I'm so sorry."

Erin's brow furrowed in confusion. "For what? Stealing that stupid painting? Who cares. You're my daughter. And I hear you saved Lena Swift's life." She looked around and then leaned in with a conspiratorial whisper. "Jemma told me all about it."

Sherry's brows shot up. "Jemma told you?"

"Well, I kind of wrangled it out of her," Erin said, a mischievous smile curving her lips. "Anyway, we can't talk about that here. So, how are you holding up? I saw Mr. Dube on the way out. He's headed straight to the US Attorney's office."

"Wait, what? The DOJ? Why?" As soon as the words were out of her mouth, she knew though. Being an unregistered meta was a federal crime. And the serum was probably a contraband substance as well. She was in deep shit. "Nevermind," she said before her mother could answer. "I know I disappointed you."

Mrs. Broward laughed and shook her head. "You've always been this way. I've learned to live with it. Now, what is that lawyer going to do for you?"

"He thinks he can convince them to knock it down to a year or less."

Erin's anger flared. "A year? You saved that woman's life, stopped that bitch ex of yours from killing anyone, and rid this city of a menace. They should pin a medal on your chest."

"Mom, stop," Sherry said, taking her mother's hand. "It'll be okay. After the motorcycles, you told me that if I got caught committing a crime, you'd let me do the time. I know what I did."

"This is different." Erin's lips were pursed in aggravation. "Now—"

"Mom, I said stop. Don't waste our time on this. I'm just glad you're here. What else did Jemma tell you? Did she say she'd come visit?"

Her mother's expression turned grave. "I don't know, honey. She's upset. But she called me. That has to be a good sign, right? I know you like her."

"I'm in love with her mom," Sherry said as the tears flowed again. "And I screwed it all up."

Erin cradled her daughter and stroked her hair. "Give it time, Sherry. If it's meant to be, it'll work out. I just hope you've learned your lesson this time."

"I suppose," Sherry groaned. It wasn't a lie, not exactly. She still felt conflicted, but she knew better than to lie to herself. She was more pissed that she'd gotten caught. She was also irritated that Malka had fucked her over, not intentionally, but the result had been the same. One day, she thought, she'd have to return the favor.

"No," her mother replied. "I came to comfort my daughter in her time of need. But if you don't need me…"

Sherry chuckled at her mother's knowing smile. "Of course, I need you, Mom. I always will."

She raised an eyebrow. "Clearly. I'll be with you every step of the way, okay?"

With a nod, Sherry hugged her mother. She was probably furious with Sherry, but Sherry was an adult. She'd torn Sherry a new rear-end when she'd been caught with the motorcycles, but now, Sherry knew, she was letting her deal with her own problem and doing what a parent should, what Sherry would owe her own adult child if she ever had one. Erin was loving her child.

Chapter Forty

Sherry sat in the US Attorney's office, feeling impossibly small in her orange prison jumpsuit. The office was pristine and professional, with its mahogany desk, neatly stacked files, and polished plaques on the walls. Everything was perfectly in place, reflecting the meticulous nature of the woman who occupied it. The sterile efficiency of the room only magnified how out of place Sherry felt. She tugged at her sleeves, trying to shrink into the chair as embarrassment and shame crawled under her skin.

How had she let it come to this? She'd gotten herself into this mess—there was no hiding that. She stole a Rembrandt. Now, she was sitting in front of the Assistant US Attorney, preparing to negotiate her own fate like it was a business deal.

Sandra Armstrong, a no-nonsense woman with sharp eyes and a crisp voice, barely looked up from her notes. "For your part in the theft of the Rembrandt, we're offering ten months in The Penthouse, plus a year of probation. This is below the minimum sentence for grand larceny."

Sherry's heart dropped. The Penthouse. Her throat tightened as she tried to find the words, but she felt utterly powerless.

Before she could speak, her mother, seated beside her, jumped in, red-faced, her voice brimming with anger. "Ten months? After she saved Lena Swift's life? Is this your idea of justice?"

Armstrong glanced up, unfazed. "That's the only reason we're offering her ten months, Mrs. Broward. If she hadn't saved Swift, I'd throw the book at her: five to twenty."

Sherry's chest tightened with shame. She couldn't stand the idea of her mother fighting like this for her. "Mom," she all but whispered, not wanting to meet her mother's gaze, "Malka's already looking at twenty years for trying to kill Lena. She's paying for what she did, but I'm the one who stole the Rembrandt."

Her mother whipped around to face her, fury and sadness in her eyes. "But it's Malka's fault you even got involved! She manipulated you!"

Sherry swallowed, feeling the weight of her mother's words. "Maybe. But Malka didn't steal that painting. I did. Ten months is no time at all. Now let it go."

Eyes glistening, her mother finally relented, placing a hand on her daughter's arm.

Armstrong's eyes flicked between them, her patience waning. "The offer stands, Miss Broward. ten months in The Penthouse. Take it or leave it. I can give you time to decide if you need it."

"I've already decided," Sherry said. She glanced at Sanele, trying to put on a brave face, but it was hard, especially with her mother sitting right there.

Sherry twisted her leg, staring at the black ankle monitor, another badge of humiliation. She was only stuck with it until sentencing, but still. At least she'd been given bail, though her mother had to put her home up as collateral.

Sitting in her childhood bedroom, Sherry felt the walls closing in on her. The posters on the walls, the familiar creak of the floorboards, it all felt so distant now. She rubbed her wrists absentmindedly, the ghostly feeling of the handcuffs still fresh in her memory. Her mother didn't understand. She wasn't just throwing herself on her sword. She was busted. She'd done the calculation. The shortest stint in prison was a deal. Afterward, she had some ideas about how to get by. She just needed to talk with Malka. She had a plan.

Her mother gave her no space, though, and paced the room. Despite how she'd acted when she'd visited Sherry, her temper had gotten the better of her, even more so than in the US Attorney's office. Probably, Sherry decided, because it was now much more real. Her daughter was going to be sentenced. She was going to prison.

"This isn't fair," Erin said. "They're treating you like a common criminal! You didn't hurt anyone. Who gives a shit about that stupid painting. This is ridiculous."

"I killed a man, Mom," Sherry whispered, her voice barely holding together. "And I committed grand larceny."

Her mother's voice softened, but the tears in her eyes were unmistakable. "But Sherry, what about Jemma? Can't she do something?"

The mention of Jemma twisted the knife deeper. Sherry hadn't been able to stop thinking about her—about whether Jemma would still be there after ten months in prison. How could she ask her to wait? And what if she didn't? Worse still, what if she did? How could she face her? She hadn't visited while Sherry had been in the city jail, which told Sherry a great deal about what Jemma thought.

"I don't know," Sherry said, interrupting her mother, her voice thick with emotion. "I just hope… I hope she'll understand. But I can't run from this."

Her mother sat beside her, squeezing her hand. "Well, if she's worth a damn, she'll see just how wonderful you are."

Sherry took a deep breath, the weight of responsibility pressing down on her. "She does, mom. She called you. She's going to testify at my sentencing. But, Mom, she's a superhero. And…I'm a supervillain now."

Her heart sank as that reality settled in. She had to face what she had done, but deep down, she held onto the fragile hope that Jemma might still be there when she came out, even though she didn't believe it.

All she could do now was hope.

Chapter Forty-One

"All rise," the bailiff called, and everyone stood. Sherry wore an orange prison jumpsuit, and her hands were bound in thick chromium steel shackles that ran halfway up her forearms. She'd been a model prisoner for the last two months. Most of the guards even kind of liked her, but the shackles were standard procedure, and they felt even more humiliating than the jumpsuit, if that was possible. Standing in the courtroom, she looked around. It was mostly empty, being a sealed proceeding. Jemma sat at the back in her Lena Swift suit, her eyes watching Sherry intently. Judge Madison stepped up to the bench and sat down, scanning the courtroom. This was federal court, so there would be no cameras, just a gaggle of reporters. Sherry's mom sat behind her, face a mixture of sadness, worry, and stoicism.

The bailiff called, "The United States District Court for the District of Massachusetts is now in session, the Honorable Judge Sarah Madison presiding. You may be seated."

"Good afternoon," the judge said. "We are here today for the case of United States v. Broward. Ms. Armstrong, I understand that you and the defendant have come to an agreement?"

Armstrong stood. "We have, your honor."

"Ms. Broward, am I correct in understanding that you wish to enter a guilty plea to these charges?"

Sherry swallowed hard and tried to wipe away a tear from her cheek without much luck. "I do, your honor." Sanele handed her a tissue. "Thanks," Sherry whispered.

The judge looked at her notes, then back to Sherry. "You do understand the serious nature of these charges, and you do realize that I may sentence you to up to five years in prison despite your agreement."

Sherry's heart skipped a beat at that. Five years was such a long time, but she would go, if for no other reason than to prove to Jemma that she wasn't the monster that Jemma obviously thought she was. She'd made a mistake, and she'd pay for it, but she hadn't killed anyone. No, that wasn't true. She'd killed Il Duce, but that had been in the defense of Jemma's life, and she wasn't going to apologize for that.

"I understand, your honor," Sherry murmured. She was doing her best, but she was stuck emotionally. She couldn't decide which was worse—going to jail or the idea of losing Jemma forever.

"Please speak up, Ms. Broward, so the court recorder can hear you," the judge said.

"I understand," Sherry repeated, a little louder this time.

"Would you like to make a statement on your own behalf?" The judge asked.

Sherry looked at her attorney, who nodded, then back at the judge. "I would."

"So noted. You may proceed."

"Your honor," Sherry began, a speech practiced for hours in front of the mirror. "I—" she paused momentarily and looked back at Jemma, who was still watching her with hawkish intent. "I did something wrong. I stole a piece of priceless art, something that should be a part of the public trust. During the commission of that crime, I was exposed to something that changed me in a way I'm not fully aware of. I'd like to say that I did it for principle or some high-minded ideal, but that wouldn't be true. I did it for money.

"In the process, I let down everyone who loved me. For the rest of my life, I'll be classified as a supervillain, ETE-898, but I'm just a person. I grew up in a good home with a good family, and I have embarrassed them and shamed them in a way I can't even begin to imagine. For that, all I can say is that I'm truly sorry. Not because I got caught but because I hurt people. Someone I love dearly almost died." Sherry paused for a moment. She'd prepared a longer speech, but she couldn't remember a word of it, so she just said, "That's all, your honor."

"Mr. Dube? Any other witnesses for the defense?"

"Yes, your honor. Lena Swift is here, and she'd like to make a statement."

The bailiff said, "The court calls Lena Swift to the stand."

Sherry looked down at her attorney and then back, her eyes following Lena as she made her way to the stand. She wore a beige skirt suit and a white blouse. Her hands were wrapped in white, but only far enough to cover her tattoo, with a matching headscarf and her typical mask.

As she entered the witness box, the judge said, "Ms. Swift, as a super, you may testify under your alias under the Enhanced Human Protection Act. Please state your alias and registry number for the record."

"My alias is Lena Swift, and my registry number is EP47."

The bailiff asked her to raise her right hand. "Do you swear or affirm that the testimony you're about to give is the truth?"

"Yes," Jemma said and sat down.

"You may begin your statement," the judge said.

Sherry watched Jemma, thinking about the time they'd spent together and wondering what she might say. Sanele hadn't told Sherry, and she and Jemma hadn't spoken since her arrest.

"Your honor," Jemma said, her voice calm and professional. "I've only known Sherry Broward for a short time. But I think the court should know a few salient points. Ms. Broward was not working with Ms. Morozov or the Rostovich's. When I arrived at their warehouse, Sherry was wrapped in thick chains. When she escaped those bonds, she could have run. I would have died, and no one would have been the wiser to Ms. Morozov's actions or to Ms. Broward's involvement. Instead, she came to my rescue, defeated the man known as Il Duce, risked her life to pull me from the harbor, and performed CPR to save my life. She was as much responsible for the capture of Ms. Morozov as anyone, as the court records clearly show. Also, she could have escaped at any time. I was, at the time, in no condition to stop her, but she didn't.

"Furthermore," Jemma continued. "I have had a personal friendship with Ms. Broward until recently, and I've found her to have a kind heart and a friendly nature. She clearly is also more principled than she'd like. She chose to come forward and confess her crimes with no promise of lenience. She could have escaped custody at any time. Harborhaven's jail is not equipped to hold her, and yet she stayed without complaint. I believe that she should be given probation and another chance. That is all."

The judge looked down at Jemma, then toward Sherry. Sherry could only see the motion through the tears that fell over her lashes. At that moment, she felt a swelling of love for Jemma. Jemma could have said nothing. She could have let her swing and washed her hands of her. But she was there, making the case for clemency. The words 'until recently,' though, stung Sherry far worse than she thought they could. It was like a punch to the gut, and she just wanted to curl up and die.

"Thank you, Ms. Swift. Do you have anything else?"

"No, your honor," Jemma said, but her eyes never left Sherry.

"You may step down," the bailiff said at a signal from Judge Madison.

"Ms. Armstrong?"

"No, your honor," Armstrong said.

"Then I will now pass sentence. Ms. Broward, please rise."

Sherry stood along with her attorney.

"Ms. Broward, you have made an impassioned plea, and it does not hurt that Ms. Swift has come forward on your behalf, given her long and distinguished record of service to this community and to the country. However, these charges are serious. In addition, your status as an unregistered, and from what I understand, new, Enhanced Person weighs heavily on my mind. I rarely sit in instances such as this, where someone shows such strength of character in the face of such accountability. And this court is not unmoved by the testimony here.

"If I had a choice, I'd have you serve your time in a different place, but there is no other place designed to hold you. Therefore, based on the recommendations of the District Attorney, I sentence you to ten months in San Fernando Federal Ultramax Security, with credit for time served incarcerated while awaiting trial. I further sentence you to one-year probation when you are released from prison. Given your lack of income and the fact that the painting was returned to Mr. Rostovich, I will set aside the typical ten-thousand-dollar fine. The sentence is to begin immediately. This case is adjourned."

They all rose, and the court officials filed out. Sherry's mother sniffed and cried, but Sherry had prepared her for this. This was better than she'd expected, and she could handle it.

"It's alright, Mom," Sherry said. "I'll be out in eight months, and we can have video chats."

Sherry's mother hugged her and they took Sherry away. On her way out, Sherry looked to the back of the courtroom, but Jemma was gone.

Chapter Forty-Two

Sherry sat in a different facility than where she'd been first kept, the walls pressing in on her, the cold concrete floor beneath her feet sending chills up her spine. The cell was small and dark, a claustrophobic space where the air seemed thicker than anywhere else. It was stifling, and the dim light from the hallway did little to fight the oppressive gloom. She stared at the ground, her mind racing, feeling the weight of everything she'd lost sinking in. She had never felt so alone or so trapped—physically and emotionally. Curled up on her bunk, she absently rubbed her rist and rocked back and forth.

She'd only been there briefly when Jemma pushed the door open and stepped inside. Her presence, typically calming, only added to Sherry's turmoil. Jemma was more than just her lover—she was, or rather had been, her friend. And yet, here they were, worlds apart despite standing just a few feet from each other.

Sherry looked up, her voice barely above a whisper. "You came. I thought you were done with me."

Jemma sat beside her on the bunk, her hand landing lightly on Sherry's knee. "I needed to talk to you. In here. Face to face."

But there was something in Jemma's voice that made Sherry's heart sink deeper. Jemma's touch was gentle, but her eyes were filled with uncertainty. "I'll call you, I promise. But,

Sherry… I don't think it's a good idea for us to plan for the future right now."

The words hit Sherry like a freight train, and a deep fatigue instantly clawed at her shoulders. She couldn't help the tears that stung her eyes, but she swallowed them back. "You don't know how you feel, huh?" She couldn't keep the bitterness out of her voice, but it was tinged with desperation, a quiet plea for Jemma to change her mind.

Jemma looked away for a moment, her hand slipping from Sherry's knee. "I'm sorry. I need time to figure this out. I don't know what I'm supposed to do here. I care for you, but this isn't something I expected."

Sherry could feel herself spiraling, the shame burning hotter in her chest. "So, that's it? You're walking away because I screwed up?"

Jemma's face softened, and she reached out, gently cupping Sherry's cheek. "I'm not walking away. I just… I don't want to make promises I might not be able to keep. I need to think."

The hopelessness Sherry had been fighting to keep at bay broke free. "I guess you don't want to wait around for a supervillain," she said bitterly, her voice cracking.

Jemma flinched at the word. "That's not it."

"Then what is it?" Sherry barked before she could stop herself.

"I told you about Callie, but I left parts out. It was my fault that Callie died." Jemma sighed. "Carnifex set that bear out on the bridge for me, specifically. I don't know how he knew I'd be there, and I'm not sure how he figured out who I was, but he knew I was looking for him, and I was close. After Callie…" she paused and swallowed, looking away. "After she died, I did something terrible. Her death made me into something I never want to be. After that…well, you know the rest. But, when I was with you, I started thinking that maybe I could be with someone, be more careful."

"But?" Sherry asked when Jemma paused for a long time.

"All of this has made me rethink that. I'm better off alone. My relationships never turn out well, and the stakes keep rising. This is a lot, Sherry. I can't pretend like it's not."

Sherry pulled away from Jemma's touch, her heart shattered. "But…" She couldn't look at her, couldn't bear the thought of watching Jemma leave.

"I'm sorry," Jemma whispered. "I don't think I can do this. But…"

"But what?" Sherry said through her tears. "But you'll write? You'll call? I screwed up, but I'm not a bad person. A bad person would have left you to die. A bad person would have just saved themselves. A bad person wouldn't have thrown themselves on the mercy of the justice system just to show how much she loved…." Sherry broke off. She hadn't meant to go that far. It had only been a few weeks, but it was true, and she knew it.

"If you don't want me to…"

"No!" Sherry almost shouted. "I do. I just…" She looked up at the ceiling and tried to dry her eyes to no avail. She sniffed and looked back at Jemma. She wouldn't push her away. She'd take what she could get. She knew she needed her. Maybe they'd never be together, but the thought of ten months in a box with no one but her mother. She couldn't take it. "I won't make it alone. I'll come apart."

Jemma nodded. "I'll call you, and I'll visit. I'll make time."

"Make sure Breit finds a good home," Sherry begged as Jemma turned to go.

Nodding once more, Jemma said, "I will. And I mean it. I'll visit."

Sherry didn't respond, her gaze fixed on the gray walls as Jemma slowly left the cell. The clanging of the heavy door banged into her heart like a coffin nail, echoing in the hollow space of the cell long after Jemma was gone.

Now alone, the cell felt even darker, more suffocating. The air was thick and oppressive, and Sherry's chest tightened as the realization hit her in full force. Not only had she lost Jemma, but she had lost everything. She really was a criminal now. Convicted. Labeled a supervillain, Enhanced Threat Entity 898. Even if she somehow made it through the eight months in The Penthouse, what then? Who would hire her? What kind of life could she possibly have after this? The world had no place for someone like her.

She sat in the silence of her cell, her head in her hands, tears finally spilling down her cheeks. She had no answers, no plan, no future—just the cold, dark reality of the choices she'd made.

It was over.

Chapter Forty-Three

Sherry liked the feeling of being in civilian clothes again after eight months in brown scrubs. Of course, it had felt like dog years. They only had one kind of cell in The Penthouse for supers like her: solitary confinement. She'd been sitting in a four-by-six-foot concrete cell for eight months straight. At least she'd gotten two hours of outdoor time a day instead of the standard one. She'd also had a nice, if tiny, view of Piute Peak, of which she'd drawn about a thousand pictures. Now she had a bus ticket back home, a hundred bucks cash, the address of a halfway house, and the name and address of her PO in Harborhaven. That was it.

She would say, "How the mighty have fallen," but she'd never been mighty, not once in her life. Saving Jemma was probably the only truly great thing she'd ever done, and almost no one knew about it. The details of the case had been sealed for national security.

Now she walked "The Gauntlet," a hundred-yard corridor of twisted steel tubing that led prisoners to the outside world, a grim reminder of the security measures in place—dormant now, but always threatening with hidden shocks and gases for those who dared to flee. Sherry was finally a free woman, with a year of probation hanging over her, a small price to pay compared to what lay behind her. But she had no idea what came next. She was a felon, and Jemma—her heart clenched—

Jemma was gone, lost to her because of the mess she'd created. Malka was locked up, too, staring down a brutal ten-year stretch, down from twenty after the sentencing board had gotten ahold of it.

God, ten years in that place might as well be a hundred, though. Sherry's mind flashed back to the isolation, those first empty days spent in her cell—drab, white, barren. Just a cot, a toilet, a sink. She had spent most of her time drawing, pen and charcoal mostly. And now, carrying a few of her best pieces—mostly sketches of Jemma—she realized how those drawings had been her lifeline. She even had a few sketches of Malka.

She breathed a miserable sigh. Poor Malka. She had none of that. Malka, without any special treatment and no need for special training, would be staring at the same lifeless walls, waiting for nothing but her lawyer's visits, therapy sessions, and an hour of exercise. Sherry had thought she was the one suffering, but now her chest ached for Malka.

"She'll go insane in there," Sherry muttered to herself, guilt creeping in like a weight she hadn't fully understood until now. At least Jemma was visiting Malka regularly, which would help—some.

Malka still had considerable finances, so she had arranged for them to see each other while inside—a few small, quiet moments that had kept them both tethered to something familiar. Despite all Malka had done, despite the chaos and manipulation, Sherry felt a pang of sorrow for her. Ten years seemed like a death sentence. And now, here she was, free, and Malka was trapped in that nightmare. The idea stung deeply, and Sherry decided that, somehow, she'd get Malka out of there. The Penthouse was better than gen-pop in normal women's prisons, but still.

It really wasn't Malka's fault. Prince Lucifer's blood had poisoned her, and Sherry was the only one who could testify to that. But, as far as Armstrong was concerned, Sherry was a co-conspirator. She'd been stuck testifying against Malka. The best she'd been able to do was to water it down some.

But what weighed on Sherry most was the loss of Jemma. If she hadn't gotten herself into this mess, maybe—just maybe—

she could have had a future. She could still feel the ache of Jemma's last touch, the way she had looked at her with both sadness and distance before walking away. That isolated cell, as miserable as it had been, was nothing compared to the emptiness she felt now. What life awaited her now, outside? She was a felon, and worse—a supervillain in the eyes of the world.

Her heart sank lower as she neared the end of The Gauntlet. She'd spent months thinking about this moment, about walking free. But now that freedom was here, it felt hollow.

As she approached the gate, she spotted a black Ford limousine parked not far away with a familiar figure leaning against the quarter panel. Sherry's stomach lurched, and her heart started to race, but from anger or anticipation, she wasn't sure.

Sherry and Jemma hadn't spoken in four months. Their early conversations had been strained—not particularly bad, but distant, the unresolved issues still dangling between them. Ultimately, Sherry decided to end the dialogue. The visits and video calls just hurt too much and drew her mind into hopeful places it needn't go, given her circumstances.

Now, Jemma stood outside in her Lena Swift outfit, waiting. Sherry honestly hoped that she was here to drop someone off or sit for a parole hearing—she wasn't sure she was ready to talk to her. It wasn't anger, she decided. It was shame. She felt ashamed for all the trouble she'd caused. The only saving grace was that she hadn't seriously hurt anyone, just some property damage, except for Rostovich. Though, despite the monster he was, guilt still niggled at her. She'd probably never get over it.

Regardless of why Lena was there, Sherry wasn't going to spend another minute in prison. She'd heard a guard making a joke about some guy who had said, "If my old lady is out there, keep me in here." It made for a good joke, but that was all. Prison was prison, and freedom was freedom. It was that simple.

When she reached the gate, it buzzed, and Sherry pushed her way through, stepping into the morning air just east of

Bakersfield. Finally, outside, she took a deep, clean breath, catching the smell of firs and wildflowers and baking blacktop. There was a faint hint of smoke. It was spring, and wildfire season had started. Still, it was like candy or a fine wine.

She took two steps forward and then pulled the crumpled bus ticket from her pocket and gazed at it. All the while, she could feel Jemma's eyes on her, watching from the parking lot.

Sherry sighed. "I guess I have to deal with this." She headed over toward the car and the woman whose life she had saved.

Jemma greeted her when she was only a few paces away. "Hey."

"What brings you here?" Sherry asked a step later.

"Visitation," Jemma replied coolly, lifting off the quarter panel and stepping toward her.

"Malka? She said you were visiting her," Sherry said. "Or is it that Amy chick? I saw her for a few minutes during group. She's really nice."

Jemma frowned briefly at that, and Sherry wished she could, for once, keep her foot out of her mouth, but Jemma recovered quickly. She said, "No. I thought you were in solitary and couldn't communicate with anyone."

Sherry shrugged. "It's more complicated than that. I wasn't supposed to talk to Malka, but we found ways to communicate. I didn't want her to be all alone."

Jemma nodded, then gave her a soft smile. "As it turns out, no. I'm here to see you. I have a friend who wanted to celebrate your first day as a free woman."

Jemma was very close, and Sherry could smell her scent. The flowery perfume she wore and the sweaty aroma reminded her of the night they'd spent at her place. Sherry screwed up her face in confusion. "Who could possibly want to see me? I don't have any friends, not anymore. Only my mother talks to me, and she's working today."

With a crooked smile, Jemma said, "That's ridiculous. I'm your friend."

"Are you?" Sherry looked up, shielding her eyes from the sun so she could see Jemma's face, well, her full lips and pretty jawline.

"Yes," Jemma said firmly. "I'd still like to be more, if you'll let me."

Sherry stayed silent, not sure what to say. Did she want that? Of course, she did, but she was afraid: afraid of having her heart broken again, afraid of not being able to adjust to a normal life, and most of all, she was afraid that none of that would happen and Jemma would just love her. She didn't know how to handle that. She'd prepared herself for the rest of her life without Jemma in it. After they'd parted, even with Jemma's calls, she steadfastly refused to believe that there might be even the ghost of a chance.

In the ensuing silence, the tension between them grew thick and fraught and cloying. All she wanted to do was hug Jemma and beg her to fly her away back to Harberhaven, but she couldn't make her body move or mouth work.

"This isn't going how I planned," Jemma admitted softly, rubbing the back of her neck. "I've been here for four hours waiting for you to get out, trying to figure out what to say, but I couldn't come up with anything good that didn't sound overly cheery or stupid."

"I'm a felon," Sherry said, the hint of humiliation tainting her voice. "Won't being seen with me screw with your good girl rep?"

"You're not a monster, Sherry. You made a mistake." Jemma shrugged and smiled. "Besides, as an out lesbian superhero, people either love me or hate me. That's their problem. It's why I came wearing this ridiculous getup." She gestured up at the prison windows. "Some guard up there will see us together and catch it on their phone. And I want them to. I want the world to know that I have your back."

Sherry was taken aback by the show of support, and her brain wouldn't let her take it without at least some sabotage. "I thought you couldn't do this."

"I'm sorry I said that. It wasn't true. I was just..." Jemma trailed off as she blinked rapidly and looked away. "I love you. I don't want to be without you. Life is complicated, and it wasn't fair of me to judge you like that."

Sherry sniffed, and her throat tugged at the lump in it. "I

should be grateful that you're here." She paused. "I am grateful. I just don't know where to go from here."

"How about we take it one day at a time," Jemma said. Then she gave a weak smile. "If you can keep your hands off this fit, government-built body."

Sherry chuckled, and a bit of genuine humor crept into her voice. "Well, it is a sexy outfit."

Jemma grinned crookedly and then held up a finger. Sherry watched, bemused, as she opened the passenger door. The cold air from the AC wafted from inside, creating ripples in the stifling heat. Jemma ducked behind the door and fiddled around inside the car, where Sherry couldn't see. So, instead, she oggled Jemma's ass for the few seconds Jemma was bent over. Then, she looked away, whistling with false innocence, just as Jemma turned to face her. In Jemma's arms, curled up and shaking, was a little calico ball of fur, meowing plaintively.

The tears that had threatened burst forth in earnest. She dropped her duffel, reaching out. "Oh, my God," she whispered, taking Breit from Jemma's hands and holding him close. "Where has he been?"

"My place," Jemma said with an incredulous, if half-hearted, scowl. "I wasn't going to let him die in your apartment while you were in jail. And I certainly wasn't going to hand him off to the pound or some pet charity. Jesus, Sherry, I'm a hero. I *save* the cat. That's like superhero 101."

Sherry hiccupped a sob as she laughed through her tears, and, for a split second, her entire body vanished before appearing once more.

"What was that?" Jemma asked, eyes wide.

"Oh, that? Yeah, I can turn invisible and stuff. I've mostly got it under control."

Jemma nodded and smirked. "That could be interesting."

Sherry sniffed and laughed despite herself, and Jemma reached out, enfolding Sherry in her arms. They stood there like that, the three of them, for a good long time. Sherry cried, Jemma cried, and Breit licked at their faces with his scratchy tongue.

"Come on," Jemma said, finally. "I have this big new

apartment, and I've got a spare bedroom if you want it." She shrugged then and added shyly, "Or you can stay with me. I mean, if you'd like it. You know. If you want."

Sherry scoffed at her. "Where'd you get the money for a big apartment? I thought you were a broke-ass superhero for your principles living in a dingy one-room hovel."

Jemma smirked at her and pointed downward. There, on Jemma's feet were a pair of brand new Nike's.

"And what makes you think I want to room with a sellout," Sherry said with a raised eyebrow and a cheeky smile. "I mean, what's next? Are you gonna get Addidas plastered on your ass? Rent out your tits to Reebok?"

Jemma laughed. "Unbelievable. You're the one who said I should do this. Besides, a girl's gotta eat."

"First, I didn't know that you were Lena Swift when I told you that," Sherry shot back. "And, honestly, you really thought I was serious?" Jemma did scowl at her for real, then, and Sherry broke into a wide grin. "You are too easy."

Jemma leaned in and kissed her on the cheek. "You bitch," she whispered playfully.

Sherry shrugged. "I'm a supervillain, you know. They even gave me a code name."

An eyebrow arched, Jemma stared at her. "Did they now?"

"Yeah. I'm ETE-898, codename: Wraith."

Jemma rolled her eyes. "Who came up with that?"

"Who else? That kid at the Bureau, Parker. Apparently, I have a fan."

In response, Jemma just shook her head. "You're going to be insufferable, aren't you?"

For a moment, Sherry and Breit disappeared. Jemma gawked at the empty spot. Sherry re-appeared, ghostly and translucent. She walked right through the car to the other side. The scientists inside The Penthouse had told her that she'd developed some kind of quantum vibration control or whatever. Apparently, it let her shift the frequency of her subatomic particles and those close to her, allowing her to pass through solid matter. It was all very technical, and she had no idea how it worked—yet. She had some reading to do.

"So, are we going to stand here all day, or do I need to catch the bus?" Sherry asked when she abruptly solidified on the other side of the car, making Jemma gasp. Then, with a chuckle, Jemma opened the rear door and waved Sherry in. Sherry charged back around and shuffled awkwardly inside, manhandling little Breit, who mewed while she got situated.

Jemma grabbed the duffel and tossed it into the trunk before climbing in with her.

"Um, what are you doing?" Sherry asked. "You can fly all by yourself."

"Yeah, but the cat doesn't. I'm riding back with you. Also, my contact at DHS wants to have a word with you, so I promised I'd at least get you to take the call."

Sherry rolled her eyes. "Well, that's a waste of jet fuel. Don't you guys ever think about global warming? And is it that guy, Jessup, or Jesse, or whatever his name is? I already told him absolutely not. You can do all that hero stuff, but I'm going home to work at the SunBean if they'll hire me."

"There's a pardon and record expungement in it for you."

Sherry looked at her askance, a pert grin curling her lips. "That's tempting, but why would I want it now? That would have been nice eight months ago. I just got out of jail. I'll save that for when I have to go back. I might want to steal another Rembrandt or maybe a Picasso this time; who knows? I'm a hardened criminal, you know?"

Jemma rolled her eyes. "At least talk to the guy, please? I promised him."

Sherry decided she was having too good a time fucking with her. "Teach you to make promises you can't keep," she said and looked out the window, but she couldn't keep a straight face. Finally, she turned back to Jemma and put a hand on her cheek. "I'll talk to him. But I can't fly, and I'm not traveling overseas; they can forget that. My ass is staying in Harborhaven. If they can arrange an art job, that'd be good. Maybe at The Met."

Jemma laughed and leaned over, pulling Sherry into a toe-curling kiss. "I missed you."

Sherry blinked back more tears. "I missed you, too."

Epilogue

Sherry took a deep breath and checked her watch. It was noon, everyone should be inside. Dressed in a tight black dress that flattered her figure and showed off her muscular legs and arms. She stalked up into Sin City on a pair of new Louboutin black patent-leather pumps, a black briefcase in one hand.

"Excuse me, ma'am, you can't be in here," a large man with a square jaw, who looked about in his forties said and put out his arm. "We're not open."

"You must be Dexter," Sherry said, her voice quiet and confident. "You should know that Sin City is under new management."

He raised an eyebrow. "Ms. Morozov owns Sin City, ma'am, and I haven't heard a single word about new management, so you'll have to leave."

Sherry gave him a broad, white smile and fluffed at the bun in her hair. "Well, that answers one question. It seems Malka's orders have been dying further up the chain, as we suspected. Where might I find Timothy?"

"He's in the office, but you can't go in there," Dexter said, placing a hand on her shoulder. Sherry snatched his hand and twisted—gently. Dexter dropped to his knees, a grimace of pain stretching his gruff features.

"No one touches me without my say so. Are we clear?"
He nodded.
She leaned down and tightened her grip. "I'm sorry, I can't

hear you."

"Yes," he grunted.

"Yes what?" She barked at the man.

"Yes, ma'am."

Sherry released him. "Now, lock the doors and round up the rest of the staff. It's time for the daily meeting. Malka is unhappy with the way the club has been run, and she has asked me to fix it."

With the lights on, the club was far less inviting. The wear and tear of years of dancing, drinking, and the rare scuffle adorned several surfaces. In addition, the club's entire look seemed old and tired. She set her briefcase on one of the cocktail tables and removed the clipboard inside. On it, she made a note to hire someone to re-decorate. This place needed more upscale clientele. Looking at it now, it was no wonder that the best it could attract from the villain community was the likes of Lull. Sin City was going to be the new neutral ground. Heroes, villains, and groupies would all be welcome.

The staff threw her a few questioning looks, but Dexter did as he was told and began making the rounds, gathering them up for the meeting.

"Oh, Dexter, darling," Sherry cooed. "Just have everyone take a seat in front of the bandstand. I'll be back in a moment."

Sherry strutted across the club, up the stairs, and stopped at the office door. She placed her palm on the scanner. Instead of the normal green, it stayed red. "Asshole," she muttered.

Something caught her attention: an odd sound from the other side of the door. Curious, Sherry pressed her ear to the wood and listened to the sounds of… "Oh, hell no!" she raged.

With narrowed eyes and pursed lips, she made a note on her legal pad to call someone for door repair, removed her right shoe, and kicked open the office door. The door crashed wide and hung, swinging precariously by one hinge.

Timothy, Malka's soon-to-be former assistant, had a young woman sprawled across Malka's desk.

"Out!" Sherry ordered, giving the young woman a pointed look and stepping back into her pump.

Needing no further prodding, the woman quickly slid out

from under Timothy and covered herself before darting past her and down the stairs.

Sherry pulled an envelope from her clipboard and held it out as Timothy struggled with his fly and belt. Her face was a mask of absolute confidence. "Timothy, you're fired. Here is your last paycheck. I have deducted the money owed to the club for your skimming, leaving…well, leaving not much, but I'm sure you won't mind. You may leave. You know where the stairs are."

Timothy didn't move, and Sherry eyed him up and down. He was a thin man, not terribly handsome, but not terribly ugly. Plain would be the word she would use. He was tall, toned, and had pretty green eyes. Unfortunately, those eyes were too close together and sat over a tiny nose and thin mouth with almost non-existent lips.

Malka had never intended for him to take over, but her right hand, Sebastian, had been arrested with her at the warehouse, so there wasn't much of an option. Unfortunately, Timothy was also an idiot and a thief. He'd run the club into the red within four months of Malka's incarceration, mostly due to mismanagement, rampant skimming, and a total lack of floor control. Once Sherry had seen the books, she'd known exactly where the problem was.

"Malka left me in charge," Tim said as he slid his belt home.

Sherry sauntered over to the massive window and opened it wide, dropping her clipboard on the couch as she went. "No, Timothy, I assure you that was not what she intended. It fell to you because there was no one else. Now, there's me."

"You can't do that, you bitch. And besides, Malka's in jail. It's not like she can fire me herself."

Shaking her head, Sherry walked over to Timothy and jammed the envelope into his waistband. Then she proceeded to snatch him by the neck and lift him straight up onto his toes. As he held onto her iron bar of an arm for dear life, she dragged him to the window and held him out, dangling him over the sidewalk below. Fortunately, it wasn't a very far drop, only about twelve feet. It would hurt. He might even break a leg, but he wouldn't go to the cops. Malka had enough on him to put him away for a few years.

"You should have taken the stairs," Sherry hissed—and let go. He landed with a sickening thud and screamed. Maybe it was further than she thought. Oh, well.

For a moment, she glanced around the room. It was nice but so sparse. It needed something; she just couldn't figure out what. It was just another thing to fix, but it was still far better than pulling shots for rude customers. And she had to be honest with herself; she was a felon and on probation. No one would hire her except someone like Malka. At least here, she knew who she was dealing with, and she was in charge and didn't have to take any shit from anyone.

Jemma, however, would have kittens when she found out. But then again, maybe not. Sherry loved Jemma that much was true, but she had to be her own woman. And working here, she could keep Jemma in the loop if anything insane was afoot.

Her adrenaline flowed from the confrontation with Timothy, and she needed to control it. She drew in a shaky breath and then let it out slowly, settling herself as best she could. She didn't know how long she could keep this up.

Carefully, Sherry reached into her briefcase and removed the photograph of her and Jemma scarfing burgers, the first thing they'd done after she'd dropped her suitcase at Jemma's apartment. She stroked the glass with a finger before setting it on the desk. She had a plan. She would hire a competent manager, clean up the place, and get on to something else. She ignored that niggling voice in the back of her head that warned her this was a bad idea. It would be okay.

Carefully, she schooled her features, picked up her clipboard, and strode back downstairs to start a fresh day, earning her half of the bar. On her way out, it hit her what was missing from the office. It needed some art on the walls. Her lips curled into a wicked grin as she thought about it.

Maybe something by Munch.

Coming 2025

The Senator's Child

**Amid walls of power, trust no one but the
woman at your back.**

Three years have passed since Miranda Rogers and her wife, Sarah, took refuge in a secluded cabin in Appalachia, hiding from the violent Patriots of the Thirteen. With those threats seemingly behind them, Senator Miranda Rogers is enjoying her first full term as the Junior Senator from Kentucky, with Sarah steadfastly by her side. Together, they've built a peaceful life with new purpose, especially after adopting Mina, Miranda's young Korean cousin. But that life takes a turn when the vice president dies unexpectedly, and Miranda is called upon to fill his role, once again thrusting her family into the spotlight.

What should have been a moment of triumph quickly turns to dread when Mina is kidnapped, mere hours before Secret Service protection would have extended to Miranda's family. Haunted by the conspiracy that nearly destroyed her once before, Sarah fears that Mina's disappearance may be connected to a dark legacy they thought they'd escaped.

Restrained by both law and procedure, Sarah and Miranda must rely on Nia Calloway, a young but tenacious Secret Service agent. Nia's only lead points to Siobhán Murphy, a.k.a. Wildwire, a notorious hacker with a personal stake in the case. Although Wildwire is distrustful of authority and on the run from the FSB, she recognizes the stakes are too high to ignore and reluctantly joins forces with Nia, forming an alliance as tense as it is urgent.

As Nia and Wildwire dive deeper, they find themselves entangled in a sinister plot, one where shifting loyalties and hidden motives leave them with no one they can trust. Forced to depend on each other as enemies close in, their growing bond becomes both a strength and a vulnerability, a spark they can't ignore and a distraction that may get them both killed. With a rogue Secret Service agent in the mix and time running out, they stand together as the final line of defense—not only fighting to bring Mina home, but to protect each other from an enemy bent on destroying them both.

Join Cait Reagan

In

DARK SISTERS: A CAIT REAGAN NOVEL

Coming Soon - Wherever Books are Sold

About the Author

Aoibh Wood lives in New England with her wife and their adorable orange tabby, Jabb. . .err. . .Papaya. She enjoys travel, the outdoors, playing guitar, and weightlifting.